Highland Lady

Hester Pennie

SIMON & SCHUSTER

LONDON • SYDNEY • NEW YORK • TOKYO • TORONTO

First published in Great Britain by
Simon & Schuster Ltd in 1990

Copyright © Hester Pennie, 1990

Simon & Schuster Ltd
West Garden Place
Kendal Street
London W2 2AQ

Simon & Schuster of Australia Pty Ltd
Sydney

British Library Cataloguing-in-Publication Data available
ISBN 0–671–71702–2

Typeset by Selectmove Ltd, London in Bembo 11/13pt
Printed and bound in Great Britain by
Richard Clay Ltd, Bungay, Suffolk

Highland Lady

Chapter One

❧

Glen Fada, 1825

SUNLIGHT FLASHED green through the thick window glass and woke her, touching her cheek like a loving hand. Sweet scents of a Highland summer, aromatic pine resin mixed with the musty scent of bracken, filled her nostrils. The white-painted room was bathed in sunshine; window curtains billowed gently in the cool breeze.

As Grizel lay collecting her thoughts, the brightness of the day was dulled for her by a heavy feeling of depression. Then, with a sickening lurch of the heart, she remembered why. It was the first day of August, 1825, the day she and her family were to leave their ancestral home, Glen Fada. With sudden resolution she sat up, throwing the covers to the floor. It seemed imperative to start the day quickly. There were only nine hours left in which to gather a store of memories to sustain her over the days and years that lay ahead.

Once dressed, she ran quickly down the twisting flight of stairs to the kitchen. In the cavernous room with its long pine table and raftered roof sat the two maids who were all that remained of the vast army of servants that once had lived at Glen Fada: Beatie, the kitchen maid, and Mrs Grey, her mother's former lady's maid who had come out of retirement to help them pack. When Grizel sat down beside them, Mrs Grey rose to pour a cup of tea which she laid on the table, at the same time patting the young woman's shoulder in silent sympathy. All feelings were left unspoken that day; only sorrowful looks sped from eye to eye. 'Your mother slept well,' Grey said.

'I'm glad of it. Let her rest a little longer.'

On the previous evening Mrs Macalpine had been put to bed in a fit of hysterical weeping after reading old letters that she found in

1

the black japanned cabinet by her bedside. They reminded her too vividly of the past, of members of her family who were now dead or far away, of the days when she had lived a life of outrageous luxury.

My last day, Grizel repeated silently to herself, over and over again. Her feelings were confused. One half of her longed for the ordeal to be over; the other dreaded the arrival of evening when the Macalpines would drive from this beloved land on the first stage of their journey.

She rose from the table and went to stand in the open kitchen doorway, staring up at the guardian mountains that ringed the house beside the River Spey. In the dreaming silence the valley looked as it must have done for thousands of years, and as it would look long after she and all the people around her were dead. Granite outcrops on the slopes sparkled and shone in the sunshine as if dusted with gold. The woods that crowded around the house were bright with dozens of shades of green. Grizel stared at them hungry-eyed and realised for the first time how many different greens there were. No painter's palette could reproduce them all.

Shaking herself slightly, she made a decision. 'The garden, I'll go to the garden,' she said aloud. From habit she slipped back into the kitchen and took a basket in which to gather the fruit she knew was ripening on the heavily laden bushes.

The garden was some distance away because in one of his costly improvement schemes, her father had placed it at a remove from the house, deciding that, in imitation of greater magnates, he wanted a lordly estate.

She went by way of the farm buildings, empty now of the crowds of workers who once laboured in them. The byres and barns stood tenantless as well except for a few clucking hens scratching the dust for leftover grain. Cavernous stables that once had housed twenty horses stood empty now.

When Grizel pushed open the wicket gate to the walled plot black-birds and finches, busy among the berries, cried out resentfully and rose up, beating the air with their wings. There had been no garden-ers at work for several years so the beds were wild with weeds and vegetables left to sprout untended from the rich earth. She pushed aside tangled branches to gather a bounty of blackcurrants, sweet red gooseberries and raspberries that gleamed among the foliage like jewels. As she picked she tasted the berries like a connoisseur, and her lips were soon stained scarlet with juice.

Time slipped past like a thief but Grizel was unconscious of it as she sat in a shady corner, tasting her fruit and twisting long stems of grass into sweet-smelling plaits. Her mind was at peace as she relived her happiest childhood days. But she could not stay in the past for ever.

By the time the sun had passed its zenith in the sky, awareness returned and the look of abstraction left her face. Memories of her favourite places began pulling at her like a magnet. It was time to say farewell. On she wandered, past overgrown banks of ornamental shrubs and along a twisting, tree-shaded path that meandered slowly by the side of a sparkling burn. She stood on its bank and watched like one hypnotised as the brown water rushed past her feet, gurgling over multi-coloured mountain pebbles and idling in shallow pools where tiny fish darted to and fro. Grizel knelt down to scoop it up in her cupped hands. The cold familiar taste was delicious. Nothing else – not even the finest champagne – tasted like water from a Highland burnie.

Her feet led her on along the path by the base of the hill called Ord Ban, over a rustic wooden bridge and down a shady lane where branches of wild cherry trees arched above her head. Ripe fruit hung down in flourishes of scarlet and crimson. Predatory birds watched her greedily as she walked beneath the laden branches.

'Good feasting,' she wished them.

Soon she found herself in what was left of the forest of Glen Fada. Its strange, cathedral-like presence claimed her, laying the balm of tranquillity on her troubled spirit. Far above her towered sky-brushing trees, the gashes in the crusted bark of their massive trunks shining red and scar-like in the diffused sunlight. All around was silence, deep and so brooding that it was almost audible. The resinous scent made her head swim. She sank down at the roots of one huge tree on a bed of soft green moss where springy tufts of blaeberry plants were already showing their autumn bounty of tiny purple fruits.

Grizel picked a few, anxious to have that taste to remember as well. The thin skin of the little berries dissolved on her tongue in an instant, the sweet taste filling her mouth like nectar.

She was drawn deeper into the forest and walked slowly on till she reached a clearing from which, like a framed picture, she caught sight of the blue and silver glimmer of the waters of Loch an Eilean. On the velvet of its distant bank stood the white-painted cottage built by Grizel's father as a pleasure place for her mother. She never used it and the children took it over, furnishing it, keeping a cow tethered on the grass at its door, sailing on the waters of the loch in their own boat which was still tied up, rotting and neglected, by the shore. It was too painful to go into the cottage for the last time alone, Grizel decided.

Leaning against an outcrop of rock, she stared across the water which rippled like slowly unfurling silk in the soft breeze. Fir trees stood right on the water's edge with their black and twisted roots reaching down into it like grasping hands. On a tiny island in the middle of the loch were the ruins of the stronghold of the Comyns, brigand descendants of Robert the Bruce and predecessors to her own family as lairds of Glen Fada. Time had ravaged the castle. Now there remained only a broken tower and a few tumbledown walls with trees growing from the tops of them, the haunt of ospreys who built their nests in the crumbling battlements every year.

The white-breasted parent birds were slowly circling above the island. She watched as one of them, spotting a fish in the waters of the loch, plunged down feet first and caught its struggling silver prey in fierce talons. Ferocity and pride of possession had marked the Comyns who for centuries held on grimly to their birthright. The same Highlanders' blood beat proudly in her veins. She loved this land with a passion that was overwhelming, almost mystical. To cherish and serve had been her inheritance and she grieved that, because she was a woman, the spreading domain would never be within her control.

How long she stayed, gazing out at the fort and dreaming in the shadows, she did not know. She shivered suddenly as a gust of wind chilled her and saw that the sun was beginning its descent behind Tor Alvie on the other side of the valley. Soon grey mists would come drifting along the river, the light would fade, and it would be time for the family to leave.

She walked down the twisting path that flanked the river running out of the loch. Ahead she saw the gate to the house and, on her left, the squat bell turret of the granite church huddling into the hillside at the edge of the park. Every stone on the path, every knot in a tree trunk, was familiar to her. Cutting these ties was painful as surgery. With bent head she climbed the path to the double wooden gate.

She lifted the latch, stepped through, and let the gate bang shut behind her. The noise of the latch clicking back into place was so familiar, and so final, that at last her tears broke, dripping through the fingers she held to her face and wetting the bodice of her dress.

Her elder brother Patrick was in a fine stew when she arrived home. 'Where have you been? Hurry, get dressed! We've only an hour,' he shouted.

There was no time left for weeping, no time to brood over the past or the future as she ran to and fro, fetching and carrying, till the dreaded last minute arrived. Then Grizel and her sister Louisa stood back while Patrick took their mother's arm and escorted her to the front door of the house.

Mrs Macalpine, dressed in a plain white gown with a deep-brimmed straw bonnet covering her thick, curling dark hair, paused for a second in the doorway. In the dim light of the hall, her children saw her bend down and lift her husband's plaid from its place on the wooden settle by the door. Frayed and old, the plaid was of red Macalpine tartan with crossings of green and blue. The laird's wife carried it proudly as she and her children trod the familiar path beneath the birch trees to the ferry.

The ferryman, John Macalpine, was leaning on his oars waiting for them. His family, like many other people who worked on Glen Fada estate, bore the same name as the laird because they had been retainers since time immemorial and regarded Grizel's father as a sort of superior relation. Over her brother's shoulder, she could see the pony carriage drawn up on the shingle of the other side of the river. Lister, the butler, stood holding the bridles of the two carriage horses. Mrs Grey and Beatie, who could not bear a last farewell, stayed hidden in the house. Only a few workers from the estate, their expressions reflecting mixed feelings, witnessed the last departure. None of them cheered or waved as they would have done in the past.

With set faces the girls climbed into the boat behind their mother and perched uncomfortably on the wooden plank seat. From long familiarity Grizel knew that it took twenty-five strokes of the oars to cross the river on a calm day and she began to count as Macalpine dipped his blades into the rushing water. Twenty-two, twenty-three, twenty-four. . . . Oh, why did the journey have to end?

Too soon the bow of the boat crunched into the gravel of the bank and Patrick leaped ashore first to help his mother. Mrs Macalpine looked over her shoulder at the boatman. She seemed to want to speak to him but he avoided her eyes, keeping his head lowered over the oars. She bent down again, lifted the plaid from the seat, and with her long-fingered white hands draped it around the old man's shoulders. When Grizel climbed out past him, she saw that he was weeping.

As the horses trotted forward with Patrick at the reins, he and his mother stared straight ahead, never looking back, but Grizel and Louisa half turned in their seats and kept the white house in view until they turned a corner and it disappeared behind a stand of trees.

Recriminations were useless but it was impossible for the sisters to appear controlled when their world and everything they held dear was so cruelly wrenched from them. Grizel felt as if her heart would crack in two. Tears scalded her cheeks, wiped away with shaking hands. Beside her, Louisa was sobbing like a child.

Though neither of them could speak, the same thoughts were uppermost in their minds. For two hundred years Glen Fada had been the Macalpine family's home and refuge. Now, denied a return to the place they loved above all others, they could only ask themselves fruitlessly how it had ever come to this and wonder what lay ahead in the world beyond Glen Fada.

Chapter Two

Edinburgh, 1806

IT WAS JUNE and the family was preparing for the summer move to the Highlands. Up and down the stairs of their house overlooking the broad sweep of Charlotte Square ran servants and porters, carrying trunks, boxes and parcels to be loaded into the two commodious carriages drawn up outside the front door. Supervising everything was the busy figure of the head of the household, Peter John Macalpine, descendant of a long line of Highland warriors and seventh laird of Glen Fada.

He did not look like a robber baron, however, more the brisk lawyer type in keeping with the profession he had studied for. Birdlike, his darting eyes flashed here and there, noticing everything. He rattled out orders with a rapidity that made his servants' heads reel. Only when everything was loaded and tied down to his satisfaction did he run up to the first-floor drawing room and begin marshalling his family, who had been watching his operations from the long windows overlooking the square.

'My dear, let me take you downstairs,' said Macalpine, gallantly offering an arm to his beautiful wife. Though they were barely thirty years old, they were the parents of five healthy children as well as the fortunate possessors of a large amount of land and money.

Jane Macalpine rose unsteadily from her day bed. She had been in uncertain health since being delivered a few months before of a six pound baby son whom they had named John. Taller than her husband, she carried herself with the stately air of a duchess. Her mass of curling dark hair grew low on the forehead of her heart-shaped face and ringlets curved prettily over each cheek. Her eyes were particularly lovely for they were triangular in shape and very pale blue which gave them an unsettling quality. Even her habitual pallor did not detract from Jane's beauty.

With a gentle hand beneath her elbow, Peter John guided his wife down the stairs while her unmarried sister Maria walked behind carrying her sister's Leghorn straw hat and fine Kashmir shawl. Bringing up the rear was a maid carrying the baby in a wicker basket and the excited children – eight-year-old Grizel, the first-born; seven-year-old Patrick, the petted heir; tomboy Anne, with her stick-like legs and pertly pretty face who was five years old and devoted to her brother. Then came stout, expressionless Louisa, aged eighteen months, whose hand was firmly gripped by the Cerberus-like governess,,bz Mrs Potter. Deep frown lines over the bridge of her nose and down the sides of her mouth gave her the appearance of an untrustworthy dog.

The children's mother turned her head when she was halfway down the stairs and said in a languid voice, 'I think you'd better take the little ones and travel in the carriage with Mr Macalpine, Potter. Patrick can go with you as well. I'm far too nervous to put up with the baby crying and his fidgetting on this awful journey. It's bad enough having to worry about the girls.'

Anne's face fell at this, she hated to be parted from her brother, but Grizel brightened for she hated Potter. It was a relief to be travelling apart from her and she determined to do nothing to arouse her mother's anger which was always ready to flare up, especially at her.

It took some further bustling about on Peter John's part before everything was finally settled to his satisfaction but, within fifteen minutes, they set off with whips cracking and horses' hooves sliding on the slippery cobbles of the square. Mrs Macalpine set up a fearful moaning and crying as the coachman struggled to control a fractious horse on the outside of his team of four splendid bays but her sister grasped her hand and said soothingly, 'Keep calm, Jane, there's no need to worry. Just close your eyes and collect yourself.'

The cries that continued to issue from their mother did not upset the two little girls who sat facing her with the lady's maid, Grey, between them. They were used to the fuss their mother made whenever they embarked on a journey and were far too happy at the thought of going back to their beloved Glen Fada to share her anxieties. A summer in the Highlands, stretched ahead of them like an eternity of sunshine and freedom.

The children hated the winters spent in the vast house that looked north towards the jagged grey outline of Edinburgh's Old Town. From their nursery windows they would stare out at the skyline of the old city with its higgledy-piggledy chimneys and towers. It looked an interesting place, perched away up there on the crag beside the castle, but they were never allowed to visit it because it was said to be full of rogues and vagabonds. Life in the Charlotte Square nursery was grim and depressing for Potter ruled despotically, without any intervention on the children's behalf by their mother. They were sporadically educated by various tutors, none of whom, except a gentle old emigré called M. Martin, imparted much knowledge to their pupils. He taught them the French language and told stories of life in pre-Revolutionary France before the *citoyens* chopped off the heads of their poor king and queen.

But they loved Glen Fada, their ancestral home on the banks of the River Spey, where life was totally different. Though Potter would be with them, her rule was less rigid and sadistic there because the faithful Highland servants allied themselves with the children against her. Besides this year, they knew, she would be much occupied with the new baby so they would be free to roam the hills and forests like little savages.

They wouldn't be worried with lessons either for in the Highlands there were no outside tutors. Their mother always had plans to take over their education herself but these dwindled away to nothing because she was so often ill in bed or lying on her parlour sofa, complaining of a headache. When she was well, she was too occupied with visiting or with guests to think of giving lessons.

To the children, another pleasant feature of their lives at Glen Fada was the amount of entertaining that went on. People were forever paying calls and the house was always full of visiting relations, of whom they had a vast number. These distant relations came from far and near to pay their respects to Macalpine, the laird, and by Highland custom expected to be entertained for the night or, even better, several nights. It was the Highland way.

No wonder the children regarded the prospect of summer at Glen Fada like a happy and riotous freedom after a long period in jail.

The two fine carriages trundled slowly along, both stacked high with boxes and bundles and drawn by four mettlesome horses. Escorting them were various attendants and outriders in fine dark green livery with silver facings. No expense had been spared on their

travelling party and at every inn where they stopped, they were met
with a rapturous reception.

'How good to see you again,' said landlords and landladies, bowing low to the laird and his lady. 'How big the children have grown
and there's another baby! What a fine little fellow,' they gushed.

Macalpine and his wife beamed graciously at the flatterers. It
never occurred to them that they were well received because of the
money they spent and not from the deference due to their exalted
rank.

Flattery relaxed the nervous Mrs Macalpine who grew more
ladylike and snobbish with each enthusiastic reception. She quickly
assumed the mantle of the laird's lady, head of a feudal hierarchy.
The looks of envy and admiration that were cast at their entourage
as it rumbled along the rutted roads pleased her and she leaned back
in her corner, occasionally regaling her daughters with anecdotes
about the various families whose houses and castles they passed en
route.

They were left with the impression that only people of gentle
birth were worth consideration and, of these, the Macalpines were
to be counted among the top rank. 'Your father's family have been
lairds of Glen Fada since the sixteenth century and my people were
great landowners before William the Conqueror came to England,'
said their mother in one of her expansive moods. She did not add
that her father was a country parson but chose only to remember
that noble Saxon blood flowed in his veins for she was a Godwin,
descendant of the unfortunate Harold slain by William the Bastard
at Senlac Hill.

Their progress was slow because of Jane Macalpine's frail health
and nervous temperament. She continued to screech in terror every
time a horse stumbled. It was a strain for the children to stay quiet
and not try her spirits further but Grizel helped her younger sister by
playing games with her and pointing out interesting sights through
the carriage window when Anne's patience was on the verge of
running out. Her solicitude earned her not the praise she longed
for, but a reprimand from her mother who told her: 'You're so sly,
Grizel! You think you can worm your way into my good graces but
you're a minx to make use of your sister like that.'

Grizel sat back in her seat, abashed. It was a problem to know
how exactly to please her mother. The rebuke was soon forgotten,
however, because the children's mother and aunt spent much of the
time gossiping together in a sort of secret language which they had

devised and which they thought was incomprehensible to the children. Sharp little Grizel soon worked out that all they were doing was adding '-vus' to the end of every word. Grown up people are so very strange, she thought as her head drooped forward and she slipped off into a doze.

When she woke they were clattering into the yard of the inn at Dunkeld where they were to spend the evening before crossing the Tay by the carriage ferry at Inver, and paying their toll to the Duke of Athol for the privilege.

'You've been good children,' their father announced when they climbed stiffly down from their seats, 'so as a treat you can stay up to hear the great Neil Gow tonight.'

The name did not mean much to them but from the note of enthusiasm in their father's voice, they guessed that they were being allowed an immense privilege and obligingly clapped their hands. There were bright smiles on all their faces when, after supper, they assembled in the inn parlour to hear Mr Gow.

At first sight the bent, snuff-stained old man with straggling grey hair and a deeply lined face was a disappointment. However, he made a special point of noticing the children.

'Have any of you a favourite tune? If so, I'll play it for you.' For Gow was a famous musician whose fame spread far and wide from his Dunkeld home. No one else in Scotland could make a fiddle speak as he did.

Anne and Patrick shook their heads. Their idea of music was chanted nursery rhymes but Grizel was already showing talent as a singer. 'Can you play *Cuchulain?* I love that tune,' she said, trying not to see the disapproving face her mother pulled at her presumption.

Gow smiled delightedly at her. 'Ah, *Cuchulain,* the story of the warrior who lived at the court of the Queen of Skye. You've good taste, my dear. If that's what you like, I'll give it to you.' And, standing up, he drew the bow across the strings of his fiddle and launched, with a gusto that belied his eighty years, into his repertoire of old Scots airs.

The inn's shadowy parlour was lit only by the fire blazing in the hearth, flashing off the brass fire tongs and warming pans hung on the wall. As Gow's music poured out, Grizel felt herself ascending to Paradise. She listened entranced, watching the nimble fingers dancing on the neck of the instrument, seeing the abstraction in the old man's eyes as he made the fiddle speak, feeling deep within himself every emotion he was trying to awaken in his audience. And he succeeded. When he played bright and cheerful tunes, they smiled and their feet tapped in time to the music, but later, when he started to call up the melancholy airs of Scotland, including Grizel's beloved *Cuchulain,* solemn looks and even tears met his performance. Gow was too much of an entertainer to leave them like that, however, and for his last piece he played a tune of his own composition, music dedicated to love and happiness.

Its sweetness sighed forth into the air like lovers' voices through the ages, and though she did not know why, Grizel was deeply moved. The music seemed to presage emotions she would one day feel herself and she was weeping softly as Gow finished his recital. Tears ran down her cheeks while the old man put his instrument carefully away into its case, accepted Macalpine's financial tribute and made his way out into the night on the arm of his son Nathaniel. When the audience rose to leave the parlour, Grizel's distress was noticed.

'What's wrong with you?' asked her mother sharply, but all she could do in reply was to sob. Her parents looked at each other askance and her mother leaned towards her, fists clenched, hissing: 'You're making a deliberate fuss. You want people to look at you. Get up or I'll box your ears! You can't sit here all night.'

Before the threat could be carried out, however, Peter John stepped in. He lifted up his weeping daughter and told his wife, 'No, no, my dear, it's the music that's affected her. I'll take her for a walk along the river bank 'til it wears off or she'll not be able to sleep. Gow does that to me as well. . . .'

They did not walk far but stood on a little path beside the Tay, watching the moonlight silver the water. Her father's hand holding hers reassured Grizel that someone understood her at last, but the moment soon passed.

'You're eight years old now,' he said to her gently. 'You must try to behave in a ladylike way and not worry your mother so much. She thinks you set out to annoy her.'

'I don't, I really don't,' she whispered. 'But Mother and Aunt Maria don't understand me. They never believe what I tell them.'

Her father, though kind, would hear no criticism of his wife. 'That's nonsense! They believe it when you tell the truth and behave well. It's when you turn mulish that you annoy them most. You know that yourself.'

She nodded, stubbornness was one of her failings, but there was one question that she longed to ask, a question that often ran through her mind. 'Father, why does no one like me? Patrick and Anne and little Louisa and the new baby are all loved – but no one likes me. I'm no one's favourite.'

He bent down over her. 'Of course you are! We all love you. You're imagining things if you think you're not loved. It's just that the others make things easy for themselves. They're not so prickly as you are.'

She longed to say she was only prickly because of the injustices forever being meted out to her. 'I don't think Mama likes me very much,' she persisted.

'Nonsense.' He was brisker now. 'You must remember that your mother's always on edge when she travels. She doesn't enjoy it and she particularly doesn't like this part of the world. She's a very nervous person and she has good reason for her anxiety.'

Grizel gazed at her father with worried eyes. 'What do you mean? Why should she be so nervous?'

He straightened up and gave himself a little shake as if he felt he had said too much. 'Just believe me. Be kind to your poor mother. When you're older you'll understand.'

Grizel's eyes gleamed with sympathetic tears. 'I'm sorry, Father. I'll be good, I promise. I'll do nothing to annoy my poor mother.'

On the following day their convoy crossed the desolate moor of Alvie and everyone's spirits rose at the prospect of reaching home at last. When a stop was made to water the horses, Mrs Macalpine yielded to Patrick's plea to be allowed to travel the last leg of the journey with his sisters and they all sat squashed into one seat, trying to be well behaved and quiet. Fidgetting stopped when the River Spey came into view and they craned forward, straining their eyes in the old game of trying to be the first to make out their home among the silver-trunked birch trees on the other side of the river.

Grizel saw it before the others but, sensing that if she won the contest she would earn a reprimand from her mother, she said nothing and a few seconds later Patrick cried out, 'Look, there it is! There's Glen Fada. We're home, we're home!' He gave a cheer which was echoed by Anne and, in a release of delight, they all leaned back in their seats and kicked their heels against the wall of the carriage until their mother reached across and pinched the cheek of the child unfortunate enough to be sitting nearest to her. It was

Grizel who received the cruel nip but such was her excitement she hardly felt any pain.

The sighting of the house did not mean the end of their journey for they had another two miles of tedious driving before they reached the carriage ferry at Inverdruie and crossed the swiftly flowing river. These two miles were purgatory even for the adults of the party and it was all they could do to stop the children leaping from the coach and charging off across country to the little rowing boat that served as their own ferry on the Spey.

When they negotiated the river crossing at Inverdruie, however, their reception on the other bank was everything that could be desired. They leaned from the carriage windows, waving and beaming, as people from the estate came running to the roadside to cheer their passing. They recognised old friends, not seen for the last six months, and cried out as they drove along: 'There's dear Betty. There's Arthur Dunn and his father. There's wee Allie Beag, the post boy. There's Maggy from the mill and Jeanie the hen wife. . . .' The Macalpines' homecoming was like the triumphal return of a Roman Emperor and his conquering army. Men stood bare-headed as their laird drove by, bonnets in hand, looking at him with love and admiration in their eyes. These Highlanders would have followed him to their deaths, in the same way as their predecessors followed past lairds.

The cavalcade rolled through the landscaped park and into the cobbled yard behind the big house. There the children erupted from the confinement of the coach like exuberant little animals, calling to each other in delight as they ran here and there, searching out their favourite places. Patrick, closely followed by Anne, went first to the stables; Grizel wandered into the garden where white heart cherry trees bowered the gate to her private paradise.

The adults allowed them to run free without chastisement because Glen Fada had a beneficial effect on them as well; its soothing atmosphere eased away tiredness, eradicated worries and rebuilt confidence. The Macalpines had come home, to the place where they had spent every summer for as far back as Grizel could remember. The routine never varied – winter in Edinburgh and the summer at Glen Fada.

Glen Fada house was shaped like a T. The projecting wing at the back was the original dwelling, the unpretentious home of the earlier Macalpines. The present day kitchens, still rooms and pantries were

on the ground floor of the old wing, with the library above. There
the previous laird, Macalpine's uncle, had been found dead in his
chair with the Bible open on his chest. On the top storey, little
apertures like winking eyes peeped out of the steeply pitched slate
roof. These were the nursery windows.

Grizel's father built a new front on the house to satisfy his wife
who complained that there were no proper receiving rooms at Glen
Fada. She wanted to copy the spacious reception rooms that their
fashionable neighbour the Duchess of Gordon had built at Kinrara,
her house two miles farther up the river.

'The Duchess holds such wonderful entertainments at Kinrara but
we can't entertain in any style at all. Even my sister Charlotte in
Glasgow has a better drawing room than we have and her husband
is only a merchant. . .though he's rich enough, I'll grant you,'
Jane Macalpine complained, and the jibe about his brother-in-law's
riches was enough to make her husband draw up the plans for a fine
new salon and dining room.

His latest improvement had been the remodelling of the kitchens.
The children loved them as they were in the old days with a low,
smoke-blackened roof and dozens of dark corners where old retainers huddled, smoking their pipes or taking snuff and gossiping,
always gossiping. The kitchen was Grizel's favourite place in the
house. She would sit there for hours listening to stories of ghosts
and fairies, magic and legend, that richly fed her imagination. But
one day a mouse dropped off a rafter into a syllabub her mother
and Aunt Maria were preparing. That spelled the end for the old
kitchens. When Mrs Macalpine was revived with sal volatile and
order was restored, she told her husband, 'You'll have to do
something about that terrible hole. It's like a crofter's cabin in
there, filled with peat reek and people, all drinking our whisky
and eating our food.'

He built a new kitchen, but fortunately could do nothing about
the people who continued to fill it to capacity, and the whisky
flowed as generously as ever. There was always a bottle with a
circle of glasses and a plate of bannocks laid at the kitchen door
for the refreshment of anyone going in or out. By nightfall, neither
drop nor crumb remained.

On a dull morning in August, 1807, Grizel stood with her back
to the others in the nursery looking down into the kitchen courtyard. She could see her father, his brown hair tied tight back from
his face with a black velvet ribbon and his legs in their tight

white buckskins and tasselled half boots in constant restless motion. He was bursting with energy and enthusiasm as he unrolled a set of papers under the eyes of his two chief accomplices. For as far back as Grizel could remember, her father had spent his summers at Glen Fada with rolls of papers and plans sticking out of his coat pockets, expounding his improvement schemes to the estate mason and the carpenter who were only too eager to carry them out. A sense of dread that she could not explain gripped the child as she watched and wondered what new plan was afoot.

Alerted by the intensity of his sister's gaze, Patrick left the group in the middle of the nursery floor and came to stand beside her. Like hers, his eyes were immediately drawn to their father.

'What's he doing, do you think?' asked Grizel.

Patrick shrugged. 'He said he was going to build a new stable. I hope he does.'

His sister turned to him. 'He builds things and then pulls them down again, and he builds things that nobody wants! Like those cottages he built for the old women at Polchar. They don't want them but he's making them live in them.'

Patrick laughed. 'They're pretty cottages. Father says the old women don't like them because they're too clean and airy. They prefer dirt and smoke.'

'That's not fair,' she protested. 'They're used to their own ways. They like black houses with deep thatches. I like them too – people feel safe in them. English cottages don't look right here.'

'That's because you're a Highlander at heart,' her brother told her, and it was true. Grizel did not like change and would be perfectly happy never to leave Glen Fada at all. Sometimes she wondered why her father undertook the trek to winter in Edinburgh every year when he could have stayed at home and run his estates the way the lairds before him had done.

Her spying from the window was rudely interrupted by Potter, the governess, who came up behind the child and roughly pulled at her arm. Instinctively Grizel cringed, as if from a blow, for Potter made the children shiver in fear when they were left alone with her. Their mother did nothing to temper the cruel regime, refusing to listen to any complaints against the governess and never climbing the stairs to the nurseries, either in Charlotte Square or at Glen Fada, to check on what was happening to her children.

Today however Potter did not cuff Grizel but pushed her back to the nursery table and told her, 'Get on with copying your letters from the alphabet book, miss.' Then she bustled about, singing in her tuneless voice of a sailor going off to sea and never returning. As she sang, the words brought her to such a pitch of anguish that she wept huge, splashing tears. Though they were kind-hearted children, the young Macalpines looked on their governess's grief dispassionately for they had too often heard her story about her young husband, a sailor with long black curls, who never came back from the war. After Potter had retreated, sobbing, to her own room, Grizel put down her pen and said to Patrick and Anne: 'I don't think he was killed at all. I wouldn't blame him if he decided to stay away.'

They were all stifling their laughter when there was a clattering on the steep wooden stairs and the door was pushed open to admit Beatie, the kitchen maid, carrying a tray of food. The smell was enough. 'It's boiled mutton again,' groaned Patrick, and Grizel felt her stomach heave. Beatie set the tray down on the table and Potter, wiping her eyes, came in from next door.

'We hate mutton,' said Grizel, staring the governess out as she started spooning the noxious food on to their plates.

'Your mother ordered it. You must eat it,' was the reply, and Potter set about cutting up unappetising chunks of mutton for her charges. The children sat around the battered table, sunk in gloom. They stared at the congealing fat on the lumps of mutton that filled their plates, their natural appetites rapidly disappearing.

'In the kitchen they'll be eating bannocks and cheese. I'd rather have that,' said Anne daringly.

'And drinking whisky,' added cheeky Patrick, but his grin disappeared when Potter gave him a slap across the hands with the back of the serving spoon for his sally. Grizel saw her brother's face contort in pain. Because he was a year younger than herself, she felt that seniority gave her the responsibility of standing up for him.

'You shouldn't hit him! You know Father doesn't allow you to hit any of us. If we're to be punished, he's the one who does it,' she told the governess, but her reward was an even harder slap with the spoon which she feared had broken one of her fingers, so piercing was the pain. Grizel refused to cry, however, for she knew that Potter enjoyed the sight of her charges' tears.

'I'll fetch your father to make sure you eat this,' snapped the governess and went in search of him.

The library was dark and dim. When Potter was admitted into its secluded shade, she had to screw up her eyes to see her way across the floor to the desk in the window where her master sat. The walls were lined with shelves stacked with leatherbound books. A deep sofa was set in front of the fireplace, and several padded chairs with reading stands in front of them were ranged on a Turkey carpet glowing with reds and blues. In one corner stood a set of library steps, and on the top shelf, between books and ceiling, were ranged Macalpine's most recent acquisitions: a series of marble busts of famous philosophers and writers.

The laird himself sat quill in hand, a bleak look on his face as he turned to stare at the governess. It was obvious that he was not in a mood to suffer needless interruption.

'It's the children, sir. They won't eat their mutton unless you order them to.'

Macalpine frowned. 'Isn't it your job to make them eat, Potter?'

'But they refuse. They won't eat it, they say. It's Miss Grizel's fault. She's encouraging them.'

'What does their mother say about this?'

Potter assumed a sanctimonious expression. 'The poor mistress is unwell, sir. She's in bed and Miss Maria is attending her. I daren't interrupt them.'

'Why won't they eat the mutton?' Peter John tried a different tack.

'They say they don't like it, but the mistress ordered that they should have it.'

That was the governess's trump card, and she knew it. The laird doted on his wife. If she ordered mutton, mutton it must be. Peter John would do nothing to countermand her instructions. 'They must eat it,' he said absently. 'Give them nothing else until they do.'

When this message was carried back to them, the children despaired. Patrick quickly gobbled up his share of the mutton but, though they tried hard, the girls could not manage. Even less could they eat the disgusting beans that were served with it. Grizel spooned some of her portion into her mouth but her gorge rose at the salty taste.

Potter's face shone with satisfaction. In her right hand she held a heavy wooden ruler which she whacked on to the table, making the crockery jump. When this did not force them to clear their plates at once, she beat Grizel across the back. The child convulsed and chewed frantically at her meat, bolting a piece down, retching as she did so. Anne tried to follow her example but the mutton was uneatable as far as she was concerned and in spite of being cut across the legs three times with the ruler, which left red weals on the pale skin, she became mulish.

'I can't eat it, I can't eat it,' she sobbed, laying her head on the table.

With relish, Potter pronounced sentence. 'In that case, it'll be served to you at every meal until you do.'

It took two days before hunger drove the girls to eat the mutton. Even worse than the horrible taste was the triumphant look on their governess's face when the plates were finally cleared. Grizel swallowed down her last mouthful with loathing and then said to Potter, 'You're a wicked woman. We all hate you.'

As soon as the words were out, she saw that she had provided the governess with another weapon. 'So you all hate me, do you? Do *you* hate me?' As she spoke she took hold of Louisa's ear and forced the child's head back. The youngest girl was fat, stolid, and very slow to learn. All she wanted to do was sit quietly in a corner playing with a block of wood that she wrapped in bits of rags. Though it bore no resemblance to a real baby as far as the others could see, it was her doll and she loved it dearly.

'Do you hate me, Louisa?' Potter crooned. She lifted the rag-wrapped log from the floor and made to throw it into the fireplace. Louisa's eyes widened in alarm. She shook her head. 'No,' she muttered.

Mrs Potter scrutinised her mutinous charges. 'Who wants to go to Kinrara this afternoon?' she asked.

Patrick shrugged. 'I don't. I'd rather go into the forest with the ponies.'

'So would I,' agreed Anne, with a conspiratorial look towards her brother. It was her bitterest disappointment that she had not been born a boy for she was even more daring than Patrick at climbing trees, better at playing bat and ball and riding the broad-backed Highland garrons over the twisting forest paths. Since babyhood she had loved horses so much that when the family were in Edinburgh, she spent hours astride a sofa back pretending she was on a saddle. She even wore her pinafore back to front in the hope that it looked like a boy's jacket.

'You shouldn't be allowed to go out in the forest alone. I'm sure it's dangerous. I'll tell your mother so,' threatened Potter, and the younger children's brief rebellion collapsed, leaving only Grizel defiant and too proud to yield to the governess's threats. 'You're saying very little, miss. You're the one that hates me, aren't you? Sly and sulky as ever, I see. It'd be better if you were left at home to get over your sulks while the family goes to Kinrara.'

Grizel knew that she was meant to beg, to grovel and take back her words of defiance, but pride prevented her. Visits to Kinrara, the home of the Duchess of Gordon, were the highlights of her summer. For days before an outing she looked forward to it. Even the adults were flattered at being invited into a social milieu that was closed to them outside the Highlands. Their enjoyment was so great that no one noticed the eager little girl's absorption in the brilliant scene the beautiful Duchess created around her. It was another world where lovely women in exquisite gowns had nothing to do but flirt, chatter, and exercise their charms on similarly elegant men.

What the child did not realise, and what her parents overlooked though they would have condemned it in less exalted society, was that the talk at Kinrara was often bawdy in the extreme, especially from the exquisite lips of the Duchess of Gordon and her daughters, the Duchesses of Bedford and Marlborough. They were as outrageous in their speech as their mother. Fortunately Grizel was too young to appreciate the nuances of the Duchess's wit which made her followers shriek with laughter. She saw only the Duchess's kindness and angelic beauty, only slightly faded though she was nearly sixty years of age.

Every word her heroine had ever spoken to her was treasured in her memory and she knew all the local stories about the grand lady. She loved the tale about the young Duchess growing up in Edinburgh's High Street where she and her sister accepted a wager to ride a large pig that rooted about among the dung heaps there. An even more thrilling story was about the days when her husband the Duke was raising a regiment of Gordon Highlanders and his Duchess attracted recruits by offering them the shilling held between her lips. Because it came with a kiss from the beautiful Duchess, many a bold young fellow who had no intention of going for a soldier, took the shilling and joined up. 'When I grow up,' Grizel had often told herself, 'I want to be as beautiful and as bold as the Duchess.'

Revelling in her power to wound the child, Potter leaned forward and hissed, 'You're to stay at home today and cool off your evil temper, miss.' At this Grizel lifted her blue eyes and stared coolly into the woman's flushed, triumphant face. Her hatred of the governess was deep-rooted, and it showed. 'Don't look at me like that,' snapped Potter, slapping the child's cheek with a hard hand. Grizel did not flinch but continued to stare.

'You impudent child! I'll tell your mother,' was the next threat, and Potter swept out of the nursery.

'I hate her. Oh, how I hate her!' gasped Grizel to the others around the table. They nodded sympathetically for they hated Potter too but had learned from bitter experience that it was best to hide their feelings. Only Grizel was incapable of doing so.

It was Maria Godwin who answered the rapping at her sister's bedroom door. She held it half closed and stared at the red-faced governess. 'What's wrong?' she asked with an irritated note in her voice.

Potter was in awe of Miss Godwin, who had such hard and searching eyes. 'It's Miss Grizel,' she replied, 'causing trouble in the nursery again. Saying she hates me, and making them all very insolent.'

Maria glanced across the room to where her sister lay in bed, propped up against lace-trimmed pillows with newspapers and books spread over the coverlet. Jane, who could not be seen by the governess, grimaced and waved her hand to tell her sister to dismiss the woman. Maria stepped out on to the landing and closed the door behind her. 'You shouldn't bother the children's mother. She's not well. She mustn't be worried. If you can't control the children –' The threat was implicit.

'I can control them very well but Miss Grizel's a real trouble-maker. She's a sly little minx, always stirring up the others when otherwise they'd be as good as gold.'

'Yes, she causes my poor sister a great deal of trouble. She's a difficult child. She'll have to be disciplined.' A look of complicity passed between them. 'She shouldn't be allowed to go to Kinrara this afternoon,' Maria continued.

'That's what I told her,' agreed Potter, 'but she didn't seem to care. She was just as rebellious after I threatened her with staying at home.'

'Then she must stay at home in a way she won't enjoy,' said Maria, turning back to the bedroom door. 'I leave it to you, Mrs Potter.'

In the nursery Grizel wondered whether it would be possible to run away, to hide herself in the forest and stay there for ever, but she knew they would find her. There was no avoiding the sentence that was about to fall on her so she stiffened her back and put on her bravest face as a jubilant Potter appeared at the head of the nursery stairs and stood in the doorway like an actress about to step onto the stage. She sounded cordial when she spoke to the younger children. 'Well, there's to be a picnic at Kinrara today. You're all going.' Slowly she turned to Grizel. 'But you've to stay at home. Your mother told me to shut you up in the nursery cupboard to teach you better manners.'

Grizel blanched. She had a horror of confined spaces and a terrible fear of the dark. Even five minutes in the nursery cupboard was enough to make her teeth chatter with terror. With a sudden dart, she attempted to dash past the governess and out of the door. Perhaps if she could find her father or her mother, she would be allowed off this terrible sentence. . . . But Potter was waiting for her. She seized the child with rough hands and bundled her towards the cupboard door which was hauled open to reveal a black and yawning hole inside.

'In you go! That's the best place for you,' said the governess, pushing the child roughly into the darkness and locking the door behind her.

The cupboard smelt of damp and was as dark as a tomb. With her heart pounding Grizel collapsed on to the floor, her arms around her knees, and made herself listen calmly to the sounds of the other children preparing to depart for Kinrara. She wanted to pound on the door with her fists but pride stopped her. Potter must not know how much the punishment affected her. She pressed her ear against the crack of the door and heard Anne whisper, 'Be brave. We'll bring you back some cake.' Then a terrible silence filled the nursery.

The darkness seemed to press against Grizel like a curtain. She huddled in a corner, terrified to move in case some spectre reached out for her. Her skin prickled all over with goosebumps and tears flooded her eyes. All the tales the servants told about Glen Fada's ghosts raced through her mind. There was a rustling behind her and she felt something brush past her feet. To her it was not a mouse but an evil spirit, one of the ghosts that haunted the locked bedroom on the floor below. Not one of the family would ever sleep there because of its fearsome reputation. Her father's uncle had tried to spend a night in the bedroom but was found unconscious on the stairway with a deep cut in his head before morning broke. 'I know the meaning of evil now,' was all he said when he was revived.

The memory of the tale set Grizel shivering. Suppose she was to hear a noise from the room below. . . ? She put her hands over her ears to stifle any sound but could not shut out fear. Tears poured unchecked down her cheeks and sobs racked her chest. She had no idea how long she spent there. It could have been an hour; it could have been a whole day. With every minute that passed, her torment increased.

When she heard another rustling behind her, she leapt to her feet with a terrified scream, hammering with her fists at the wooden door panels and kicking with her feet until the toes of her satin slippers were torn away. But in the nursery outside, silence reigned.

In the evening, the picnic party from Kinrara rolled up the drive to Glen Fada in three large carriages. People spilled out into the house, laughing, joking, full of friendship after a sunfilled day among the heather. Jane Macalpine, showing no sign of ill health, was deeply gratified that the Duchess of Gordon was so kind as to take tea with her neighbours. She entered the house in a frenzy of activity, snapping her fingers at the butler to tell him to bring immediately the best china service, the silver teapot, and the finest Malmsey wine.

The lovely Duchess knew how to charm. She took Peter John's arm and toured the new salon, making congratulatory comments on the appointments, exclaiming with admiration over the heavy brocade curtains and pausing to scrutinise the paintings on the walls. When she reached a portrait of the laird's great-grandmother she stood before it and said, 'What an amazing likeness between this lady and your oldest daughter – the pretty one with the golden hair. Where is she today? She's not been in our party, has she? I do hope the child's not unwell. She's a great favourite of mine.'

Maria Godwin, wearing her society face, said, 'She was left at home, Your Grace, for being disobedient to her governess.'

The Duchess smiled. 'Children! They're such monkeys sometimes. But, poor little thing, she's missed a lovely day. Do let her come down now.'

'The governess will fetch her,' said Jane Macalpine, turning to Potter but Peter John forestalled her.

'No, I'll go up and fetch Grizel. Potter can stay here with the little ones.'

As he turned to leave the room, the Duchess grabbed up her silken skirts in one hand and followed him. 'And I'll come with you!' she exclaimed. She knew what a thrill it would be for the little girl to be summoned from punishment by a Duchess.

They heard the strangled sobbing as they neared the top of the nursery stairs.

Finding the room empty, the laird did not at first know where his daughter was, but her terrible gulps and gasps of misery guided him to the cupboard. When he ran across to it and turned the key in the lock, she fell out on the floor at his feet. Her hands were broken and bloodied and so were her toes in their torn slippers. With her filthy, tear-stained face and clothes streaked with dirt and cobwebs, she was in a state of abject terror and near collapse. The Duchess gave a cry of pity and knelt down on the floor beside her.

'Poor little thing! What a place for her to be shut up. Lift her up, Macalpine. The child's half dead.'

Grizel stared in disbelief at the lovely face staring pityingly into hers. She saw her heroine's huge blue eyes and porcelain skin with its artfully placed black patch on the left cheek; she saw the high-piled powdered hair and the curving red lips which came closer still to press a kiss on her own forehead.

'You're safe now, my sweet. We've come to save you,' said the Duchess.

Peter John bent down to lift his child's limp body. The Duchess watched closely as he cradled Grizel to him, his face concerned. The Duchess's eyes were guarded, her mind busy with her own speculations on what manner of parents her neighbours might be.

Macalpine himself was kind enough, that she could see, but what of his lovely wife with the ice blue eyes? The tea party broke up in confusion when Peter John carried his daughter downstairs and the Duchess's manner was cool as she bade farewell.

Peter John was furious. 'Who shut the child up like that?' he raged after the Duchess and her party drove away. The women of his family quailed before him for he was normally a placid man who did not interfere with their orders.

His sister-in-law tried to explain: 'Grizel has been very insolent and troublesome. Potter can do nothing with her. She came to ask for permission to punish her and make her stay at home. I'm sure it was all a mistake. Perhaps the child locked herself in.'

'And left the key on the outside of the door? Fetch Potter here.'

The governess was terrified of him. 'I'm sorry, sir, it was a mistake. I only meant to shut her in the cupboard for five minutes. . . .'

Jane Macalpine swiftly intervened. 'Go back to the nursery, Potter. I'll speak to my husband about this.

'My dear, she's a good governess with excellent references,' Jane coaxed when the servant had gone. 'She made a mistake forgetting to let Grizel out, but the child is very sly and in need of discipline. If we send Potter away, it'll be difficult to find another woman to come up here and take over such difficult children.' She turned pleading eyes on him to their usual effect. Peter John gave in to her for he could deny her nothing. He pushed aside the niggling doubt at the back of his mind about the governess and the way she treated his children.

Before breakfast next day he climbed the stairs to see Grizel and ordered that she should be allowed to rest until her hands and feet healed. Even better, she was to be given all the choicest things to eat – her favourite cheese, delicate home-cured ham and, luxury of luxuries, a cup of tea with milk and sugar! While she was enjoying this repast, a huge basket of hothouse fruit from the gardens at Kinrara was delivered for Miss Grizel Macalpine. There was no message, not even the Duchess's compliments, for her parents.

In the evening came the best surprise of all. Patrick and Anne came running upstairs to her bedroom, panting and gasping for breath. 'You must get better quickly,' they told her. 'Aunt Lizzie's arriving tomorrow.'

Grizel's face broke into a beatific smile. 'Aunt Lizzie! Dear Aunt Lizzie. Everything will be better when she's here.'

Chapter Three

THE CARRIAGE that drove into the yard at Glen Fada the next day was old-fashioned and slightly shabby. The lady who alighted from it was dressed in plain style and travelled with only one maid servant but was greeted with reverence by the people of the household, for this was the laird's only sister, Miss Lizzie Macalpine.

Despite the lack of ostentation, Lizzie Macalpine was extremely rich. Her fortune came from her mother's side of the family and she was the proud possessor of two large Leicestershire estates. But she did not believe in vulgar displays of wealth and secretly scorned her brother's status-conscious wife who was never satisfied unless she had everything bigger, better, and more fashionable than anyone else of her acquaintance.

Dressed in plain gingham, she knelt down on the cobbles and held out her arms to the children who rushed into her embrace. First came little Louisa who was exclaimed over and called 'You darling'; Anne was told she was growing into a beauty; then Patrick was enthused over as being a fine little man. Grizel hung back, afraid of appearing too forward, but Aunt Lizzie gave her a specially warm embrace and many kisses. 'My darling, my sweet! You're so pretty, and so lady like. I've missed you since I was last here. Come with me, I've a special present for you.'

The child's hungry heart silently responded to her aunt's warmth and cheerfulness. She felt safe in Lizzie's love, uncriticised and secure as she never did with her mother or Aunt Maria. As she clung to Aunt Lizzie's hand she wished that her aunt would come and live with the family all the time instead of only for a month in the summer. Her aunt, however, was very much an English lady for her mother had died giving birth to her and she had been taken over by her great aunts, while her brother, Peter John, two years her senior, stayed in London with their father. On his death, the orphaned Peter John had gone to live with his uncle at Glen Fada from whom he inherited the estate.

Surrounded by her court of children, Lizzie entered the house by the kitchen door. There was no standing on ceremony for her. Jane Macalpine and her sister were waiting in the drawing room. Their eyes met in wordless condemnation of her nondescript clothes and unceremonious way of making an entrance. They treated her with condescension born of the knowledge that they were beautiful and desirable while she was sparrow plain and looked every inch the old maid she was destined to remain.

Aunt Lizzie did not waste time in chatter with her adult relatives. She spent only a few minutes in the drawing room and was soon upstairs in the nursery with her basket of gifts.

'For you, Patrick,' she said, giving him an oddly shaped parcel that turned out to be a trumpet; Anne received a basket with ribbons round the handle, and Louisa a real doll that made her normally impassive face break into a smile of pure joy. 'And now for my pet,' said Aunt Lizzie, and handed a paper-wrapped parcel to Grizel. She unwrapped it slowly, wanting to prolong the pleasure, for she received few gifts. She unpeeled one corner of the paper to reveal a box beneath. It was made of red lacquered wood with a design painted on it in gold. Grizel pulled away the rest of the paper and a sewing box was revealed. With a gasp of delight, she put it carefully on the floor and threw her arms round her aunt's neck.

'A sewing box! It's what I've always wanted. How did you know?'

There were tears gleaming in Lizzie's eyes as she said, 'I've seen you working away so diligently at your patchwork, I knew you'd appreciate this. But look inside, my dear. Look inside.'

Grizel lifted the lid and found miniature reels of silk, needles in black paper, a silver thimble, scissors and crochet hooks. But the real glory was a picture of a full-rigged sailing ship painted inside the lid. It rode on a sea of cerulean blue and she thought it quite the most beautiful thing she had ever seen.

The arrival of Aunt Lizzie meant that the rigours of the nursery regime were much relaxed. The children's aunt was their guardian angel for Potter was afraid of the plump little person with the discerning, intelligent eyes and during Lizzie's visit did not dare to treat her charges too harshly. Grizel was well aware of the effect her aunt had on the governess and one day overheard Lizzie asking Mrs Macalpine, 'Why do you allow that woman such power over the children?'

'Potter came highly recommended. I trust her completely,' the children's mother replied in her creamy voice, but Lizzie was unconvinced.

'In my experience, when people are anxious to rid themselves of troublesome servants, they're very ready to write glowing references.'

Jane Macalpine was affronted to have her judgement called into question but was too much in awe of Lizzie to give a sharp answer. Her sister-in-law was possessed of a fortune worth almost £1,000 a year as well as her estates.

Later, sharp-eared Grizel heard her mother complaining about Lizzie's interference to Aunt Maria who replied, 'It's best not to annoy her. She's never likely to marry. Such a spinsterish little thing, and so old fashioned! All that money will have to go somewhere. The children are her only family – the girls are the obvious choice for her to leave it to. . . .'

Both Godwin sisters had a strong respect for money, in their eyes the ultimate measure of standing and importance, for they came from a family where it had always been in short supply. They envied Lizzie her fortune and her freedom however much they appeared to condescend to her.

Aunt Lizzie caught a cold a few days after she arrived and was forced to spend most of the time indoors on the drawing room sofa. She did not enjoy idleness and one morning looked up with a welcoming smile at the approach of her favourite niece.

'Come and sit by me, my dear. Tell me what you've been doing all morning,' she said, holding out her hand in welcome.

Grizel sat on the floor and played gently with her aunt's fingers. 'I've been sewing with your workbox. I do love it so, Aunt Lizzie.'

'I thought you might! What are the others doing?'

'They're in the nursery. Potter's making them stay in because Louisa did something naughty – I forget what it was, but she didn't mean it.'

'Oh, poor things! It's such a lovely day. If I was feeling stronger, I'd go up there and tell Potter to allow them out.'

The child looked up and whispered, 'I wish you could stay with us always.'

Aunt Lizzie laughed. 'But I might have a family of my own some day. If I do, you must come and stay with me. . . . Oh, I think I can hear a carriage coming to the house, my dear. Go over to the window and tell me if I'm correct.'

Grizel stood in the window bow and stared out over the broad sweep of gravelled drive. Her aunt was right. A carriage was drawing to a halt and a tall thin man in smart cream nankeen trousers was climbing out. He was heading for the front door.

'There's someone coming – a tall man, a stranger,' she called back over her shoulder, and was surprised to see a warm flush come over Lizzie's pale face as she sat up and adjusted the lace wrapper around her shoulders. Like a girl, she patted her hair with nervous hands and said in an excited voice: 'He's come to see me. Go and play now, my dear. I'll see you again later.'

The two sisters sat together in Jane Macalpine's parlour with their heads bent over their sewing and their tongues wagging as fast as bell clappers. They were so engrossed in their conversation that they hardly noticed the child slipping in and sitting down beside them. Grizel had mastered the art of staying as quiet as a mouse and listening to her mother and aunt chattering together. When they eventually noticed her, they switched into the 'vus' conversation which they had perfected into a flow of words, rattled out without hesitation.

'Itsvus the oddestvus thingvus evervus . . . suchvus a queervus couplevus . . . nevervus wouldvus havevus believedvus . . . mustvus bevus accidentvus, not seriousvus . . .'

'Novus beautyvus,' said Aunt Maria biting off a length of silk thread with her pointed little teeth.

Mrs Macalpine gave a superior smile. 'That's true – I mean, truevus. Dumpyvus littlevus thingvus – quitevus spinsterish-vus. . . .'

'So we thought,' agreed Maria, and then her eye fell on Grizel who stiffened in anticipation of hearing more and as a result was abruptly sent off on an errand which she knew was spurious.

Bursting with news she ran up to the nursery and announced to her brother and sisters: 'Aunt Lizzie's going to be married.'

Patrick laughed in disbelief. 'Never! Not her. I heard Mother telling Aunt Maria that she'd have Lizzie round her neck 'til she died.'

'You wait,' said Grizel mysteriously, and sure enough when the

nursery supper tray came up that night Beatie brought an item
of news with it. 'Your auntie's getting married,' she announced,
thumping the tray down on the table.

Mrs Potter, who was busy with John, turned quickly around and
asked in obvious relief, 'When? Who to?'

'It's the nice man who came today. He's from London and his
name's Mr Warden. They're all talking about it down there and
toasting the couple in champagne. It was quite a surprise but Allie
Beag says she's had a lot of letters from London since she arrived.'

Grizel clasped her hands together in excitement. 'I'm so glad! I've
seen him and he was wearing lovely nankeen trousers.'

Aunt Maria and the children's mother were thunderstruck by the
news and talked about it constantly.

'It's awful. She'll probably have children of her own now,'
mourned Jane Macalpine, seeing the fortune she had earmarked
for her daughters disappearing out of her grasp. Maria was jealous
and more concerned about the character and appearance of the
bridegroom. To her fury, she could find little fault with either
for not only was Edmund Warden tall and handsome but also
pleasant-tempered, rich, and well-connected. The sisters were so
astounded at Lizzie's unexpected coup that they forgot to use their
secret language when discussing it in front of Grizel.

'How did she manage it? She couldn't flirt to save herself and she's
no sense of fashion at all. Have you seen the bonnets she brought up
from London? A hen wife wouldn't wear them!'

What was worse, they soon found out that Lizzie's visit to Glen
Fada had another purpose than announcing her engagement. The
sisters sat stony-faced in the parlour while she went through the
house collecting things that belonged to her. These were to be boxed
up and sent down to the house Mr Warden had bought in Brunswick
Square, London. Under Jane's resentful eyes she happily swept up
china and silver, pictures and tapestries, little tables and a delicately
carved whatnot that had stood in the drawing room. Everything
was sent south on the carrier's cart, and, though the sisters fumed
and fretted in private, it was impossible to argue because Lizzie was
only taking what had been left to her by the same uncle who had
raised Peter John. Unfortunately it turned out that she owned most
of the really pretty things in Glen Fada, and when they were gone
the fine reception rooms looked empty and cheerless.

Aunt Lizzie's visit was a short one for she was dashing back
south to be married. Before the month ended, she was mounting

her carriage again and Grizel stood fighting back her tears as she watched her aunt's bags and boxes being loaded in the front. She knew that she must not weep openly for the sight of her crying over Lizzie's departure would infuriate her mother and Aunt Maria who were scarcely able to contain their chagrin at the latest turn of events. Sensing the child's sadness, and feeling great pity for the niece whom she felt to be sadly neglected and unloved, Lizzie leaned out of the carriage and held out a hand to her. 'Come, my dear, ride with me to the park gate. I'm sure your mother will allow you to do that. You can walk back. She can come, can't she, Jane?'

With an effort, Mrs Macalpine put on a smile and nodded her head in assent. Grizel clambered in and sat on the seat beside Lizzie whose arm held her close as she said to the coachman, 'Drive slowly, Johnstone. There's no hurry. I don't want you to be sad, my sweet,' she said to Grizel. 'When I'm married, I'll make sure that you come down to visit me and Mr Warden in London. You'd like that, wouldn't you?'

Grizel nodded but could not speak because of the tears that threatened. Lizzie kissed her and whispered, 'I love you, Grizel. You must remember that. You're a very sweet, kind child. Don't let people tell you otherwise.'

'But no one else loves me, Aunt Lizzie. No one at all.'

Lizzie held her more tightly. 'Your father loves you. He really does. And he's very proud because you're such a good scholar.'

'But my mother. . . .'

There was a pause as Aunt Lizzie considered what to say. 'Your mama is often unwell, my dear. She's had a lot of sorrow. She broods about it, but it's not your fault so you mustn't worry. Just remember that I love you very much. And, Grizel, try and help the little ones – especially now.'

The horses stopped at the main gate where the child jumped down. She stood waving as her aunt's carriage receded along the tree-lined road towards the ferry, the words 'especially now' ringing in her mind. What did Aunt Lizzie mean? What was about to happen?

When Aunt Lizzie asked Grizel to help the other children, the girl realised that her aunt knew something of the misery they daily endured under Potter. Grizel dreaded what would happen now that there was no watchful adult to intercede for them but she need not have worried because the day after Lizzie's departure, another visitor arrived. This time it was their Uncle Edmund, Jane and Mary's youngest brother, a lanky, boyish fellow of sixteen who liked nothing better than frolicking with the children, letting them ride on his back and leading them in noisy hallooing parties around the house and garden.

The minute Edmund's horse was taken away to the stables, Patrick attached himself to his uncle, crying, 'Let's play Red Indians. Let's see who can get the dirtiest.'

Edmund laughed. 'Yes, let's see who can get most berry juice on them!'

This open invitation to become hoydens did not go neglected and daily Edmund's charges were brought home at sunset, filthy, staggering with tiredness, and delightfully happy. What was even more delicious was that neither their mother nor Mrs Potter addressed a word of reproach to them for, as far as his sister was concerned, Edmund was perfect. He brought a blessed respite to nursery life for he was always organising jaunts and urging his nieces and nephews into more and more adventures.

Grizel was puzzled by her mother's tolerance that glorious summer. She was always easier with the children when Edmund was there but this year she was even more indulgent than usual. She fussed round him like a mother hen, granted his every whim, and never scolded even when he and his little followers made a terrible racket running backwards and forwards along the corridors of the huge house – something they would never dare to do without Edmund to lead them on. With the short memories of childhood, they quickly forgot the unhappy times and every day stretched before them full of golden promise. They were happier than they had ever been.

The only day when even Edmund was expected to behave with circumspection was the last Sunday in each month when the minister came to preach a service at the little church tucked away in the corner of Glen Fada park.

Religion did not play a large part in the lives of the working people who lived on Glen Fada estate. They stuck to ancient superstitions, beliefs and rituals more faithfully than they adhered to Christianity, and the presence of a man of religion was not considered necessary even at burials or weddings. The Holy Days of established ritual were disregarded. Like most of his landed neighbours, with the exception of MacIvor of Carn Dearg who had married a very religious wife, Peter John Macalpine paid lip service only to religion.

It was quite sufficient for him that a monthly service was held in his estate church.

The Reverend Alistair Grant officiated at these occasions, coming down from Duthil, eight miles away, with his freckled, red-haired son riding pillion behind him. Father and son looked forward to their visits and made a weekend of it, arriving at Glen Fada on Saturday afternoon and not leaving till Monday morning.

The children of the big house took much pleasure in the arrival of the minister's son, Murdo Grant. He and Uncle Edward were almost the same age and when they were together, all kinds of games were organised.

Tremendous excitement filled the nursery on the last Saturday of September when the Macalpine children hung around the stable yard all morning waiting for Murdo's arrival on his father's sway-backed chestnut mare. When they heard its hooves clip clopping over the cobbles, they almost dragged the boy off the horse's back.

'Come on, Murdo, we're going for a picnic and to race the ponies. Come and help us saddle up. Grizel's afraid to ride on her own. Will you lead her?'

The minister's son was a good-natured lad and not above playing with younger children. He grinned at Grizel who had blushed with shame when Anne mentioned her cowardice. Since babyhood she had suffered from an unaccountable terror of horses. Everyone else in the family, except her mother, was at ease with them but they made Grizel shrivel up inside with fear. She did not know why. Murdo did not laugh at her. He only asked, 'You'll not be frightened if I go with you? Ride the pony and I'll walk beside you. I'll make sure nothing happens.'

She nodded, reassured, and soon they were on their way along the twisting road that led by Speyside to a cluster of farms in the distance. They knew where there was a big field that was ideal for holding races. With Murdo walking by her side, Grizel's nerves calmed and she sat easily on the ambling old pony, listening to the excited chatter all round her. When they reached the field, she was even brave enough to take part in a race and came second – a great triumph, though she was sure that Murdo had arranged it. When they tired of racing and were about to go back again, a girl came walking out of the thicket by the side of the field, driving a couple of black cows before her with a hazel branch.

'Oh, it's Annie,' cried Grizel, waving her hand. 'Annie, hello. Come and talk to us.'

The girl smiled back and walked towards them, tall and straight-backed with a glowing golden complexion and glossy dark hair tied up in a neat snood secured by a narrow strip of velvet ribbon across her forehead. Her legs and feet were bare under her calf-length black skirt above which she wore a looped up apron and a white cotton blouse.

In a soft Highland voice she said, 'Good day to you, Miss Grizel. You're looking very fine up there on your pony. I saw you galloping about just now. Just like the Duchess of Gordon, you were.'

Annie and Grizel were friends although the cow girl was about five years older. Ever since she could remember, Grizel had been meeting the other girl in the fields around Glen Fada house for Annie lived in one of the estate farms and spent her time herding in the fields that bordered the river bank. She was a bright, intelligent girl who always had a smile for Miss Grizel, as she called her. On fine days the two of them would sit together under the hazel trees. Grizel loved to hear Annie sing Gaelic songs and tell old Highland tales that had been passed down through the generations.

Now Grizel asked her friend, 'Come and play with us, Annie.' The girl looked tempted by the prospect. Her eyes sparkled and her lovely lips parted in a smile. Grizel became aware that Murdo and her young uncle were staring at the cow girl in admiration. Annie disappointed them however. 'I'm sorry. I can't stay with you today,' she said. 'I'm on my way to the milking. My mother's sick and I've her work to do. I'll see you all at church tomorrow.'

When she walked away Edmund asked, 'Who is that girl?'

'It's Annie – Annie Macalpine. She lives in that farm over there.'

'And she's a relation of yours,' added Murdo.

'She's got the same name. Is that what you mean?' asked Edmund but Murdo shook his head. 'No, most of the people round about here are called Macalpine but Annie's one of the laird's own family. I suppose she's a sort of cousin to you bairns,' he said, looking at Grizel who gave a gasp.

'I never knew Annie was my cousin. She never said anything.'

'She's an accidental daughter,' said Murdo gravely, 'and she's a good lassie. She doesn't make anything of it. Her father was your great-uncle, youngest brother to the old laird, and her mother was his housekeeper after his wife died. They never married so that's why Annie's driving cows instead of sitting in a drawing room doing needlework.' There was an unusually bitter note in the boy's

voice but Grizel was too amazed at finding out she was related to
the beautiful Annie to worry about it.

They all stared after the girl's departing figure until Patrick said,
'We don't have to go back home, do we? It's too early.'

No one relished the thought of a sunny afternoon being wasted
under Mrs Potter's eye so the children pleaded with Edmund and
Murdo: 'Take us to Loch an Eilean, please. It's such a lovely
day.'

The boys looked at each other and laughed. Then they nodded
and said, 'All right. Lead the way, Patrick.' The children knew
their way to the loch by heart for the little cottage on its banks was
their favourite playing place though they were not permitted to go
there unaccompanied. Like property owners, they were delighted
to show it to Murdo and Edmund, rushing to and fro proudly
pointing out the tea things, the little chairs, the books and toys
they'd brought from the big house to furnish it. They sat round
the table and pretended to take tea while Louisa happily consented
to being tucked up in a doll's cradle where she promptly went to
sleep. Such childish games soon bored the older boys, however,
and Edmund jumped to his feet saying, 'There's a rowing boat tied
up on the bank. Come on, we'll row you over to the Comyns'
castle.'

Squealing in delight, they ran down to the loch side where Murdo
and Edmund pushed out the boat and rowed them over the water
to the island and its ruined castle. It was the first time they had
ever explored its mysteries – they'd been warned not to go there
because it was dangerous – and it was thrilling to creep into its dark
corners, climb up the broken stairways that snaked up the sides of
the crumbling walls and ended in nothing. The children stared up
at turret rooms with their ceilings open to the sky and ran across a
cobbled courtyard where a huge tree burst through the stones and
raised its branches to the sky like a supplicant. When they were
tired out, they sat in the shade and Murdo told them stirring tales
of brigands of long ago.

'In those days to be a Highland gentleman you had to be a robber
as well,' he began, and Grizel listened with parted lips and wonder in
her eyes as he launched into the story of a cattle-thieving ancestor of
his who was never caught by his enemies though the whole country
was out seeking him.

'My word, they must have been great fighters in those days,' she
sighed, and Murdo laughed. 'Aye, they were bold lads.'

She gazed at him and said, 'I think they must have looked like you, Murdo,' for she greatly admired his strong-boned face and bright red hair.

Edmund had been twisting skeins of grass together in a long plait while Murdo told his story. Now he looked up to ask the minister's son, 'What are you planning to do when your schooling's over?'

Murdo frowned. 'My father hopes I'll follow him into the ministry, but I don't want to preach sermons to people who nod and smile, then go out and do exactly what they like the minute the minister's back's turned.'

Edmund laughed. 'It *is* a bit like that, isn't it? I'm off to India in a couple of months but sometimes I wonder if I shouldn't stay at home and look for a comfortable parish somewhere. My father was a clergyman like yours and I'd like a quiet life, I think. I'm no robber baron.'

It was the first time the children had heard about the imminent departure of their young uncle and they were suddenly sober as they gazed from one boy to the other. Murdo Grant smiled as he told Edmund, 'I'd go to India if I had the chance. Perhaps you and I should change places.'

Edmund sprang to his feet and laughed, his old cheerfulness returning. 'I wish we could, but I don't see the uncles who've paid for my cadetship letting me change my mind.'

The following day was Sunday and Grizel sat in the laird's pew beside her father. She listened with love and pride when he stood up to sing the hymns in his tuneful tenor voice. On her left sat her mother in a white gown trimmed with blue satin ribbons and a dashing large hat set with nodding plumes. Next was Aunt Maria, equally well turned out, for she was very fashionable. At the end of the pew sat a solemn-faced Uncle Edmund who kept turning his head to look at the girls crowding into the church behind them. Grizel knew he was looking for the lovely Annie Macalpine, and she didn't blame him.

Behind her, in the body of the church, she could hear the shuffling feet of the standing congregation who filled it to the door. They brought their children and dogs with them and some of the old women took snuff throughout the proceedings, coughing and sneezing so much they almost drowned out the voice of the minister. Everyone was dressed in their best – strong, upright men in plaids, and their handsome women in dark flannel skirts

and white cotton jackets. Few of them wore a bonnet but most
had their hair braided up and snooded like Annie Macalpine's and
a delicious smell of birch tree buds, out of which the women made
a lotion for washing their hair, mingled with the aromatic scent of
snuff and the odour of damp in the church.

In the middle of the sermon, a baby started to cry and a couple of
dogs began to howl. That was the signal for the minister to wind up
the proceedings with commendable speed and, with raised hands, he
blessed them all before stepping down from the pulpit.

Later that afternoon, when everyone had eaten, slept a little and
re-emerged ready for more food, there was a clatter of china as the
butler and a battery of maids bore in the tea trays. Plates of cakes and
scones, pots of jam, and green and gold patterned cups and saucers
were set out on side tables, flanked by silver tea pots and water jugs.
Mr Grant the minister stood with the laird at the drawing room fire
as Mrs Macalpine and her sister, in their Sunday finery, presided
over the tea-taking ritual.

'I do enjoy a cup of tea,' sighed old Alistair Grant, his eyes
shining. At this there was a stifled giggle from Patrick because the
minister said the same thing every Sunday he visited Glen Fada.
Grizel flinched. She felt only pity for the good old man. It was a
joke in the family that he had the same unquenchable thirst for tea
as most Highlanders had for whisky. She dropped her eyes and tried
to steel herself against Anne's sharp little elbow prodding her in the
ribs because she did not want to join in the laughter. Murdo was not
in the room for after church service he had taken himself off to the
farm where he had friends among the servants and the gamekeepers.
She was glad he was not there for he was far too sharp not to realise
when his father was being laughed at.

'We know how you enjoy your tea,' cooed Aunt Maria in her
most cordial voice. 'Drink up your cup and I'll give you another.' As
she spoke she shot a sly glance at her sister who sat smiling benignly
in her comfortable arm chair. Grizel stiffened, sensing some devilry
afoot between them. Obligingly the minister drank and Aunt Maria
rose from her seat to take the fragile cup from his hands and fill it up
again. He sipped at the second cup with equal relish, greatly flattered
at the attentions being paid to him by the ladies of the house who
were past mistresses at the art of pleasing when they so chose.

'My word, this is a fine brew of tea. My wife finds it difficult
to buy good quality tea these days, even in Inverness,' he said,
completely unconscious of the fact that he was detected in an

outright lie for everybody knew his miserly wife never spent a
farthing on tea. It was unknown in his manse.

'This is Souchong. We have it sent up specially from William
Law of Hanover Street in Edinburgh. We find it more to our taste
than Congou or Pekoe. Don't you agree?' asked Mrs Macalpine in
apparent innocence.

Alistair Grant sighed and sipped his cup as if it contained nectar.
'I do indeed. It's the finest Souchong, I'll be bound.'

His hostess's sister interjected, 'I should hope so at six shillings
and sixpence a quarter pound!'

The minister spluttered. It was more than was spent on his entire
household's living expenses for a week for it was common knowledge that his wife kept a miserable home where sparse fires were always smoking, minute candle ends spluttered, and the meagre meals
were badly cooked from the cheapest ingredients. The only time
they ate well was when some parishioner gave them a present of a
piece of mutton or a brace of grouse. The minister never breathed a
word of complaint and apologised for his wife's poor housekeeping
by saying that she was a scholarly woman whose interests lay more
in books than in her kitchen or still room. If he drew any invidious
comparisons between the life of plenty lived by the people at Glen
Fada and his own neglected existence in Duthil Manse, he never
acknowledged it nor did his loyal son. Their obvious enjoyment of
the monthly visits to the Macalpines spoke volumes, however.

Grizel felt taut with shame as she watched Aunt Maria filling the
silver spirit kettle with water and ringing for more cream. Peter
John murmured his excuses and, saying he had papers to attend to,
slipped away to the library.

'You'll take another cup?' she asked the minister.

Oh no, don't tease him. Don't tease the poor old man! Grizel
pleaded silently, and lifted her eyes to stare accusingly at her aunt
who returned the look with a smile of ingratiating sweetness. It was
the special smile that she bestowed on children when visitors were
with them. It would have been difficult for strangers to imagine the
other face she could present when, if annoyed, she would tweak
a child's cheek between her thumb and thimbled forefinger. The
painful pinch she administered left a mark that stung for hours.

Grizel felt grateful that the minister's son was not in the room to
see his father being patronised in this fashion. Uncle Edmund who
was sitting at the back of the party was as alert as she to what was
going on, and with a murmured apology he rose from his chair to

leave the room, unable to watch an innocent and kind-hearted old man being pilloried. The children could not depart until they were given leave to do so and Grizel had to sit unprotesting, wishing herself a thousand miles away, as Maria and her mother plied the minister with cup after cup of tea. What satisfaction could they be deriving from their game? she wondered. They were like people baiting a chained and confused bear.

'Could you manage a seventh cup? I've had this new pot brewed specially for you,' Maria asked in her fluting voice, and poor Grant was too polite to refuse though Grizel could see that he felt quite sick of tea. She breathed a sigh of relief when eventually he worked up the courage to say, 'I've taken a sufficiency, thank you very much.'

But by then Mary had pressed ten cups on him and she and Mrs Macalpine could scarcely conceal their glee. He'd set up a tea-drinking record for Glen Fada! Grizel knew that as soon as he left the room the sisters would shriek with laughter at his gaucheness and Mary would imitate the way he stood with the tiny cup grasped in his enormous hands; the way he sipped the tea, rolled his innocent eyes and made congratulatory comments on its flavour. 'Six and sixpence! A tea fit for a king, I assure you,' Maria would say, imitating his Highland accent and never thinking how lucky she was to be able to afford such indulgences while he scarcely earned six and sixpence in a week. The revelation about Annie Macalpine came back to Grizel's mind with great force as she reflected on the inequality of people's situations.

When the minister refused the eleventh cup, Grizel could stand no more of the pantomime with its innocent chief actor. Asking her mother's permission, she slipped from the room and ran into the garden where she sat in a rose arbour, gritting her teeth and fuming against the cruel teasing. The injustice of it hurt her sorely and she longed to have had the courage to stand up against her mother and aunt.

As she sat alone, nursing her anger, Murdo came whistling up the path. She watched him from her secret perch, and could see how determined his face looked; how firm the chin and guarded the eyes. He had none of the naive defencelessness of his open-faced father. No one would ever dare to make a joke of Murdo Grant. From his hand swung a pair of partridges which one of the estate gamekeepers had given him to take home. Grizel moved and he spied her, holding out the birds and saying, 'Look at this pair that Angus MacNicol gave me. Aren't they fine?'

She smiled with an effort and replied, 'Yes, very fine. They'll roast well. Your father's in the drawing room, drinking tea.'

'He likes his tea. He doesn't drink it at home. My mother says even the blackest Bohea's more than we can afford. Poor Father, he loves it so! Ministers live on other people's bounty, you know – like your mother's tea and the gamekeeper's birds.' The angry note was back in Murdo's voice again and this time Grizel understood why.

The girl lifted her eyes to his face and a great liking for him filled her. He was as straightforward and honest as his father but he would not be so easily deceived. 'Don't go for a minister, Murdo,' she said, 'it wouldn't suit you.'

'I don't intend to!' he replied, and together they walked up the garden to a small hill from which they could see Glen Fada park spreading before them. Grizel sighed, a sudden wave of love for the place seizing her and damping down her anger. 'The summer's nearly over,' she said. 'We'll soon be going back to Edinburgh.'

'Cheer up. There's next year, and the year after that – and before then, there's the harvest festival.'

The children always knew their summer idyll at Glen Fada was coming to an end when preparations began for the harvest festival. It was the most important event of the year and the laird always provided a gargantuan supper. For days the kitchen was a hive of industry. The maids stood stirring up vast bowls of syllabubs made of cream, white wine, nutmeg and sugar, as well as *crannachan* which was a Glen Fada favourite, a speciality of the cook, Mrs Macdonald. She made it from toasted oatmeal, cream, honey, and of course enormous libations of whisky. All the children except John, the youngest, were allowed to accompany their parents to the party which was held in the great barn and, though the distance could easily have been walked, their carriage was drawn from the house by a gang of men, all well primed with whisky.

They sat closely crammed up together on the seats feeling as grand as royalty while the team of sweating men heaved and pulled them along the rutted track. When they dismounted at the barn door, their ears were filled with the loud cheers of people assembled at the long tables. Inside a scene of wonder met their eyes. The interior was decked out with flowers and fruit. Branches glowing with scarlet rowans arched over the door to keep out evil spirits, and wreaths of gold and russet beech leaves were looped around the walls.

The food was delicious, and in its lavishness a luxury to the laird's children even more than to the children of the farm workers, but it was the dancing after the feast that Grizel most enjoyed. The sound of fiddles striking up in a spirited Strathspey made her heart lift and her feet start tapping, for she shared a love of music and dancing with the people of the valley who instantly leapt to their feet and rushed on to the floor, heel-ing and toe-ing with enthusiasm and elegance that would not have been outdanced in any London ballroom. The old folk and the bairns, the lads and the lassies, all danced well and virtuoso steps were watched with admiration and greeted by applause.

From babyhood Grizel was a spirited dancer and so was Anne but Patrick could never do more than lollop around like a young colt, barging here and there in an uncoordinated way. Louisa was incapable of making her feet do what she wanted so she sat on the sidelines watching, but their father danced every reel with his body straight, his legs bent and his feet moving so fast that it was hard to see them. His wife was much more stately, weaving to and fro among the other dancers like a brig in full sail, very conscious of her dignity and beauty. It was hard for her with her English ideas of class and status fully to understand the open uncomplicated relationship between her husband and his estate people.

Grizel saw Annie Macalpine in the crowd of dancers and ran over to her. Annie beamed, saying, 'You look bonnie tonight, Miss Grizel. I like your gown.'

The child ran her hands down the skirt of her white muslin dress and flushed with pleasure. Annie was wearing her usual dark skirt and white blouse but tonight there was no apron. A wreath of yellow roses was twined around her snood of hair. 'You always look bonnie too, Annie,' said Grizel with absolute truth because she believed that the other girl was the most beautiful person in the room, outshining even Mrs Macalpine.

Annie giggled and laid a hand on Grizel's cheek. 'You're a flatterer,' she said, 'But one day you'll be the bonniest woman hereabouts. Just you wait. You'll be tall and fair-headed, and that's what the queens of fairyland were like, you know.'

Before she could say any more she was swept off to dance by a red-faced lad who kissed her full on the mouth when the music struck up. Grizel knew that did not mean there was any romance between them for every Highland gallant kissed his partner when they stepped on to the floor.

She watched Annie's progress round the room with a strange yearning in her heart. Soon she would be back in grim Edinburgh and there would be no Annie to talk with. Since Murdo had told the children of their kinship to the cowherd girl, Grizel had wished more and more for Annie to be with her all the time. Perhaps she could be taken into the family like an older sister? She longed for someone to confide in. Her mother and aunt never ceased to criticise her, to accuse her of pettiness and duplicity, of sullenness and jealousy, when truly she was none of those things. When she was with Annie she felt free to speak without fear of being misunderstood; she felt herself blossoming because she was with someone who truly liked her.

She sat on a bench in the corner to watch the revellers and her eye picked out Geordie Dunn, the head gardener, sitting with his wife and daughters. Hovering over them was his eldest son Arthur who had started working as a houseboy at Glen Fada when he was only ten years old. He had proved so efficient that when a supercilious butler their father brought up from London refused to stay because the place was too remote and the people too savage, Arthur had been promoted to his exalted position. Now, at the first harvest supper he'd attended as a butler, he glowed with pride and his family glowed with him. Grizel liked Arthur well enough but she was fonder of his dignified father, a genuine Highland gentleman, handsome as an earl, whose majestic grey head towered above all the others at the gathering.

After the next set, Daniel Macintosh, the head forester, stood up with a beaker of whisky in his hand and proposed the laird's health.

'And here's good fortune to him when he fights the election. Let's hope he becomes the Member of Parliament for Fraserburgh!' he cried out to a roof-raising cheer.

Duncan's toast was the first intimation Grizel had received of her father's latest scheme. He was standing for Parliament! That must have been what Aunt Lizzie meant when she said 'especially now'. If father won a seat in Parliament he would have to go to London and would be away from home for long periods. A dreadful blackness settled over Grizel's party spirits at the thought of being left to the care of her mother, aunt, and cruel governess.

The depression was still on her next morning when the children were summoned from the nursery to say goodbye to their Uncle Edmund. This was another shock for they had expected him to travel south with their own party but Edmund was going away early, it seemed. Grizel stood at the breakfast room door and saw to her surprise that although it was early, her mother and aunt were already dressed and sitting at the table. Normally, neither of them rose before noon so this must be a very special day. She looked closer and saw that their faces were flushed and their eyes swollen as if they had been weeping.

When Edmund saw the children he rose from his place at table and came towards them, embracing each one in turn and kneeling down in front of Louisa, his special pet, to ask with a catch in his voice: 'When will I see you again, my little woman?'

His words had a strange effect on the children's mother who rushed over and hugged him close, tears flowing down her cheeks as she did so. Grizel and Anne looked at each other in dread. By now their mother was sobbing convulsively and even Aunt Maria could not calm her. Between them Edmund and her husband led Jane back to her chair and sat her down. Patting his sister's hands, Edmund said: 'It's not for ever. I'll come back one day. I'll write to you.'

'No, no,' she sobbed, 'I'll never see you again. I know I won't.'

A grim-faced Aunt Maria took Edmund's arm and whispered to him, 'You'd better go quickly. She'll put herself into a fit if you don't.'

Peter John nodded in agreement. 'Yes – go, my boy. The carriage is ready. It's time.'

Hurriedly he embraced his sisters for the final time. Jane Macalpine's face went whiter than the tablecloth while her hands desperately clutched at his coat. She clung to him as if trying to prevent his departure but he gently loosened her grasp before turning back to the children and kissing them once more. When he pressed his lips to Grizel's cheek, she saw that he was crying too. Edmund's tears shocked her more than her mother's hysterics for she had never seen him cry before. Then he turned abruptly on his heel and followed Macalpine from the room.

The children and their aunt rushed to the window to watch as, with bent head, the young man ran across the gravel and leaped into the carriage. As he was driven away his head was still lowered and his shoulders drooped as if he carried a heavy load. Behind them, Jane was sobbing as if her heart would break. Her sister tried to comfort her, patting her hands and saying soothingly, 'Don't cry, Jane. He'll be quite safe. He's young and strong. He'll do very well in Bombay. It's a future for him.'

'But he's only a child, a little boy. It's a terrible country. I'll never see him again – never!'

The sobbing went on for a long time, engaging the attention of everyone except Grizel who stood stunned in the window, gazing up the drive at the disappearing carriage. Her tender heart was touched to think of Uncle Edmund, their playmate, going far away to an alien place. It was the first time she had had to part for ever from someone she loved. The pain of parting, and misery for Edmund's desolation, made her eyes brim over.

It was a while before Grizel realised that Edmund's departure meant there was no protector to stand between the children and Potter now. The bad days were about to begin all over again.

Chapter Four

∽

Edinburgh, 1810

PETER JOHN MACALPINE lost his election although it was many months before the children heard about the defeat. All they knew, in their cold nursery, was that he rarely appeared at home and when he did, he was too busy with business affairs to pay much attention to them. His abstraction gave Potter a free hand to practise her cruelties and life became doubly miserable because a regime of strict economy had been introduced to the previously free-spending household. Jane Macalpine's idea of cutting down on expenses had no effect on her own comfortable way of life but imposed privation on parts of the house which she did not visit, notably the nursery.

These measures did little to recoup the vast expense of a lost election but the economy measures lasted for some three years. After the Fraserburgh debacle, Grizel was surprised to find that a large brass plate had been nailed to the front door of their Edinburgh home. 'Mr Macalpine, Advocate', it announced in large letters.

'What's an advocate?' she asked Mrs Potter.

'It's a man of the law. Your father's going into practice as a pleader in the courts.'

Grizel knew that Edinburgh's law courts were situated on the top of the craggy hill of the Old Town that faced their home across Princes Street. Law cases were fought out there and many of her father's friends were lawyers whose conversation centred around the doings in those courts. But Peter John Macalpine had never worked before. His time had been comfortably filled with making plans for Glen Fada, entertaining and being entertained. Tentatively Grizel asked her mother about the brass plate.

Jane Macalpine was defensive.

'You really are a stupid little girl! Didn't you know your father
is an advocate? He studied here at Edinburgh before we married.
His friends have suggested that he go into practice. He'll be much
in demand because your father's a brilliant man – brilliant.'

Unfortunately though the plate was polished every day till it
shone like a new guinea, neither its brilliance nor her father's
attracted many clients and as the months passed, talk of the law
courts gradually died away.

When the family returned to Edinburgh after the summer holiday
of 1810, the children were surprised when their carriage drove past
the Charlotte Square mansion and drew up in front of a tall grey
townhouse in Heriot Row. It had no similarly gracious outlook for
its windows stared bleakly into an untidy patch of grass used by
laundry women for drying clothes. Grizel hated it from the moment
she stepped into the hall because it was cramped, dark and cold.
Nor was she alone in her dislike of the change. Little Louisa was
convinced that the new house was haunted.

'It scareth me,' she lisped, clinging to Grizel's hand every time
they had to negotiate the dark nursery stairs. Her obvious terror
gave Potter a new weapon against the child and there was no
interference from any adult to stop her sadistic cruelty. She made
Louisa sleep in a room on her own where she was denied a candle or
a nightlight because of the need to save money. 'On your mother's
orders,' was Potter's favourite justification. Cruellest stroke of all,
she made a point of sending the little girl up and down the dreaded
stairs to run errands on her own, though Grizel always offered
to go in her stead. Naturally this was never permitted. 'Louisa's
only being silly. She must learn to be brave. There's nothing
to be frightened of,' said Potter, ignoring the child's obvious
terror.

It was some time before Grizel discovered why Louisa was so
afraid of the stairs: in a dark corner halfway down stood the object
of her special terror – a large travelling trunk made of cow hide
with the bristles still on it. It had been kept in the attics at Charlotte
Square but there was nowhere else to store it in Heriot Row. Even
in daylight it was a horrible sight with its mangy-looking skin
covering, but when a hand was laid on the stiff hairs in the dark
it was enough to make one's skin creep. Louisa was reduced to
a state of gibbering terror whenever she had to pass it and when
Grizel discovered the reason for her sister's fear, she made a point
of leading the child by the hand past the trunk if she could.

In Heriot Row, the only time the children saw their parents was during fifteen minutes after dinner when they were sent downstairs as the dessert was served. They were expected to sit on a row of chairs against the wall and were rewarded for good behaviour with a piece of fruit, a cake or a handful of nuts.

No one enjoyed this ritual, neither adults nor children, and it was rarely prolonged. After fifteen minutes were over they were ordered back upstairs – without a candle, for their mother said there was no need to waste money on one. If her husband protested she told him, 'Children can see perfectly well in the dark. It's good training for their eyesight.' He never contradicted her. One winter evening, after they left the dining room, Potter held the older children back in the hall and ordered Louisa to go up the stairs alone.

'I c-can't,' she stammered.

'Of course you can, you're only being stupid. It's time you learned to do things on your own,' said the governess. Their mother, hearing raised voices, came out to add her authority to Potter's.

'Do as Mrs Potter tells you and don't be silly, Louisa. You're nearly six years old and still behaving like a baby. Go up the stairs at once.'

The other children watched in silent sympathy as their little sister in her frilled white dress put one foot tentatively on the lowest step. Though she paused and looked back beseechingly her tormentors were adamant.

'Go on, go on,' they ordered.

Very slowly she disappeared around the bend of the stairs and there was silence for what seemed like an eternity. Then they heard a single anguished cry. When there was the sound of someone falling, Grizel struggled from Potter's grip with a strength born of urgency and ran up the stairs. Louisa lay collapsed in a heap on the landing floor beside the hated trunk.

Grizel bent over her crumpled body, calling out, 'Bring a light. She's fainted. . . she's so afraid of that trunk.'

But it was not just a faint. Louisa was twitching and quivering in a strange way, and when the adults reached the landing they found her, blue-faced and unconscious, in a fit.

Peter John's face hardened as he bent over his youngest daughter and lifted her gently from the floor. 'The children will be given candles from now on,' he said in a voice that brooked no argument, not even from his wife. For once he was standing up for the children.

Louisa was carried away and put in bed but her condition was so worrying that a maid was sent running out to fetch a doctor. The contrite parents sat up with the child all night and, mercifully, in the morning, she regained consciousness.

Their father came to the nursery to tell the other children the good news and then took them down to the landing where he opened up the old trunk and showed them innocent-looking striped paper inside. 'It's just a trunk, nothing to be afraid of. I've given orders that it's to be taken away and stored in the basement,' he assured them.

After Louisa's fit, Grizel became even more bitter against Mrs Potter. Now that she was older, she was learning to value her own judgement. The depths of perverted cruelty in the governess were obvious to the girl who constantly asked herself, Why is our mother so blind? Does she not care what happens to her children? The more she pondered the question, the more she came to realise that the only way they could hope for a happy life was to rid themselves of Potter. The question was, how to go about it. Grizel spent many long hours planning ways and means.

One cold winter morning, she leaned across the nursery table and whispered to the others, 'I've a plan but you must help by doing exactly as I say. Don't let me down.' Potter was out of the nursery so they bent their heads together while Grizel talked urgently to them. When they nodded in agreement, she asked anxiously: 'Now you all understand? You know what you've to do?'

Their father's dressing room was adjacent to the nursery. When he was at home, his habits were very regular. He spent the period between nine and nine thirty there every morning, preparing himself for the day ahead. He had been away from home for some weeks on unspecified business. On his return, Grizel planned to stage her rebellion. He came back on a Sunday. When the following morning she heard the sound of his dressing room door opening, she slammed down her spoon on the table top and said, 'This gruel is disgusting! I can't eat it. I'll not eat it ever again. Why can't we have a cup of tea for breakfast like you do, Potter?'

The governess reeled in shock. Not only was a child addressing her disrespectfully, but she was refusing to eat. Fury made her forget that the children's father was in the next room for he had been more absent than present over the past months. 'Disgusting, is it?' she screamed. 'Disgusting is quite good enough for you!' And she came up behind Grizel and grabbed the golden hair which had grown long enough to make a convenient handful.

Eyes watering with pain, the child deliberately overturned her plateful of watery gruel and watched with satisfaction as it slopped over the table and dripped down on to the rug. Any shred of self-restraint remaining to Potter snapped, and she gave one of the eldritch screeches with which she so often terrified her charges. At the same time she swung out an arm and sent Grizel flying off the nursery chair. Then she turned on the other children who were also pouring their gruel over the table, hauled Anne off her chair and slapped Patrick so hard that the marks of her fingers could be seen on his cheek.

They did not stay silent as they normally would, out of fear of worse punishment, but set up a united wail that rang through the house. The governess was still frantically slapping and kicking them when their father, alerted by the din, came rushing in from next door with his half tied cravat dangling from his neck. He stood in the nursery doorway, face blank with shock, as he took in the appalling scene of his children being beaten by their governess.

Astonishment turned to outrage, his eyes flashed and he ran forward to restrain the woman, shoving her back into a corner with an angry hand.

'I've long suspected this, Potter,' he roared in a tone the children had never heard before. 'You usurp your authority! Only I am allowed to beat these children. Pack your bags and be out of here at once. Go now, go before I do something that I might regret.'

The children, huddled together in the corner of the room, watched as their governess collapsed before their eyes like a straw doll. She put up both hands in a beseeching gesture and wailed, 'It was a mistake, sir, have pity on me.'

But Peter John was adamant. What he had just witnessed had pricked his conscience, and he realised guiltily that he had been closing his eyes to unpalatable facts for too long. 'Go now,' he said firmly, unaffected by the huge, splashing tears the governess began to weep. When they realised that their ogre was truly defeated, joy and hope rose in the children. Grizel wanted to shout and cheer. She wanted to rush across to her father and throw her arms around him, but in his guise of avenging angel he seemed altogether too stern and unapproachable. He did not leave the nursery until the cowed governess was ready to precede him downstairs. Soon they heard the men servants heaving her trunk after her. They never saw her again.

That day they celebrated, laughing and cheering when, on their father's orders, the downstairs servants rushed in with trays of delicious food. Aunt Maria arrived in the nursery to supervise them and they were allowed to go out to play wild games in the garden at the back of the house. Meanwhile, unknown to them, their father was for the first time remonstrating with his wife for her neglect of the children. Even so, his protests were very mild. 'I know you're not strong, my dear. I know how difficult it is for you to go up to the nursery, but perhaps Maria could help. That woman was a brute. I could hardly believe what I saw. If it hadn't been for Grizel standing up to her, there's no knowing what damage she could have done. The children were terrified of her – she was beating them like a maniac.'

Jane Macalpine made little protest but her resentment against her elder daughter burned fiercely in secret. 'It was Grizel who caused the trouble of course,' she said later to her sister. 'That child has brought grief to me from the day she was born, the sly, scheming little minx! Potter was perfectly suitable. Her references were excellent, and it's far from easy to find a woman who'll work for the wages Macalpine pays. Now I'm to be put to the trouble of finding a replacement for her.'

Maria sympathised. 'Grizel needs disciplining. She's a trouble-maker. The other children would be perfectly well behaved without her example before them. She's jealous of Anne, you know. She's always trying to cause trouble and make herself important. She needs to be taught a lesson, one that she'll always remember.'

Mrs Macalpine and her sister took a series of petty revenges against the children for ousting the governess. They pinched their cheeks, denied them treats, and arbitrarily cancelled outings. Anne and Patrick soon tired of the restrictions on their lives when denied the hire of ponies and forced, reluctant scholars both, to spend boring hours with mumbling tutors. As their mother intended, they soon came to regret the passing of Potter whose rule in retrospect seemed less fearsome.

'All right, so she hit us and made us cry, but we could do what we liked when she was busy with John,' grumbled Patrick, and Anne added her voice to his, saying to Grizel, 'All this is your fault. You shouldn't have made us drive out poor Potter.'

She could hardly believe her ears. As far as she was concerned they had triumphed over evil, and even the petty restrictions of nursery life were trivial annoyances compared to Potter's cruelties.

'Poor Potter you say! You were as anxious as I was to see the back of her!'

'She wasn't so bad. When she was here things were better than they are now at any rate,' said Patrick.

Grizel erupted into fury. 'That's the last time I do anything to help you! You should be grateful to me instead of saying she wasn't too bad. What short memories you all have when it suits you!'

The campaign of retribution against the younger children gradually died away but there was no lessening of the antagonism which both mother and aunt still felt towards Grizel. They told themselves that she needed disciplining; convinced themselves that everything she said or did had an ulterior motive. Mrs Macalpine never once examined why she felt such an antipathy towards her oldest child. She always had, she felt justified in her dislike and did not wish to examine the reasons for it.

Because she sensed the coldness in her mother's heart, the growing girl became guarded and defensive. When she was younger she had tried every way she knew to ingratiate herself but now she was beginning to realise that friendship between them would never be possible and retreated behind a facade of self-possession that Mrs Macalpine found even more annoying than the earlier craving for love.

'Some way has to be found of breaking Grizel's temper,' she said to her sister. The two of them took every opportunity of criticising the girl and made cutting comments about her looks. 'Too much of a Highlander to be really well bred,' they agreed, for Grizel was growing tall and thin. The resemblance to the portrait at Glen Fada was even more marked.

They scoffed at her aspirations to learning. Grizel enjoyed nothing better than spending hours in his library with her father who had no prejudice against educating women and encouraged her to browse freely among his precious books. His wife and sister-in-law never read anything except newspapers and popular novels and they felt that Grizel regarded herself as superior to them because she read poetry and the Greek classics. The fact that Peter John encouraged the child in her search for knowledge infuriated her jealous mother.

'You'll never find a good husband if you make a show of being clever,' she warned. 'Men don't like blue stockings. It's going to be difficult enough to find someone to marry you as it is. You're not pretty like Anne, you're far too tall and skinny.'

Grizel recalled Annie Macalpine telling her she was going to look like a fairy queen. Something awful must have happened to change her as she was growing up, she thought, for she accepted without question that her tomboyish, pert-faced sister was the prettier. Everyone liked Anne, everyone admired her spirit and her looks. No one admired Grizel.

After the dismissal of Potter, Aunt Maria took on the task of trying to teach Louisa to read and write. The child was very slow to learn, she was even reluctant to speak, and more than one visitor to the house went away shaking their heads and saying, 'What a pity the youngest girl's an idiot.' Potter's regime had intimidated Louisa who retreated into sullen silence from which only Grizel could coax her. Aunt Maria's tactics of sarcasm and bullying were quite the wrong way to treat her. One day Grizel found Louisa weeping, her hands over her face, in a quiet corner.

'What's wrong?' she asked, bending down to her little sister. Louisa dropped her hands and showed angry red spots on each cheek. 'Aunt Maria nipped me with her thimble. It hurts,' she whimpered. Grizel knew only too well how painful it was.

'Why did she nip you?'

'Because I couldn't read my alphabet book.'

'But you *can* read it. You read it to me yesterday.'

'I know, but when Aunt Maria asks me to read it, the letters all jumble up. I can't see them properly.'

'I'll tell her you can read it. Come with me and you can read it in front of her,' said Grizel, pulling Louisa to her feet.

Maria and Jane were together in the boudoir and were frankly astonished at Louisa's ability to read the letters so long as Grizel guided her finger along the lines. They looked at one another with raised eyebrows during the recital. When it was finished, Grizel said, 'You see, she can read very well. You shouldn't be hard on her, Aunt Maria.'

As soon as the words were spoken, her mother's face darkened. 'You're only a child, you've no right to criticise your aunt.'

Grizel floundered. 'I'm not criticising. I just think Louisa needs gentleness. It's not fair. . . .'

'How do you know what is fair? You're trying to make trouble again. You're trying to turn Louisa against her aunt. You're a sly minx but you don't deceive me,' her mother said angrily.

Tears sparkled in Grizel's eyes. 'I'm not sly, Mother. I'm truly not. I'm only trying to help.'

'To help yourself, you mean! You need to be taught a lesson, and I know how to do it. Go and fetch your work box,' her mother ordered.

A look of desperate pleading crossed Grizel's face. 'Not the one Aunt Lizzie gave me?'

'Exactly that one. Have you any other? I'm going to take it away from you for a month as punishment for your impudent behaviour to your aunt.'

Jane Macalpine knew how the child treasured the pretty box and could not have devised a more painful punishment. Grizel went slowly to the nursery and fetched her treasure which she handed reluctantly to her mother. Jane lifted the lid and examined the pretty things inside before handing the box to her sister. 'I'm sure you'll be able to use this,' she said, knowing that if Grizel saw her aunt using the box every day her punishment would be even harder to bear.

The month took a long time to pass and Grizel counted the days until the box would be restored to her. Aunt Maria and her mother wasted no opportunity of exclaiming over its prettiness and how useful it was – far too good for a child, they said. Maria had taken a great fancy to it and was storing her silks in the little drawers. She used it as freely as if it were truly hers.

On the day the box was due to be returned, Anne urged Grizel, 'Ask for it back. The month is up.'

Grizel knew that both her mother and her aunt were waiting for her to make some protest. A feeling of cold pride settled around her heart. 'No. I won't give them the satisfaction of hearing me ask for it,' she said.

'You're stupid,' said Anne. 'You want it back, don't you? Ask her for it.'

But Grizel shook her head. The box was a symbol of her integrity. Even if it meant she would never have it back, she was not going to be made to plead and grovel for it. As the weeks passed the look of satisfaction on Jane Macalpine's face became almost cat-like every time she saw her sister using the work box. Neither of them mentioned it to Grizel who put on a brave front, pretending not to notice when Maria ostentatiously lifted the lid and exclaimed at the prettiness of the ship painted inside.

'I don't care if she goes on using it for ever. I'll never forget how she came by my box,' Grizel told Anne, and neither of them ever did.

Grizel had satisfaction over the Potter affair, however, when they returned the following summer to Glen Fada and found the people in the kitchen all gossiping about an item of news that had been kept from the inhabitants of the nursery. Beatie the kitchen maid asked Grizel, 'You remember that woman who was governess here?'

'Do you mean Potter?' Grizel asked, and the maid nodded, her eyes agleam with the joy of having a juicy bit of news to impart.

'She's in trouble. High time, we all say. We knew how cruel she was to you bairns. After your father sent her away, your mother found her a position in the household of the Duke of Lauderdale. She was looking after the heir. He might have been a difficult child – he was very petted, they say – but that wasn't any reason for her to try and drown him!'

Grizel was gratifyingly astonished. 'Potter tried to drown a little boy?'

'She did that, and him only four years old! She was holding his head under the bath water when a footman broke into the room and saved him.'

'What happened then?'

'They took her away and locked her up in Bedlam – she'll never get out because she's insane. The Duke's very angry at your mother for recommending her.'

When the other children heard the story they laughed at first, but later the full implication of Potter's madness struck them and they were sober and silent. 'I think we've had a lucky escape,' said Louisa, the first perceptive comment she'd ever made.

It took more than a year before a suitable replacement governess was found for the Macalpine children. Some of the candidates were too gentle for children who had learned under Potter's rule how to defy authority; others refused to spend half of the year in isolation in the Highlands. With each failure, Jane Macalpine became more and more testy. Eventually a friend in London recommended a young woman who was in sore need of a position.

It did not matter that Dorothea Alfred had neither training as a governess nor even a good education. At her interview she showed herself to be of the character Mrs Macalpine preferred – malleable. She was prepared to put up with the cramped nursery in Edinburgh and to accompany the family to Glen Fada. For her part, Mrs Macalpine was prepared to overlook the woman's many faults: an untidy, barely clean appearance, rough way of speaking and obvious lack of refinement – not to mention her scanty education. It was sufficient that the position was filled by a grateful candidate who could be relied on to do what Jane Macalpine ordered.

The children were horrified by their new governess. 'She only washes herself once a week and she never seems to change her underwear at all,' Grizel complained, and was amazed to receive the reply, 'That's good. She's saving soap. You're all far too keen on washing yourselves. It costs your father a fortune.'

Patrick and Anne disliked Alfred because she hated exercise and was reluctant to go out in the open air. Confinement in the Edinburgh nursery weighed heavily on them. While the others complained, Louisa did not say much, content to sit quietly in her chair staring into space. She was only really happy when presented with food and would clean her plate of anything but the most disgusting meals. When sweet things came her way it was difficult to prevent her eating so much that she was sick, and she could consume an entire plateful of cakes when one made a rare appearance in the nursery.

It was with Louisa, however, that Miss Alfred scored her greatest success for she managed to coax her out of her semi-idiot isolation and teach her to read and write fluently. When this triumph was revealed to the child's parents, Miss Alfred was assured of her post.

Grizel was lonely after losing Louisa to the governess for she had concentrated all her love and attention on the little girl. Instead she took up John who was quite happy to allow her to cosset him like a doll. She taught him to read far more quickly than she had managed with Louisa for though he looked like a wrinkled little changeling, he had a sharp intelligence. He was able to read nursery rhyme books without help when he was three and Grizel was so proud of him that she beamed like the sun when visitors remarked on the little boy's remarkable capabilities.

From Grizel's point of view Miss Alfred's greatest fault was her ignorance. Not only was she poorly read, she was also bull-headed and incapable of being corrected. Because of the hours she spent in her father's library, Grizel was well informed for a child and had a good grasp of history so when the governess told her charges that Queen Elizabeth lived before King Henry VII, Grizel rebelled and protested loudly: 'That's wrong. He was her grandfather. How could she have lived before he did?'

The governess reddened and stared at the child, almost shouting with rage, 'Do not contradict me! You're only a child. I'm the teacher.'

'But you're teaching us a lot of nonsense.'

'How dare you! I'll report your insolence to your mother, miss.'

So Grizel was in trouble again. Her father was called upon to
reprimand her during one of his flying visits home from yet
another electioneering attempt, and made her weep when he said
sorrowingly that her promises to be good never lasted very long.

Inside the Macalpines' house there were two worlds, adults' and
children's. News from the adult realm only filtered through to the
children's gradually, usually via the servants' gossip.

In the summer of 1812, all the talk in Glen Fada kitchen was
of Peter John's second attempt to win the seat at Fraserburgh.
Though she did not grasp all the facts, the girl knew that her
father's two attempts at entering Parliament were costing him dear.
She guessed that it was because of these that Charlotte Square had
been sold and half-hearted economies been made in running their
two homes.

The need to save money however did not affect the life of luxury
lived by her mother and aunt. Bored in their Highland isolation,
they gossiped together and made plans for the fine clothes that
would be bought for the Edinburgh season. They liked nothing
better than spending hours with dressmakers and jewellers, discussing the correct shade for new gloves or the right sort of fan to be
worn with the latest gown. Mrs Macalpine's dressmaking account
was enormous for she sent to the well-known modistes the Miss
Stuarts of London for her best gowns – magnificent creations of
lace and satin embroidered with pearls or diamanté rosettes, and
trimmed with gauze and swansdown.

It was a cruel shock to her when Maria, who was in her late
thirties and almost reconciled to spinsterhood, appeared in her
sister's boudoir one morning with a letter in her hand. It was a
proposal of marriage from a distant cousin who had just left after
spending a few weeks in the Highlands with them. He was a man
of her own age, well off, an Oxford don. Altogether a very suitable
match.

'But you can't leave me,' Mrs Macalpine cried.

'Jane, you've three daughters growing up to keep you company.
Grizel's nearly a woman and it's time you began taking an interest
in her. I won't have another chance to marry and our cousin James
is a very pleasant man.'

Her sister was inconsolable, 'Grizel's only a child still, and so
awkward and prickly. She'll never be any company for me.'

'Then you'll have to rely on Anne because I've decided to accept this offer. When we return to Edinburgh in the autumn, I'm to be married.'

Peter John Macalpine came home from electioneering so jubilant and cheerful that strangers would have thought he had actually won the Fraserburgh seat. In fact he withdrew at the last moment in favour of a candidate put forward by his friend and distant relation, Charles Grant, a Director of the East India Company.

When his wife protested at his rashness saying, 'But you've spent thousands! You've thrown your money away for nothing', he made an expansive gesture.

'What's money? I'll soon make it back. I've a plan to cut down some of the forest. Contractors are paying big money for trees because of all the ships that are needed for the war. The felling gangs are moving in next week.'

His resiliance in the face of defeat had to be admired. Infected by his enthusiasm, his wife suggested: 'Perhaps, then, it'll be possible to send Patrick to Eton? He should be educated with boys of his own class, and he's growing too big for Alfred to cope with here.'

So plans were made and the news was broken to the nursery that not only were they about to lose their Aunt Maria but Patrick was to go as well to start school at Eton College.

The two oldest girls were made miserable by this news. Anne, who had been Patrick's closest friend and playmate since babyhood, spent every possible hour with him that summer. Grizel had not been particularly close to her brother but tried to help Anne because she knew how fond she and Patrick were of each other, and how lonely his departure would make her. Patrick was clearly excited at the prospect of going away.

'But won't you miss home?' asked Grizel.

'Not much. Mother says Eton College has very fine buildings and there'll be plenty of good fellows there.'

His sisters gazed around at their beloved Glen Fada and wondered what could be better. He sensed their reservations and told them, 'There's a whole new world out there. I can hardly wait.'

Grizel nodded. 'You're lucky,' she agreed, 'and you'll be able to learn so much. All those books. . . .'

Patrick grimaced. 'That won't be much fun – but the games will be, and boys are allowed to keep their own dogs and horses.'

Grizel's mind still ran on the world of learning that was about to open to her brother. 'I wish I could go to school,' she sighed.

Patrick laughed. 'Girls don't go to school. They don't need to.'

A worm of envy stirred in her. How unfair that she was being left to the haphazard teaching of Miss Alfred while Patrick, with neither interest nor aptitude, would be guided by men of real learning.

'You're lucky. When you're finished at Eton College you'll go to university,' she told him with a sigh. Anne felt sorry for her sister. Though she herself was not a scholarly child and her greatest interest was horses, she appreciated Grizel's hunger for books.

'Girls never go to universities,' she said comfortingly, and Grizel nodded.

'That's true, but isn't it a pity? All we've to look forward to is another winter of Miss Alfred filling our heads with rubbish.'

'And then we'll have to worry about finding someone to marry,' laughed Anne.

On the last weekend of the summer, the Reverend Grant and his son rode down from Duthil. Grizel was surprised to see how much Murdo had grown. He was almost a stranger with the look of approaching maturity on his angular face. This time he sought out the Macalpine children who had grown too big to wait clamouring for his arrival.

There was obviously something on his mind and eventually it came out. 'This'll be the last time I see you, Grizel. I'm off to the East India College next week. I'm very grateful for the chance because I won't have to be a minister now.'

Grizel looked at him admiringly. 'I'm so glad. When will you go out to India?'

'In about two years, I think. They'll send me out as a cadet providing I do well enough at the College.'

She had a sudden presentiment of the sort of man he could become, an impressive one indeed. Her imagination was sparked into life by thoughts of the places he would visit, the sights he would see. In an impulsive gesture she put out her hand and took his. 'I wish you well, Murdo Grant,' she said, 'I'm sure you'll be a great success.'

He smiled but there was something in his eyes that struck a chord of sadness within her. It seemed for a moment as if he was trying to tell her something. Then she knew what it was: Murdo was torn in two at the thought of leaving the Spey valley. He longed to make a success of his life but he was a boy who loved his Highland homeland and took a fierce pride in his heritage. He would cherish its memory in his heart no matter how far he travelled.

All these things she saw in his eyes as he lifted his head to stare at the summit of Ord Ban, the hill that rose beyond the spreading park. She followed his gaze and drank in the view of the lovely valley, the glittering river and the guardian mountains with their distant gullies and purple-tinted flanks aflame in the setting sun. As she did so, she felt his pain.

'It'd be hard to leave this place,' she said, and he nodded.

'I knew you'd understand. I'm trying not to think about it.'

When he and his father left Glen Fada on the Monday morning, Grizel slipped out of the nursery and ran to the yard to take her farewell. Murdo leaned down from the back of the horse and shook her hand. 'I hope we meet again one day, Miss Grizel.'

'I hope so too. I'll think of you when I look at the hills,' she told him.

Through that summer of departures, Grizel's friendship with Annie Macalpine flourished. They met nearly every day and Annie taught her how to knit on one needle stuck under the elbow as they wandered through the woods herding the black cattle and their sweet-faced calves. Annie's mother had married the tenant of one of Macalpine's farms after the old uncle died and he was a good farmer who tilled his land with care and bred the best cattle in the district.

It was from Annie that Grizel heard the gossip, and even the news, about her own family. It was Annie too who told her about the beginning of the felling work in the forest.

'They say your father's selling the trees to a timber company from Hull. They're paying well for wood,' she informed Grizel whose face reflected her consternation.

'But everything will be different if the trees are cut down,' she cried.

'Don't worry. They won't take them all,' Annie consoled her. 'Your father needs the money and they're paying three shillings a tree.'

Grizel stared at her. 'You don't think that makes it worthwhile do you?'

Annie shook her head. 'No, I don't, but I haven't your father's responsibilities. I just hope the same thing doesn't happen here as is happening in other parts of the Highlands. There was a peddlar at our door yesterday talking about the felling that's going on up north – the hillsides are bare, he says. He sang us a song about it.'

'Do you remember the song?' Grizel asked, and Annie nodded. 'I'll sing it for you,' she said, and raised her voice in a sad sounding lament. She sang it in Gaelic but because Grizel only understood a few of the lines, Annie translated it for her.

> *Yonder's the little glen, kindly and sweet,*
> *Haunt of full grown harts,*
> *My curse on the bands of men that*
> *Have robbed it of its glory.*
> *Now instead of the song of birds,*
> *And the murmur of deer in the thickets,*
> *Our ears are stunned by the crash*
> *Of falling trees and the clamours*
> *Of the Sassenach.*

Every time she recalled that sad song during her winter in Edinburgh, Grizel's spirits sank. She dreaded what she would find on the next return to Glen Fada.

When the carriages turned the last bend on the moor of Alvie and the Spey valley spread before them, the children's faces showed consternation as they gazed out at the hills around their Highland home. Huge patches of land were laid waste; wounded trees lay tumbled like ninepins as if snapped off by a giant hand. Across the fields and up the hillsides was the raw torn earth of pathways made by carts that hauled massive trees away to the river on which they were floated to the sea. As she looked at the ravaged land, Grizel felt as if a war had been waged over her beloved forest. She tore her eyes away from the long swathes of destruction that cut like bleeding scars and turned to Peter John to ask, 'You're not cutting down all the forest, are you, Father?'

He did not answer her directly and she detected a shifty air as he explained, 'There's a tremendous demand for timber because of the war, my dear.'

She sat silent, contemplating that reply. Did he mean he was being patriotic and cutting down his forest to help his king and country or was the desecration that she saw before her for money alone? She was not too young to realise that their convoy of coaches drawn by the finest horses and attended by an army of servants would not have disgraced a Duke.

When she was at liberty she walked the old paths, noting with a sinking heart how the clearings were growing wider and the trees less thickly crowded together on the mountain slopes. Everywhere she went gangs of men were shouting and hacking at the trunks of ancient trees with enormous axes. At the turn of the century, there had been more than twenty square miles of forest on Macalpine's lands. Now, thirteen years later, the sawmills were grinding away all day and the acreage of forest had halved.

She climbed to a secluded glade in a part of the forest that was still untouched and, leaning against the trunk of a massive fir, stared up into its branches and reflected. Only three shillings for a tree that has taken three hundred years to grow!

The post of head forester was now occupied by a stranger called Duncan Bain, whose loyalties seemed to lie more with the Hull timber company than with Glen Fada. He called at the house one afternoon to tell the family there would be a log run the following morning.

'Wrap up well,' he warned them, 'because it'll be gey cold. There's rain in the wind.'

A log run was a great event and the news spread round the district like a forest fire. When morning broke groups of men, women and children could be seen gathering on the path leading up to Loch an Eilean. They were eager to watch the spectacle of the huge logs being sent down the stream that ran out of the loch to the River Spey.

The sluice gate at the head of the loch was kept closed until there was a big head of water behind it. Then, when the people were all on the safety of high ground, the gates were opened and the water came gushing out in a torrent that raged and tore at the heightened banks of the stream, bearing the stacked logs along with it like tossed toys. Young men and boys stood ready with long poles to help things along, and it was exciting to see them skipping down the banks, pushing and thrusting at the jostling logs. It was all too exciting for regrets and even Grizel thrilled as her ears were filled with the sounds of gushing water, shouts, laughter and Gaelic curses of the crowd.

The mob followed the logs down to the confluence with the Spey where local labour was left behind and professional Spey floaters took over the management of the forest harvest. It was their job to lash the logs together into long rafts and set them on course for the sawmills farther down the river.

She had seen this operation many times before, though on a smaller scale, and the sight of the tall floaters always thrilled Grizel. They were handsome, hardy men who lived rough through the logging season and withstood the rigours of their lives by fortifying themselves with whisky. In spite of hard physical labour and having to live most of the season in bothies with only heather for a bed, scarcely ever knowing the luxury of having dry clothes to wear, they were healthy and long lived. Few of them, even in old age, suffered from rheumatism and they were pointed out to people who preached against whisky-drinking as evidence of the beneficial qualities of the native brew.

The Macalpine family stood on the river bank and watched the floaters at work. On the opposite bank, the floaters' families were watching too and every now and again, a bottle of whisky was passed from hand to hand among them. Even the children were given a sip for floaters' bairns developed a taste for whisky when very young. The little babies were soothed to sleep with it.

As she watched, however, Grizel felt that something was wrong, something was missing – what was it? She looked around at the faces of the people on the river banks and knew what was amiss. A sense of their hostility towards her family came creeping through, as slow and insidious as a winter frost. Faces which always used to be open and laughing were now grimly set. Groups of people were standing apart, their eyes hard and critical as they looked at the laird and his lady. There was none of the happy banter and camaraderie that had gone on in the past.

Later Grizel found herself beside Duncan Bain and asked him, 'There seems to be some trouble with the people today. What's wrong, Mr Bain?'

He said only, 'Oh, it's nothing, they'll soon forget. It's just that I've been speeding up the logging run. Your father gave orders for a big rock in the middle of the river to be blasted by dynamite last week. Maybe you remember there used to be a rock in the middle that jammed up the logs when they cam' into the Spey.'

She remembered the rock. It had risen out of the middle of the rushing river like a grey island and crowds of laughing, shouting men and boys used to arm themselves with spars and cling to it like monkeys so that they could push the logs away from its sides.

'But surely taking the rock away makes things easier. Why should they object to that?' she asked.

Duncan explained, 'Well, the people who live where the wee river joins the Spey have always had the job of pushing the logs off the rock. They got paid for their trouble, you see. It wasn't much but they won't get anything this year.'

Grizel was silent. That explained the resentment. The payments handed out to the people could not have amounted to much more than a pound a year but it meant a lot to them.

'I wonder how much it cost Father for the dynamite?' she asked, but Duncan Bain did not reply.

Grizel was growing up, emerging from the chrysalis of childhood and beginning to look at the world through independent eyes. From her earliest days she had been taught by her mother that it was unseemly for a gentlewoman to show any feelings and the lesson had been well absorbed. Her face revealed none of the conclusions that she was daily reaching, about the people and things she loved, and why she loved them.

I love Glen Fada. Nothing will ever change that, was the central tenet of her life. Every morning she rose from her bed in the Highlands, there was something fresh to enchant her outside the window.

I love Annie, I love Anne, I love Louisa and I love John. . . . Those emotions were true and growing deeper with the years. Annie was her dearest friend; her sister Anne was growing close to her as well; Louisa was still a pet, and young John delighted her with his amazing intelligence. She and he had a special bond for they shared a common devotion to Glen Fada. When he looked up at their sheltering ring of mountains he saw the same awe and wonder in his eyes that she knew was in her own.

I love Father. . . . That still held true, but not in the same uncritical way as she had done when small for as she grew older she was able to pick out Peter John's faults and discern his weaknesses. As time passed her love for him changed, resembling more that of a parent for a wayward child than a daughter's for her father.

When she told herself she loved Patrick, doubt crept in. She was not blind to her elder brother's severe defects of character. He was naturally idle, had no interest in learning, and was happiest hanging around the stables with the lads, throwing dice. In the days when they had had to lie and dissimulate in order to survive Potter's regime, Patrick had been the ablest villain of them all, quite without conscience.

I love my mother. . . . Do I love my mother? All children must love their mother, Grizel told herself, but while that argument was being put by one side of her mind, the other riposted with: Why must they go on loving if their mother does not love them?

Chapter Five

ALLIE BEAG, the post boy, came running along the drive to the house. They called him 'boy' although he was almost forty years old, but in stature he was no bigger than Louisa, a wizened-faced little gnome just over four feet tall.

He was waving the newspaper as he approached Grizel who waited in the yard to collect the mail for her mother.

'Have you heard the news, Miss Grizel? Have you heard? The Duchess is dead! It's right here in the paper – look.'

Mrs Macalpine had always suspected that Allie Beag had a good read at the newspaper before he delivered it to the house. In his excitement he was giving the game away but Grizel was not going to tell tales on him; she was too distraught by the news to think of anything else.

He unfolded the large sheet of the *Edinburgh Advertiser*, closely printed with black type, and pointed. 'Look here. It's in here.' And he read aloud, 'The Duchess of Gordon has died in London. She expired in Pulteney's Hotel, Piccadilly, with her children around her, in the sixty-fourth year of her age. The Duchess is to lie in state for three days before her cortège proceeds to Kinrara where she will be buried.'

Grizel was devastated. The beautiful Duchess could not be dead! The valley had not seen her for about two years because she had been spending most of her time in England but memories of the times she kept open house for her neighbours at Kinrara, and especially of the day when she helped Peter John rescue Grizel from the nursery cupboard, were precious. In her mind's eye she could still see the beautiful, concerned face bending over her; smell the soft scent and admire the porcelain complexion.

'It's awful sad,' she told Allie Beag who nodded.

'A lot of folk'll agree. She was well liked. There'll be a grand funeral, just you wait and see.'

Instead of going into the house Grizel set off across the fields looking for Annie Macalpine whom she knew would be in the long meadow by the river. Her friend shared Grizel's fascination with the Duchess and the two girls had often spoken of her. Now Annie received the bad news with a solemn face and the words, 'Oh, the poor soul. She wasn't old but I don't suppose folk as lovely as her are meant to grow old and feeble. Perhaps they wouldn't want to. Don't take on so hard, Miss Grizel. She had a wonderful life and she enjoyed herself.'

Grizel's spirits were low and she shook her head. 'She was beautiful and rich but I don't think she was happy. She and her husband were miserable together. They say he's up in Castle Gordon with another woman, and that's why she spent her time at Kinrara or London. They've not met for years.'

Annie nodded. 'So they say, but she didn't look like a woman who was sorrowing to me. Remember all those grand parties that your family used to go to? They went on for days, those parties.'

But Grizel, her mind filled with the novels she sneaked away and read avidly as soon as they fell from her mother's hand, asked, 'What went wrong? The Duke and the Duchess must have loved each other when they were young. Something very sad must have happened to them.'

Annie put a comforting arm round her friend's shoulder and said, 'You think too much about things. Come on, I'll walk you back to the house. They'll be talking about this for days at Glen Fada.'

The news had reached the nursery before Grizel, and even Miss Alfred was eager to discuss the Duchess.

'Such a lovely woman, so stately and kind,' she enthused. 'I saw her once driving along the road to Kinrara and she bowed to me most graciously.'

John, who had been reading in the window seat, looked up and said, 'You're all talking a lot of twaddle. The woman's dead. Lots of people die every day but because she's a Duchess the whole county's in a state about it.'

Anne and Grizel rounded on him. 'She was beautiful, everyone loved her.'

The boy gave a strange sort of laugh that made his sisters stare at him apprehensively. John sometimes sounded like a little old preacher because he spent a great deal of time with the Macalpines' close friends and neighbours, the MacIvors of Carn Dearg. They lived eight miles up the road to Kingussie and often 'borrowed' John for days at a time. They were convinced he was a genius and enthused over his intelligence but Grizel was secretly disapproving of the effect the puritanically religious Mrs MacIvor had on her little brother. In Grizel's opinion, she filled his head with prejudice and intolerance.

'You shouldn't laugh because someone has died, John,' she protested.

'I'm laughing at you women,' he said, staring at his sisters. 'I'll tell you something about the Duchess of Gordon if you really want to hear it. Do you?' When they nodded, he closed his book, carefully keeping a finger between the pages to mark his place.

'You're such a goose, Grizel. You're all geese. Even Mother and Father are dazzled by the Duchess and her daughters just because they're in high society and wear fine gowns but they're just *loose women*. I've heard Mrs MacIvor say so many times and I agree with her. Arthur Dunn told me something too. You know that handsome serving man of the Duchess's, the one they call Long John?'

Their brother held them spellbound. It was hard to believe that such a small boy could have such self-possession – and such worldly knowledge. He said with a man-of-the-world air that made Miss Alfred gasp, 'Long John was the Duchess's lover. That's why he was always so cheeky to her.'

There were gasps from the girls too but John was not finished.

'And you know her daughter, the Duchess of Marlborough, the bonny one you're always talking about?' They nodded again. 'Well, Arthur says she's run away from her husband and children. Guess who she ran off with? *Her* footman. Like mother like daughter, Mrs MacIvor says. They're loose women, all that set, and you don't want to be like them because they'll *burn in Hell*. That's where your beautiful Duchess is going, mark my words.'

The girls felt cold at his words though they knew they were just the reported wisdom of Mrs MacIvor. Though a good friend and neighbour, in matters of religion she was stern and unyielding. In her eyes, all sinners were headed for Hell and no act of repentance would save them.

A week later it was again Allie Beag who came running into Glen Fada with the news that the Duchess's cortège had passed through Kingussie and would soon be visible from their side of the river. The entire household ran out to stand on a hillock and strain their eyes towards the distant road. Grizel's sight was sharp and she was the first to pick out the snaking black line on the dry white road leading down the hill from Kingussie. The black-covered hearse carrying the draped coffin was drawn by eight ebony-coloured horses with black plumes on their heads, and followed by a line of dark win-dowed mourners' carriages. It had traced a painfully slow progress from London to Speyside where a vault and memorial stone were prepared for Jane Gordon on the river bank at Kinrara. The horses drawing the coffin trudged forward with terrible deliberation as they slowly turned in at Kinrara's gate, and from over the water the watching party could hear the mournful drone of pipes sounding up a long lament for the Duchess.

Grizel felt herself shaking with emotion, especially when she glanced at John's face and saw a look of satisfaction there. He was so patently sure that the Duchess was receiving her full punishment in Hell at that very moment that his sister's heart was gripped with pity, both for the dead woman and for her puritanical little brother.

The interment took place next day and every able bodied man in the countryside turned out for the ceremony but, as was the local custom, no women attended at the graveside. Peter John Macalpine went with his friend MacIvor and youngest son, John.

When they returned to Glen Fada a couple of hours later, Macalpine looked as cheerful as if he'd been at a wedding instead of a burial. He could barely contain his glee as he burst into the drawing room to tell his wife and daughters, 'Good news! Very good news, my dears.' Then, turning to the amazed Jane, he said, 'You're going to be the wife of Peter John Macalpine M.P. after all.'

'What do you mean?' she asked him, wondering if the whisky had been flowing too generously over at Kinrara, but he was completely sober.

'I met the Duchess's son-in-law, the Duke of Bedford, at Kinrara. We got to talking about politics and he's promised me the prefer-ment of the seat at Tavistock! It's in his pocket and it'll be va-cant soon because the fellow who's got it now is on his death bed. I wager I'll be in the House of Commons within this three month.'

Jane Macalpine was delighted. All thoughts of mourning fled and she rose from her chair to throw her arms around her husband's neck. 'It's what you wanted and what you deserve, my dear,' she told him. 'You need a wider field for your talents. My word, won't those folk in Edinburgh be jealous when they hear this.'

Her father turned to Grizel and put an arm round her waist. 'Don't look so solemn,' he told her. 'There's no point grieving over the Duchess for ever. Aren't you pleased about my news?'

With an effort, she smiled. It was not just sorrow over the death of the Duchess that oppressed her. She was remembering the economies that had followed her father's previous attempts to get into Parliament. The ravages of the forest were plainly visible on the hills behind her, eloquent witness to his profligacy. What would it cost before he won the seat for Tavistock?

There was not long to wait for an answer. When the harvest festival was over, there was no sign of the family's trunks and boxes being hauled out and packed for the trip back to Edinburgh. As the days grew colder, the children huddled round the nursery fire wondering when the great journey south would start but the horses stamped idly in the stables and the carriages gathered dust in the huge sheds.

Eventually Grizel asked her mother, 'When are we going back to Edinburgh, Mama?'

Mrs Macalpine, with her armchair drawn up close to the blazing parlour fire, looked up from her sewing and said, 'Oh, didn't you know? We're staying here for the winter. Your father's decided to sell the house in Heriot Row. I never liked it.'

Macalpine was away fighting the Tavistock election and funds were needed. Not only was Heriot Row being sold but Jane Macalpine was also given the task of cutting down on running expenses at Glen Fada. There was nothing she liked better than exercising petty economies, provided they did not affect her own comfort. One of her first orders was that there were to be no fires in the nursery unless it was very cold, and even when the bitter weather arrived, nursery heating costs were to be kept to a minimum.

Mornings were the worst. When winter held the valley in its cruel grip and covered the mountains with caps of glistening snow, the children rose to windows painted with ice patterns and rooms so cold that a miasma of frost hung around the bed curtains. They had to break the ice in their water jugs before they could wash, and then huddled round a fire of damp peats which gave out hardly any heat.

One freezing afternoon an old cousin of their father's who lived on a nearby estate came visiting and saw the children gathering twigs in the park.

'Playing bonfires, are you?' he asked jovially. 'When I was a boy we loved lighting bonfires.'

John gave him a grave stare. 'It's for our nursery fire,' he said shortly.

The old man stumped up the nursery stairs behind the laden children and what he saw appalled him. 'Haven't you any proper peats for this fire?' he asked, glaring at the miserable little glimmer in the hearth.

Miss Alfred bristled for she resented any criticism, even implicit, of the children's mother. 'Mrs Macalpine doesn't believe in coddling children,' she announced in a righteous tone.

'Woman, the bairns in the poorest cottar house are warmer today than these poor creatures,' was the angry reply, and the kind old man rushed home to his own farm where he ordered his carter to deliver a load of the best dry peats to Glen Fada, with the orders that they were to be used by the nursery alone. The children rejoiced in their fuel pile and jealously guarded it against the servants who often tried to take peats from it because they were drier and better burning than the ones provided for the house. It was no chore to Grizel and Anne to toil up the nursery stairs with buckets of these peats, and as they hauled them upward they blessed their old relative.

Grizel had never spent a winter at Glen Fada before and during the long dark months when it was not possible to wander far afield, the kitchen was her haven. Everyone there treated her with kindness and affection, for there was no unctuous deference in their attitude towards her. She was the laird's lassie, the eldest of the family, one of their own. They knew she hid herself in the kitchen away from sharp-tongued Alfred and her indifferent mother.

The servants were her friends. She admired the poise of Dunn, the handsome butler; loved kind old Beatie, the kitchen maid, and often sat with Chrissie, the sewing maid with the sweet, pensive face and the badly crippled body that made her lurch when she walked. In spite of her crooked arms and claw-like hands, she was a wonderful seamstress and made stitches so tiny they were almost invisible. Presiding over the kitchen was the goddess of the hearth, Mrs MacDonald, the red-faced cook, who was attended by a ragged army of local girls. This army changed every year and when Grizel asked why the kitchen maids were always different every time she came back to Glen Fada, it was Chrissie who told her, 'It's because of the harvest supper. They all fall with bairns then and they've to get married about the time the Old Year ends.'

Also in and out of the kitchen at regular intervals through the day came Annie Macalpine, wrapped in her woollen shawl, to see Grizel; Allie Beag, who refreshed himself with whisky after he delivered the mail; people from the farm who were sent on errands, and Arthur Dunn's father Geordie, the head gardener. He was a particular favourite with Grizel's mother who went into raptures over the bouquets of flowers and hothouse fruits he provided for her during the summer, and the pots of flowering plants that filled her rooms with delicious scents throughout the dark winter days.

The most idle member of the staff was the piper Roderick Macalpine who spent his day sipping whisky at the kitchen table. When the laird was away from home his morning duty of greeting the dawn with a skirl of music was banned because the lady of the house did not like to be disturbed before noon. When he was not playing, Roddy did nothing but drink, other tasks being beneath him for they might damage his fingers. He was always genial towards the children and Grizel liked to sit at the table beside him because there she was sure to hear all the local news from the crowd of passers by who trooped in and out. Each visitor, man, woman or child, was invited to take a glass of whisky and a slice of cold beef from the bottle and plate beside the piper's elbow. He accompanied them in their toast and grew more and more indiscreet with the passing hours.

One cold winter morning Grizel arrived in the kitchen and went to warm herself beside the range. The cook was angrily berating the maids.

'This place was in a huddle guddle when I came down, the plates never washed, the hearth all covered with soot, no water drawn!' she spat in rage, and aimed a swipe at the head of the youngest maid who ducked and ran into the yard, howling.

'Och, it's not the lassie's fault,' said the piper soothingly, 'it's the brownie getting fashed again.'

'That brownie's a grand excuse for lazy maids,' snapped the cook, but she looked over her shoulder at the glowing fire as she spoke for it seemed that even she was afraid someone hiding in the chimney breast might be listening to her. Every house in the Highlands had its own brownie and if it was not kept placated with kind words and saucers of cream laid out on the hearth at night, it was liable to cause chaos.

The altercation was stilled when running feet were heard clattering across the cobbles. Such haste was not normal and everyone was hushed expectantly when the door opened to reveal a tousle-headed little boy who gasped out, 'Whaur's Arthur? He's to come now, the auld man's dead.'

All heads turned towards the butler who was polishing silver at the long table. His face blanched as he asked, 'What auld man?'

The boy replied, 'Your auld man, your father. A tree they were cutting down fell on him. Come on.'

At the news the maids and the cook wailed in unison like a Greek chorus for Dunn's father was a popular man. As the piper poured out a large glass of whisky and pushed it into the butler's hand, Grizel felt herself go numb with shock. No one in their household had ever died before and the gardener was an old friend, very much part of her world. He had guided her baby steps among the flowers, picked her his choicest raspberries and cherries, and made nosegays for her every time the family returned home after a sojourn in the south.

Anxious to share the awful news, she slipped out of the kitchen and ran into the main house where her mother and Anne were sitting together in the parlour. They looked up in surprise when she paused in the doorway and then announced in a portentous voice: 'It's awful, so sad – Geordie Dunn is dead.' They gazed at her with round eyes and then, to her horror, her mother gave a histrionic scream and collapsed in a heap on the floor, her embroidery frame crashing down with her.

'You shouldn't have broken the news like that, you know how nervous she is,' scolded Anne as she leaned over their moaning mother, smoothing the hair back from her white face. 'Help me get her up. Call for the maids. . . . Do something useful, for goodness' sake!'

It was difficult for Grizel to sympathise for she suspected that there was an element of play acting in her mother's dramatic reaction. True, Geordie and Mrs Macalpine had agreed well together but it was with her husband that Dunn had spent so many long hours planning and re-planning the Glen Fada gardens. The mistress only enjoyed their bounty and rarely walked in them.

These thoughts were thrust aside however as the girls helped the maids to lift their mother and settle her in bed. Overcome with compunction, Grizel sat at her side and tried to take her mother's hand but it was snatched angrily away from her and with a white face and set teeth, Mrs Macalpine said, 'Get Grey. She'll know what to do.'

Without asking the reason for summoning the lady's maid, Anne ran out of the room and Grizel anxiously watched beads of sweat coursing down her mother's face. The dark head twisted and turned on the pillow and the pearly teeth were ground together with a terrible grating noise. Terrified, the girl tried again to help and bent over the bed as her mother said, 'Sit me up. It's the pain, sit me up.' Frantically she pulled at the bell and then tried to put her arms behind her mother's shoulders. As she did so the bedclothes slipped to the floor and she saw to her horror that a large patch of blood was staining the sheet. Grizel's head swam, she feared that she was about to faint, but at that moment the door opened and Anne came in with the sensible Mrs Grey who took one look and ushered the girls out.

'Go to the kitchen. Get them to send up hot water,' she called after them.

Grizel felt incapable of movement and leaned against the wall on the landing, her stomach heaving and her heart pounding. When Beatie came charging up the stairs with a steaming jug, she saw the girl and said, 'Go to the kitchen, miss, you shouldn't be here.'

'Oh, Beatie,' she sobbed, 'is my mother going to die?'

'Not at all. Just go away and don't worry about it. She's going to be all right.'

Mrs MacDonald gave Grizel a cup of tea with a nip of whisky in it, and she sat at the table listening to the chatter with her head in a swim. No one seemed very worried about what was happening upstairs.

'It's not the first time it's happened and it's not very far advanced. Your mother loses lots of bairns,' said Beatie when she came down. Grizel did not fully understand what she was talking about. The other servants were all far more interested in the arrangements for Dunn's burial.

'It'll be a big affair. Folk are coming from all around. He's one of a big family and he's well respected. Someone from the family'll have to go to his house and pay their respects to the widow.' All eyes looked at Grizel who paled in terror. Who would go? Her father was away; her brother was at school; her mother was lying in bed dangerously ill; her other brother was too young. . . . 'There's only me,' she thought.

'What would I have to do?' she asked reluctantly. The excitement in the kitchen had summoned people living round about. One of them was Betty Cameron, the grieve's wife, who had briefly acted as nursemaid to Grizel in one of her earliest summers at Glen Fada. She put an arm round Grizel's shoulders and said reassuringly, 'Just come to his house with me and give Mrs Dunn the respects of the family. It'll be much appreciated.'

'Oh, must I? I've never seen a dead person.'

'You'll not have to see him. Just speak to his widow, that's all. It's nothing to be worried about. I'll go with you. I'll come in this evening when the work's all done and we'll go together,' promised Grizel's old nursemaid.

Dread filled the rest of the day. Betty arrived with the evening, majestic in her long black skirt and shawl and stiffly starched white cap. She held Grizel's hand as they walked the short distance to the gardener's cottage at the west gate. The girl's heart was thudding in her throat as the green-painted door was pushed open.

Inside the dim parlour Mrs Dunn sat enthroned in a high-backed chair by the fire with a pristine handkerchief pinned over her grey head and her calloused hands lying listless in her lap. The room was full of familiar faces – people from the farm and the saw mill, the boatman and his wife, the piper, the house servants, the other gardeners – all jammed close together, talking and drinking as if they were at a party.

Betty elbowed her way through, drawing Grizel behind her, and presented the young girl to the widow. 'Miss Grizel's come to pay her respects, Minna.'

Grizel took Mrs Dunn's hand, whispering, 'I'm so sorry. My father will be grief-stricken. Mr Dunn was such a good man.'

The widow acted with dignified restraint. She kept her harrowed face averted and not a tear escaped her eye as she thanked Grizel. In a soft voice she said to Betty, 'Take a look at him, there's not a mark on him. He looks as if he's asleep, a grand-looking corpse.'

In terror Grizel looked at Betty and saw the dismay on her face. Annie Macalpine, whom Grizel had glimpsed in the throng, came up and put an arm around her friend's shoulders, saying, 'Oh, I don't think that's necessary.'

But the other mourners clustered round and added their requests to the widow's. 'Go on ben and see him. It's like he was asleep,' they urged.

Not to look at the corpse would be a great insult to the house and, as far as the Highlanders were concerned, children were not shielded from the facts of life and death.

There was no avoiding it. Holding Betty's reassuring hand, and accompanied by Annie who whispered, 'There's nothing to be afraid of,' Grizel went into the adjacent room where Dunn's body stretched out its six foot length on a trestle board in the middle of the floor. Two candles burned at his head and, because the window was closed tight, the room was filled with a musty, unpleasant smell that choked in Grizel's throat. Panic seized her. Some primitive fear made her want to scream and she drew back, on the verge of turning and running away. Behind her pressed the other mourners and she knew what offence it would give if she did not go through with the viewing. Bravely she walked on between her two concerned companions and stood looking down at the face of the dead man.

What nonsense to say that Dunn looked as if he was asleep! The sheet that covered him hid any evidence of broken limbs but his once tanned skin was bluish grey, the lips that normally curved in a cheery smile at the sight of her were heliotrope-coloured, and the bridge of his proud nose rose up bonily from his fallen cheeks like the skeletal backbone of a bird she and Anne had found on the moor. This was the face of death. Particularly frightening was the saucer that lay on his chest. It contained a little heap of salt and another of earth. All Highland corpses were provided with those last offerings. Grizel yearned to shut out the sight by closing her eyes. She glanced in wordless terror at Betty who was still holding her hand.

'Don't cry, Miss Grizel, he's at peace,' she said, and led the way back to the mourning party where the piper, who was even drunker than he would normally have been at that hour of the day, thrust a glass into her hand. 'Have a whisky, lassie,' he slurred.

It was normal for Highlanders to give children, even infants, a taste of the water of life and Grizel sipped the liquor gratefully. As its warmth went slipping down into her chest, it heartened her, gave her strength and sufficient will to stop the trembling that gripped her entire body.

She and Betty were on the point of leaving when another mourner who had been induced to go in and see the corpse came rushing out with a terrible scream. 'He's sat up. He's no dead at all. He's sat up!'

The male revellers in the parlour abandoned their whisky and rushed next door while the more superstitious women ran outside howling in terror, leaving the widow sitting impassively by the fireside.

Betty abandoned Grizel and strode up to the crowd jamming the door of the room that contained the body. She was so tall that she could see over their shoulders.

'Och, he's dead all right. They sometimes sit up like that. Just put him back and lay something heavy on his chest to weigh him down,' was her sensible advice. Then she went back to Grizel, who was white-faced with shock, and took her charge back home.

That night and for many nights afterwards, the girl would wake screaming from a dream about Dunn's corpse sitting bolt upright, scattering its saucer of salt and earth to the floor and pointing a bony finger in her direction.

Peter John Macalpine's delight at coming home with the good news that he had won Tavistock was soon dissipated when he discovered his weeping wife confined to bed having suffered a miscarriage. She was full of complaints against their eldest child.

'She's so insensitive, rushing in with the news that Dunn was dead, almost as if she enjoyed it. That child's not natural. From the beginning she's brought trouble with her. Remember what happened to my mother, and now this! She's made me lose my baby!'

He held her hand and consoled her. 'Your mother's death had nothing to do with Grizel. She was only an infant when it happened.'

'But she was there. She brings bad luck.'

'Grizel wasn't to know that you were carrying again. It was only a few weeks anyway. She didn't mean to upset you,' he protested.

Her mother was determined, however. 'She wouldn't have cared if she did. She's so insensitive. Miss Alfred agrees with me. That child's sullen and sly and doesn't care about anyone except herself. You must speak to her, point out the trouble she's caused. And Anne tells me that she even went to Dunn's wake with Betty. She should never have been there.'

Peter John sent for Grizel to attend him in his library and lectured her soundly. 'You frightened your mother so badly that she lost the baby she was carrying. You're fourteen years old, you must think about the effect your actions have on other people.'

'But I didn't know Mother was having a baby. No one told me.'

'You should be more sensitive, you should've noticed she was unwell.'

Grizel hung her head and said, 'I'm sorry,' for indeed he had made her feel that she had caused unnecessary anguish and the guilt oppressed her. Though he saw her remorse, her father was not finished with her yet.

'What were you doing at Dunn's wake?' he asked.

She lifted her head and looked at him proudly. 'I went for the family. Betty said there was no one else who could do it. I didn't want to go but I went for your sake.'

This made him pause. Her family pride was pronounced, the strongest of all his children's, he knew. Perhaps the child was not being sly and pushing herself forward as his wife suspected.

'Very well,' he said in a more kindly voice, 'but don't do anything like that again. It could have waited 'til I returned or your mother was well enough to go to see Mrs Dunn. It was not your place.'

Grizel knew he meant to say, 'You're only a child – and a daughter at that.' How she wished that she had been born a boy! Not like Anne, so that she could ride horses or go shooting, but because a man might inherit responsibility for Glen Fada. Then even going to wakes would have been a duty she would have borne with pride.

The fright over the miscarriage changed the family's plans. Peter John decided it was too risky to leave his wife alone in the Highlands while he went on Parliamentary business in the south, so it was decided that a house should be rented in Edinburgh for the rest of the winter.

'You'll be nearer all your friends there,' he said, 'I'll be able to come up and down more easily, and Lizzie and her family want to visit for a few weeks over Christmas. It would be difficult for them to reach Glen Fada at that time – the roads might be blocked by snow.'

When Grizel heard this piece of news, her face lit up. A visit from Aunt Lizzie and her indulgent husband was always a delight, and she had not seen her beloved aunt for about two years. The anticipation of this pleasure softened the blow of hearing that they were leaving Glen Fada so unexpectedly. When she sought out her friend to break the news, she said, 'I'll miss you,

Annie, but it won't be long 'til it's summertime again and we'll be back.'

Annie's face looked unusually solemn as she replied, 'Summer seems a long time off to me. My stepfather's ill, we might have to give up the farm. If anything happened to him, my mother wouldn't be able to run it alone. She's been very poorly these past few years. The pains in her legs and back are so bad that she can hardly walk.'

'What will happen if you leave the farm?' The thought of Glen Fada without Annie was a bleak one for she treasured their friendship. Annie was the only friend in whom she could confide, the only person whose advice seemed sensible and true.

The tall, stately girl gave a gentle smile. 'Wherever I am, I'll not forget you, you can be sure of that. I won't go anywhere without letting you know.'

That winter the Macalpine family rented an imposing house in Edinburgh's fashionable George Street. It boasted a music salon and a ballroom which delighted Mrs Macalpine's heart. 'This is very fine,' she told her husband. 'Most suitable for a Member of Parliament. You've chosen well, my dear. When the girls are presented in society, we must take this house again because we'll be able to give the best dances in town. Anne's sure to be a great success, but –' and here she lowered her voice a little but not enough so that her eldest daughter could not hear – 'I'm not so sure about Grizel.'

The arrival of Aunt Lizzie drove away all Grizel's worries. With her she brought her husband Mr Warden and their two delightful children – a little girl and an infant boy – whom they treated with such indulgence that Jane Macalpine pulled faces behind plump, matronly Lizzie's back and predicted the children would turn out wilful and spoiled.

'Children need discipline. They need to be brought up firmly and without luxury. Lizzie's far too soft with those brats. They'll catch the first illness that comes around,' she predicted to Anne and Grizel, and hinted as much to Lizzie hersel'. Unworried, however, Mrs Warden went her own sweet way and her children grew rosier and more lively every day. Grizel loved to watch her aunt while she played with the children, tickling their little toes and cuddling them in spontaneous outbursts of love.

One morning in the nursery she spoke her thoughts aloud. 'My mother never played with us. She's never come into the nursery at all. Not once, so long as I remember.'

Lizzie did not want to criticise her sister-in-law outright so she said, 'She's always been delicate.'

The girl nodded. 'I know. She has those terrible headaches. We're often sent away when she's lying down in the drawing room.'

Lizzie said nothing and put her face down to plant a kiss on the cheek of her baby daughter. The sight of such open love made Grizel's heart yearn and though she did not want to pursue the subject, she said suddenly, 'My mother doesn't like me, Aunt Lizzie. She's never liked me, and when she had her miscarriage at Glen Fada she said I brought her bad luck. What did she mean?'

Lizzie sat back on her heels on the hearthrug, her pleasant face clouded with concern. The time had come to talk to Grizel, she could see, and she felt annoyed that her brother had not shown more awareness of his daughter's bruised feelings.

'Has no one ever told you about the carriage accident?' she asked.

'What carriage accident? I don't understand.'

'When you were six months old, your father and mother were travelling with you and your grandmother – your mother's mother – from Edinburgh to Glen Fada. There was a terrible accident. Your mother was in one carriage with you and the nursemaid. Your father, Mrs Godwin and her maid, Chrissie, were in the second. Their horses were frightened by a bird flying out of a hedge near Blair Athol and they bolted. The carriage was upturned on a bridge and your grandmother fell over into the river. She was killed outright.'

Grizel put her hands up to her face, leaving only her blue eyes visible. They were round with horror.

'I never knew how my grandmother died!' she gasped.

Having started the story, Lizzie had to finish it. 'Your mother's carriage was just behind and she saw everything. She jumped down and ran to the ravine. She climbed down the rocks like a mad woman, your father said, and found her mother lying dead. They thought she was going to lose her senses.'

A feeling of infinite pity for her mother filled Grizel's heart. 'Oh, my poor mother. No wonder she's always so upset when we travel. But you said a maid called Chrissie was in the carriage – is that the Chrissie who's at Glen Fada still?'

Lizzie nodded. 'Yes, poor thing. She was terribly injured. That's why she's so crippled. Your father and mother keep her on in the household but your mother won't ever see her. She's given orders that Chrissie's to be kept out of her way. The sight of the girl upsets her.'

Her final question was the most important. 'And me? What about me?' Grizel whispered.

Lizzie bent over her baby and carefully wrapped her up in a knitted shawl before turning to Grizel and cuddling her close. 'Your mother was distraught after the accident and could not nurse you. You'd been there, you see. . . . She's never got over it. It's not your fault but – she remembers. She was very close to her mother.'

It was a cruel revelation for Grizel. She shook her golden hair and a deep frown marked her forehead. 'My poor mother, I'm so sorry. But, Aunt Lizzie, it wasn't my fault, was it? Surely it wasn't my fault.'

Lizzie kissed her on the forehead. 'It wasn't your fault, my darling. Of course not.'

In spite of her aunt's reassurances, however, Grizel felt she knew now why her mother was always so distant and cruel to her. The mystery was solved at last but her new knowledge brought Grizel little comfort.

For the rest of her stay Aunt Lizzie spent a great deal of time with Grizel, trying to cheer her up. 'You must come and stay with us when we go back to London. When will you come?' she asked her niece. Grizel's face brightened at the prospect, then as suddenly sobered again.

'I'll come next year but I'll have to go back to Glen Fada first. It might be Annie's last year there.'

Lizzie laughed. 'You're a real Highlander at heart, my dear, aren't you?'

Grizel nodded. 'Yes, I am. I love Glen Fada. I'm worried Father might sell it, Aunt Lizzie. I heard him and Mother talking about how much it was costing to fight the election at Tavistock.'

Lizzie frowned. She disapproved of her brother's prodigality and had warned him about it. 'Don't you worry about that,' she told Grizel, 'he can't sell the estate. If he could, he'd probably have done so by now but our uncle tied it up well with an entail. Uncle Patrick was very canny.'

After Lizzie and her family departed, spring came to Edinburgh, and clusters of cherry blossom decorated the trees in the squares at each end of George Street. Miss Alfred allowed the children to go walking alone there every day. One afternoon they were returning in the soft sunshine when Anne suddenly halted and said, 'I think that's Patrick standing in the street outside our door.'

Grizel's eyes followed her sister's pointing hand and, sure enough, there was the dark-suited figure of a boy obviously waiting for them. Although it was over a year since they'd seen him and he had grown very tall, they knew him at once by his glowing mop of golden hair and the fidgetty way he was swinging one foot to and fro as he waited.

Anne ran towards him with arms extended, calling out, 'Patrick, Patrick, why have you come home? Are you ill?'

He didn't look ill. His cheeks were glowing with rude health. He hung his head and said, 'No, I'm not ill. I was waiting for you. Is Mother alone? I want to see her.'

The children rushed him into the house and presented him to their mother in the drawing room with as much clamour and excitement as if they were magicians producing a rabbit out of a hat. She was thrilled to see her son and held him in her arms, exclaiming over him, so it was some time before she asked, 'But why are you here? You should be at school.'

He looked shifty and said, 'Can we talk about it alone, Mother? Please ask the others to go away.'

He was confident again when he arrived in the nursery later. 'I'm not going back to Eton,' he said. Grizel imagined his departure from school must have some connection with her parents' much discussed but never implemented economy drive but she was proved wrong. 'In fact, I can't go back. I had a little trouble. They asked me to leave,' said her brother.

'Why?' Everyone asked the same question at once. He adopted a man-of-the-world air. 'Oh, you children wouldn't understand. It was a little bother over money. Nothing much. They didn't understand when I said my father would pay it all back.'

Peter John arrived home in a hurry to deal with the problem of the prodigal son but found his wife prepared to defend Patrick.

'It's not his fault,' she protested. 'He was led astray by boys older and richer than himself. He's only a child.'

It was their father who explained the position to the other children. 'Patrick was deceived into thinking he had unlimited funds at his back and his debts would be easily cleared,' he said with a slightly shame-faced air as if he remembered something similar happening to himself. Then he brightened as he added, 'His fees at Eton were very high anyway. I'm just as glad he's come home. We'll send him to school here in Edinburgh.'

Grizel wondered how much exactly Patrick had managed to owe before his creditors foreclosed on him. Judging by what he told them of the lavish way of life of some boys at Eton, it must have been considerable if he was expelled because of it.

The prodigal son was soon forgiven. His mother would forgive him anything anyway; his father deferred to her as usual, and his brother and sisters treated him like a saviour because with Patrick in the nursery Miss Alfred's authority was destroyed. Taking their lead from him, they did exactly what they liked.

Soon it was time to leave for the Highlands again but before they did so, Patrick was installed as a lodger in a flat owned by a widowed friend of Jane Macalpine's. He was to stay there during the summer and concentrate on his school work as a belated punishment for his transgressions at Eton. Terrible warnings against misbehaviour were heaped on him as he parted with his parents.

The summer of 1815 at Glen Fada was one of jubilation. The war against Napoleon was coming to a victorious end and patriotism was running high. Elated by victory, Macalpine and his wife dined out with the gentry all over the countryside and at Glen Fada house, hospitality was dispensed with a generous hand. Visitors came and went in a steady stream and the children were left to range over the estate like wild things.

There was so much to see, so much to find out. Who was married, who had died, who'd had a baby or gone away since they were last at home? They ran to and fro, visiting, sailing on Loch an Eilean, and holding make believe parties in their tiny cottage. Only Grizel was subdued because Annie Macalpine had gone away. Both her mother and her step-father had died during the winter but she left a note for Grizel with Mrs MacDonald the Glen Fada cook. The note said she had gone to Elgin to live with her natural father's sister who had taken a fancy to the girl. 'She's going to turn our Annie into a lady,' said Arthur Dunn with a touch of envy in his voice.

Grizel was in her seventeenth year and growing up fast. The confines of nursery life chafed upon her and she found it difficult to keep a grip on her temper when left with only Miss Alfred and the younger children for company. Her father recognised the unsettled look on his daughter's face and sensed her hunger for new experiences, so one morning he said, 'You're growing too big for the nursery, my dear. You write a good clear hand and my clerk and I have papers that need to be copied. You can help us.'

The chance of escaping Miss Alfred and nursery rules delighted Grizel. Even though it was eye straining poring over papers, spending half the day with her father and the clerk, Willie Crawford, seemed a wonderful release and she grasped at it eagerly.

Every morning she went in the library, and, working at a little table in the corner, listened to the conversations between her father and Willie. Their talk and the words that formed beneath her pen as she painstakingly copied letters and papers made the scales of childhood fall from her eyes. Some inkling of the true state of Glen Fada's affairs were revealed to her.

'I'd no idea that it cost so much to win an election,' she said to her father one day after calculations with a pile of bills revealed that Tavistock had so far cost him over £25,000 – a Pyrrhic victory indeed, she thought.

He looked up sharply to see if there was any criticism in her face but she was innocent of irony so he explained; 'Only gentlemen can stand for election, my dear. The House is full of men of property; it keeps the adventurers out, you see. That's why it's expensive to gain an entry there.'

'But why so much?'

'There's payments to be made to the electors – and sometimes they can be greedy. Rivals have to be bought off and agreements made. There's the expense of the hustings, the posters, the campaign, the travelling to and fro. . . .'

If the explanation satisfied him, it unsettled her and she profoundly wished that he would give up his dreams of Parliamentary glory. She fervently prayed that the expense of being an M.P. would not drain Glen Fada dry.

When she was freed from the library there was no Annie to divert her so she found she was spending more time in the kitchen where she heard everything that was going on and was often able to tell items of news to her parents first. That was certainly the case when Chrissie, the crippled sewing maid, confessed to the cook that she was pregnant.

Mrs MacDonald did not believe her at first but stood with her hands on her vast hips and gazed in a sceptical way at the crooked young woman. 'What makes you think that?' she asked.

'I know I'm pregnant,' said the maid. 'I only wish I wasn't. It'll be born in the spring. I'm three months gone.'

'Do you want to have it?' was the next question.

Chrissie seemed to hesitate. 'I don't know. . .perhaps if I have it, the father'll marry me.'

'That's the usual way,' agreed Mrs MacDonald. 'But who's the man?' It was beyond her imagining who could have put Chrissie in the family way. The poor thing had no beau, she never went out, she was not even in her first youth any longer. But Chrissie wasn't giving anything away. 'I'll only tell the mistress that,' said she.

Jane Macalpine was outraged when the news was broken to her by Grizel and, overcoming her aversion to seeing the maid, she sent for Chrissie and berated her in no uncertain terms. 'I'm really surprised at you! I thought you were above this sort of thing. It's all very well for the scullery maids and laundry women – but you're better than that. What's going to happen to you now? You can't bring up a baby on your own.'

Her rage was all the stronger because she felt that she had been very kind to Chrissie. Instead of sending her away after the accident, when a payment could have made amends for her injuries, the Macalpines had given her a home. Now, it seemed, their kindness had been abused.

Chrissie stood, stoney-faced. She did not look particularly ashamed or grateful nor did she weep. Her only excuse was, 'I couldn't help it. I love him, you see.'

'Who's the father? You'd better tell me at once and we'll see what can be done,' scolded Mrs Macalpine.

This was what Chrissie wanted. She lifted her head, hope in her eyes. 'He said I mustn't tell or you'd punish him. You won't do that, will you?'

'So it's someone in the house?' The mistress's mind ran through the gamut of male servants – the gardeners; the pot boys; the farm hands; the foresters; the game keepers; the groom in the stables. Most of them were married already and only a few were so ill-favoured that they would be likely to spend time wooing a crippled maid. Then she thought of Allie Beag, the dwarfish man who ran with the mail bags. He was over forty years old though he had never shown any interest in women. It must be Allie Beag.

'Was it Allie Beag?' she asked.

Chrissie looked insulted. 'No, of course not. It's Arthur Dunn.'

Mrs Macalpine put her hand to her throat in sheer astonishment. The gardener's son, the handsome butler who, as every year passed, was growing more polished and poised. Her first thought was that

Chrissie lied but there was a look in the girl's eyes which denied that. Dunn was the father of this ill-favoured servant's child.

Next it was Dunn's turn to be summoned to the mistress's presence. It was an awkward interview. 'I understand that you're the father of Chrissie's baby,' Jane began sternly. He looked down at his well-polished shoes and tried to bluster but the cold eye of his mistress deterred him. He did not deny the charge.

'You will, of course, immediately marry her. She's under my protection and we've kept her in the house for years because she was injured in our service. I expect you to put this right directly.'

It was not an unreasonable request because hasty marriages were quite normal among the people who lived at Glen Fada. Arthur Dunn's brothers had both married girls well advanced in pregnancy but he was an ambitious young man with his eye on greater things. His promotion to butler had shown him a world beyond the confines of the gardener's cottage at Glen Fada and he liked what he saw. A crippled bride did not fit in with Dunn's plans for the future.

'I won't marry her,' he said firmly, and no amount of brow beating would make him change his mind. He said he would provide money to help with the birth, he would even arrange for one of his sisters to raise the child if the mother did not want to keep it, but he would not marry Chrissie. Nothing would shift him from that resolve, not even the hostility of the other servants who drew away from him every time he stepped into the kitchen.

Grizel had never seen her mother so infuriated. When she argued with Dunn, her face went scarlet and her ladylike code of concealing her feelings was nearly cast aside. She was almost prepared to box her butler's ears in the same way as she boxed her children's.

In the end, thwarted at every turn, she threatened him: 'If you don't marry her, you'll have to leave our service.' It was a hard sentence and one with drawbacks for the Macalpines as well as for Dunn because he was the best butler they had ever had at Glen Fada. The threat did not work. Dunn knew he had enough expertise to find himself another post easily enough – he'd been thinking of moving on anyway though he did not say so – and the threat of dismissal was not much of a worry to him. By the end of the month, he had left and was replaced by a butler called Robert Lister who came with a warning from his previous employer that he was fond of the bottle.

'Then he'll be quite at home here,' said Mrs Macalpine tartly.

She was even more furious when she heard that Dunn quickly found himself another position with a titled couple in Morayshire where he was highly prized. The question that occupied every mind after he left was, 'What will be done about Chrissie?' Peter John Macalpine was away in London and his wife turned for advice to her friend Mrs MacIvor. With such a judge, Chrissie could not hope for forgiveness.

'She's sinned against God and morality. She should've known better, and her a cripple too. It would have been bad enough if she was normal but for someone like that to yield to such feelings!' said a scandalised Mrs MacIvor. The idea that crippled Chrissie with her crooked body should feel passion offended the two women immeasurably. Chrissie was dismissed and sent back to her outraged aunt in Edinburgh.

Grizel spent many hours pondering the story of Chrissie and Dunn. Who was right? She knew that it was outrageous for Dunn to act as he did; she knew that Chrissie had been loose moralled – but, yet, she felt pity for the girl. She wished there was someone sympathetic with whom she could talk about it all but Anne was too young, their mother as unapproachable as a basilisk. With Annie gone from Glen Fada, Grizel felt more friendless and alone than ever.

Chapter Six

ON THE MORNING of Grizel's seventeenth birthday, she was invited into her mother's boudoir and told; 'You're not a child any longer. You've reached the age when you ought to be introduced into society. I'm going to order you a wardrobe suitable for your station in life. Now stand still while Grey and I measure you.'

Grizel had always admired fine clothes. Before she was able to read, she paid keen attention to the outfits worn by visitors to her parents' house, and some of her earliest memories were of seeing her mother dressed for special occasions in gowns trimmed with pearls and beading that filled her with wordless admiration. Later, her special delight had been to visit Kinrara where she sat entranced by the beautifully attired Duchess and her friends, by their lace and silk flowers, their ostrich feather plumes, their painted fans and glittering gem stones.

When any member of her own family, male or female, appeared in something new, it was always Grizel who noticed their finery first and now her heart soared with delight at the realisation she was about to be provided with pretty clothes of her own.

Nursery wear had always been plain and economical. The Macalpine girls were always dressed the same and no allowance was made for self-expression in their clothes. Unadorned white muslin dresses were worn in summer; dark gabardine, cut from a bolt of mourning cloth bought in bulk and trimmed with red braid to brighten it up, provided winter wear.

She would have stood still for days, weeks if necessary, while Mrs Grey and the dressmakers crawled round her feet and circled her with tape measures. She was not given any choice in what was to be ordered, but that was not a cause for resentment. Her mother had always shown a high fashion sense and was frequently complimented on her fine appearance. She would not allow her eldest daughter to appear looking like a dowd for the hook was being baited for a husband. Whatever arrived from the dressmakers would be pretty and suitable and the girl gloried in the excitement of being fussed over at last.

Boxes and packets poured into Glen Fada from Inverness where the clothes were made up by two Miss Macalpines, distant cousins of her father, who had a dressmaking establishment. The delicate materials were fingered and displayed with an almost sensual pleasure.

In the white-painted bedroom that she shared with Anne, Grizel dressed and re-dressed herself in the delightful new clothes, unable fully to believe that they were hers. To a girl who had never owned more than three dresses at once in her life, the new wardrobe seemed immense. Mrs Macalpine did not stint her daughter for she ordered three flounced gingham dresses in the colours of sweet peas; two high-waisted muslin dresses, one pink and one blue, with delicate rosettes of embroidery around the ankle length hems; three simple white muslin dresses with coloured ribbon sashes, the long ends of which trailed almost to the ground when she put them on. The most glorious outfit of all and the one which delighted her so much that she hung it up where she could see it every morning as soon as she opened her eyes, was an evening dress made of pale lilac silk. Its full skirt ended in a small train at the back and there were elaborate love knots on each shoulder. When she put it on, Grizel smoothed her fingers down the soft material and pirouetted in delight. It was not a gawky girl who looked back at her from the mirror but a starry-eyed young woman, glowing with high hopes and expectations.

As well as dresses there were silken petticoats; delicate-looking flat slippers made of stiffened silk with paper thin soles; a chip straw bonnet lined with white satin and adorned with clusters of pale pink roses that nestled against her cheek; hand stitched gloves; silk neckerchiefs with delicately frilled edges, and a parasol with deep flounces of pale pink and cream inside that made it look like an upturned rose when she raised it over her head. As a child she'd owned a Chinese paper umbrella with flowers painted on it and once again she experienced the special thrill that comes from owning something very pretty. The old Chinese parasol was still in the nursery cupboard, tattered and ripped because it had survived many vicissitudes including being used as a sail on the make believe sailing boat in the laundry pool, but the arrival of the lovely silk parasol marked the formal ending of Grizel's childhood. A new chapter was opening before her.

Anne received most of Grizel's old clothes – not that she had many to give away – but there was no jealousy between the sisters because fashion interested Anne very little. Her idea of a suitable dress was something that was easy to wear and did not restrict her outdoor activities. Even when it was necessary to dress up and look smart, Anne always had an untidy look. Louisa was not a great deal better though she still had youth as her excuse.

Adulthood, however, proved to be less exciting than Grizel had hoped. Banished from the nursery because she was now too old to take part in the childish routine, she found herself very lonely. Her mother kept to her bed till noon and was as remote as ever when she did get up; her father was nearly always in London on Parliamentary business, and few visitors called during his absence from home.

In her pretty muslin gown, Grizel sat in ladylike idleness in the drawing room every morning. The delights of doing embroidery and reading books soon palled and she stared out of the window at her old haunts which beckoned her enticingly. Her eye travelled up the lanes leading up to the brooding woods and she longed to run along them as she had done in the past, but when she looked down at her feet in the silk slippers and at her body encased in embroidered muslin she knew that the delights of the forest were forbidden to her when she was dressed in such finery.

In the nursery Anne, John and Louisa would be giggling over their lessons while Miss Alfred tried to cram learning into them. After a few weeks of drawing room idleness, even those boring lectures seemed appealing.

In desperation, Grizel gathered her full skirts in her hand and manoeuvred her way up the narrow nursery stairs. When she pushed open the door, the group inside looked up in surprise. Her eye took in the familiar scene. Framed Mercator maps, their edges stained with damp, hung crookedly on the walls. The carpet was threadbare and faded, the fire a sullen glow, and the table and assorted chairs were chipped and battered but it looked comfortable, safe and familiar.

At the sight of the visitor, Alfred's sallow face took on an expression of malice. 'Here's the lady of fashion come to visit us,' she said. 'What fine clothes we're wearing today – it's the pink muslin, I see.'

Grizel ignored the jibe and said in a placatory tone, 'I came up to ask if there's anything I can do to help? Perhaps I could teach John his mathematicks. My father's been giving me some lessons. . . .'

'Mathematicks! My word. So you've been learning Euclid, have you? I doubt if he'll help you find a husband. You've become quite a lady but if you think you'll catch a fine husband with your mathematicks and your flounces, you'd better think again. When you go out into the world, you'll find there's girls prettier and cleverer than you. Being Miss Macalpine of Glen Fada won't be enough when you're launched in society.'

The governess's sarcasm closed the nursery to Grizel and loneliness grew acute. Even the servants seemed to treat her with a new reserve now that she was officially grown up. So, after a few more days of misery, she went to her room, took off her new dress and laid it carefully in her trunk before searching through Anne's things for her old muslin gown.

Wearing it once more she felt able to return to the familiar routine, sitting in the kitchen with the servants, wandering in the forest and sketching on the banks of the loch. She could hitch up the skirt and steel her courage to ride the pony along the mountain paths. It was only the nursery that she avoided, afraid of Alfred's cutting tongue. She knew she could give as good as she received but mindful of her mother's admonitions about the behaviour of young ladies, felt it would be demeaning to exchange insults with a governess.

Sometimes outward placidity was hard to sustain for she was stricken with a deep self-consciousness, frightened that everyone around her was, like Alfred, making fun of her behind her back. The acquisition of a new wardrobe had not helped turn her into an adult overnight; inside she was still a child and it was difficult to steel herself to deal with the world on adult terms.

She did not know how to cope with the rules of society for though the Glen Fada children were used to visitors coming and going in their home, they had never mixed with adults at social occasions. When their parents gave parties, the children were brought in for only a few minutes to be displayed like well-behaved pets. Yet Grizel's transition from the nursery to the adult world was expected to be achieved without coaching. When people called and she sat with her mother in the drawing room, terror of doing the wrong thing practically paralysed her.

How can I switch overnight from eating nursery bread and butter to taking drawing room tea or dining with lords and ladies? she asked herself. But Jane Macalpine acted as if her daughter ought to know by instinct how to eat exotic dishes that had never passed her lips before. She ought to be able to handle the range of dazzling cutlery and battery of glasses that lined up at her place at the dinner table like a menacing army. Grizel, who had never been used to anything but the talk of her siblings and the governess at meal times, was expected to blossom into someone who could manipulate conversations with people older and more experienced than herself, ask the right questions but refrain from parading her own knowledge – if she had any – of a particular topic. She was expected to know how to be entertaining – but not too entertaining; how to be charming, ladylike and demure.

Her parents decided that Grizel's first outing into society would be by accompanying them to a grand dinner held by the newly married Marquis of Huntly, the Duchess of Gordon's eldest son, and his new wife, the daughter of an immensely rich merchant who had brought a fortune with her as a dowry. The dinner was to be at Kinrara which the Marchioness's money had extended and re-furnished in most luxurious style.

The Macalpines were anxious to attend in order to see the improvements at the house and to meet the young lady the Marquis had married. He had been a rake in his youth and his rank could have brought him the pick of well-born young women but rumour had it that the bride he settled on was plain and awkward. 'But rich, of course,' said Mrs Macalpine, with a knowing peck of the chin.

'I can't face it. Let me start by going to the MacIvors,' Grizel pleaded with her mother, but no refusal was brooked.

'Don't be silly. You can go to Carn Dearg any time. Kinrara dinners are attended by the most fashionable people. It's the best society and it'll be an excellent introduction for you.'

Grizel's legs were shaking and her stomach so tightly knotted with fear that she was afraid of collapsing while she followed her parents up the flight of shallow steps to the imposing front door of the house.

She had not been at Kinrara for years and was amazed at the changes. When the Duchess and her daughters first moved there, it was only a modest farmhouse with two big rooms and a kitchen tacked on at the back, but over the years they extended it till it resembled a country house in the English style. Now, as they drove around the curving sweep of drive, Grizel saw that it had been recreated into a mansion. Huntly had imported an architect and an army of labourers and craftsmen from the south. They'd been working for a couple of years and the fruits of their labours were on show for the first time.

The new house had two colonnaded wings gazing down at the river and its once homely interior was transformed. In the reception rooms were ornate plaster ceilings thickly encrusted with swathes of flowers and fruit, crystal chandeliers glittered like ice crystals, falls of brocade hung at the windows and the polished wood of the mahogany double doors gleamed like satin.

The host and hostess awaited their guests in their vast drawing room, the walls of which were decorated with pale blue figured silk set in gilt rimmed panels. Above the fireplace hung a Rembrandt portrait of an old man surrounded by panels of glittering mirror glass that reflected the flickering candles of the wall sconces. Huntly greeted each arrival with his peculiar laugh that sounded like a comb being scraped against a wall, and his dumpy young wife stood by his side, strangely immobile and expressionless with a fixed smile on her face, offering her hand to the guests in the manner of an automaton. A sufferer from nerves herself, Grizel recognised the symptoms in the Marchioness.

The dining room was so magnificent that it looked as if it had been uplifted on a magic carpet from one of the huge London ducal houses that Grizel had read about in her mother's novels. The walls were covered with scarlet paper on which hung enormous gilt-framed portraits, and a long white-clothed table stretched the length of the room with brilliant batteries of candles standing along it in multi-branched silver candlesticks. Garlands of roses and ivy leaves were looped around the tablecloth skirts and Grizel's heart sank when she saw the array of wineglasses at every place. An army of liveried menservants was lined up, one behind every chair, and a group of maids stood by under the direction of a high-nosed, imposing butler who resembled engravings she had seen of the national hero, the Duke of Wellington.

Acutely conscious that her lilac silk frock and the wreath of artificial wild roses in her hair looked girlish and insignificant beside the silks and diamonds of the other female diners, Grizel was shown to a chair between two drawling English bucks at Kinrara for the shooting. They looked her up and down, dismissed her as of little interest and, after making the most perfunctory of remarks, pursued a conversation about shooting over her head.

She was glad to be neglected because words froze on her tongue and she could think of nothing to say that could possibly interest the young men. Left to concentrate on the food, she watched her neighbours to see which knife and fork, which wine glasses were picked up for every course, and ate delicately, remembering always to leave half the portion of food on her plate as was polite. The wine flowed abundantly and she sipped it gratefully for it calmed her fluttering nerves.

She was almost beginning to enjoy herself by the time the battery of sweets appeared. There were blancmanges and cakes, tarts and pies, fruit salads, ices and jellies. She chose wine jelly which quivered gently on her plate as if shaking in terror at the prospect of being eaten. Grizel stared back at it helplessly for all the other guests who had selected jelly were tackling their helpings with fork and spoon but there was no fork on the tablecloth at her place. She could quite easily eat the jelly with only a spoon and would have done so without self-consciousness at home, but she was afraid of being thought ignorant and ill bred so she whispered to the footman behind her chair to bring her a fork.

Though her voice was very low, sharp-eared Huntly, a most conscientious host and an exacting employer who dismissed maids if so much as a thread was found on the carpet, overheard her and shouted out loudly in his braying voice: 'Miss Macalpine of Glen Fada has no fork. Get her a fork at once. There should have been a fork at her place.'

The other diners downed forks and stared at Grizel as the servants ran to and fro. Three of them came back carrying forks and attempts were made to press all of them into her hand. The man who succeeded almost scooped up the jelly for her in his anxiety to smooth over the mistake.

Her face bright red, Grizel dropped her eyes and wished that the floor would open and swallow her up. She dreaded the thought of what would be said to her by her mother during their carriage ride home but she need not have worried. To her surprise, she was almost congratulated for her behaviour.

'It was quite correct to ask for a fork. Huntly's servants deserve to be reprimanded for their error. In a household like that, such things should never happen. You did very well, my dear,' said Mrs Macalpine approvingly. But Grizel knew that if such a situation ever arose again, she would try to make do with the spoon and never again risk causing such an eruption.

'I was very proud of you, my dear. You did us great justice.' said her father softly when he bid Grizel goodnight after the Kinrara dinner. His words filled her with delight and she gazed at him with brilliant eyes. To be congratulated by him was worth any amount of nervous suffering.

Next day her parents were cordial and talked to her like a grown up. All at once she was no longer an awkward child but had earned the place of an adult. Grizel basked in the warmth of their regard.

'You did so well at Kinrara that, though you're still a little young, your father and I have decided you'll go with us to the Northern Meeting this year,' her mother told her.

Grizel gasped and clapped her hands together in delight. The Northern Meeting at Inverness was the greatest social event of the year for the best families in the Highlands. It had been started long ago by the Duchess of Gordon who every year brought a party of her fashionable friends up North for the occasion. As always, society eagerly followed her and lords and dukes, clan chiefs, rich merchants, generals, bonnet lairds and belted earls and their ladies converged on Inverness for the first week of October. Many people travelled long distances for the event and everyone brought a party of friends, some of them from as far away as London.

Festivities lasted for an entire week and every day there was either a ball, a grand dinner party, a concert or an outing. Many friends met only during the Meeting and there alliances were cemented, marriages arranged and deals struck. The week of gaiety and sophistication did not have an equal in the Highland year.

While preparations for the trip were going on, news came that Annie Macalpine was unexpectedly coming back to Glen Fada to stay with Betty, the grieve's wife, who had been a friend of her mother.

'Poor lassie, she's having no luck,' Mrs MacDonald told Grizel. 'That relative of hers has died as well and Annie's out of a home again.'

When Grizel heard this news, she ran to her mother and pleaded, 'Couldn't we find Annie something to do in the house? We need another sewing maid now that Chrissie's away and Annie's a wonderful needlewoman.'

To her surprise she did not have to plead very hard. Mrs Macalpine knew Annie well and was quite prepared to recognise her as a distant relative, though an illegitimate one. 'She's a pleasant girl and very skilled. She'll be useful at such a busy time, especially now that Grey's left me,' she agreed for Mrs Grey, the faithful lady's maid, had surprised everyone by marrying Peter John Macalpine's valet and the pair of them had left to take the tenancy of the inn at Aviemore.

When Annie stepped out of the cart that brought her home from Elgin everyone stopped, open-mouthed with amazement, at the sight of her. She had always been a pretty girl but now she was a beauty with a perfect oval face and almond-shaped dark eyes, serene beneath sweeping brows that looked like the wings of a bird. She no longer wore the dress of a farm lassie but was gowned in a smart travelling costume of dark blue serge with a looped up skirt, and a cheeky little hat with a long pheasant's feather pointing up from the brim.

With a cry of delight, she rushed towards Grizel, calling out, 'How you've grown. . .how pretty you are with your golden hair.' Despite her newfound sophistication, Annie was not afraid to show her affection. Though Grizel was at first a little intimidated by the new Annie, it did not take long before she realised that the veneer the well-bred aunt had imparted had not changed the friendly and unaffected girl.

In the nursery Annie's charm even turned aside the jealousy of Miss Alfred who was soon treating the newcomer like a friend, asking her advice about how to trim her gowns or dress her hair because, through living with her very clothes conscious aunt, Annie had become a source of infinite knowledge about fashion. Everyone said it was a miracle that she showed no resentment about being returned to servant status and went busily about performing menial chores for Mrs Macalpine or Miss Alfred without a word of complaint.

All the children warmed to her, even undemonstrative John who crowded up to her knee when they sat before the fire and said, 'I love you, Annie.' She put her arm around him and squeezed him close so that Louisa rushed over too, anxious to share in the giving of love, something that was rare for the young Macalpines.

Grizel and Annie made a toy theatre for the younger children and cut out paper dolls with their limbs held together by string so that they could leap and dance like stage acrobats. Annie made clothes for the dolls from scraps of material and when they were set to perform on their make believe stage, Louisa laughed and clapped her hands

in delight, casting aside her usual lethargy until she became almost
as lively as John.

Annie accompanied them on their walks and while they wandered
along, told them the stories her mother had told her about brigand
lords and their fierce women. She told about the White Witch who
lived in the lee of Ord Ban and the lady of the Rowan Tree who
must never be annoyed. Their favourite of her stories however was
about their mutual ancestress Barbara of Rhynettan, a beauty who,
when abducted by her father's enemies, laid a trail for her lover by
tearing threads from her shawl. He rescued her, married her, and
they lived happily ever after raising a large brood of children that
was the start of the family of the Macalpines whose blood Annie
shared.

John and Louisa particularly enjoyed stories about the fairies, the
little people who lived beneath mysterious grass-covered mounds
that could be seen rising like big molehills in the fields on their
father's estate. Annie said the fairies had the power of transforming
ugly people into beauties, of conjuring up gold for the deserving
poor and removing sickness from the grievously ill, but you had to
know what incantations and pleas to make to them. Louisa believed
in fairies completely and went about chanting spells to herself in the
hope that they would hear her and turn her into someone as loveable
as Annie.

Even Grizel half believed in fairy power as she sat with Annie,
putting the finishing touches to the clothes she was to wear at the
Northern Meeting. One tweak of Annie's skilful hands and a wreath
of flowers took on a new beauty. 'Wear it like this,' Annie said,
arranging a lace fichu becomingly at Grizel's neck. The difference
was astounding. 'Hold your fan in this way. Your hair would look
so pretty if you coiled it up around your ears.' Annie was always
right and she was generous in her advice.

'You really have magical powers,' Grizel told her admiringly. 'If
I looked like you, Annie, I wouldn't be so frightened of going to
Inverness.'

'You mustn't be afraid. You'll be a great success. All the young
gallants will be wanting to dance with you.'

Grizel frowned. 'Oh, I do hope so. If no one dances with me, my
mother will be so angry. She expects me to catch a fine husband and
I don't know how.'

Annie laughed. 'You don't need to know how! Just be yourself.
Someone will spy you out quick enough.'

'It's all so confusing being grown up. I feel just the same but the world around me has changed. I wish I could go back to being a child again. I don't want to worry about getting married or finding a good husband yet. How do I know if someone's a nice person or not? In novels people fall in love with each other and they seem to be so stupid about it. Will that happen to me, Annie?'

'You're such a sweet girl that you'll fall in love one day without even noticing it. You'll fall in love with a fine young fellow and he'll fall in love with you. Don't worry about it, just go to the Northern Meeting and enjoy yourself.'

Grizel looked at the serene face of her friend and asked, 'Have you ever been in love, Annie?'

The fine brows tightened a little and there was a trace of wistfulness about the mouth as Annie paused and said, 'There was a time not long ago. In Elgin, in fact. I liked a young man and he liked me but his family wanted someone better for him.'

With a rush of sympathy, Grizel put out a hand and said, 'You're so brave. You never gave a hint of it.'

'There's no point moaning about things you can't change,' said Annie briskly. 'If someone's to be your fate, you'll meet him, come what may. Remember that, Miss Grizel.'

Jane Macalpine was taking no chances. A letter was sent to Oxford commissioning Aunt Maria to travel to London and select three of the prettiest dresses for Grizel from the dressmaking workrooms of the Miss Stuarts, the capital's most fashionable modistes. When the parcels arrived Grizel was tearful with astonished gratitude for the first dress was white muslin with a blue sash and shoes to match; the second was white gauze with pink shoes and a wreath of hyacinths for her hair, but the third was the most beautiful of all – a pink gauze gown with long fitted sleeves that ended in points on the backs of her hands. Its neckline and hem were heavily embroidered with pearl beads.

When she put this dress on she felt herself transformed, especially when she added the crown of bacchus leaves that Annie made for her as a hair decoration. The dark glossy leaves showed up her abundant golden hair to its best effect.

'That's the one for the Grand Ball,' Annie told her. 'You've never looked so lovely.'

All the servants turned out to wave Grizel off as she drove away with her parents to Inverness. The coming out of the laird's eldest daughter was a big occasion for them and she felt buoyed up by their admiration and confidence, especially by the fond embraces she received from Annie and from Betty who came down from her hillside home to add their good wishes to the others'.

The first call was at the inn in Aviemore where Mrs Grey and her husband stood in the yard, delight on their faces as they admired the transformed Grizel. 'My word, you're looking so fine that you'll catch the eye of a lord,' said her mother's maid.

Grizel held all their admiring words in her mind to give her confidence on the evening of the Grand Ball. A broad staircase covered with deep red carpeting led to the assembly room. Grizel slowly ascended it, wearing her pearl-fringed gown and clinging tightly to her father's arm, fighting against the impulse to turn around and run away. From the ballroom above came the sound of chattering voices and the strains of music; not the reels and strathspeys that were usual in the Highland parties she'd been to at home, but sophisticated quadrilles. Fortunately she had been taught to dance to such music in Edinburgh and her nerves calmed a little.

As Grizel and her father stepped on to the broad landing, she looked into his face for reassurance and what she saw there raised her spirits for Peter John was gazing at her with love and admiration. His eyes were brimming with unshed tears and she knew she must not fail him, but must live up to his expectations. Swallowing the lump in her throat, she raised her laurel-trimmed golden head high and swept bravely into the ballroom. Within seconds she was swallowed up in a crowd of admirers. A few minutes later she was on the dancing floor in the arms of a beaming young man. In no time she was surrounded by friends. Miss Grizel Macalpine was a success!

Everyone liked her. They flocked to her, brought her ices and complimented her on her dress. They danced her round the floor and pleaded with her to dance with them again. Far off, as if in a mist, she saw her mother's face, clearly showing incredulity at the success of her ugly duckling daughter.

Grizel was floating on air and felt as if she had been touched by magic. On such a night it was easy to believe in Annie's fairies.

Chapter Seven

THE FEELING of being in favour with her mother for the first time gave Grizel a sparkle that made everyone warm towards her. In Inverness, passers by turned in the street to stare after her; even people who had known her since childhood paused and looked at her twice. Her parents fussed around her as if she was made of precious china, so delighted were they with her debut in society for, at the ball, everyone said she was without doubt the most sought after young woman present, outshining even the daughters of title and vast estate.

When the week was over she could hardly wait to reach home again and tell Anne and Annie about her conquests – who she danced with and what they said. Her eyes were bright with excitement as their equipage rolled down the drive towards the house. But her home looked strangely bleak under a grey sky and there was an unnatural stillness in the yard which dampened all their high spirits as they alighted from the carriage.

Her father was giving his usual rapid fire orders about the unloading of the baggage when the kitchen door opened and Patrick walked out. Mrs Macalpine saw him first and her face registered surprise, delight and then doubt as he walked towards her with an ingratiating smile on his face. He was anxious to reassure her and his first words were, 'There's nothing to worry about, Mother.'

'But why are you here? You should be at school in Edinburgh,' she cried.

'I'm quite all right, Mother, it's just that – '

'It's just what?' asked Peter John, a hard edge to his voice.

'It's just that I had to leave my lodgings. I hadn't anywhere else to go so your lawyer Mr Guild told me to come here.'

Jane Macalpine took a step back in outraged astonishment. 'Do you mean to tell me that woman allowed you to go out into the streets of Edinburgh without arranging for someone to take you in? I thought she was a friend of mine.'

'She knew I was coming home. She wrote to Mr Guild about it.'

The clerk Willie Crawford appeared in the doorway behind Patrick. He was holding a letter and there was a solemn, bearer-of-bad-news look on his face. Macalpine walked towards him, took the letter, and the two men moved off into the house together, talking earnestly.

Grizel's grown up status was fully confirmed that evening when her father took her into his confidence.

'I don't know what to do about Patrick. He's been sent home because his landlady would keep him no longer,' he said sorrowfully.

Grizel was surprised. 'She's such a pleasant woman. I'm amazed she's acted in this way. It's all so sudden.'

Peter John shook his head. 'I don't blame her, though your mother will hear nothing said in her defence. The letter that came with Patrick said she could no longer keep him because of his behaviour towards her daughter.'

Grizel remembered that the widowed landlady had a very pretty daughter of about fifteen and her heart sank. 'What happened, Father?'

'The mother found Patrick and the girl in what she calls a compromising situation. He swears that he intended no harm, that it was merely innocent flirting, but the mother is not prepared to keep him. She's right, I suppose.'

Patrick was in disgrace for a few days but he knew how to win over his mother. With tears in his eyes he pleaded his innocence and begged forgiveness. 'I'll never do such a thing again, even by accident,' he promised.

His mother made excuses for him to his father. 'From what Patrick tells me, the girl was a clever little minx in spite of her youth. She knew what she was doing though Patrick didn't. Thank heavens no permanent damage has been done because it would never do for the heir to the laird of Glen Fada to mix himself up with the daughter of a lodging house keeper! Anyway, he's far too young to be thinking about marriage.'

Her husband was forced to agree. 'We can't risk him making a hasty alliance,' he said, forgetting that he and the beautiful Jane had themselves formed such an attachment when they were only nineteen. In fact, the marriage had been very much to Jane's advantage for her background was humble and her dowry non-existent. She herself knew the power of young passion, but it did not suit either her or her husband for their son to become infatuated with a penniless girl.

'There's only one thing to do,' announced Peter John, 'We'll have to establish ourselves in Edinburgh again 'til Patrick finishes school. He can live at home and you, my dear, can keep an eye on him. He's been running wild these past few years.'

Mrs Macalpine beamed. Edinburgh was far more to her taste than Glen Fada, especially now that the Inverness season was over. 'Edinburgh is best,' she agreed. 'We'll take the George Street house again and bring Grizel out in smart society. If she's going to make a good match, it's best to launch her in the capital – especially now that she's such a success with young men.'

The mother had relented towards her daughter and began to dream of an exalted marriage that would repair the faltering family fortunes.

'Perhaps you'll find a lord, or failing that a rich manufacturer's son,' she speculated to Grizel. 'Remember, it's your duty to marry well so that you can pave the way for your sisters.'

Back in Edinburgh Jane Macalpine was in her element. More dresses, more artificial flowers, more dancing slippers were required, and she and her daughter became almost companionable as they embarked on an exciting round of shopping, buying gloves and lace, fans and slippers, perfumes and pretty jewellery. Shopkeepers bowed and scraped when the Macalpine carriage drew up at their doors. They well knew that money would flow with extravagant largesse for it must not be thought that the family were counting the cost of the eldest daughter's debut.

The end of the war had brought a feeling of euphoria to everyone, a feeling that was entirely infectious, affecting even to the most sober-sided citizens of a city not known for its lightness of heart. In the general enthusiasm, Patrick was quite restored to favour and was soon rushing out every evening to meet his friends. It was when he began mooning around after the lovely Annie Macalpine that his mother scented danger.

'Not that I blame him, Annie's a lovely girl, but she's only a servant really and certainly not for our son. We'll have to find her a position well away from here,' she said to her husband. With the connivance of her sister Maria it was arranged that the Miss Stuarts in London would take Annie on as a dressmaker's apprentice.

This news was broken to the girl as a *fait accompli*. 'You're to go down south with Mr Macalpine when he travels to London on Parliamentary business next week,' she was told.

Annie looked astonished. There had been no thought in her mind of leaving the Macalpine household, far less of leaving Scotland. 'But I've never been to London,' she said.

'Of course you haven't, and isn't it a grand opportunity! The Miss Stuarts run the most fashionable business in the city. You're very lucky for them to give you a place, but of course they know me well and I recommended you highly,' Jane Macalpine said gaily.

Grizel, who had been listening as the news was broken, stepped in on her friend's behalf. 'Perhaps Annie doesn't want to go,' she suggested.

'Of course she wants to go! She's a very courageous girl. Besides, there's not going to be a place here much longer. You girls are growing up and we'll need to find a proper lady's maid soon,' was her mother's pointed reply.

So that was it. Annie was being sent away. There was an unspoken threat lurking behind the charm. Either Annie went to London or she was to be abandoned without support. Grizel's anger rose in her throat but there was nothing she could do.

Annie appreciated the nuances of the interview as quickly as her friend and put on a brilliant smile, 'Thank you very much indeed for your help, Mrs Macalpine,' she said. 'I'll be glad to go to London.'

Everything happened so quickly that the friends barely had time to discuss the situation before Annie was driven away in a post chaise with Peter John. Their last words were cheerful admonitions to keep in touch and promises that they would always remain friends but tears were shed in private by both of them.

As Annie's dangerous loveliness was whisked away, Jane Macalpine gave a sigh of relief. 'I'm having such a year,' she said. 'What with the excitement of settling Grizel and now the worry with Patrick – I wonder that my health will stand it.'

In fact it stood it very well and she was blooming like a rose on the night of the first ball the Macalpine family gave for Grizel. All the children, including John, turned out to receive their guests. The outfits worn by Grizel and her mother cost more than the laird of Glen Fada received for the felling of three square miles of forest. Jane looked magnificent in her mature beauty, robed in plum-coloured velvet trimmed with luxurious fur and lace and with a huge aigrette of ostrich plumes standing up from a diamond-studded band around her brow. Grizel, virginal and sweet, wore yet another London gown afloat with transparent gauze and French net. On her head was a wreath of roses that made her look like a Botticelli angel.

Everyone who was anyone in Edinburgh came to the ball – the city's Lord Provost was there - Mr Richard Arbuthnot, their old neighbour from Charlotte Square whom they knew as Dickie Gossip; Lord and Lady Gillies; Sir David and Lady Brewster; the Molesworths; the Grants of Kilgraston; Lady Ashburton; Lady Gray; Lord Wemyss and the Melvilles all attended. The faces that were seen in the George Street house that night belonged to the highest in the city's society and what was even more gratifying, they looked on the young Miss Macalpine with favour. Their admiration warmed her, lending her a glow which only enhanced her good looks.

Days and weeks of a hectic social round followed. Grizel and her mother were invited everywhere. Not a party or ball could be counted a success unless Miss Macalpine attended. Hostesses vied for her acceptance and young men lined up for the honour of leading her on to the dance floor. Her mother was giddy with speculation, wondering whether it would be best to make a quick match with the son of a Sheffield steel magnate or wait for the heir to a dukedom to declare himself? She decided to wait because though there was more money in steel, the dukedom meant good blood and, as far as she was concerned, blood was of paramount importance.

As Jane and her daughter drove from party to party, from call to call, she impressed on the girl: 'You've excellent breeding and a Highland heritage to match any in the land so you must be careful where you bestow yourself. There's many people who would be honoured to associate themselves with our family and you're in a position to pick and choose, my dear. But above all, you must find someone of our own sort – a gentleman, a man of good birth.'

Grizel smiled. She was nearly eighteen years old and deliriously happy. Never in her life had she known such success and she was savouring it so much that even wistful memories of the distant Annie and Glen Fada were temporarily forgotten.

'I don't want to fall in love yet, Mother, I don't want to tie myself down in marriage,' she said. 'I'm enjoying all this far too much.'

Her mother leaned back wearily in the carriage seat. 'I'm not talking about falling in love! I'm talking about making a good

match. Don't leave it too late. Girls in their second season don't
have such a wide choice because it's well known that the best ones
are all snatched up in their first year. I wouldn't want you to be
regarded as a second rank girl.'

What she did not say was that her husband would find it difficult
to sustain the expense of a second year of hectic entertaining and
outfitting for Grizel. After all, Anne was developing fast and giving
every sign of being as pretty and successful as her sister. If Grizel
could make a good marriage early and be off their hands, they'd be
able to concentrate on Anne. Jane sighed in happy speculation.

'Now I wonder if it would be possible to marry both my girls into
the aristocracy?' she asked aloud. 'I think the Duke of Hamilton has a
son that might suit Anne. And then there's Louisa. She's a little slow
but men don't look for intelligence in a girl. Louisa won't be difficult
to place if both of her sisters make dazzling marriages. . . .'

He was so tall that he could lean one elbow on the high marble
mantelpiece without straining. Around him clustered his friends,
laughing and joking but slightly in awe of him it seemed, for with
his imposing height he towered above them like a tree.

To Grizel, the stranger gave off some unaccountable attraction.
Her eyes were drawn immediately to his mobile, laughing face.
He had a high-bridged patrician nose, a wide mouth, and a broad
forehead beneath a mop of thickly curling black hair which would
have given him the look of a blackamoor had it not been for the
pallor of his skin.

She stood in the doorway of the little room where Patrick brought
his friends to take tea with his sisters in the afternoons, and the stranger turned towards her. They stared at each other for what seemed
like an eternity and then he smiled. Long laughter lines crinkled
pleasingly at the corners of his eyes. Grizel's stomach lurched.
She hesitated and felt a rush of colour suffuse her face. Something
momentous had happened to her in only a few seconds.

Patrick turned away from the fireplace when he heard the door
opening and gave a grin. 'Here's my other sister. She's the one
that all the Edinburgh gallants are mad about,' he said to the
group of boys at the fireplace. She knew most of them, fellow
students of her brother's, and was accustomed to the languishing
looks they threw in her direction but the tall stranger was older
than the others and far more polished. He took his elbow off
the mantelpiece and stepped towards her, still smiling. There

was frank admiration in his eyes as he said, 'It's easy to see why she's such a success.'

It seemed to be difficult to breathe and Grizel's legs felt strangely weak but she managed to smile back at him and hold out her hand, saying, 'How do you do. . . .?'

Hearing the question in her voice, Patrick stepped between them. 'This is my friend Tom Falconer. He's in his final year studying law at the University. I've been telling him about you, Grizel.'

'Good things, I hope,' she joked. It was Tom Falconer who answered. 'Very good things,' he said, and turned his fascinating smile on her again.

Anne, who had been flirting gaily as she poured out cups of tea, looked from her sister to the tall man still holding her hand. She too knew immediately that something important had happened.

Grizel felt unaccountably light-hearted, as happy as a bird freed from a cage. She had just come in from a bracing walk. She knew that she looked well with sparkling eyes and flushed cheeks, and was glad that today she had chosen to wear her new scarlet pelisse trimmed with black braid, Hussar-style hat, from which her hair escaped in fetching curls, and tasselled black boots.

Tom Falconer helped her off with her pelisse and laid it carefully on a chair before turning to her again and pointedly picking her out of the whole company as the one he wanted to talk with. It was as if they had known each other for years for there were no barriers, no constraint between them. They could chat with ease; they were eager to exchange ideas and when the time came for the callers to leave, it was a painful wrench for both of them to break off their conversation.

'We must meet again and talk some more. This has been a delightful afternoon,' Tom Falconer told her as he left.

As Patrick was showing his friends out, Grizel stood at the fireplace gazing into the glowing coals with a strange expression on her face.

'Is something wrong?' Anne asked gently.

The face her sister turned to her was transformed, no longer guarded but open and hopeful, 'No. Oh, no. It's wonderful. I don't think I've ever met anyone as interesting as that friend of Patrick's. He makes me feel alive somehow.'

'You have the same effect on him,' laughed Anne. 'He couldn't take his eyes off you. What were you talking about?'

Grizel frowned. 'I don't remember really. Nothing important.

About what it felt like to grow up, childhood, Edinburgh. . .nothing really. It wasn't what was said, it was how we seemed to understand each other. Oh, Anne, I do hope I'll see him again.'

'I'm sure you will,' said her sister knowingly.

He came the following afternoon although Patrick had told Grizel his friend was not fond of going into society. This time they played cards and when the tables were set out, Tom Falconer laid a hand on her arm and asked, 'Please play as my partner, Miss Macalpine.'

Heavy snow was falling but the little party sat warm and snug indoors while huge white flakes drifted past the window. Knowing how bitter it was outside gave them a sense of warm comradeship and they played on amid much laughter until evening came and the lamps were lit along the snow-piled street. Tom Falconer held her hand before he left and said, 'You're a wonderful partner. It's been such a pleasure. Can I come again tomorrow?'

It was all natural and inevitable. They fell in love over a space of a few afternoons, while Mrs Macalpine, unsuspecting of what was going on, slept off the exhaustion of her round of morning visits.

On the seventh day of their acquaintance, when snow was still banked on the pavements and the whole city was in the grip of a sparkling frost, Tom arrived, all wrapped up in a huge muffler, and invited Grizel to walk with him. She knew her mother would be furious at her for not acting with more reserve and asking permission to go out with this stranger, but she cast aside convention and agreed immediately.

Like children they ran out together, their faces alight with laughter as they made fresh footprints in the unmarked snow. She bent down and took a fistful of it to make a snowball which she threw at him, taking care to hit him on the shoulder where it would not hurt.

He brushed the flakes off his coat with a gloved hand and said, 'You've made a hit, a palpable hit.' Then, his expression serious, he added, 'But you know that, don't you?'

She shook her head and asked coquettishly, 'Have I? What sort of a hit?'

'Don't tease me. I've never felt anything like this before. Since the first afternoon we met, I've not been able to think of anything but you. I've not been able to work. I've cut classes every day so that I can see you. Miss Macalpine, you've made a very great hit indeed.'

And then he laughed the wonderful laugh that lightened his whole face and made her heart leap. She wondered whether he was serious or only making a joke but her speculations were swept aside when he took her hand and said earnestly, 'I used to think all that talk about falling in love was nonsense, but now I've seen the light, truly I have. I'm in love with you, Grizel.'

She gazed at him in wonder, admiring his bravery in speaking out so boldly. 'I wondered about love as well. I wondered what it would be like,' she whispered.

He bent his head towards her and asked in an urgent voice, 'And do you know now?'

'Yes, I think I do.'

Anxiously he asked, 'Have you known for long?'

She shook her head. 'Not long.'

'How long?'

'A week,' she whispered.

'Who do you love? I hope it's me – if it's some other man I'll not be able to stand the jealousy,' he told her.

She looked at him with eyes that glowed like jewels. 'No need to be jealous. Of course it's you!'

He clasped her hands in his and swiftly bent towards her to plant a kiss on her lips, both of them oblivious to the passers-by.

For Grizel, the next few weeks were divided between a fever of longing to see Tom and the pure bliss she felt in his presence. How strange, she thought, that all her parents' efforts and expenditure on her behalf might as well have been saved because she met the man of her dreams through Patrick. She lived for meetings with Tom, and though her social round went on unabated and she sparkled and charmed as much as before, when Tom was not there part of her was absent too, longing for the next time they would meet.

The pleasant afternoons in George Street continued but they were too irregular for the lovers' liking because Patrick could not be relied upon to bring his friend home every day. Secretly, they arranged to meet during her afternoon walks along George or Princes Street, and when they bumped into each other would laugh out loud at the happy 'accident'. At every meeting they talked and talked, words pouring from them in torrents. They agreed on so many things: liked the same sort of books; thrilled at the same poems; were delighted to find that strange level of communication that binds lovers together.

Sometimes they met at dances or parties because Tom put aside his dislike of going into society for Grizel's sake. To dance with him, or even better sit out beneath the potted palms and covertly let him hold her hand, was unadulterated bliss. Sometimes, very daring, they managed to exchange a kiss in a secluded corner while Mrs Macalpine's eyes were turned away. These snatched embraces made both of them burn with longings they could not express.

'I can't bear not to be with you. We'll have to tell our people how we feel,' he said with passion in his voice. 'I want everyone to know we love each other. I want to marry you, Grizel.'

'And I want to marry you,' she whispered as she tentatively put out a hand to stroke his curling hair. She was eighteen and Tom twenty-two, old enough for marriage surely. 'My mother was nineteen and my father the same age when they married, so they can't tell us that we ought to wait,' she told him.

'I want to come and speak to your father,' he said, but this interview could not take place until Peter John came home from London.

He was due to arrive on Christmas Eve and on the following night the Macalpine family were invited to a *bal-masqué* given by a trio of rich maiden ladies. They owned a large house in Abercromby Place and were famous for the originality and extravagance of their entertainments. To celebrate Christmas 1816 they were holding a Shakespearian entertainment and guests were instructed to dress up as characters from the Bard's plays. Patrick and his friends, with Tom among them, were to wear Elizabethan dress and provide an entertainment for the partygoers.

Grizel, her mind fixed on an evening in Tom's company, half hoped that her parents would plead off the ball but it was too big an occasion to miss. Her father rested from his travels most of the day and emerged in the evening dressed all in black as Hamlet; her mother swept downstairs as Cleopatra in a toga-like gown that suited her magnificently; Grizel was a virginal Juliet in white muslin with a lily wreath in her hair. She and Tom had decided that this was the night when her lover would be formally introduced to her parents. Having done that, they could then go on and arrange a private meeting between Tom and her father.

The first person she saw when she entered the ballroom, waiting beside the door for her arrival, was Tom. He looked like a gallant in a miniature by Hilliard. His fine head was surrounded by a huge white lace collar, and he wore a velvet cape over one shoulder of his embroidered surcoat. When their eyes met Grizel was sure that the charge of excitement between them filled the room but no one else in the party seemed to notice. She tried to guide her parents towards him but they had spied other friends in the throng and were hurrying over with cries of delight.

'I'll meet you later,' she whispered to Tom, and went after them.

It was difficult for Grizel to hide her excitement and apprehension but her parents appeared oblivious. Her mother was too busy scanning the faces of the crowd for potential suitors she had set her sights on. The possibility that her daughter's heart was already pledged never seemed to occur to her.

The entertainment took place at midnight and Grizel's heart beat faster when Tom stepped out in front of the group of players to read a poem dedicated to the beautiful young ladies of Edinburgh. In his hand he held a long scroll. Delighted laughter and clapping swept through the gathering when each verse named one of the girls of their set. The young ladies in question blushed, bent their heads and held their fans up to their eyes when their names were called.

The name of Grizel Macalpine was kept to the last. The praise for her was longer and far more fulsome than it had been for anyone else. As Tom read, he looked at her with such devotion that everyone knew the words were those of a lover to his lady. There was no mistaking the feeling in his voice.

Grizel felt the colour flood into her cheeks but did not simper or pretend to hide. She gazed back at him, as open in her response as he was in his compliments. For a few minutes, both of them forgot that they were surrounded by curious onlookers.

Later, when Tom approached her and requested the pleasure of a dance, their steps matched perfectly and they took the floor with such assurance that several old chaperons on the sidelines nodded their heads together in a kind of complicity. Kindly couples smiled at them as if they were already acknowledged lovers but when she came off the floor, Grizel's arm was grabbed by her mother in a vice-like grip and the angry voice hissed in her ear, 'You're making an exhibition of us. It's shameful! You must come home at once.'

With a backward glance over her shoulder at Tom, Grizel was hustled out of the ballroom and into the waiting carriage by her furious parents. They would brook no explanation and certainly were not in the mood to be introduced to a suitor.

Next morning Grizel was apprehensive of trouble but confident of eventual success when her parents were told of the seriousness of Tom's intentions.

Her mother's attack began quietly enough. Mrs Macalpine called her daughter up to her bedroom after breakfast and asked, 'Who was the young man who read the poem? Your father and I thought it very unseemly of him to heap such praise on you. It set people talking. Such things are not correct when a girl is unengaged. He's made no approach to us – it's all very irregular.'

Grizel stood at the side of the bed and said softly, 'His name's Tom Falconer. His father's a professor at the University. He's been many times to this house, Mother. You've even met on the stairs once or twice with Patrick, don't you remember?'

Mrs Macalpine lay in a stiff and hostile silence which frightened her daughter. When she began talking again, her voice was heavy with malice. 'That doesn't alter the situation. He's attached gossip to your name.' She warmed to her theme. 'He talked of you as if he was your lover. He talked in most intemperate language. It was unsuitable. Your reputation is quite sullied. . . .' Her voice was rising now. 'Your father and I have decided that you are not to meet that young man again. You will not speak to him, and you are certainly never to dance with him again. He's too forward. It was ill-bred presumption on his part to make an exhibition of you like that.'

'But, Mother, we're very fond of each other. He wants to come to speak to Father about me.'

Her mother reared up in the bed and screamed, 'What? You're mad! Did you hear what I said? You are *never* to meet that man again.'

'But there must be some mistake. They can't have anything serious against me. They must only be annoyed at us taking things into our own hands,' said Tom consolingly when she met him in Princes Street that afternoon, for she had no intention of keeping to her mother's ban.

'My mother's a strange woman. She's fixed her mind on marrying me to some Duke's son or Sheffield manufacturer's heir,' Grizel told him.

Tom flinched. 'Don't even speak of it. I can't bear the idea of you with anyone else. You must marry me and none other. Promise me that.' He grasped her hands painfully in his.

'There'll never be anyone else for me but you.'

They looked yearningly at each other, both longing to be able to kiss there and then in front of the passing crowds of people.

'I feel exactly the same. I want to be with you forever. I'll come to speak to your father today,' he said.

She shook her head. 'No, not yet. It's best to allow things to cool down a little. I'll test the ground with him first. He's far more reasonable than my mother.'

The glory of being in love lent Grizel an added sparkle. Sometimes, when she saw her brilliant face reflected in a mirror, she felt that her happiness in Tom's love was almost tangible. Even the atmosphere of brooding disapproval in the house did not sully her delight.

Several times she tried to speak to her father about Tom but he brushed her away as if he dreaded the subject being brought into the open and continued to avoid her until the time came for his return to London.

In a desperate attempt to force the issue she waylaid him on the stairs on his last morning and pleaded, 'Please, Father, won't you listen? I want you to see Tom Falconer. You'll like him. He's most suitable.'

Her father flinched as if she had hit him and said, 'No, Grizel, I can't. Your mother's against him. You must do as she says.'

As she stared after her father's receding figure, Grizel felt the cold grip of fear around her heart. For the first time she began to doubt that her dream of marrying Tom would come about. The realisation that she was young and unprotected, still very much at the mercy of her parents, frightened her. She had been carried away on a dream of love, buoyed up with hope and Tom's certainty that one day they would be together. Now she saw that there were fearsome obstacles in their path.

I'll have to be very strong, she told herself, but her love for him never once faltered.

Her only ally was Anne. She dared not risk confiding in Patrick for Mrs Macalpine had instructed him that his importunate friend would not be welcome at George Street. Her sister sympathised and volunteered to act as go-between for Grizel and Tom. Fortunately she was friendly with Tom's sister and between them they carried notes for the lovers.

'I love you. I love you. After you left me in the garden at the end of George Street this afternoon I wanted to run after you, to lift you

up and run away with you. I must marry you. We must be together.
The pain of being kept apart is killing me,' he wrote.

'My darling,' she wrote in reply, 'in my heart I am already your
wife. I looked out of my window tonight and gazed over to where
you are and wished I could fly across the rooftops to you. Oh, how
I long to be with you! My heart is breaking.'

Tom arranged a meeting place in the house of a mutual friend
and they rushed there every day, as eager for the sight of each
other as if they had been apart for years. When the tactful friend
left them alone, they would embrace passionately. Tom kissed her
without restraint now, on the cheeks, the eyes, the lips, and Grizel
felt herself burn with a desire that frightened her with its intensity.
The fact that their meetings were forbidden and had to be kept short,
made them even sweeter to the lovers. The longing to be together
grew so strong that when they were apart they were unable to eat
or sleep. Tom's studies suffered and she grew thin and white with
anxiety and stifled desire.

'Has your mother said why she objects to me?' he asked over and
over again but Grizel could only shake her head.

'No, she won't say. She only tells me that I mustn't see you. If she
knew we were meeting now, she'd lock me up in the house. She's
threatened to send me away to stay with Aunt Maria in Oxford, and
she'd do it if she knew we were meeting each other like this.'

He frowned. 'It can't only be because of the poem. Perhaps I was
a little too outspoken then but I love you and I don't care who knows
it. I'll write to your mother.'

When his letter arrived Mrs Macalpine only glanced at it then tore
it into shreds and threw it on the fire.

'If you meet that man again, I'll send you to India to your Uncle
Edmund,' she warned Grizel, and the girl knew the threat was a real
one but still the secret meetings continued and loyal Anne covered
up for her sister.

Tom was unable to bear the secrecy and pressed for the matter
to be brought to a conclusion. 'I want to marry you. You want to
marry me, don't you?' he asked her. She nodded, unable to speak,
and he pressed her: 'Why don't we marry then? We're both old
enough. They wouldn't be able to do anything about it.'

When he held her in his arms, she knew there was nothing she
wanted more in the world than to marry him but she was reluctant
to defy her family. A last faint hope that everything could be arranged amicably still remained.

'Wait 'til my father comes home. If I have the chance to explain everything to him, I'm sure I can make him understand. With him to our side, we'll be allowed to marry openly.'

Tom's face showed his doubts. 'I'd rather we ran off and married. At least then we'd have done it.'

It was their first disagreement. In spite of her longing for him, Grizel wanted her family to accept the match.

Tom was anguished in case her family forced her to marry another suitor, and time after time he pleaded: 'Promise they'll never part us. Promise you won't agree to a match with anyone else.'

'Of course I won't marry anyone else! You needn't even think about that. I'll wait for you even if I have to wait for years. Don't worry, I've asked Anne to speak to my mother. If we can arrange a meeting between her and your mother, everything might still be smoothed over.'

Tom looked grave. 'I wish you'd just marry me in secret. It could easily be arranged,' he pleaded, but Grizel thought of the scandal that would ensue if she did such a thing, the pain it would cause her proud father, and drew back. 'Let's see what Anne can do first.'

Anne spent a long time alone with their mother but when she returned to Grizel, her expression was gloomy. 'I don't know why she's so against him. I told her how clever Tom is and what a brilliant career at the Bar lies before him. I told her how everyone we know thinks highly of him. I said his parents are well-bred and rich. I thought I could counter any objection but she's absolutely set against the match and won't tell me why. It's a mystery.'

Grizel wrung her hands sorrowfully. 'I thought she'd be pleased to know that I was fixed so early. She used to warn me not to have a second season. Now I've an offer of a good marriage, she won't hear of it.'

'I did try, Grizel,' her sister said. 'I asked if she wouldn't pay a call on Tom's mother. I said her daughter's a good friend of mine and that Mrs Falconer's a very highly placed woman, an heiress in her own right with thousands of acres in Tweed-dale. I described their lovely house and all their fine pictures but Mother wouldn't agree. She said it's not her place to make the first advance.'

'That sounds as if she might agree to a meeting if Mrs Falconer was the one who made the move!' cried Grizel.

Tom's sister was duly delegated to broach the subject but no call was ever made nor invitation received from Mrs Falconer to

Mrs Macalpine. It began to appear that Tom's family were as against the marriage as Grizel's.

Throughout the days of dispute at home, Grizel was forced by her mother to keep up an outward show of composure. Together mother and daughter went out calling. They attended lunches and dinners daily, and Mrs Macalpine's ability to assume a party face when only minutes before she had been hissing and spitting at her daughter like a cat, amazed the girl. Her mother had missed her vocation, she decided. Jane Macalpine could have been another Sarah Siddons and made a fortune on the stage.

Although she was all cordiality and sweetness outside, however, in private Mrs Macalpine intensified her campaign against her daughter. When they planned an entertainment at home, she took exquisite pleasure in making Grizel watch her dashing her pen through the name 'Tom Falconer' which Anne and Patrick had tried to insert in the guest list.

'But why? He's done nothing wrong. He's Patrick's friend. If you allow him to come, I won't dance with him, I promise,' pleaded the girl. Her mother only smiled cruelly and replied, 'He's a man without looks, breeding or intelligence. There's no one of judgement who gives a groat for him. Such upstarts are not entertained by the Macalpines of Glen Fada.'

At a ball given by friends, Mrs Macalpine never left her daughter's side for a minute and when she saw Tom approaching through the crowd, her fingers dug viciously into the girl's arm, bringing back memories of the days when nips and slaps were administered by those same hands 'Don't speak to him. Do not dance with him tonight or any other night.'

So the lovers were forced to meet in a few snatched secret moments and to pour out their frustrated feelings in writing. Grizel lived for the arrival of Tom's letters, smuggled to her daily by Anne. One morning however he wrote to say that his family had finally pronounced themselves as much against the match as hers. Grizel put down the letter on her desk and burst into a storm of tears. It seemed as if her world would come to an end.

She longed to write him a letter that told everything in her heart – all the love, all the pain, all the terrible confusion – but when she took up her pen the tears fell and nothing she wrote expressed her emotions. In the end she only scrawled a note: 'I am waiting. I will go anywhere with you. Come, please come. Grizel.'

This time Tom counselled caution. 'Grizel, Grizel, Grizel – I cannot write your beloved name enough. Be brave. Do nothing to antagonise your mother. I have persuaded my own mother to meet you at last. I'm sure if you could only speak to each other, all this ill feeling and confusion would come to an end. She is writing to your mother today to ask for an interview. I love you. I will always love you. When I am not with you, the sun does not shine and no birds sing. You are my wife already although we have been through no ceremony. Write to me, wife, and tell me that you have received this letter and will do as I ask.'

Secretly she had been making preparations to leave but now she could only wait, counting the hours and the minutes until she learnt the result of Tom's mother's letter.

The following afternoon, she was at the window of her room when a carriage drew up at the door and a fashionably dressed woman alighted. She was admitted to the Macalpine house and immediately closeted with the mistress. The interview was short. Within a quarter of an hour the stranger drove away again and Jane's maid arrived to summon Grizel to her mother's parlour.

'Mrs Falconer has been to call on me. She and her husband are as concerned about this foolish connection as your father and myself. She has requested an interview with you, Grizel, and I've agreed. She'll come tomorrow morning and I hope you listen well to what she has to say.'

Hope blazed in Grizel's heart when she heard this plan. Surely reasonable women could find some grounds of agreement; surely Tom's mother would realise how much she loved him?

'May I see her alone,' she asked daringly, and her mother nodded agreement.

A pretty and fashionably dressed woman, Mrs Falconer nevertheless wore an air of sorrow as she entered the Macalpines' drawing room. She sat down on the sofa beside Grizel and after they had exchanged stilted greetings, opened her reticule and brought out a letter from her son.

'Thomas asked me to give you this. He said you were to read it and then burn it. I expect it's because he doesn't want any other eyes to see it,' she said passing the letter over to the girl. Grizel held the thin sheet of paper between her fingers and wished that she could keep it, cherish it in her sandalwood box beside every other note he had ever sent her, but she nodded and tore open the seal.

It was a heartfelt letter, one of the most passionate he had yet sent.

His handwriting was bold and open, and as she read the words scrawled on the page, it was as if Grizel could hear his beloved voice speaking them to her.

'My dearest heart, my wife, this is a message of love. No matter what is said to you, stay firm. Remember that I love you with all my heart and will always do so. If we are firm in our resolve they can never part us. If only I could be with you! I want to kiss you, to hold you close and tell everyone that you are mine. I keep a place empty in my bed at night for you. One day you will fill it. Be mindful of me, my love.'

While she read these words Grizel looked up to see if his mother had any suspicion of the message she carried but Mrs Falconer sat with head averted, staring out of the window at the traffic in George Street below. There was no way that Grizel was going to burn this precious letter and she folded it up small and slipped it into the tight-fitting sleeve of her dress. Tom's mother watched as she did this but made no protest. There were other things on her mind.

Leaning forward she took Grizel's hands in hers and said gently, 'Listen to what I am going to say, my dear. I know you love my Thomas and I appreciate what pain this must be for you both. In other circumstances I would welcome you into my family with complete confidence because I can see how much you love him. But my husband would never endure such an alliance.'

With an anguished expression Grizel asked, 'But why? I've done nothing to antagonise your husband.'

Mrs Falconer soothed her. 'His quarrel isn't with you. It's of much longer standing than that. Did you know that my husband and your father were friends when they were at College? They had a quarrel, I don't know why, but since that time they've conceived a violent hatred of one another. My husband's refusal to allow this marriage isn't because of you, but because of who you are. Tom's father is a vindictive man, I'm afraid, and he has told me that if our son marries you, he will never speak to him again. Not even I would be able to prevail on him to relent. He'd cut off his son completely. Thomas would lose his inheritance, his family – he'd lose everything he holds dear. Surely you wouldn't do that to him?'

This came as a bitter shock to Grizel. Her mother, though she must have known, had not prepared her in the slightest for this revelation. The girl's head was spinning but still she tried to plead her case. 'But surely your husband will change his mind in time? Surely if he could see how happy we are together. . . .'

But Mrs Falconer sadly shook her head. 'It's too late for change, my dear. If you persist in this connection only unhappiness lies before you both. A marriage based on such a sacrifice could not possibly be happy. You must set my son free, I beg you, because he'll never give you up. He's too much a man of honour for that. The act must come from you. I've come here today to plead with you to do it.'

Grizel was unable to sit still. Such a decision! She rose from her chair to pace the room. If she said, 'I won't give him up. I'll go with him without money, without approval,' she knew he would back her up, but Mrs Falconer's warning about the future of such a marriage struck home. She loved Tom too much to take him away from everything he held dear; from his parents and his loving home, from his inheritance which would be wrested from him because of a love affair.

But her feelings revolted against parents who would forbid a marriage because of their own feuds. How prophetic it had been for her to dress as Juliet at the Shakespearian ball. But *Romeo and Juliet* was only a play. She and her Tom were alive and in love. The words of his last letter increased the agony of their separation. . . . 'I want to kiss you, to hold you close.' He truly loved her. She loved him. To go on living without him would be impossible.

His mother saw the conflicting emotions on the girl's face and waited anxiously for her decision. Eventually, with unshed tears glittering in her eyes, Grizel said, 'I love your son. I can't renounce him unless he tells me that's what he wants me to do. If we're allowed to discuss it ourselves, we will give you our decision. That's all I can say.'

Peter John Macalpine came posting home in answer to a frantic message from his wife. He found his house in uproar with Jane having hysterics in her bedroom and Grizel stone-faced and impassive, refusing to go out, refusing to speak, refusing to do anything until she was permitted to meet her lover.

'Look at this. Heaven knows what's happened between them. He writes most intimately to her,' cried Mrs Macalpine, waving a sheet of paper beneath her husband's nose as soon as he entered her room. It was Tom's love letter which she had filched from her daughter's room. 'He calls her his wife! I think she's married him – and almost certainly worse from the other things he says.'

Peter John sought out his daughter and asked, 'Have you married this young man?' She stared at him for a long time as if considering her reply. It would, they both knew, be quite simple for them to have married because in Scotland all that was necessary was for a couple to stand up before witnesses and call themselves man and wife. But this was her father and she could not lie to him. 'No, I have not, but how I wish I had.'

'He calls you his wife. Has he called you that in front of anyone else?' If they had been presenting themselves publicly as a married couple, Falconer's claim to be her husband would be established in law. Grizel shook her head wearily. 'It was something we talked about between ourselves, Father. I haven't married him and I've not given him any liberties though I know my mother suspects I have. He's too honourable for that. He's not a seducer.'

Macalpine sat down heavily beside his daughter and sunk his head in his hands. 'My heart is breaking, Grizel,' he said in a faltering voice. 'You are my eldest daughter and I love you dearly. I do not want to see you contract some hole in the corner marriage with a man whose family refuses to acknowledge you. Remember our family pride. Remember too that I was wronged by his father.'

She turned to him eagerly. 'Won't you tell me the whole story, Father? No one will explain it either to Tom or myself. At least tell me why you think I should give up the man I love so dearly.'

Her father looked pityingly into her grief-stricken face and shook his head. 'It's between Falconer and myself. Believe me, daughter, I was sinned against most grievously. I cannot blacken Falconer's name by going into the sordid details but he played me false, very false. His is bad blood. I would not want you to bear the name.'

She stared bleakly at him as he continued, 'You know me to be a man of honour, and that I have never done anything to harm you. Believe me, my child, if you persist in this connection, the shame of it will kill me. You might as well take up a knife and drive it into me as marry that man's son.'

Grizel rose from her seat and stared sightlessly through the window, twisting her hands together until they were white and bloodless. She remembered Tom's mother's warning about the dire consequences for him if they married. She had no wish to cause his estrangement from his family. Then her father's words echoed in her head, and her own deep held family loyalty smote at her. But the love she felt for Tom was so terribly strong.

She wished there was someone else she could consult in this awful dilemma but Annie Macalpine, the only outsider she could trust, was far away in London. Oh, Tom, cried her aching heart. If only you were here to stand by me. Oh, what will I do?

Her father walked up beside her and put an affectionate arm around her waist. When she made no move away from him, he knew he had the advantage. She rested her head against his shoulder. 'Whatever I do, I'll cause someone pain,' she said in a broken voice. 'Tell me what to do for the best, Father.'

'Write him a letter, telling him that for everyone's sake you've decided to give him up. Trust me, he wouldn't want to lose his family either. It's for the best,' Peter John assured her.

So simply the die was cast. Tears spotted the single page of Grizel's letter as she gave him up 'for our own good, dear Tom, as I'm sure you'll realise in time.' On her father's advice she told him it would be best if they never communicated with one another again. She longed to add that every word of the letter was torn from her like a piece of flesh but struggled to keep her tone impersonal. It was better that way, her father said.

As Grizel signed her name with faltering hand she had a last wild impulse to tear up the note and cast it on the fire.

Quickly Peter John took the piece of paper, folded it up and hauled on the bell pull. 'I'll send it over immediately,' he told her.

She stood before him with bent head as he swept her into a loving embrace. 'You've been a good daughter, a brave fine girl. Few of us marry the very first person we fall in love with. Later, we look back and realise that it was as well. God bless you, my dear.'

But you married your first love! Why do you deny me the same privilege? she cried silently.

When he left her, she sank sobbing into a chair. She felt that the heart within her breast was broken, as jagged and irreparable as a smashed dish. Outside the sky was eggshell blue and there was a feeling of summer in the air, but all around Grizel was deepest winter.

Chapter Eight

❦

'GET UP, you're imagining that you're ill. You're not the heroine of some novel.'

Grizel's mother stood at the bottom of the bed and railed at her daughter who lay whey-faced against the pillows, refusing to open her eyes. Her impassivity angered Mrs Macalpine who stepped up to the head of the bed and shook the girl by the shoulders. She might as well have been shaking a puppet, so little response was there.

'In my day, girls did as they were bid without putting on silly airs and graces. You're not ill, I know you're not. You're only play acting.'

But Grizel lay unmoving with her eyes closed. She could not bring herself to open them and see her mother dressed up like a duchess, for she was about to go to yet another reception and was frustrated by her daughter's refusal to accompany her. There was no shifting the girl however and eventually her mother had to depart with the caustic comment, 'Everyone thinks you're sulking because you weren't allowed your own way. Don't be a fool and wreck your chances after all the money we've spent on you.'

Grizel could not move. Grief weighed her down like a lead weight. According to the maids, Tom had called after he received her letter but Mrs Macalpine had given orders to turn him back at the door and to say that Miss Grizel had no wish to see him. Then Patrick came home from his University classes and said that Tom was bitter and angry. He could not understand why she had renounced him so firmly.

'He's always talking about you, Grizel. He says you were only flirting with him, toying with his affections all those weeks.'

The pain of hearing that was even worse than the decision to part with him.

She could not eat, could not bear the company of other people. She wanted only solitude, to lie alone in bed and grieve. There was no cure for what ailed her, she knew that well enough. Even if time restored her to an appearance of her old self there would always be this aching void in her heart where once love had reigned. 'I'll never love like that again, I know it,' she told Anne, and no whispered consolation could sway that certainty.

A doctor was summoned. He prescribed rest and an invalid diet, followed by gentle exercise. 'She's overtired, exhausted. Been doing too much gadding about, I dare say. It would be best if she could be sent away to the country for a while.'

Grizel wanted to clasp his hand in gratitude and urge him to insist on a change of air. If only she could be sent back to Glen Fada where in early summer the woods would be soft and green, and bluebells in bloom beneath the beech hedges. At Glen Fada, her pain would not disappear but it would be less agonising to bear. When Grizel drifted off into an uneasy sleep, she dreamt that she was being rowed across the Spey by their boatman and the house loomed up in front of her like a sanctuary.

Her father, silent, tactful and almost shamefaced, sat by her bed and attempted to divert her with cheerful conversation. He never once referred to the unfortunate love affair but she could sense by the way he looked at her that he sympathised with his stricken daughter.

The question that was uppermost in her mind – what exactly had happened between her father and Tom's – hung unspoken and unanswered in the air between them but she was grateful for his kindness and most of all for the way he shielded her from her mother's rage. She was furious at Grizel's insistence on turning down all invitations.

'When I think of the expense we've been put to on your behalf – all wasted! When I think of the trouble I've taken, my drained energy. All those eligible men asking how you are, eager to see you, and you lying up here like a sulking child. There's nothing at all the matter with you except ill temper. You've always been sly and sulky.'

Her father bought a quiet little pony and took her out riding with him but the effort exhausted her. He arranged for her to be driven to the seaside at Portobello for baths but they did nothing to bring the colour back into her face and, in late June, it was decided that they must take the doctor's recommendation and return to Glen Fada.

The city Grizel would be happy never to see again lay behind her as she half sat, half lay in her seat, without an ounce of energy in her body. After the tedious crossing of the River Forth at Queensferry, however, her spirits began slowly to rise. When the horses' heads were turned for home, they tore along as if they were as eager to reach the Highlands as their passenger and Grizel sat swaying to the motion of the carriage, listening to the hooves rattling and thudding along the rutted road. With each step they took the rawness of her grief felt less. On the second day, when they were near Aberfeldy, she felt her heart rise at the sight of the first ridge of granite-studded hills, the first line of tall pine trees.

She inhaled the champagne air deep into her lungs. It was like being given a healing draught. For the first time she knew that she would survive this terrible blow after all, and something resolute in her decided that not only would she survive, she would be stronger as a result. But she would also be guarded. Never again would she leave herself open to such wounding. In the opposite corner of the carriage her mother was nodding in sleep, propped up by a battery of cushions. She could see her mother more clearly now. The old fear had gone. Grizel closed her eyes and drifted into a dreamless sleep.

Everyone but Anne thought Grizel fully cured of her malaise by the time summer was over. The girls enjoyed a full programme of social events, in which Anne was often included for she would soon be seventeen. They whirled from Kinrara to Carn Dearg and back to Kinrara again with Grizel talking and chattering, laughing and flirting like someone possessed. Her frantic desire to appear light-hearted and flirtatious worried her sister who saw the shadow on her sister's brow when Grizel thought she was unobserved.

Miss Alfred was still in charge of the nursery and now that Grizel was transformed from a skinny child into a golden-haired beauty, her dislike deepened into jealousy. Mrs Macalpine played upon this by telling the governess tales of her daughter's ungratefulness and trickery in entering into an unsuitable engagement without the consent of her parents. In conjunction they never ceased to upbraid and annoy her. Mrs Macalpine's favourite ploy was to parade would-be suitors and force Grizel into their company. She was determined to find a suitable husband for her daughter before a second winter season commenced in Edinburgh. Her favoured candidate was a loud-voiced young fellow who owned great stretches of land along the River Tay. His houses with their huge policies, the property he owned in Edinburgh and the town of Dundee, his rich elderly relations who would leave him even better off in time, were all talked of incessantly at the Glen Fada table. It seemed it was of no account that his clumsy approaches repelled Grizel. He was invited to shoot and included in every party where he was always seated beside her. They were ushered out into the garden to walk in the twilight, paired off for outings, card games, or anything else in which it was necessary for two people to come together.

'I don't like him,' she said, but her mother ignored her protests.

'He's very rich. You'll come to like him. You just need to see more of him.'

If that's what you want, then that's what you'll have, thought Grizel, and started encouraging the young man, leading him on while at the same time watching her mother's delighted reaction. Mrs Macalpine really believed that Grizel was seeing sense at last. The sums of money being constantly tallied in her head could almost be seen in her eyes, and she was forever questioning the young man about the extent of his acreage, the size of his house, the number of horses in his stables, the age of his aunts and unmarried uncles. She computed that his fortune was even bigger than she had originally imagined.

'A brand might be snatched from the burning after all,' she wrote to her sister in Oxford. When the suitor finally made his offer for the girl's hand, her mother was enraptured but Grizel received the news coolly.

'I'll have to think about it,' she told her parents, and stayed out of sight for a day until her mother, unable to bear the suspense, sought her out and asked for her decision.

'You'll have him then, miss? When will the wedding be?'

Grizel shook her head as if she was refusing a jelly at dinner. 'No, I don't think so. I've written and refused him.'

'What do you mean? You must be mad! How can you refuse a fortune of three thousand a year and more to come?'

'I'm afraid I have. He doesn't suit.'

'Doesn't suit! You wicked girl. That marriage would've been of great benefit to the entire family.'

Grizel stared hard at her mother, a cold light in her eyes, as she said firmly, 'My happiness has been sacrificed once for the benefit of this family. It will not happen again. Please remember that, Mother.'

When Grizel was in her third season and still without a serious suitor, it was decided that her field of operation should be widened and at last she was despatched to London for the long promised visit with Aunt Lizzie. The motherly soul was horrified by her niece's emaciated looks and evident unhappiness.

'Don't let your mother worry you. While you're here you needn't give a thought to marrying. You and I will have a lovely time,' said her kind aunt. Grizel's recovery of health and spirits was aided by regular visits from Annie Macalpine who was doing well at her dressmaking and was the most prized employee of the fashionable Miss Stuarts in their St James' establishment. Clients clamoured to be attended by the dark-haired girl whose discriminating taste created exactly the right clothes for them.

When Annie heard the sad story of Tom Falconer, she told Grizel, 'It's been cruel for you but I can see that you've come out of it a strong woman. Life's not finished for you, not by any means. I'm sure your future is going to be a happy one. You deserve it after all that's happened.'

'But what about you, Annie?' asked Grizel, feeling guilty for she had talked at length about herself while her friend had been reticent about her own hopes and fears. Though she was so lovely there was little chance of her meeting anyone suitable in the dressmaking establishment.

Annie laughed. 'I believe in luck! It's served me well enough so far. If I'm meant to meet a husband, I will. If not, at least I'm able to look after myself. One day I hope to have my own dressmaking business. I'm saving for it, and I've money put away from my aunt's legacy.'

Before Grizel left London to return to Scotland, Annie's luck took an unexpected turn. The eldest Miss Stuart died and her sister felt unable to continue the business alone. Annie came to Aunt Lizzie's to discuss what she should do.

'I haven't enough money yet to buy the business from Miss Stuart but I don't want to work for anyone else,' she said with a downcast expression. Lizzie and her husband had a long talk together and then they presented Annie with a proposition. One of their friends had a daughter who was being sent out to India to live for a time with her brother, for the East was a good place for catching husbands and young girls often took trips with matrimony in view. A suitable companion for the voyage was needed – would Annie consider going?

The two friends debated the idea. 'India's so far away and very unhealthy,' said Grizel, for she dreaded losing her friend for ever. Uncle Edmund had disappeared there and Murdo Grant after him. Now dear Annie was about to sail off to that country which seemed like a bourne from which no one ever returned.

'Oh, I'm strong enough,' her friend assured her. 'I'm not worried about getting sick. What holds me back is the terrible distance. Six months' sailing before you reach land! I doubt I'll ever see the Highlands again if I go.'

Both girls were silenced by that thought then Grizel said, 'Don't go, Annie. Stay here. Something else will turn up.'

Annie's eyes were dark and brooding as she continued to mull over the problem. 'There's arguments on both sides. It will be hard to go into a world where I know no one but what is there to keep me here? I don't want to be a dressmaker's assistant for ever. I'm an accidental daughter, Miss Grizel. Do you know what that means? Here I've no place and no future, but in India. . . ? They're not so worried about accidents of birth there, so I'm told. I'll miss you dearly, and I'll miss my home, but I think I'll go to India and take my chance there.'

Grizel returned to Edinburgh after Annie's departure a month later. Mrs Macalpine, in the thick of another social season, was loud in praise of her second daughter.

'Anne's such a success. She's so many admirers.' This litany was directed at Grizel who continued to play the same game, building up high expectations about one man after another before shattering her mother's dreams with an adamant refusal. She and Jane rarely talked in a friendly way; all their exchanges were of the thrust and parry variety.

In fact, though she would not admit it, Anne was causing Jane Macalpine almost as much concern as pleasure. She was flirtatious and very pretty, with gleaming reddish gold hair and slightly hooded blue eyes which gave her a challenging and enigmatic look, but she was as fussy as her sister when it came to accepting the addresses of any particular young man. Time and again it looked as if a match was about to be made, and time and again, Anne cried off.

The reasons she gave were often trivial. One suitor was sent packing because his taste in literature did not agree with hers; another received his marching orders because he reached across the dining table and helped himself to potatoes by sticking his fork into a particularly fine specimen. The silence as he did this was pregnant with meaning and when he attempted to engage Anne in conversation after the meal, she swept past him with a contemptuous twitch of the skirt. 'No Macalpine of Glen Fada could ever marry a man who doesn't know how to behave properly at table – even if he does have an income of a thousand pounds a year.'

Patrick was attempting to study law with a view to a career at the Bar – though without any great success – and clever John was away at Haileybury College being prepared for a career in India. Louisa was the sole occupant of the nursery, slow and placid, interested only in food and Miss Alfred's gossip. She had grown so plump and rosy that her mother was concerned in case she ate herself into a state of unmarriagability, for she would be the next to be launched.

The two oldest girls, free now of nursery restrictions, delighted in each other's company though their interests were very different. Anne remained as tomboyish and fond of horses as ever, an interest that Grizel could never share, but they were united by their devotion to the Highlands. Their sisterly affection gave them a bulwark against the caprices of their mother and the extravagant whims of their father. They tolerated Miss Alfred who was growing openly anxious at the prospect of Louisa's escape from her care.

One autumn day the mail bag that was carried into the Glen Fada dining room by an ageing Allie Beag contained two letters from India. The first, from Bombay, announced the marriage of Uncle Edmund to the daughter of a well-placed gentleman in that city. The news was received with rapture by Mrs Macalpine who set about speculating on the girl's family connections. The second letter was from Cawnpore, a city where they knew no one. It was addressed to Grizel. When she opened it, she gave a cry of delight.

'It's from Annie. She's married! Isn't that wonderful news?'

Her family all gaped in astonishment and Mrs Macalpine commented, 'That didn't take long. Who's she married to? Some young clerk?'

'Just a minute. Oh, yes, here it is. Her new husband is called General Arkwright.'

'A General,' gasped Louisa. 'That's very senior, isn't it?'

Grizel read the letter out loud, '"He's forty-five and very fine-looking. . . ." She says, "We're coming home at the end of the year and I'll bring him to Glen Fada to meet you all. He's a fine gentleman. I'm sure you'll like him."'

Jane Macalpine was looking decidedly glum. A general in the army of the East India Company would have a good pension, even if he had no money of his own. Annie Macalpine, the cow herd girl, had done very well for herself while her own two daughters, launched on the marriage market at vast expense, hadn't yet managed to secure themselves so much as a bonnet laird. Her chagrin was made even worse when it turned out that Annie's husband was one of a family of rich Midlands industrialists. He owned a fine house in Nottinghamshire and had extensive mill interests. He was rich, even richer than the rejected Tayside landowner, and that was a bitter pill to swallow.

When the girls were together they talked of nothing but the news about Annie.

'It makes me believe in fairies after all. They must have been guarding her,' said Louisa with a sigh.

'I can see from her face that Mother wishes they'd start looking after us,' Anne joked. 'We'll have to write and ask Annie for the magic spell.'

'I'm too old to marry now. I'm sure I'll end my life as a spinster aunt. I couldn't marry the man I wanted and I'm not prepared to settle for second best,' said Grizel with finality.

Anne nodded her head. 'Mother only wants to see us married off to money but I don't feel like sacrificing myself for her.'

Grizel's worry, and one that she had voiced to no one, was whether she and Anne would have any substance behind them when their father died, because she could see quite clearly that Patrick was not shaping up very well as a provider.

Later that day, when they were walking along the little path beside the church, she hinted as much to Anne who only laughed and said confidently, 'You worry too much. There's always Glen Fada behind us. We'll be quite safe.'

But there was cause for concern and the eldest girl knew it. As year followed year their forest shrank but with the end of the war against France, the demand for timber had fallen off sharply and the trees of Glen Fada no longer represented an unfelled fortune. Grizel had noticed how, over the past two years, the work force on the estate had dwindled alarmingly. Her father and his agent spent long hours shut up in the library, puzzling over their bills, and Grizel was no longer encouraged to read her father's papers. She had the uneasy feeling that things were being hidden, if not ignored by the laird of Glen Fada.

When there was another election and the Tavistock seat had to be contested once more, an estate Macalpine owned near Nairn was sold up but he explained that, as they never went there, it was no loss. 'Far better to convert it into money,' he said airily. Of all the large spreads of land he had once owned, he was left with one estate which he was systematically milking dry. But no one, least of all himself, seemed to realise what was happening. He bustled about, full of confidence and enthusiastic plans that were more trouble than they were worth.

The row of cottages he built at Glen Fada for his workers looked pretty but would have been more suitable on an English estate than a Highland one. His greatest mistake was to force four old widows, estate pensioners, to give up their dark little homes and move into the white-painted houses.

The crones hated their new homes, nothing about them suited. 'They're too cold, they're too open, people can see in the windows. . .' they constantly complained, but the laird was determined that they should stay where he put them. When people started calling the cottages 'Macalpine's almshouses' the widows rebelled. One night all of them were mysteriously destroyed by fire though the old ladies managed to escape with their possessions intact.

Shrugging his shoulders, and leaving these frustrations behind him, Macalpine headed off for London in his private post chaise on Parliamentary business. His travelling costs in a year would have kept a more modest family travelling for a decade. Money still flowed as if Macalpine had a reservoir of gold at his fingertips but eventually he was forced to realise the gravity of his position.

Her father's brow was furrowed and streaks of grey showed clearly in his brown hair on the morning he decided to take Grizel into his confidence.

'Would it matter very much to you, my dear, if we made our home at Glen Fada for a while? Young ladies like to be in society, I know, but the rental of the George Street house is heavy.'

To his relief, she sounded delighted when she replied, 'I love Glen Fada, Father, and I never much cared for Edinburgh. Giving up the house there won't disappoint me at all.'

In the time of retrenchment, Patrick abandoned his studies and came home to Glen Fada. He eagerly took on the responsibility of overseeing the work of the estate while his father was away in London. Like a whirlwind he set about building a new saw mill, reorganising the forest operations and trying to bring the farmwork into some sort of order. Without regard for old loyalties, he cut the already depleted work force.

When Grizel protested, her brother dismissed her objections with a wave of the hand. 'We don't need the people I've sent away. We don't need a household piper. He never did anything but get drunk anyway. I've given him a job in the stables and he can play the pipes at his leisure. We don't need so many women in the kitchen either – what do they do all day but gossip? Or all those people hanging about the farm yard.'

He was right, she supposed, but she felt for the folk who had lived in and around Glen Fada for as long as she could remember. In the past it was never expected that they should earn their keep for they were old retainers, many of whom shared the family surname. Their ancestors had performed the same nebulous duties for the laird with never a thought of being turned off.

Even Miss Alfred had to go, for Louisa was too old for a governess any longer. Alfred had served the family well by bringing on the youngest daughter so much. It was only Grizel, having smarted too often under her tongue, who felt no sadness at her departure.

As she watched her brother busying himself from early morning till late at night, Grizel saw he was modelling himself on his father. But Patrick lacked one essential trait. He did not have the sense of feudal responsibility that had been passed on from the old lairds to Peter John. His son had only the same bustling way of walking, the same headlong manner of talking, the same rashness in rushing into things without planning carefully beforehand. He covered sheets of paper with detailed plans, he wrote reams of letters and instructions, but his improvements were often self-defeating and his plans had to be undone.

He did not like Grizel or Anne interfering with the running of the estate and guarded his privileges jealously. In an effort to help they took over more menial duties, running the house and attending on their mother who was without a lady's maid. Anne also ran the stables and Grizel, with the assistance of Louisa who had to be restrained from gobbling up all the sweetest and most succulent dishes, supervised the work of the kitchen and the dairy.

They were out of doors during all weathers and their mother, who continued to spend most of the day in bed, bemoaned the radiance of their complexions. To be pale was much more fashionable. 'You look like dairy maids,' she sighed, eyeing their homespun plaid cloaks and disordered hair.

On a brilliant summer's morning Grizel saw a tall, lean figure marching along the driveway leading to the house. She shaded her eyes with her hand and watched the approach of the stranger. If she had not known that Uncle Edmund was far away in Bombay, she would have thought it was him but when the figure came nearer, she gave a cry of delight and ran out to greet her little brother John. Not so little now though. He was nearly six feet tall and had outgrown his clothes. His wrists protruded bonily beneath his sleeves.

Three years at Haileybury had matured him markedly, but he had retained his dry wit and keen eye that missed nothing. Often his sister saw him sceptically watching the bustling figure of Patrick charging to and fro across the stable yard and guessed what thoughts were running through the younger brother's head. John was not encouraged to help manage the estate so he spent most of his days at Carn Dearg where he dazzled the MacIvors with the breadth of his knowledge and understanding of affairs.

There was a touching wistfulness in Jane Macalpine's face as she folded up *The Scotsman* one morning after spending half an hour scanning its closely printed columns. The sight of her mother's melancholy touched Grizel's heart in spite of the resentments that still lurked there.

'What's the news, Mother?' she asked.

'The King's coming to Scotland in the summer. There's a great to-do in Edinburgh, everyone's so excited – committees and organisations are getting up to give him presentations and put on balls.'

Mrs Macalpine's voice was full of longing. She would have loved to be part of the hustle and bustle, the coming and going, the dressing up and displaying oneself in fashionable circles.

Her husband rose from his seat at the dining table and walked over to tell her, 'If you want to be there, my dear, it can easily be arranged. I'll take a house.'

Jane's face brightened a little but she sighed and said, 'I don't think I'll be well enough to stand it.' For the past year she had been prey to a succession of strange ailments; fits of weeping, depression, faints and hectic flushes confined her to her bedroom most of the time. She only showed animation when her husband was at home.

'But it would be such a chance for the girls. They so rarely meet anyone suitable up here,' Macalpine urged.

'Are you sure it will be possible?'

'Of course. Things will be straight again soon. I'll write a letter about it right away,' he said in an optimistic tone of voice, and no one presumed to argue with him.

So in early July 1822 they set out from Glen Fada to see the King who was due to arrive in Scotland in the middle of August. The road south was thronged with traffic, coaches and carriages full of fashionably dressed and excited people heading for the city.

The house they rented was a grim-faced mausoleum in Picardy Place, not so fashionable an address as any they had previously occupied but Macalpine excused it by saying, 'We'll have the best view of the King receiving the freedom of the city. The ceremony's to take place right outside our front door. We'll put a platform outside the window and all our friends can come to watch.'

On Thursday, 15th of August, after a hold up of a day during which the King could not leave his yacht, the *Royal George,* in Leith Roads because of bad weather, he finally stepped ashore to a tumultuous reception from the hundreds of thousands of people who had thronged down to Leith to see him. There was not a lodging house room to be had in the city and people who left it too late to book accommodation were reduced to sleeping in their carriages.

'Edinburgh's gone quite mad,' said Grizel as she stood on the top plank of the scaffolding at Picardy Place, straining her eyes down the length of Leith Walk to catch sight of the outriders of the vast procession that was to escort the king from his landing stage to Holyrood Palace. In the distance could be heard the booming of cannons, the sound of massed bands and a frenzied shouting and cheering from crowds who had come from all over Scotland to greet the first crowned king to visit their country since Charles II.

On their viewing platform, the Macalpines were surrounded by a group of friends – several lawyers; Willie Crawford, the clerk; and Mrs Siddons the actress whose brother owned Edinburgh's Theatre Royal where magnificent entertainments were to be staged during the Royal Visit. With her was her delightful nineteen-year-old daughter Sally who was fussed over attentively by Patrick, susceptible as ever to a pretty face.

The girls exclaimed over the gorgeously robed dignitaries who gathered beneath their window at the gate which had been erected in the middle of the road to mark the boundary of the City of Edinburgh. Mr Arbuthnot, their old neighbour from Charlotte Square who was still Lord Provost of Edinburgh, stood robed in scarlet and ermine with a massive golden chain around his neck, waiting patiently to hand over the keys of the city to King George IV.

'There's Dicky Gossip. Doesn't he look fine?' cried Anne, waving her gloved hand. 'And there's Mr Guild with his sons, and Willie Melville and his brother!'

The Royal Procession came into sight, a line of brilliant colour, and its magnificence silenced even the most vociferous of their party. Carriage after carriage of colourfully robed gentlemen accompanied by their fashionably dressed ladies rolled up the street. Horsemen in uniform or other extravagant costume pranced at the sides of the carriages and great bodies of kilted Highlanders marched in proud display.

'There's Scott! No show without Punch,' cried Anne as the carriage containing the organiser of the whole event passed by. Sir Walter Scott's French wife was dressed in gleaming cloth of gold, they noted. Scott was not a favourite with the Macalpine family. Taking their lead from their mother, they considered him an outrageous social climber.

The children were sorry that their father was not riding in the smart procession but he had turned down the opportunity to take part for reasons which he did not divulge.

The girls were to be officially presented to their ruler at Holyrood House on the following afternoon, however, and would follow that with an attendance at the Peers' Ball in the Assembly Rooms of George Street.

Unable to dance attendance on the King, Macalpine showed his loyalty by sending fifty brace of ptarmigan shot on his estate and a large barrel of his finest old Glenlivet whisky to await His Majesty's arrival at Holyrood Palace.

Grizel had been against giving away their whisky. 'But there's only two barrels left. Its been in the cellar for eighty years at least. It's a shame to give it away,' she protested.

'Gifts to kings are never wasted, my dear,' her father reassured her, 'We'll be showing our family to good advantage, and there's no telling what benefits it might bring us.' The whisky was duly sent off in spite of her protests.

As she stared down at the florid-faced, rotund personage who was their ruler, Grizel could well imagine the relish with which he would attack their Glenlivet. King George IV was grossly fat. His tightly corsetted body was squeezed into the uniform of an Admiral of the Fleet with an absurd cockaded hat perched on top of his flaming red wig. He paused at Picardy Place, obviously enjoying himself hugely, and as if he knew that there were female eyes surveying him from their house, he flirtatiously lifted his pouched eyes and rolled them upwards at their viewing platform. When he saw the line of pretty women smiling down at him, one pudgy hand removed the hat with its decoration of thistle and heather and swept it across his chest in a courtly bow. Even the sceptical Grizel was suffused with loyal admiration at his attentions and the women smiled, giggled, gave discreet cheers and fluttered their gloves in his direction. It was not every day that they were ogled by a king.

After the long procession had straggled its way towards Holyrood, a party of young people came to call on Anne and Grizel. They were led by James Guild, son of Mr Macalpine's old friend and fellow Edinburgh lawyer, who said that he had a favour to ask of the elder Macalpine girls.

'Do you remember how we used to give exhibition quadrilles at the balls? You were both so good at all the French steps! Well, we've decided to get up another set and give an exhibition at the Assembly Rooms when the King attends the Great Ball. We want you to join us because no other ladies in the city can dance as well as you.'

It was true. Both Grizel and Anne were exquisitely light on their feet and looked graceful and elegant on the floor. Anne's face showed her eagerness to join in this latest venture but Grizel drew back. 'We haven't time to practise. It's been so long since we danced, I'm sure I've forgotten how.'

She dreaded such a public re-entry into society.

'You've not forgotten at all! We were practising our steps just the other day at home,' protested Anne.

'But what about dresses? Everything we have is out of date and. . . .' It was not possible to remind Anne publicly of their parents' reluctance to spend money. They'd brought their best gowns down from Glen Fada but while they were good enough to wear to mingle in a crowd at the official reception, they could not be worn again in an exhibition quadrille. New dresses would cost a considerable sum of money.

This objection was overcome by Mrs Siddons who burst out, 'You must do it! I'll help you find really splendid gowns, I'll make it my project to dress you. We've two days, after all. It'll be easily done.'

The girls' father nodded in agreement. He was intensely proud of his lovely daughters and his heart would be full if he could see them dance in front of the King. Any money it cost would be well spent, he said, and from that moment the decision was made. They were to be part of the quadrille.

The festivities of the Royal Visit were giddying. After the procession passed by and darkness fell, the family took to the streets to walk around and admire the illuminations that turned Edinburgh into a glittering fairy-land of lights. Every public building, every shop, every imposing private house was decorated with banners and devices lit from behind by fluttering candles or hissing little lamps proclaiming messages of loyalty and good wishes to the Royal visitor. Bonfires blazed on the summits of Arthur's Seat and the Calton Hill, fireworks flashed like meteors across the sky and the girls felt they had been transported into an *Arabian Nights* tale, a feeling that came over Grizel even more strongly on the following afternoon when she and Anne, escorted by their father, waited in the slowly moving queue of more than 450 women at Holyrood Palace to be presented to His Majesty.

In the sweltering summer weather, the heavy satin of their court dresses clung to their legs and the eight enormous ostrich feathers that Sir Walter Scott's protocol ordered they should wear upon their heads, felt unmanageable and as heavy as lead as they inched forward into the vast receiving room. After an hour and a half's queuing, Grizel caught sight of the immobile figure of George IV at the end of the room. She blinked in horror for he was incongruously got up in a full costume of Stewart tartan. He wore a plaid, a jacket and diced hose of tartan. His chest was glimmering with brooches, and the final horror was his kilt which was too short. Instead of showing manly legs, it revealed that the costumiers had covered his Majesty's unattractive nether limbs with prim pantaloons of pink gauze. He was like a painted figure from a pantomime and behind her Grizel heard the stifled giggles of a group of ladies.

'My God,' said one, 'the King's displaying all of himself to us today!'

Her companion whispered back, 'Perhaps that's because he's only spending a short time with us, and thinks we ought to see as much of him as possible.'

Grizel tried not to look at the King. Her mind was full of the glorious figures of Highlandmen she had known all her life. Nothing was more becoming than a kilt on a handsome man but this was a shameful travesty and she shrank from the Royal embrace when the King pressed his moist rouged lips against her cheek.

Next day was spent in frenzied preparations for the Grand Ball with an excited Mrs Siddons fluttering around Grizel and Anne. Tickets for the event had been hard to come by and Macalpine had been privileged to secure sufficient for his family.

The girls both looked lovely when the actress was finished with them. Their silken skirts, swiftly made up by the theatre dressmaker, swept the floor; soft white gloves reached up to the middle of their upper arms; their necks were encircled with borrowed jewellery from her stage props and their heads adorned with more ostrich feathers dyed a pearly opalescent hue that matched the blue and silver of their gowns.

As they were ushered into the gorgeously decorated Assembly Rooms, the trembling in Grizel's legs was so strong she was afraid people could see them shaking under her skirt. But when the familiar music was struck up by the massed orchestra of Nathaniel Gow, son of the famous old fiddler who had once moved her so deeply, she was filled with an energy that lightened her spirits. Her head lifted high and proud, her trembling disappeared and she stepped on to the floor with all the aplomb of an actress.

Judging by his drooping eyelids and sagging jowls, the King was tired. He sat in a gilt and red-upholstered throne at the side of the room to watch the exhibition quadrille. The dancers stood in a line, four young women in pastel-coloured dresses and long flowing satin sashes facing four men in dark blue jackets with high white neckerchiefs round their throats.

The massed musicians swung off in brisk time. The couples bowed in unison and began weaving the pattern of their dance. The hours of practising proved worthwhile for they moved in easy unison, brushing past each other, bending gracefully, clasping outstretched hands, moving from side to side with perfect confidence.

Anne was dancing with James Guild, the leader of their group, who took their exhibition very seriously; Grizel's partner was his younger brother George, a more easy going young man but equally as good on the dance floor.

Above their heads hung chandeliers of such brilliance that the heat from their candles warmed people standing far away from them. The walls of the ballroom were painted palest green and cream with huge flourishes of ornamental gold stucco around long mirrored panels. The audience stood at the sides of the room or sat in fragile-looking gilded chairs, watching the King to take their lead from his reactions. King George leaned forward in his armchair, hands on his massive thighs and eyes lighting up with interest as he watched the prowess of the golden-headed Macalpine girls – to and fro, back and forward, crossing and re-crossing, always smiling, always graceful, always pointing their feet with precision and care.

When they finished their first set, tumultuous applause greeted them and Grizel felt her face go crimson as, for the first time, she became aware of how many people were watching. There was one more dance to perform, one more pattern to be woven on the floor, and James Guild whispered to them to line up again, to extend their hands to each other and wait for the first note to sound. This time, their initial nervousness had dissipated; they were even more confident and there was a lightness in their dancing, a gaiety that transmitted itself to the watching crowd. Grizel was progressing down the middle of the floor with one hand held up high by her partner when, in the forefront of the crowd, she saw Tom Falconer. He was staring straight at her, his dark eyes burning with the pain that was in her own heart too. Clinging to his arm was a pretty young woman.

Grizel felt as if he had struck her with his stare. She faltered, dropped George's hand, put the wrong foot out at the turn and felt herself starting to trip. Fortunately her partner reached out for her and saved her from sprawling full-length on the floor but the near disaster unnerved her.

She stumbled again and took up the wrong place in the set, throwing the other dancers out in their carefully prepared plan. Anne, the quickest witted of the women, realised what had happened and rearranged her moves in time but the others bumped against each other in confusion. James Guild was furious. Grizel could see the anger on his tight set face as he danced past. When their set finally ended, the applause was less enthusiastic than it had been the first time.

Grizel barely noticed. She had seen Tom again, accompanying another woman, and she wanted to die.

How she longed to run into the crowd and take his arm. If only she could stop the thundering music and tell him how she was coaxed into writing that letter. If only he could know that she did it for him and that her heart would never recover from the pain dealt to it that day. If only she could assure him that no matter where she went or who she met, she would always remember him.

At that moment Grizel made a bitter promise to herself: If ever I marry, it will not be for love. I'm done with that. I'll seek out safety and security, calmness and affection, but never, ever love!

With her head lowered, not daring to glance in Tom's direction, she walked off the floor while James Guild followed her, hissing, 'You ruined it! You made fools of us all.'

Anne restrained him with a hand on his arm and asked, 'Are you quite well, Grizel? You looked ill halfway through the set. Do you feel faint?'

'Yes, I do feel ill. I'm sorry if I spoiled everything. I'll go home, there's sedan chairs at the door. I'll take one of them.'

'I'll come with you,' said Anne, and though her sister tried to persuade her to stay, she was firm. The sisters went home together although the ball was less than halfway through

During the night Grizel shed bitter tears, feeling them slide down her cheeks like rain. Anne sensed her distress and climbed into bed beside her, whispering, 'I saw him too. I know why you're upset. But you mustn't cry. It's all over now. You must look forward to the future, not back into the past.'

'Oh, Anne,' sobbed Grizel, 'I love him so! It's as bad as ever. When I saw him there, in the crowd, I thought my heart would stop. How could he find someone else so soon? There'll never be anyone else for me but Tom.'

She fell asleep, still crying, and in the morning woke feverish and ill with a malaise that lasted for the rest of the Royal Visit so she was excused any more outings into society.

Her appetite disappeared and once more she looked as if she was wasting away. Her father was alarmed by her rapid decline and it was decided to accept the invitation that arrived from Annie Macalpine, Mrs Arkwright as she now was, who had returned from India with her husband and was living in style on his property near Nottingham.

Peter John personally escorted Grizel to Annie's new home and when he took his leave of her, his face was concerned and his eyes full of love and sympathy for he knew what was ailing his daughter.

'Enjoy yourself with Annie,' he said. 'I've left a gift in your dressing room. I hope it will help you recover your spirits.'

The gift was a purse containing ten golden sovereigns, money his daughter knew he could ill afford.

Chapter Nine

'OH, ANNIE, how wonderful to see you, and how well you look! I'm so glad that things have turned out happily for you!' Grizel sat on the sofa in Annie's pretty drawing room and grasped her dear friend's hand. Dear Annie had changed – but in a wonderful way. She had become a great and gracious lady, at ease in the most exalted circles for she and her husband were friends of members of the Royal Family who treated Annie like a lady of exalted birth. There was no hint in her appearance or behaviour to tell them otherwise. But Annie was not play acting for she was naturally refined and had always been so even when she walked barefoot across the Glen Fada fields. This illegitimate daughter of a maidservant was a living refutation of Jane Macalpine's theories about the pre-eminence of birth.

It was comforting to be cossetted by Annie and her bluff, kindly husband with his twinkling blue eyes and considerate manners. They sat for hours with Grizel, listening sympathetically as the normally reticent girl poured out the story of her unhappy romance. When the telling grew too painful, Annie took her hand and sympathised with soft words.

'My dear, even when things look at their blackest, you must have faith that they'll improve. I know it's hard but it's true. In my own life there were times when I cried as many tears as you are crying now and thought I could die, but I didn't and I'm glad of it.'

'But you're so good and patient, Annie. Everyone loves you and you deserve all the good things that have happened to you. I'm not like you – I'm not a good person. Perhaps my mother's right. Perhaps I am cold and wicked and ungrateful!'

'That's nonsense! You're a dear, loving girl. You mustn't believe all the things that people have told you.' Annie did not want to criticise the girl's mother directly though she had often noticed the unfeeling treatment that was handed out to Grizel. Mrs Macalpine was a careless mother to all her children at the best of times, but she seemed set on being deliberately hurtful to her eldest daughter.

Grizel protested again, 'But everyone prefers Anne or Patrick, Louisa or John. They can't all be wrong. There must be something about me that turns people away – even Tom Falconer.

'He looked at me with such hatred when I was dancing at the ball. It burned into me like a branding iron – but it wasn't my fault, Annie. I did it for him. I've suffered so much. If only he knew.'

'Oh, my dear, how sorry I am. If you'd only believe that people do love you – people like me and your sisters, your Aunt Lizzie and Betty at Glen Fada. Your father too – he loves you. I saw from his face how concerned he is about you. You mustn't give way to this, Grizel.'

Grizel was brought up short by her friend's firm tone. 'Don't think me self-indulgent, Annie. I'm not, truly. It's just that I've had no one but Anne to talk to about Tom. I wish I could be as brave as you. I remember how much I admired you when you made up your mind to go to India. I could never have been so courageous.'

Annie laughed. 'Courageous? If only you knew how I was quaking inside! Come on now, we're going to take you in hand. And no more tears.'

Annie's strength and good sense helped Grizel and soon she was able to go into society, pay calls and actually feel enjoyment at the supper parties they held in their elegant home. Every time her eye fell on her hostess in one of her lovely silk dresses, with an adoring husband at her beck and call, Grizel remembered the girl she used to see tending the black cattle in the meadow near Glen Fada and was glad that, for Annie at least, miracles did happen.

The General was fond of entertaining old army friends from India who came to shoot on his estate and sometimes stayed for weeks at a time. One particular friend was so devoted that he bought a place only two miles away and the two veterans spent a great deal of time together, fighting and re-fighting old campaigns. The friend's name was Griffith Bingham, a retired Colonel from the East India Company cavalry. It was he who was recruited by Annie to divert Grizel.

Although he was grizzled and old and slightly shabby, Bingham was kind and thoughtful. Every day he offered to take her driving, and if she refused would happily sit with her and discuss the books she read though the only reading he himself enjoyed was bloodstock manuals or racing lists. He was madly keen on horses and was establishing a breeding stud on his new estate.

The Colonel and the girl from the Highlands shared a feeling of displacement and loneliness. She did not feel at home anywhere except in Glen Fada and he, after thirty-five years in India, had left all his friends behind and only had one unmarried and reclusive brother living in London. He clung to General and Mrs Arkwright because they represented his past and could talk with him about the things he loved. They appreciated how much he yearned for the burning Indian sun, the smiling faces of his old servants and soldiers, and the Anglo-Indian social round that they had shared.

He felt at ease while talking to Grizel, too, because she smiled sympathetically and did not excuse herself when he launched himself on his Indian tales. He was intrigued by the air of sadness that she carried with her and questioned Annie about her background. What he heard of her childhood and her unhappy love affair engaged his sympathies totally.

By the end of September Grizel had totally recovered her health and spirits and the time had come to return to the Highlands. Before she left the Arkwrights, however, she pressed Annie to bring her husband to Glen Fada for the General had never been farther north than Edinburgh. When they accepted she extended the invitation to their friend Bingham as well.

'I know you'd relish our Highland life. There's good shooting and you'll particularly enjoy meeting my sister Anne. She's as enthusiastic about horses as you are!'

Her journey home was slow, travelling via her mother's cousins in Derbyshire before going on to Edinburgh where she met up with Patrick so they could travel north together. He was silent and unusually subdued during their trip but it was not until she was able to talk with Anne that she discovered the reason for her brother's reticence.

The family's financial situation had taken a turn for the worse. Some of the people to whom her father owed money had started pressing for repayment. Glen Fada estate was teetering on the verge of ruin and, as he descended into chaos, Macalpine was taking with him many loyal friends and even employees who

had loaned him money to tide him over his financial embarrass-
ments.

'If the estate wasn't entailed it would be sold up by now,' said
Anne bitterly as she stared out of the window of the nursery where
the sisters had taken refuge from the prevailing gloom downstairs.

'I'd no idea things were as bad as this,' Grizel said sadly. 'Patrick's
looking very glum. He'll have to shoulder it all when father's dead.'

'Before that. Father's asked him to take over some of the debts.
He's had to take on the responsibility for sixty thousand pounds.'

The extent of the sum staggered Grizel. 'Sixty thousand! But
that's a fortune. He'll never pay it back.'

Anne nodded in sad agreement. 'And that's not all. There's far
more than that outstanding apparently, though I doubt if even
Father knows how much. When I think what's happened to our
family, I feel so angry! None of this should have happened. You
realise what it all means, Grizel? It's not only Glen Fada that stands
to be ruined, but us as well. There's nothing left, nothing at all,
we'll have not a penny in dowry. We've missed the opportunity of
good marriages, you and I. Sometimes I feel like laughing when I
think of how we went along in blissful ignorance. . .believing what
Mother told us about being able to pick and choose!' Anne's voice
was hard as she went on, 'We're too old and too poor now for
anyone to bother about us. Haven't you noticed how our suitors
have dropped away these last twelve months? They must have heard
about all this before we did.'

Grizel felt a wave of sympathy for her embittered sister. 'Oh,
Anne, don't worry. You're still young and so pretty. Someone will
want to marry you.'

For herself she'd given up all hope and desire for marriage, but it
hurt Grizel to see Anne's naturally cheerful nature so changed.

'I'm not so sure, but I can tell you this. It'd take more than poor
table manners for me to turn away an offer now. I don't relish
growing older and poorer here with the house falling down around
us and the servants disappearing one by one because their wages
haven't been paid for months.'

She pointed down onto the deserted courytard. 'Look there. Not
a soul to be seen. It wasn't so long ago that it was full of people from
morning till night – pipers and grooms, maids, governesses, tutors,
butlers. How can things have changed so much in such a short time?
I can't see hope for any of us, Grizel.' Anne stared bleakly at her
sister who shivered.

A feeling of disillusion and apprehension seemed to seep through every room and corridor of the old house but, because she wanted to soothe her sister's fears, she assumed a reassuring air as she said, 'Things never stay bad for ever. We've had alarms before and they've blown over. Glen Fada's stood for a long time and it'll stand for many years longer. Cheer up. Can you guess who I've invited up for the shooting – Annie and her husband. They're bringing a friend with them whom I'm sure you'll like.'

Annie Arkwright brought happiness with her wherever she went and the fortnight she and her husband spent at Glen Fada was like a light in darkness. Every day of that October was golden, warm and sunny and Annie led them all out on expeditions and picnics to the most distant glens where they sat on tufts of purple heather and forgot their troubles.

As expected, Colonel Bingham found a community of interest with Anne who took him off to the stables and talked horses to him from morning to night. One day, from the drawing room window, Grizel saw them driving off together in the little gig. The brown-faced Colonel sat in the passenger seat while Anne stood up at his side, her straw hat on the back of her head, cracking a long whip over the galloping pony's back. They stayed away for hours and came back fresh-cheeked and beaming, full of tales about the places they had visited and the sights they'd seen. Never once did Grizel feel any jealousy at Anne's taking her friend over. She was only glad that the lonely Colonel and her angry sister were finding such pleasure in each other's company.

Griffith Bingham stayed a week longer than his friends and when he left Anne seemed nervous, pacing the house as if his departure had opened a gate in her mind, allowing all the old worries to come flooding back. Grizel attempted to distract her but made no headway. In a strange way, it was as if her beloved sister had left her.

On a dull November afternoon, the mail bag was brought in as usual by Allie Beag. Lister, the butler who had replaced Dunn, emptied the letters out on to the dining room table but from the corner of her eye Grizel saw him palm one and slide it into a silver bowl on the mantelpiece. When she went to retrieve it later, wanting to know to whom it was addressed, the letter had disappeared.

The first intimation of trouble ahead was her mother's shriek from upstairs. It sounded as if she was being tortured. This was followed by an urgent undertone of conversation, then the chatter of angry voices. As Grizel ran up the stairs to her mother's room, she could hear her parents' voices raised in anger.

'Anne, you can't mean this!'

'You must be mad. It's impossible.'

Grizel pushed open the door just as Anne, standing stiff and controlled in the middle of the room, said calmly and very quietly, 'Yes, I do mean it. You must accept it because it is going to happen one way or another. I had hoped you would take it in good part.'

Mrs Macalpine was pacing the floor, her hair disordered and her face bright red. 'Good part! How could you expect us to take it in good part, as you call it? It's a scandal.'

She turned and saw Grizel standing amazed in the doorway. 'You might as well hear the latest news. Your foolish sister has agreed to marry that wizened old stick Colonel Bingham!'

With red, chilblain-chapped fingers, Grizel held the open cookery book towards the glow of the hearth to make it easier to read.

Even close to the fire, she shivered in the chill draught which came creeping like a thief beneath the door leading to the echoing denuded house where the other members of her family slept, wrapped up against the cold in cocoons of shawls and plaids. The silence in the kitchen was broken only by crackling wood in the grate and the chop, chop, chop of Miss Alfred's knife cutting its way through a pile of carrots, a task which was awkwardly performed because of the gloves she wore to protect her plump little hands against the bitter cold. Grizel felt anger rise like bile in her throat at the sight of the governess's ineptitude but she bit back the exasperation which she longed to express, for on this occasion the governess deserved gratitude instead of dislike. She had kindly taken leave of her new school and come north to assist at the wedding celebrations of her favourite pupil. Alfred had never made any secret of her preference for Anne.

It was even more kind of her to stay up all night to help prepare the wedding breakfast. In Glen Fada's cavernous service quarters only Lister and Beatie, the kitchen maid, remained. They hung on through affection for the family though they had not been paid for months and Grizel privately doubted if they would ever see a farthing of what was owed to them.

The hour before dawn was the worst. Leaden tiredness weighed down Grizel's shoulders and her eyelids drooped as she stirred and tasted, chopped and sieved, but still she persisted doggedly. This must be a memorable meal, the best she could concoct with the aid of the *Cuisinière Bourgeoise*, for the wedding breakfast was her present to her sister. She had no money to provide any other. As she turned the book's stained pages and deciphered the receipts by the fire's flickering light, she silently thanked the memory of old M. Martin, their French tutor.

When Grizel reached her lowest ebb, when she felt total exhaustion claim her and was almost ready to follow Alfred's example of snatching a nap on a long bench against the wall, energy surged miraculously back at the sight of dawn streaking the sky outside the window. She knew the sun would be rising over the mountain called Carn Bheadhair and, grabbing her shawl, ran outside and stood watching streaks of pink, yellow, gold and orange trail like bridal ribbons across the bowl of sky above the mountains. On every side surrounding her home, as far as she could see, the outlines of their jagged peaks rose to the sky, range upon range, like paper cut outs, dark blue and purple against the dawn light.

Grizel ran quickly up the mound of earth beside the house. From its vantage point it was possible to catch a glimpse of the most magnificent mountain of all, the mystic and brooding lord of the land: Cairngorm. There had been a fall of snow during the night and the mountain's flanks were streaked in white which made it look like a huge wedding cake dribbled with icing. Cairngorm had decked itself out in honour of Anne's wedding.

She was asleep when Grizel crept into the room they shared. She held back the bed curtains and stared at her sister's blonde curls tumbled on the pillow and her vulnerable sleeping face. Though Anne was nearly twenty-four years old, sleep made her look like a child for it removed the veneer of stern resolve that had carried her through the last few weeks. From the day she had broken the news of her impending marriage to Griffith Bingham, she had stood stoically firm while a storm of reproaches rained down on her.

'He's not rich enough,' said her father.

'He's too old and too ugly,' said her mother scathingly. When Anne attempted to defend her choice by saying she respected him for his mind, her mother retorted, 'It's a pity he hasn't more body to go with it!'

It had been a bitter time.

Could I have done what she did? No, I couldn't or I would never have given up Tom. I gave in to them. I yielded. Anne would never

be so weak, thought Grizel with fierce love and pride as she looked
at her sleeping sister.

She had suffered for her sister and taken her side wholeheartedly
during the weeks before the wedding, but privately Grizel too
wondered at her choice. The beauty of the family could still have
had her pick of Edinburgh's lesser young gentlemen, but she had
chosen to marry an old man, without even a vast fortune to sweeten
his disadvantages. Grizel wondered why Anne had so deliberately
turned her back against the sort of physical attraction that she had
felt for Tom. There was no hint between Anne and Bingham of the
urgency, the passion that Grizel knew only too well could draw a
man and woman to each other. In this case there was another bond.
To Anne, Griffith Bingham represented her escape from the family
troubles. As his wife, she would be able to live far away, to remove
herself from the problems which beset Glen Fada on every side.

As if Grizel's scrutiny could penetrate slumber, Anne opened her
eyes. 'What's the time?'

'Nine o'clock. The sun's risen. It's going to be a fine day but cold,
very cold.' Grizel sat down on the edge of the bed and took Anne's
hand in hers. 'Everything's ready. Alfred and I've been up all night.'

Anne sat up and put her arms around her sister. 'Oh, Grizel,' she
said with a sob in her voice. It was the first sign of emotion she had
shown since the day she announced her engagement. They clung to
each other in silence for several minutes before the question she had
not meant to ask slipped from Grizel's lips. 'Are you sure, Anne?
Are you really sure?' She felt Anne draw away from her as the
words were spoken.

In spite of his short stature, Colonel Bingham, brown and wrinkled
as an old pickled walnut after his many years' service in Bengal,
looked stern and imposing in the scarlet uniform of the East India
Company's army. He stood, sword by his side, keenly studying his
new relatives who seemed apprehensive of the pious-looking young
Episcopal minister from Inverness who had travelled forty miles to
marry the couple. The Macalpines were all fairly tepid adherents
of the Scots Reformed Church and suspicious of High Church
preachers but Bingham had insisted on being married according
to his own rites.

The wedding party was not large and the majority of them were
relations of the bride, most of them bearing the same surname. It
seemed to the Colonel that everyone he met in their part of the Spey

valley was called Macalpine, from the humblest wood cutter to the exalted laird. The only guests at the wedding with a different name were Mr and Mrs MacIvor from Carn Dearg.

Peter John Macalpine, who was about to become Bingham's father-in-law, was seven years younger than the Colonel himself. The laird had tried to call off the wedding when his lawyer discovered that Bingham's fortune amounted to only £25,000. On this, his wedding day, the Colonel nearly laughed aloud for he calculated that his bride's father's debts came to at least four times as much and were still growing.

On her daughter's wedding day Jane Macalpine was conducting herself like someone at a funeral, her face red and swollen with weeping. While the Colonel stared at her, she did not trouble to disguise the dislike she bore him but shot him a venomous glance. Bingham was too much of a realist not to appreciate that his clear-eyed wife was well aware of the state of her parents' fortunes. He knew her awareness had gone a long way to persuade her to accept his hand but he trusted that the genuine love he felt for her, and the liking he knew she felt for him, would make their marriage a happy one.

At the drawing room door, the bride's brothers Patrick and John stood waiting to admit her. The Colonel studied them with the eyes of a man used to assessing the potential of young officers. There was hope for John, the youngest, a gangly eighteen-year-old lad fresh from the East India College at Haileybury but the demeanour of the heir, twenty-six-year old Patrick, boded ill for the estate of Glen Fada. He was a handsome young man but as prodigal as his sire and with even less probity.

The member of the family whom Bingham liked best after Anne was not present for she was upstairs helping her sister dress for the wedding. His face softened when he thought of Grizel. If she had not invited him to her home, he would never have met Anne. He felt a wave of kindness and gratitude towards the elder girl, remembering her habitually wistful expression, the pallor of her skin and how drawn she often looked. She was much too thin and anxious for a young woman of her age and class, and he hoped that fate would soon be kinder to her.

In Mrs Macalpine's boudoir on the first floor the sisters were preparing to descend the stairs. As the bride stood back from the glass to survey her neat figure in its blue and silver silk gown with Brussels lace trim, Grizel remembered how, when Anne was small, she always wanted to dress as a boy and wore her pinafore back to front. Now she was a lovely bride in a pale blue gown, the one she had worn when they danced their exhibition quadrille before the King.

Louisa wore sprigged muslin and the privations of the recent months had slimmed her down so that she looked almost pretty. Grizel's own gown was the one she had worn to the Grand Ball and when she ran her hands down its soft skirt she could still feel her anguish at the sight of Tom Falconer. That pain would never leave her, it seemed.

'Will anyone notice my slippers?' Anne asked her sisters anxiously, pointing one toe from beneath the hem of her gown.

Grizel shook her head reassuringly. 'No, don't worry. The stains don't show. No one will guess we dyed them with ink. You look lovely, a beautiful bride. Oh, wait! Take off one shoe – I want to put a lucky coin in your heel.'

She bent to slip a worn silver sixpenny piece under the frayed lining of Anne's slipper and then, limping very slightly, the bride walked down to her wedding.

A gentle rustling outside the drawing room door made Peter John Macalpine jump to his feet, readying himself to lead his daughter to the clergyman. The December sunlight shone with cruel clarity on the shabby, shamefaced man, his greying hair drawn tightly back from his face. He was wearing a shiny, greenish-black jacket that strained tight over his shoulders and his dejected manner clearly showed his disappointment in his daughter's choice of a groom.

The pitiless winter sun also picked out the sad pretensions of the once magnificent drawing room. It glinted off the chipped and damaged plaster work, highlighted the stains on the silk-covered walls where damp had seeped down from the broken roof, revealed the frayed upholstery, the flaked gilt on the frames that surrounded the family pictures. Here and there less faded squares marked the places on the walls where pictures used to hang before they had been sent away for sale.

The bride walked beneath the painted gaze of her ancestors with her head held high while her mother sobbed and hiccupped hysterically into a handkerchief. Anne did not give a backward glance. She stood proudly beside her ageing bridegroom and when the clergyman asked her to make her bridal pledge, the resounding firmness of her 'I will' startled the gathering.

*

Whisky, drawn off the last barrel of pale yellow Glenlivet that had been brewed from the waters of the Spey and stored for years in the cobweb-hung cellars of Glen Fada, softened prejudices and loosened tongues. Malt fumes rising to the brain persuaded the most reserved or resentful wedding guest to put out the hand of friendship so that differences were at least temporarily forgotten. Like so many weddings held in the house in the past, Anne's marriage feast could have continued all day, all night and through the next day as well, but after the toasts, the Colonel sprang his surprise. 'My carriage is waiting on the river bank,' he announced. 'I promised to dine with my brother in London on Christmas Day.'

'But that's in five days' time and it's more than four hundred miles away,' protested his new father-in-law.

'Exactly. I've good horses and we're leaving now,' was the groom's reply. No amount of pleading would make him change his mind. As Grizel glanced across at Anne, she saw from the glimmer of a smile on her sister's lips that this precipitate exit had been pre-arranged.

Sun was glinting on the walls of the huge house behind its sheltering bank of fir trees as the wedding party poured out into the garden. It threw sparks of light off the gilt lacings of Griffith Bingham's braided jacket and danced festively on the river, making the rippling water shine and sparkle like shot silk. Surrounded by members of the Macalpine family, the bridegroom led his new wife towards a little boat tied up on the bank of the Spey. Waiting at the jetty was a small crowd of estate workers with a piper blowing away manfully at his pipes.

On the wooden landing stage the grey-bearded ferryman stood with his hook tethering the rowing boat close to the shore. It was decked out for the occasion with ribbons and holly branches and the people who had known and loved the bride since birth were beaming with pride.

As Anne stepped into the frail little craft Lister, trying to look imposing though he was incoherent with whisky, graciously took her hand and helped her to a seat in the prow while the equally drunk piper, on the verge of collapse, squeezed out a last alarming skirl. The groom climbed in after her and the crowd on the bank raised a cheer.

The ferryman's oars neatly sliced the water. The river was not broad, though in rough weather the other bank could seem as unattainable as America, and the spectators saw Bingham's carriage drawn up on the shingle opposite. Ribbons were fluttering from its lowered hood and the coachmen were sporting large white wedding favours in their hats.

A sudden hush fell over the watchers when the bride alighted from the rowing boat on the other side of the water. They strained their eyes to catch a last glimpse of her as she climbed easily up a little rise and was handed into the carriage. Then a whip cracked like a pistol shot, someone in the crowd gave a shout, the piper managed to gather himself sufficiently to strike up his most haunting lament, and the four harnessed horses on the opposite shore sprang forward together, their hooves sliding and plunging in the shifting pebbles. The newly weds were off.

The family waved and tried to cheer although their throats were tight with tears but the bride sat staring forward, her shoulders squared and her back straight. She never looked back once, threw not a single glance over her shoulder at her old home. Grizel, straining for a last glimpse of her sister through a veil of tears, could not tell whether Anne was steeling herself against weakness and sentiment or whether she was genuinely glad to leave.

Chapter Ten

⁓

THE PEOPLE of Glen Fada always made a great occasion of Christmas, which was marked by two weeks of drinking and celebrations.

They observed two major festive days. The first, and least important, was December 25th but there was no church service for in the Highlands they did not mark Christmas Day as a religious occasion like people farther south. For Highlanders the most important day was Old Style Yule or Uphalieday – January 6th.

The Christmas fortnight of 1825 however was a sad and diminished occasion for the Macalpines. Not only was Anne missing but Patrick and John set out for Edinburgh on Christmas Eve, leaving their parents, Louisa and Grizel in a cold and empty house. The weather too had taken a turn for the worse and rain teemed down constantly, swelling the river till it was impossible to cross by rowing boat. The skies were grey and leaden. There seemed no cause for celebration at such a dismal time.

On previous years Grizel would have been bustling about on Christmas Eve, supervising the festive preparations. Now she sat alone and watched the flames flickering around the Yule log which her father, as head of the family, had dragged in from the soaking wet woods that afternoon. The log must be kept alight until Old Yule or else ill luck would befall the house so Grizel knelt and blew red fire into it with a heavy pair of bellows. It was so wet that it would need continual nursing.

And we've enough ill luck already without adding to it, she told herself. This year it was impossible to summon up any genuine feeling of cheerfulness. She was acutely conscious that, for the first time in her experience, the house felt echoing and sinister.

A strange dread gripped her heart as she recalled the old superstitions and stories which had been told to her by the servants over the years. In the dark shadows around her, she imagined that eyes were watching and shivered at the thought of the bedroom above her head where the spirit of a long dead Macalpine was said to storm and rage. She remembered her terror in the nursery cupboard all those years ago and foreboding gripped her. She knew that throughout the days of Christmas she would be watching out for ancient signs and omens, filled with dread in case they were portents of more ill fortune ahead.

As was their habit, on Christmas Day the Macalpines drove to Carn Dearg to dine with the MacIvors but it was a gloomy party for the talk was all of ill weather, lost money, days of prosperity long past and of friends now dead or gone away. Even the hospitable kindness of old friends could not bring consolation. On New Year's Eve, after her parents and sister went early to bed, Grizel sat alone watching the banked up fire. She felt relief at seeing the charred remnants of the Yule log still burning in the back of the hearth and attended it carefully, dreading any sign of its going out. All around her were creaks and groans as the house settled itself for the night. Mice scuttled in the wainscoating and a bitter wind came sighing like the voice of a lost soul through the cracks of the window ledges.

Grizel sat before the fire till morning. When dawn came the log was still glowing red. Anxiously, she knelt beside the heap of grey ashes in the fireplace, scrutinising them to see if there was any mark resembling a human footprint there. An indentation with its toes pointing towards the door would mean that someone was to be removed from the family circle before the year's end. Though she found nothing, the feeling of dread did not leave her but stalked her continually, a sinister shadow that marred the holiday for her.

The festive season ended on Twelfth Night, the traditional day of revels and pageants. The MacIvors always celebrated it with the Macalpines and arrived early to lend a hand with the ceremonial burning of the branches of greenery with which Glen Fada house had been decked during the Christmas period. Every branch and every twig had to be heaped on the fire and reduced to ashes if the luck of the house was to hold. As Grizel watched her flushed father supervising the burning, she wondered what luck they had to keep.

After the ceremonial burning, she and Louisa dressed in long plaid cloaks and accompanied their father and Mr MacIvor to a large flat field behind the farm for the traditional New Year game of *camanachad* – shinty – which was played by two unruly teams of local men armed with curved sticks. The players had to hit a hard ball through a goal marked by piles of plaids, and play was always fast and furious. In past years it was a famous occasion and spectators enjoyed it as much as the most enthusiastic member of either team. People came from far away to witness the game at Glen Fada.

Wrapped up in her plaid, with the cold seeping through the soles of her broken boots, Grizel watched the estate workers trickling in through the gate and was saddened to see how few there were compared to previous years. It took special occasions like the shinty match to reveal the real extent of the depredations Macalpine's mismanagement had brought to his estate. Where there had once been hundreds of workers, now there were only tens. The youngest and most agile men had all left the glen, gone not without bitter regret, leaving the aged and infirm behind. It seemed as if the fairies had spirited Glen Fada's best people away.

Grizel's father noticed the diminished crowd and said anxiously to his friend, 'I hope we'll be able to raise two ba' teams this year. There has to be a match, everyone expects it.'

Mr MacIvor peeled off his jacket and said, 'Come on then, get off your coat and you and I'll take a stick each – we'll swell the teams.'

Though they played with a will, there was little joy in the game. The cheers had a forced sound and people began to drift away before it was finished. Grizel felt her depression deepen as she compared this shinty match with similar occasions in years gone by when play went on for hours, whisky bottles were passed about among the players and the spectators howled themselves hoarse in delight at each goal scored. Only the coming of darkness would bring an end to their game then but this year it was over when the players ran out of enthusiasm and the crowd moved on to the barn for the next event of the day – the dinner and ball, an annual celebration given by the laird for his outdoor workers.

The family had discussed the possibility of cancelling the feast on the grounds of expense but both Grizel and her father were adamant that it should continue. 'It's my duty, a symbol of the link between the laird and his people. If we break it, it might never be repaired. But who's to make the preparations?' said Macalpine

'I'll provide the feast,' offered Grizel, and she spent days working in the kitchen with the help of Louisa and anyone else she could enlist. Miss Alfred had gone back south with Patrick and John so her assistance was not available, but a baron of beef and several sheep from the park were roasted; pies and puddings were baked; bowls of *crannachan* mixed; barrels of ale breached and bowls of steaming punch, reeking with the scent of cinnamon, brewed. Louisa, who had grown thinner from months of hard work around the house, was quite giddy with anticipation of the feast that lay ahead and had to be warned not to keep dipping her spoon into the bowls of cream.

'There's not enough to go round. We've only three cows left remember. Stop eating it,' scolded Grizel. 'This might be the last Christmas feast we'll give our people. It has to be a good one.'

After the shinty match, when the barn door was swung open and she saw how grandly the board was spread, she felt proud of her efforts. The workers trooped in and took their places at the table but again there was a subdued air over the proceedings. The old joyous spirit was missing from the gathering. Peter John tried his best, putting on a broad smile and acting as if nothing was changed, but the eyes that looked back at him were guarded. Sensing his people's resentment, he strove to win them over, calling out: 'Blow up, Macalpine.'

The piper, with bows of ribbon tied to the chanter of his pipes, came marching in playing *The Prince's Welcome* which was usually guaranteed to bring tears of sentiment and pride to every Highland eye. This year, however, there was no weeping. Then, in a manly voice, the laird sang his party piece, *The Skye Boat Song*, the music he always rendered at the Christmas feast, and Grizel stood up to sweep the gathering along with her sweet rendition of the Gaelic favourite *Cuchulain*.

She had first sung that song at an estate party when she was eight years old, but the love which had then united the laird and his people and made them a community was now disappearing. Clan loyalties were dying as people worried about their future. Later, when Grizel rose to leave the party, the crowd parted unsmiling before her. At the door, she felt her arm being gripped by a hand and turned to see Macalpine, the old ferryman.

'Miss Grizel,' he whispered close to her ear, 'I've just heard that the river's changed its course.'

'Which river?' she asked fearfully.

'The one out of the loch. It's burst its banks at Inverdruie and taken a new course through the meadow. You know what that means, Miss, don't you?'

She nodded but did not speak. There was a local legend that when the river burst its banks, ruin would engulf the family of the laird. It had only happened once before when the Macalpines defeated the Comyns and wrested Glen Fada from them. She told herself that such superstitions were stupid – 'The river's burst its banks because of all the rain,' said her logic – but a feeling of dread overwhelmed her and a little voice inside her head jibed back with, 'It means disaster. But what more can happen to us?' She tried not to think about the answer.

The rain stopped next day but the river still ran in its new channel. Snow began falling on January 10th and from the window of her refuge in the old nursery high up in the top storey of the house, Grizel looked out at a pristine landscape, frozen in the grip of a bitter frost. The bare beech trees of the park seemed to be holding themselves in, drawing the tips of their branches back into their trunks like old men clapping their arms about their chests as protection from the cold. In the distance a few sheep, survivors from the killing for the estate ball, were pulling wildly at piles of hay she had dragged out to them earlier that morning. A pheasant, startled by some unseen danger, rose squawking from the birch trees lining the river bank. Its shriek sounded like the cry of the damned.

Even the mountains, those protective giants, failed to reassure her and she shivered with fear as well as cold as she walked to the hearth where a fire of damp twigs gathered from the park flickered miserably. She squatted down on her heels, holding her sore hands out to the fitful warmth and, with a rueful smile, remembered the reluctant fires that had always burned in the nursery grate. Perhaps it was a good thing after all that she had become inured to discomfort while young.

Her reverie was interrupted by the noise of her mother loudly blowing her nose as she opened her bedroom door. The nose blowing ritual was the herald of her rising but today she was even later than usual for it was nearly three o'clock. Soon it would be dark and time to serve dinner in the library. They had given up using the dining room and huddled round the library fire, eating on a little table drawn up to the heat.

It was not time to go to the kitchen yet, however, and Grizel could concentrate on her writing. Louisa spent most of her day attending on their mother and rarely came into the nursery which was Grizel's private bolt hole. In her loneliness she had begun to compose stories. They helped her forget the worries and troubles of

her day to day life. Composition came surprisingly easily to her and
when she read over the first stories she wrote, it struck her that this
might be a way of earning some money. Tentatively, without any
great hope, she sent off three of them to the *Inspector* in Edinburgh.
Her heart beat fast each time a mail delivery was expected. As yet
she had heard nothing and nursed her secret for fear of ridicule,
never telling anyone how she passed her leisure time – what little
there was of it.

In spite of their troubles, Peter John Macalpine and his wife were
good companions. As their eldest daughter watched them together
she realised that they were totally absorbed in each other, did not
really need her or anyone except as servants. They were, and always
had been, sufficient unto each other. Their children, apart from the
valued heir and the still babied Louisa, were irrelevancies, burden-
some consequences of their marital pleasures. The realisation of
what her place in life would be in the future filled Grizel with dread.
She felt lonely and useless, shut out from love and company.

After they had eaten supper, the mail was announced. Allie Beag
was greeted with delight for letters were their lifeline, their only
link with the outside world. Grizel kept the key of the mail bag
and she jumped up to sort out the letters into their separate piles.
'Three for me,' she said, trying to hide the sparkle in her eye for
one of the letters was in an unknown hand and she felt sure it was
from the *Inspector*.

'Two for you, Mother, one from Annie and the other from Aunt
Maria in Oxford. The rest are for you, Father.'

His mail was imposingly addressed to the Member of Parliament
for Tavistock. If it were not for his holding that position, contact
with the outside world would be minimal for the family could
no longer afford postal charges. Fortunately for them Members
of Parliament enjoyed the right of sending letters free under the
official frank. Grizel's spirits sank at the sight of the bundle of papers
in her father's hand – all the letters that came for him nowadays
seemed to contain bills or bad news. He tore impatiently at the
seal of the first letter and perused the contents with a swift glance
before moving on to the others which he cast aside as negligently.
The last one stopped him short and he gave a gasp as he read it, his
face ashen.

'What's wrong, Father?'

'It's Patrick. He's been arrested in Edinburgh. He's in the Calton
jail.'

None of them had to ask the reason for the arrest. They all knew that it was for debt. While her mother wailed in terror and Louisa sobbed, Grizel fixed her eyes accusingly on her father who hastened to reassure her.

'No, don't look like that. He's not been arrested for my debts. My creditors'll wait. It's for sums he ran up himself when he was at College – he didn't realise. . . .'

Grizel tried to hide her anger and dismay. I was the first born. Why shouldn't I inherit Glen Fada? I wouldn't let it be ruined for petty debts, she thought bitterly.

As soon as the snow melted off the valley floor, the laird left Glen Fada. His daughter loaded him with plaids and packets of food, her anger and irritation now replaced by pity. A man accustomed all his life to travelling in great style in his own equipages, he was going by mail coach to Edinburgh to free his son from a debtor's prison. To sit with his feet in straw among the common people would be hard for him, she knew, but he seemed only slightly crestfallen when he rode off to join the coach at Kingussie. His last words to her were, 'Look after your mother and Louisa, and don't worry. I've a plan for putting everything right again.' She stared after his disappearing back, wondering at his indomitability and capacity to dismiss from his mind all the mistakes that had gone before.

Alone and even more lonely after her father left, she lost herself in the stories which she was turning out in a spate for the *Inspector*. The unknown letter in the mail bag had brought good news. Her first submissions were accepted and the editor asked for more. What was even better, he sent a draft for £20 in payment for her first efforts. Grizel had hidden the money and delight filled her whenever she thought of it. Encouraged by her success, she spent her nights in the nursery scribbling away by the flickering light of a candle-end stuck on a nail.

In the bedrooms below, her mother and sister slept, read novels or stitched away at their embroidery. No visitors called and neither Louisa nor her mother walked out or took any exercise. Mrs Macalpine was especially slothful and her way of living was ruining her health.

'I'm ill. You don't understand how feeble I am,' she complained when Grizel suggested that they go out driving in the old gig.

'But spring's coming. Look how the buds are bursting on the trees. Don't be afraid. You used to drive with Anne.' However nervous a passenger she might be, with her second daughter at the reins Mrs Macalpine would travel in perfect composure.

'My dear girl, you could never drive the gig the way dear Anne did. You always were envious of the way your sister could handle a horse,' was the dismissive answer.

Sometimes, up in the nursery on spring nights, Grizel would turn around with a start, thinking she heard voices speaking to her. The room was haunted but not by spectres. It was full of memories of the childhood games they played there. In her mind she could still hear her sisters' and brothers' laughter, remember their shrieks of delight when their father came bounding up the stairs to play Giants and Castles with them.

It was difficult not to shed tears at the memories, such a mixture of happiness and pain. In her solitude Grizel leaned her head on folded hands and thought of the forbidden subject – love.

How is he? Where is he tonight? she asked herself. In her mind's eye she saw Tom at some dinner table, so fine-looking in the lamplight, his face alight with intelligence and humour. He breathed life and energy into everyone with whom he came in contact. . . . The thought of him was like a stab at her heart and she scolded herself abruptly.

'It's not necessary to marry for love. Look at Anne with her Colonel. She seems happy enough to judge by her letters.'

Grizel's life was generally too busy for fits of repining. Not only did she have to look after the house, help Louisa with their mother and cope with Lister's fits of drunkenness, she ran what was left of the farm as well. In a strange way she did not resent this turn in her fortunes for the work was a labour of love and she revelled in tasks which used to be performed by the most poorly paid servants.

One day she was hurrying across the yard with buckets of food for the hens when she saw Patrick coming up from the ferry. They stood and stared at each other in surprise. His face expressed horror at the sight of his aristocratic sister dressed like a peasant woman in a plaid cloak and with huge working boots on her feet. Grizel saw that her brother wore immaculate buckskins and a smart blue jacket with silver buttons, but though his clothes were as dandyfied as ever his face showed the marks of strain and his blond hair was unbrushed and tousled. His usual devil-may-care manner was replaced by a dejected attitude.

'They let you out of the Calton then?' she asked. He nodded. 'There wasn't any point keeping me any longer. Mr Guild arranged it.' Her father's long-suffering lawyer had come to their aid again, thought Grizel, vainly hoping to see some signs of new maturity in Patrick's face after two months' imprisonment. But the fatal weakness was still about his mouth; the laxity in his eye. She could also see that something was troubling him deeply.

'What else is the matter?' she asked.

He shrugged like a man bringing news of a defeat. 'Bad news, I'm afraid. The Duke's taken back Tavistock. Father's had to flee the country. He'll be in France by now.'

She looked around as if to check that the world about her was the same. Yes, the mountains were still there and the river still ran.

'If he sets foot in this country again, his creditors'll catch him. They're all out looking for him now,' Patrick said gloomily.

As if the shame of debt was not enough, Peter John Macalpine, laird of Glen Fada, was now exiled from his ancestral home and the estate which he had comprehensively ruined. With the loss of his seat, her father had also lost his immunity from prosecution for debt.

The news of Patrick's arrival roused his mother from her bed but not for long. When she heard his news, she fainted and had to be carried back again. Propped up by pillows she wept and held her son's hand, repeating all the while her litany of condemnation, the people whom she blamed for her husband's downfall.

'He was cheated out of the seat at Fraserburgh. It was a disaster for your poor father. That wicked scoundrel of an agent made him sell his English estate to pay for that election.'

Grizel listened with a stony face for she had heard it all before. According to her mother, none of the prodigal waste of hundreds of thousands of pounds was ever her father's fault. Grizel wanted to ask, Why did he go on pouring money away on buying votes for elections that he couldn't win? Why did he want to go in Parliament in the first place? Why didn't he content himself with running this estate like the lairds before him?

But she knew what the answer would be. Her mother always said the same thing. 'Your father's abilities are too great for him to be cooped up here. All his friends told him he ought to go south to practise at the London Bar. They advised him to go into Parliament to have proper scope for his mind. I expect they were jealous. Your father's a great man.'

Grizel accepted without question that her father was a good scholar, a man of many interests, a man of energy and enthusiasm which needed outlets. She had often sat in his library watching as he translated from leatherbound volumes of Greek and Latin. She had assisted him in drawing up his legal briefs or preparing the notes for his books on jurisprudence. But somehow nothing ever satisfied him and nothing was ever quite finished. There was something incomplete in all Peter John's enthusiasms. He sparked off in all directions without restraint or direction.

'What are we to do now?' sobbed Mrs Macalpine from her nest in the huge bed shrouded in its tattered green silk curtains.

'We've to wait here. He'll send for us. He said he was trying to arrange something through Charles Grant, some appointment or other. He'll send a message as soon as he can,' Patrick told her.

'Where's John?' Grizel interrupted.

Her mother nodded, the existence of her younger son only brought back to mind by the question. 'Yes, where is he?'

'Abroad with Father.'

That evening, when darkness was falling, Grizel heard her brother's footstep on the nursery stairs. Putting away her writing, she turned to greet him with a serious expression. Patrick pushed open the door which yielded to his shoulder with its familiar, high-pitched squeal. It was a long time since he had been in the nursery and he had grown so tall that he had to bend his head to avoid the low lintel.

He gazed around the room, eyes wide with surprise, for the nursery was not as he remembered it. Buckets were placed on the floor to catch water where the roof leaked, the window glass was cracked or broken, with rags stuffed in the holes to keep out the wind, and the paint was peeling and discoloured. Only the old brass-edged fireguard and the Mercator maps hanging crookedly on the walls were the same.

'I'd no idea,' he said.

Grizel shrugged. She had grown used to the decrepitude of the room. 'Oh, it's not too bad tonight. At least it's not raining or snowing. In the winter drifts of snow came through the skylight and nearly blocked the stair.'

He pulled a chair close to her side and sat down heavily, lifting his boots up towards the fire. 'I've been round the farm and up at the saw mill but there's not much left.'

She recognised an echo of her own regret in his voice. Her face was sad as she gazed into the fire, replying in a faraway voice, 'There used to be forest for twenty square miles all round here. The trees were so beautiful.'

He looked at her strangely and replied, 'Yes, I do remember. Those were good days.'

She enjoyed having someone new to talk to. Louisa was poor company. 'Do you remember the picnics we went on? We used to gather geans and blaeberries and hazelnuts. How the berries stained our clothes!'

They both laughed then Patrick sighed. 'We'll go berrying again, Grizel. Summer's coming.'

'Yes, but things can't go on like this. We might not be here when summer comes. You know something else, don't you? You haven't told us everything.'

'You're right, but it's not bad news. I didn't want to raise Mother's hopes yet but it's been hard keeping it to myself.' He leaned forward, all animation and excitement now. 'There's a chance that Father will be offered a judgeship.'

She laughed, the idea seemed so ridiculous. 'A judgeship? Surely that's not possible!'

'It's in India. Charles Grant is a director of the East India Company and he's trying to arrange it. He owes Father a favour over some election or other.'

She nodded. 'I know. It was the start of all this.'

Her mind was in turmoil. India was thousands of miles away. If her father went there, she would have to go too, whether she wanted to or not. But, even in her father's present straits, to leave Glen Fada was unthinkable, surely?

Her brother sensed her reservations and asked quickly, 'Surely you're pleased? If Grant manages the appointment it will be the saving of us all. It'll mean that honourable recovery is possible for Father, and our mother will be ensured a safe and comfortable future.'

The parroted words came from him like a well-rehearsed speech and she knew that they were not his own but his father's. Peter John had already made up his mind. Patrick was merely repeating what he had been told to say.

Grizel smiled though the thought of leaving was sharp as bereavement. 'Of course I'm pleased. There's money to be made in India, but what about this house? What about the estate?'

Patrick made a dismissive gesture, casting off their past and all it had meant. She could see that already all his hopes were invested in India.

'We can sell up the contents of the house and then we'll let it out for the shooting. There's plenty of gentlemen from the south who'd take it on. Bedford's interested already. We'll have no trouble.'

So they had it all arranged! They'd been organising it in the south while no one up in the Highlands had the least idea of the changes that were about to beset them.

Pointedly she asked her brother, 'But what about the people? Our servants, the farm workers, the floaters and the wood cutters – what about them?'

'As I said, the forest's almost gone. There's little work for them any longer. Some can stay for the shooting parties but the others'll have to go.' Her silence made him uneasy and he tried to jolly her along with something of his old jauntiness, saying, 'India'll be good for you and Louisa. You'll catch fine husbands there.'

'I'm too old now for husband catching,' she said sharply.

'Don't be silly. You're only twenty-seven and could've been married long ago if you weren't so hard to please. You're as bad as Anne, difficult to suit,' replied her brother.

'I never met a man I wanted to marry after. . . .' Thomas Falconer had been her brother's friend first but when the association between him and Grizel ended, Patrick had never mentioned him again. Now he said roughly, 'You should forget that Edinburgh fop. He's married anyway. I heard it when I got out of the Calton.'

Who did he marry? Who took my place? She longed to ask the question but could not speak the words for her mouth was too dry. Her brother was impervious to her distress. He had other matters on his mind. From his pocket he drew a sheet of folded paper and held it out to her.

'Father asked me to give you this. He wants you and Louisa to sign it.'

She took it slowly. 'What is it?'

'It's nothing, only a legal document for you to sign. It won't cost you a penny; everything will be settled long before it's due.'

She straightened up and stared angrily at him. 'Don't talk to me as if I'm a child. Tell me what this is.'

'It's a deed making you securitor for a small debt our father has with Lord Lauderdale.'

'That's ridiculous! You know I've no money and neither has Louisa. How can we secure any debt?'

'But it's not to be paid now, it's only your names that they need. You won't be responsible unless Father dies before the debt's discharged, and he's going to pay it off soon. The Trustees are quite agreeable to settling Lauderdale's interest 'til it can be cleared by Father. This is only a formality. Sign it, Grizel. It's your duty to sign.'

She had been writing a story before he arrived and he saw the pen and ink pot on the table at her side. He lifted the goose quill and thrust it between her fingers. 'Sign it,' he repeated more firmly.

Her love for her father, undiminished in spite of his shortcomings, made her want to help him but an inner voice warned her that she must protect herself as well. Her eyes had been opened over the past months and she was seeing more clearly than she had ever done before.

'Let me think about it. Let me read the paper alone first. When I've done that, I'll sign it,' she told her brother.

Next morning she sought Patrick out in the stables and, without speaking, handed him the folded paper which he put into his pocket with a smile. He patted her on the shoulder and said fondly, 'Good. That's done. Lauderdale was pressing and he might've stopped India.'

She stood her ground and looked him in the eye. 'I didn't sign it and I won't let Louisa sign it either,' she said quietly. His face reddened and she thought for a moment that he might strike her but she outfaced him with her calm assurance.

She kept her gaze steady as she said, 'I didn't sign it because it's improper and unfair to ask us to take on that debt. That piece of paper might leave us penniless – and any husbands who marry either of us could be in trouble because of it.'

Her brother stared angrily back and then, faced with such resolution, dropped his eyes. From his demeanour she knew that he and their father had hoped she would not understand the significance of the paper.

'Debt's a cruel master, Patrick,' she said sadly, and turned on her heel.

In the next mail delivery there was a copy of *The Scotsman* sent up from Edinburgh. Patrick seized the paper first, turning its stiff, crackling pages anxiously as he scanned the columns. 'It's here!' he shouted jubilantly. 'We're saved, we're saved!'

His mother, leaning languidly in her usual invalid manner on the library sofa, sat bolt upright and asked: 'Why? What's happened?'

Her son thrust the newspaper under her nose with his finger on a small paragraph at the bottom of an inside page. 'Read that. Father's been made a puisne judge in Bombay. He'll be knighted – Mother, you'll be Lady Macalpine.'

Never was a swifter change seen in anyone's demeanour. Grizel could scarcely believe her eyes as her mother leapt to her feet and started rushing around like a girl. All the ailments, all the infirmities which had plagued her since Anne's wedding, were totally forgotten.

Letters from Macalpine in France arrived with the next post and, as soon as she read them, his wife started issuing orders left and right. 'We've to go south as soon as possible. Passages have been booked on an East Indiaman out of Portsmouth in two months' time. There's packing to be done, there's clothes to be ordered for all of us – we'll have to appear in the latest style. Write to the Misses Macalpine in Inverness, send a message to Lynch, write to Anne and my sister Maria, write to Annie Arkwright. . . .'

Laughing, Patrick put up a hand to stem the flow. 'Wait, Mother, wait. Think a little. As few people as possible must know we're leaving or our creditors'll be on us like bees round a honey pot.'

His mother calmed down at once and accepted the need for secrecy without a qualm, but Grizel's face showed how badly she felt about the small people who would be left in want of the money due to them – Robbie the grocer at Inverdruie, the wine merchant in Inverness, dressmakers, blacksmiths, even servants who had put their faith in the family of Glen Fada, were now to be disappointed.

The news of Macalpine's good fortune spread quickly among his friends and letters poured in with every mail. They were read with jubilation for they were all highly congratulatory. If any sceptic among the letter writers saw the humorous side of the appointment of a penniless bankrupt to a richly paid judgeship in Bombay, they gave no hint. After all, patronage and lobbying were a way of life. Macalpine's salvation had been achieved through the good offices of his distant relative Charles Grant, Lord Glenelg. His case had also been helped by the long memory and taste for good whisky of King George IV. As he approved the appointment, the monarch remembered the gift of ptarmigan and Glenlivet.

'A good fellow, Macalpine. Sent me some fine whisky in Edinburgh,' he said, signing his name with a flourish. Gifts like that were not forgotten. Such was the way the world wagged its tail.

It was important that no hint be given abroad that Peter John Macalpine was not going to India alone. As far as the outside world was concerned, his family were not to accompany him. But, in secret, their plans were being laid. Patrick was to stay in Scotland to run the estate but the girls and Lady Macalpine were going to India.

Mrs Grey came up from Aviemore to help with their packing. She was absolutely trustworthy and not a word of what she saw or heard inside the house would escape her. She helped her lady sort through the contents of Glen Fada.

'The silver, the pictures, the china and the books will all go for auction in Edinburgh. They should fetch a fair sum,' announced Jane Macalpine who showed no trace of sentiment when packing up the things that had been with her all her married life.

Grizel and Louisa regretted even the smallest trinket leaving its appointed place in Glen Fada but for Grizel the greatest loss was her father's library. She handled the leatherbound volumes with love for some of her fondest memories were of sitting with Peter John while he turned their rustling pages. She had been his chief assistant when he decided to catalogue his books. The notebook with the marbled cover in which she had carefully listed the books was in her father's writing desk, and when the library was finally packed for delivery to the auctioneers, Grizel sadly laid it on top of the pile, hoping that the buyer would be someone who would love the books as much as she did.

Her days were too full for brooding. The hustle and bustle also meant that she could spare no evenings for writing beside the nursery fire, but to her delighted surprise her earlier labours were bearing fruit and two more payments, amounting to £40, arrived from the *Inspector*. She hoarded the money, concealing her jubilation at receiving it. If Patrick, with his insatiable need for ready cash, found she had it, he would coax it from her. A warning voice told her that there might come a time when she would need ready money in her pocket.

Much of the expense of the removal to India was met by the kindness of other members of the family. Colonel Bingham, forgiving

past insults, paid the passage money – a considerable sum, for
the family must sail in the most expensive accommodation in
keeping with their exalted position. Aunt Maria sent £60 to be
used to provide wardrobes for India, and most of the new clothes
would be bought from fashionable modistes in London. Travelling
robes were needed however and orders were sent off to the Misses
Macalpine who were gratified to receive payment of their account
for Anne's meagre trousseau. They had been doubtful of seeing any
of it and now, with the money in their hands, hurriedly set about
supplying this new commission.

Busying herself here and there, Grizel had little time for sad reflections. She gave instructions to Mrs Grey, she packed and re-packed,
took notes of her mother's orders to be sent off to the pharmacist –
for Lady Macalpine was not going to India without a cure for every
disease that might attack her there!

All too soon, however, came the last day when she woke with the
summer sunshine gilding her cheek and knew she must spend some
time alone, filling her mind and soul with memories to sustain her
when she was far away from her beloved home.

When the gig bore her away from Glen Fada, she felt as if her heart
were being wrenched out of her chest. At the moment the house was
lost to view, Grizel made her secret vow.

I'll come back. I'll see this place again.

Chapter Eleven

THE FIRST STAGE of their journey was mercifully short, only the few familiar miles to Carn Dearg where they were greeted with affectionate embraces and fond kisses by the normally undemonstrative Agnes MacIvor. There were tears in her eyes as she cried out, 'Come in, come in, my dears. Dinner's waiting for you.'

Her husband extended an arm and escorted Jane Macalpine through the hall of the fine but parsimoniously shabby house which had been built by his father.

The banquet spread out for their reception touched the heart of each guest. Wine sparkled in the glasses, favourite dishes were passed around the table, and even the strained Grizel began to relax under the cajolery of Mrs MacIvor, stately in the silk gown and scarlet turban with dangling rajah-style chains which she wore only on special occasions.

No one mentioned Glen Fada, no one talked about the journey that lay ahead. It was the aim of their host and hostess to make the evening like so many happy occasions that the two families had shared in the past. Concern and sadness only touched the faces of their kind hosts when they thought themselves unobserved.

The childless MacIvors had always taken a deep interest in the young Macalpines but especially in John, and Grizel knew what pain it must be for them not to be able to take formal leave of him. She knew that John too would regret not being able to say farewell because he was closer to the couple at Carn Dearg than to his real parents.

After the meal was finished they played whist, Mr MacIvor's favourite game, but the strain of the day had been too much for the female visitors. Louisa slumped in her chair and Lady Macalpine could not restrain her yawns. Patrick leaned anxiously across to her and asked, 'Are you tired, Mother?'

Immediately Mrs MacIvor jumped to her feet, scattering her hand of cards on the floor. 'How thoughtless of us! Let me take you to your room, dear Jane. And you too, Louisa – there's a long journey in front of you all tomorrow.'

It was the first mention of what lay ahead and every face saddened at the thought. Patrick announced his intention of checking on the horses in the stables. As Mrs MacIvor escorted two of her female guests from the room, she put a restraining hand on Grizel's shoulder with the words, 'You stay a little longer, my dear. It's not yet ten o'clock.'

There was obviously something she wanted to say to Grizel alone. After Patrick and the ladies had left, the three of them sat staring into the embers of the fire. Mr MacIvor filled their glasses with velvet soft Madeira wine and his wife removed a large package from her bureau.

'We want you to have this, Grizel.' Inside was an elegant writing case covered with shagreen and with fittings of finely chased silver.

'It's to help you compose your stories, my dear, and to remind you to send letters home to us from India,' said Mr MacIvor for he was one of the few people who knew of her authorship of the stories in the *Inspector*. He had encouraged her from the beginning and used his Edinburgh connections to help her work gain a reading.

As she held their gift on her knees, tears prickled behind her eyelids but she blinked them back, remembering her mother's warning, 'A lady is always restrained.' So it was with a serene face but a sore heart that she thanked them for their gift.

'I've something else for you. I've already given one to Louisa,' said Mrs MacIvor, taking from her pocket a little golden locket with a glass-covered face. Inside was a tendril of dark hair, Agnes MacIvor's own, a remembrance of her love to be carried away with the Macalpine girls.

'It's lovely,' whispered Grizel, 'I'll wear it always to remind me of you.' The tears were very near now and Mrs MacIvor too was struggling against emotion as she took a long gold chain from her neck and threaded it through the locket before handing it to Grizel.

'Put it on now for luck,' she said, and the two women clasped hands, giving up the fight against tears that could not be denied.

Mr MacIvor, embarrassed by their emotion, cast his eyes down, coughed and said, 'I think I'll take a turn outside, my dear.'

Holding Grizel's hand in hers, Agnes nodded to her husband's disappearing back and said in a sad voice, 'He's as affected as I am. How we're going to miss you all! I know what a trial this is for you, my dear, but you must be brave. They depend on you so much. Going away is the best thing, I'm sure of it.'

Grizel wondered how she could ever have found the concerned face before her hard and unyielding. 'Sometimes I'm afraid that I can't keep up my courage,' she whispered. It was the first time she had openly voiced her fears.

Her hand was squeezed tightly in reassurance. 'You will, you will. You're the bravest girl I know. I felt for you when your attachment to Falconer was broken, and I can guess how you feel about leaving your home. You've always loved it – perhaps more than anyone else in your family. My heart's sore for you but I admire you for the way you're bearing up to it all. Your mother is depending on you and so is your father – they need your support.'

The young woman shrugged sadly. 'Do they? They don't seem to but I know I've to help them so I don't weep and cry. It's not seemly.'

That was Agnes MacIvor's style as well. She was a Spartan whose shield was her uncompromising religious belief.

'You must pray,' she said firmly. 'When we've had troubles, when my husband was nearly overwhelmed with the debts his father left, I prayed and God listened to me. Things came right in the end.' The handsome, strong face beneath the flamboyant turban gazed resolutely at the girl. Prayer and her belief in God were Agnes's comfort in all troubles but she forgot that Carn Dearg's problems were overcome by hard work and self-sacrifice as well.

The night was long and disturbed by sad dreams but eventually Grizel drifted off into a deep sleep only to be wakened, almost immediately it seemed, by her brother shaking her shoulder. In the dim light of early morning she sat up, confused.

'Wake up,' he whispered. 'I've harnessed the ponies. We must be off before the MacIvors waken. Mother can't bear to say farewell to them. It would be too painful.'

They slunk out into the grey dawn like thieves, carrying the parcels and presents the MacIvors had heaped on them. Patrick led the ponies over the grass to muffle the sound of their hooves on the gravel. It was a beautiful morning. The sun was rising in all its glory, wraiths of mist swirled up from the river bed and early morning birds were singing as he helped his mother and sisters into the gig.

Lady Macalpine sobbed pitifully into her handkerchief with Louisa's arm around her but Grizel sat half turned in her seat, watching the façade of Carn Dearg disappear behind them. No smoke rose from the chimneys, there was no movement around the door, but in the window of a first-floor bedroom she thought she spied a figure in a long white nightgown watching them drive away.

Every sight on the road to Perth brought back memories. When they stopped at the little inn at Inver, waiting to be ferried across the Tay, she remembered hearing Neil Gow play in the low beamed parlour of the inn.

'Do you remember him?' she asked her brother who nodded.

'A red-faced old man with lots of sons? Yes, I remember him, but most of all I remember the smell of peat reek that always filled this parlour. And it's still here,' he said, inhaling deeply on the threshold and giving the characteristic laughter that had been unheard during the past troubled days.

Later, as they crossed the high arched bridge over the Tay, Grizel saw her mother shrinking back in her seat, her face tense. From the blithe way Patrick handled the galloping ponies, it was obvious he had no inkling of the tragedy that had overtaken the family on a bridge – perhaps even that very one. Sympathetically, Grizel leaned across and tried to grasp her mother's hand but it was withdrawn sharply.

As the journey passed the distant imposing mountains dwindled into softly rounded hills. The road followed on the valley of the Tay which, though beautiful, was too douce for Grizel's savage taste. By the time they had covered forty miles and Perth was reached, everyone was in a state of exhaustion and depression.

They put up for the night at the Salutation Hotel. Next day Lady Macalpine, attended by Louisa, breakfasted in bed. Grizel and Patrick were taking their meal in the parlour when an ostler from the yard entered with a message. He bent over and whispered in Patrick's ear and Grizel saw her brother's face suffuse a deep shade of red. 'Who's taking it?' he asked.

'Men from Methven the feed merchant,' was the reply.

Patrick threw down his napkin and cursed. 'God dammit! Are they still here?'

'They're in the yard,' was the reply, and her brother ran out with the ostler while Grizel sat on, trying not to notice the interested

faces of the servants and other breakfasting travellers in the parlour. It was obvious that everyone except herself knew what this
latest mystery was about. When the tension became insupportable she rose and went out to the yard at the back of the hotel
where she found Patrick arguing with two rough-looking men. It
took only a few words before she knew what the argument was
about.

The men were obdurate. 'We're seizing your carriage 'til Mr
Methven's paid. There's a bill outstanding for hay and corn. He's
been waiting near two years for settlement.'

Patrick tried blustering. 'There must be some mistake. My father
merely overlooked it. Your master had better watch how he goes.
If he annoys us, he'll lose a lot of business.'

'He'll no' mind that loss,' said the older and more confident-
looking of the men. 'Business like yours isna' missed, Mr Macalpine.'

'How much is due?' Grizel asked her brother.

'Go away,' he snapped. 'This isn't any concern of yours.'

She ignored him and turned to the oldest man. 'How much is
due?' she asked, and he consulted a piece of paper in his hand. 'It's
for fifty pound. The master said to seize your carriage if there was
no money, and that's what we've done.'

'If you let them take the carriage we won't be able to travel any
further,' Grizel said, turning to her brother.

'I'm well aware of that,' he replied shortly.

She gave a hopeless sigh. It hurt her to do it but there was no
other way out. 'Wait here. I've forty pounds. If you'll settle for
that, I'll pay your bill.'

There was a flicker of assent in Methven's man's eyes. It was more
than he had expected to receive and he nodded grudgingly. She ran
indoors to take the precious *Inspector* money from her purse. When
she handed it over, she felt dangerously unprotected with the little
she had left but it was essential to keep the carriage. They still had
a long way to travel.

The journey to Edinburgh was silent and gloomy, each of them
sunk in their own bitter thoughts. Grizel was deeply worried about
how many more angry creditors would present themselves before
the journey's end and sorry also for the tradesmen who had been too
trusting in extending unlimited credit to her father.

The crossing of the River Forth at the Queen's Ferry by the
new steam boat service was rough and made them all nauseous,
so misery had them well in thrall by the time they eventually

reached the capital. It was nearly dusk when Grizel looked out at the familiar streets of the New Town. The city was as smart as ever, full of imposing new buildings, thriving and bustling, redolent of money and success. The crowds on the pavements were immaculately dressed and affluent-looking. Many of them were people she knew but, as the gig drove past, she shrank back in her seat, not wanting to be recognised.

The family were reduced to putting up at Douglas's Hotel in St Andrew's Square where regret for past glories made Mrs Macalpine retire to bed, weeping and complaining. Though the hotel was comfortable and the servants attentive, nothing could console Macalpine's wife for the loss of prestige.

The scene at the inn had been an eye-opener for Grizel. Unprotected by the security of money and respect, she felt as if she was stripped naked against a cold wind. Never before had she been so aware of the necessity of cash. In all her previous travels, the question of how to pay had never arisen. They had been the Macalpines of Glen Fada, a family with vast land holdings and a proud position in society. Their credit had always been good and the need for cash payment virtually unknown.

Looking back, Grizel acknowledged that they had all taken their supposed superiority for granted, as a kind of birthright. Not for them the anxieties of the poor. They worried about things like table manners, elegant conversation, fashionable clothes and who was well bred. Snobbery was so much part of their thinking that it was unconscious. A feeling of shame swept over her as she remembered those days. Now the blinkers had been rudely stripped from her eyes, the protecting wall around her was well and truly down, and she looked at a new world in which people disdained her, pointed fingers at the family because her father was a debtor. Money mattered more than good breeding when you had nothing in your purse.

'But it's so shaming! Why is it always me who has to speak to them?' Grizel twisted her hands together in anguish as she stared at her brother.

He put a reassuring hand on her arm and spoke soothingly. 'It has to be you. Louisa couldn't manage it, and we can't allow Mother to be worried.'

'But they want to speak to you or to Father, not to a woman. It's obvious that I can do nothing to help them.'

'That's why it has to be you. They mustn't see me. You don't want me to go back into the Calton, do you? Besides, even the roughest men will show more consideration towards a woman. They won't treat you as harshly as they'd treat me.'

Her stomach was churning as she walked slowly down to confront yet another gathering of angry tradesmen at the hotel door. Their faces were lifted towards her as she descended the stairs and for a moment she fought against the desire to turn on her heel and run away – run, run from all her troubles, run as far and as fast as she could. Her head swam but her upbringing sustained her and nothing of her agony of mind could be read in her face as she stepped up to them and listened politely to their pleas for payment.

'My bill has been waiting for three years!' said one man.

'That's nothing. Mine's been out for six! Macalpine promised payment in a six month and that's four years ago. . . .'

'I trusted him and this is what I receive in return!' shouted another who was less restrained in his fury.

Grizel wanted to put up her hands to halt the flow and tell them: 'I too trusted him. I've been disappointed as well!' but instead she nodded solemnly and promised to do what she could.

'My father's new position in India will enable him to make full payment to you all,' she said soothingly. 'If you will just be patient a little longer, I promise you'll be paid.'

Her ladylike demeanour and courtesy disarmed them and, like others before them, they drifted away, muttering among themselves. What else could they do? Grizel's legs were shaking when she turned to mount the stairs, trying not to notice the hard eyes of the hotel proprietor and his wife watching the ugly scene from their parlour. They had already seen a harness maker who was owed hundreds of pounds seize the pony carriage; they had listened while a creditor came to demand the ponies but crafty Patrick foiled that move by gifting them to Lady Guild at Riccarton. It was obvious that the hotel keeper was speculating on his own chances of being left with an unpaid bill.

Oh, if only the days would pass quickly, if only the money from London would arrive and make it possible to pay and be gone, Grizel thought.

'Well done,' said Patrick exultantly when she reached their sitting room on the first floor. 'You fobbed them off well.' He treated creditor-dodging like a game of skill in which points could be scored, and seemed to have little conception of the justice of the tradesmen's claims. As far as he was concerned, they were all importunate rogues.

'I only hope my promises will be honoured,' she said stonily, deeply resenting the position into which she was thrust.

Her brother hastened to reassure her. 'Of course, of course. I wouldn't have told you to promise payment otherwise, would I?'

The shame of being importuned for money, and the dread of meeting someone she knew on the street, confirmed Grizel's hatred of Edinburgh. It was difficult to remember that at one time she enjoyed every moment of her time there and looked forward to the excitements of each new day. In Douglas's Hotel she prayed for release from her torment. We must get away soon, we must, we must, – she told herself over and over again.

The strange tremblings that seized her legs, the odd way her heart would suddenly begin thumping for no reason, worried her but she hid her concern. Besides, there was no time to dwell on her own ailments because her mother had caught a cold and lay in bed, moaning and demanding medical attention.

'I'm too ill to travel,' she whispered when Patrick came rushing in to tell them that passages were secured on a ship sailing from Leith to London the following day. Her children looked at each other aghast for they all longed to escape from Edinburgh.

'You must go,' snapped Grizel, forgetting her usual politeness towards her mother. The least intimation of illness always made Lady Macalpine take to her bed, convinced that death was stalking her. As she lay wan-faced in the hotel bed, even Patrick's usual consideration for his mother wavered. She must not delay their flight from Edinburgh.

'You must get up, Mother. The passages are booked and paid for. If we don't take them up it could be weeks before other arrangements are made, and the sailing from Portsmouth is next month. Father is to join us there. . . .'

That decided the issue. The thought of London's bustle and, most of all, meeting with her husband, seemed to restore Lady Macalpine. In a faint, reproachful voice she agreed to be transported to the ship, at the same time warning of the heavy responsibility they would bear should her illness prove fatal. Grizel was unworried by the threats. She had heard them before. In a reassuring voice she told her mother that she had packed their old medicine chest from Glen Fada.

'But I've tried everything in it and nothing does me any good.'

'Then I will go out and buy you something that will,' said Grizel shortly, and throwing on her shawl she went to Butler's the chemist in Princes Street, where she found an assistant who listened sympathetically to her request for a nerve tonic for her mother.

'I've just the thing,' he said. 'Dr Fothergill's Tonic Female Pills. Excellent for headaches, loss of appetite, spasms, tremors, fainting fits and languid circulation.'

Grizel considered the list. Everything applied to her mother's case! 'I'll take a bottle, the largest one you have,' she said. It cost the immense price of eleven shillings. She bore it back to the hotel in the fervent hope that it would live up to its promises.

It was no sorrow to leave Edinburgh. On the last morning, the Guilds, attended by their grim-faced son James who had been so angry with Grizel at the quadrille exhibition, came with some other lawyer friends of the Macalpines to say their farewells. When he was on the verge of leaving, James Guild said to Grizel, 'You might be interested to know that I bought your father's library in the auction. Tell him I'll take good care of it.'

They left Scotland on a glorious late summer day with sunlight glittering on the city buildings and a heat haze swimming over the trees edging the south side of Princes Street.

Terrified in case they were waylaid by more creditors, Grizel kept repeating to herself, Hurry, hurry, hurry, as the wheels of the carriage lent to them by the Guilds rattled over the paving stones of Leith Walk heading for the docks. In a fever of impatience she watched the cargo and baggage being loaded. Her tension did not ease until the hawsers were cast off and their ship slid with the tide into the Firth of Forth.

The fates which had harried her so relentlessly now granted her a respite. Two days of peace and sunshine spent sailing on silken water with only the faintest motion to tell that they were at sea, restored her spirits. Like a bare fist boxer resting between rounds, she knew she must concentrate on growing strong again to build up her defences for what lay ahead. There were further obstacles to be surmounted before the family's escape was assured.

Part of her cure came from meeting new people. She realised that, in spite of the long months of isolation with no society except that of her mother and sister, she could still flourish in the company of strangers. Fellow passengers were friendly towards her and Louisa, especially a genial American author who seemed very smitten with the youngest Miss Macalpine and pressed copies of his books into her hands. Grizel's particular friend was a delicate-looking, lame woman who seemed very shy and always appeared on deck wearing a deep straw bonnet with a thick green veil hiding her face. They took a liking to each other and lingered in the sunshine, talking companionably.

On the last day of the trip, the stranger came to stand beside Grizel on deck. Her soft-voiced greeting was drowned out by the sound of the anchor being let down into the rippling river. They had to wait in mid-stream till the tide turned. The two women leaned on the ship's rail staring up the estuary of the Thames towards their landing point at Blackwall. Into view came two tall and magnificent full-sailed ships, serenely breasting the tide. They watched in admiration as the vessels bore down stream together, stately as swans, silent as ghosts. They looked deserted, with no one on deck. For a moment Grizel wondered if she had dreamt them.

'Aren't they beautiful? They're the kings of the sea. They're East Indiamen, my dear,' said the woman at her side.

'I'll soon be on one of them. We're going to Bombay next month,' Grizel said in a rush of confidence.

The other woman said nothing for a moment but reached into her reticule and took out a little pocket book. When she spoke, her voice was urgent.

'My husband's in Bombay. He's called Dr Forbes. It would be a great kindness to me if you give him this to let him know where and when you met me.'

As she spoke, she scrawled her name, 'Mary Forbes', and the date, on a page which she roughly tore out and handed to Grizel.

'I'll give it to your husband with pleasure if I meet him. Is there any other message?' she asked in surprise, wondering why the couple could not communicate more directly.

Mrs Forbes shook her head. 'No message, my dear. Just give him the paper. And I'm sure you'll meet him. Bombay society is small and everyone knows my husband. He's doctor to all the people of quality.'

'In that case, I'm certain to meet him,' said Grizel thinking of her mother who was at that moment lying complaining in her cabin. She longed to question the doctor's wife about her circumstances, ask why she could not write to her husband herself. What kept them apart? But it was obvious that her questions would not be welcomed when Mrs Forbes deliberately changed the subject, gazing after the disappearing East Indiamen with shining eyes.

'They're lovely ships going to a strange and mysterious place, but it's cruel, very cruel. I hope God is good to you there, Miss Macalpine, and keeps you in His care.' As she spoke, she raised her veil a little and leaned forward to give Grizel a kiss. When they brushed cheeks, the girl saw that the stranger's face was deeply scarred with the disfiguring marks of smallpox.

Setting foot on land was to return to harsh reality. Two hackney carriages were engaged at the wharf, one for Grizel, Louisa and their mother; the second for Patrick and the baggage. Lady Macalpine's tight-lipped face told only too clearly how lowered she felt at having to travel in a hired carriage for she had never ridden in one before, but her spirits rose when eventually they clattered into Dover Street, Piccadilly, where a comfortable set of rooms had been reserved for them by the Arkwrights who waited to receive them.

'Annie, dear Annie,' Grizel whispered, embracing her. The tears on her cheeks were seen, sympathised with, and gently wiped away.

'We're here to help,' she said softly, and all Grizel could do was hold her friend's hand and gulp back her sobs, afraid that the pent up emotion of the past weeks and months would shatter her thinly maintained reserve.

Annie understood. 'Things will be better soon. They don't stay bad for ever.'

Her husband, as kind as she was herself, immediately reassured the newcomers: 'Good news! Macalpine's in London and will be with you tonight – but he can't come 'til after dark. If the debt collectors catch him, he'll be in prison and not on his way to India.'

The news sent Lady Macalpine into a transport of fainting and Mrs Arkwright had to bring out the smelling salts before she was restored to consciousness. Then she lay on the sofa, saying, 'Oh, Annie, little did I guess when I first saw you herding cows that you would turn out to be my saviour!'

Good-natured Annie only laughed and replied, 'I didn't guess it either.'

After Lady Macalpine was settled, Annie looked with concern at her friend. 'You're very pale and far too thin. This must have been a great strain for you.'

'Yes, it's been hard, but now at least Father's back to take over our affairs. Patrick isn't able to manage things very well.'

Annie had no delusions about the capacities of either of these Macalpine men. 'Your father's impulsive. You'll have to make sure he doesn't show himself out of doors. My husband is worried that the laird's being followed for he owes a great deal of money to some very influential people.'

'How could this have happened?' Grizel burst out in despair. 'I never remember a day when money mattered a fig to Father. There always seemed to be plenty available.'

Annie had an old head on her shoulders. 'He was spoiled from the day he was born. He'd only to express a wish and it was granted. Your mother hasn't helped either. She's never restrained him. They're like children, in a way. Ruin came on them like a stone down a mountain side. The farther it fell, the more trouble it brought with it. It's up to you to help them all you can, my dear.'

'Oh, I will, of course. But I do worry about the future,' said Grizel with anguish in her voice.

Annie took her hand. 'This Indian appointment will make all right again, and in Bombay you'll meet a good man to marry. I found my General in India and the day I married him was the best day of my life. Believe me, things work out. I know it.'

The firm voice had never lost its Highland lilt and Annie's 'I know it!' was to ring in Grizel's ears for a long time.

When the chimes of midnight were ringing over Piccadilly, Sir Peter John Macalpine arrived, a sombre-looking John in tow. The rest of the family greeted them enthusiastically and Macalpine embraced his wife, hugged his children, beamed and smiled like a victor returning from battle. Excitement was still running high next morning and it was all any of them could do to keep him indoors. When he decided he must go abroad, they made him muffle up in drab clothes, told him to stick to back streets and dark alleys and not seek out his friends at the popular meeting places of the capital. Even with their warnings, however, he grew careless and was soon spotted.

Late that night Grizel was wakened by the sound of knocking at the street door. She hung over the banisters to listen as the landlady enquired who was without. 'We've come for Macalpine. We know he's here. Send him down at once,' cried a gruff voice.

Grizel's heart was beating in her throat as she waited to hear the landlady's response. Would she give them away? There was a pause and the woman said in a surprised voice, 'What Macalpine? There's no one of that name here.'

'You're lying, woman. He was followed here,' cried another man's voice.

The landlady drew herself up, all outraged dignity. 'Don't you call me a liar. I've only a General and Mrs Arkwright here. Their trunks are in the hall. You can see the labels for yourself.'

She drew back the bolts and a gleam of light shone out as a brand was held over the trunks which were indeed marked with the Arkwrights' names for there had not yet been time to re-label them. The bailiff's men were confused and started muttering among themselves. Eventually they withdrew. The frightened family huddling upstairs almost gave a cheer as the sound of their footsteps died away.

The visit alerted them to the danger of capture, however, and it was decided to split the family up. Louisa and their mother were whisked away to stay with Anne and Colonel Bingham at their new home in Hampshire while Macalpine, his sons and Grizel stayed in London to complete the arrangements for equipping the family for Bombay.

This situation lasted less than three days for once again Macalpine sallied forth, once again he was followed, and this time chased through the streets. Thoroughly shaken, he agreed to leave England and Patrick smuggled him out to Wapping Steps where he boarded a ship for Boulogne early on a Sunday morning before the town was awake. Young John was sent along as a sort of nursemaid to watch his father and restrain him from doing anything foolish. It was a heavy task for a boy not yet twenty years old but he was equal to it.

Before he left, Macalpine gave his daughter a long list of instructions. She was to re-equip the medical chest with cures and potions suitable for an eastern climate, and she was to consult a doctor herself because he was worried about her state of health. She was to collect his judge's wig from Ede and Ravenscroft in Chancery Lane; view, arrange and fit out in high style their cabins in the ship; find a lady's maid for her mother because the task of attending her was too onerous for Louisa; order their linen from a special outfitter in the Strand; order wine and dry stores from another supplier in Piccadilly; and arrange for the trans-shipment of items sent down from Glen Fada, among them the last of the old Glenlivet whisky.

'That'll be a fine solace in the East,' her father said.

Special silk stockings for Sir Peter John were to be bought from Clarke's; special pomade, gloves, shoes, and stationery were required as well. A canteen of fine silver, a crate of best china and

a travelling library were all to be bought. The list seemed endless
for they were travelling to India in the grand style, as lordly as in
the past.

'Don't worry about the expense,' said her father dismissively.
'The bills will be met from the Government's fitting out grant.'
All appointees to high positions in the East India Company service
were given £2,000 with which to equip themselves. Using it, the
Macalpines were able to forget for a little while that they were
penniless bankrupts but as she contemplated her father's list, Grizel
knew that even the princely grant would not satisfy his extravagant
tastes.

'How am I to do all this without money?' Grizel asked her brother.
Though only a few days had passed since the short respite of the
voyage from Leith her face had resumed its drawn and anxious
look.

Patrick reluctantly reached into his pocket and withdrew a thin
sheaf of bank notes. 'Here's another hundred. That'll be five hundred you've spent. I've still to pay the balance of the passage monies,
you know.'

'But Father gave you £2,000 and Colonel Bingham's paid the
passages. What have you done with the rest?'

His face was sullen as he turned on her. 'Go and do what
you've been told! Ask for credit where you can. The money's my
business.'

'Ask for credit!' Her face was angry too now and she was shaking.
'You have no right to send me out to ask for credit when this whole
family is hiding from people who are owed money already! Have
you any idea what I endure going into shops where bills are due?
Have you any idea what it means to be refused and insulted by
shop keepers? You send me, your sister, out to do these odious
tasks because you haven't the stomach for them yourself. I'll not
ask for credit. That's what brought us to this pass. That's why we're
going to India instead of staying at home on our own lands.'

He turned away and she could see that he had closed his ears to
her. There was nothing to do but take the notes and set off on her
final commissions.

Generally a little money carefully expended as part payment of
bills eased hostility in establishments where the Macalpines were
old customers. Grizel fobbed off her mother's supplier of artificial
flowers with ten pounds; the miniature painter was pleased with

thirty; the watchmaker with ten; the parasol shop with fifteen; the ribbon weaver with five. The New Bond Street chemist required the remainder of her hundred before he would make up the latest order – tooth powder, lavender water, Ching's Patent Worm Lozenges and Perry's Essence which was a wonderful specific for treating toothache to which Louisa was a martyr.

The last call was at her father's hosier, Mr Clarke, who had supplied them all with stockings of silk and cotton for as long as Grizel could remember. Although she had no cash left, in her reticule she carried a ready money order for most of her father's debt to Clarke because he wanted a dozen pairs of silk stockings with clocks on them. They had to be the hosier's best; nothing else would do. She was smiling with no anticipation of trouble when she saw the pleasant-faced old man standing behind his high wooden counter.

Grizel walked up to him, holding out the money order along with the note of her father's new requirements, but he stared blankly at the papers in her hand, his expression changing from benevolence to hostility.

'What's this?' he asked rudely, as if talking to an urchin off the street.

'It's a ready money order from my father,' she stammered.

'I don't want his pieces of paper. All I want from him is cash – real money. I've had enough of his paper promises to last me a lifetime.'

Acutely conscious of the young male assistant looking on, Grizel fought to conceal the tears that filled her eyes. To be treated in such a way by kind Mr Clarke whom she had always liked, was agonising.

'But my father wants to order a dozen pairs of stockings,' she said in a voice that quavered in spite of her resolution to remain calm.

Clarke rested both hands on the counter top and leaned towards her. 'Your father is a rogue. Your father is little better than a common thief. If he was a poor man without friends, your father would have been in prison long ago. You can tell him from me that I don't want his business. He'll never put another pair of my stockings on his legs even if he pays every farthing he owes me – and that's a big sum.'

'But this is sure money. And my father will be well able to save enough money to pay you in full for we're going to India to repair our fortunes,' she whispered.

The hosier shook his head. 'Huh! It'll take a lifetime before your father's fortunes are repaired. I won't live to see it and I don't want his orders. I don't want fine speeches either, so save your breath, Miss Macalpine. Promises are worth nothing and I'm not the only shop keeper in London who knows it.'

To his horror, as soon as he had delivered this speech, the girl seemed to crumple like a paper doll. Her head drooped, her knees bent and she collapsed on to his shop floor in a pathetic heap, one arm outflung with the rejected piece of paper still grasped in the gloved hand. With a gasp of consternation, for he was a kind man at heart, Mr Clarke rushed round the counter and bent over her, telling the shop assistant to run into the back shop and fetch his sister. He was filled with remorse for having vented his anger against an innocent young woman.

'Poor girl, it isn't her fault,' he told his sister when she came rushing in, 'I didn't mean to make her faint. It was her father's effrontery in sending her that angered me.'

Miss Clarke knelt and gently raised the girl's head on to her knee. 'Oh, there's not a drop of colour in her face,' she said sorrowfully, patting the cold hands.

Grizel opened her eyes, stared around for a little while before realising where she was. Then, with a superhuman effort, she gathered her dignity. She tottered to her feet, brushed her skirt with trembling hands and refused the glass of wine which Clarke brought from his back shop. With a stately air she walked out of the shop like a princess, leaving the hosier and his sister staring after her with shame and regret plain on both their faces.

That was the last straw for Grizel, however, and back in Dover Street she collapsed again so badly that a doctor had to be called. He looked at her gravely and diagnosed exhaustion and mental turmoil. 'It's essential for this young lady to rest and not to be worried,' he told Patrick who was sufficiently concerned to rule that his sister should be spared any more traipsing around London and must be sent off to spend the last few days before sailing with Anne and the Colonel. Aunt Lizzie offered to leave her family and accompany the invalid.

Peace, stillness and tranquillity after turmoil. . .the quiet atmosphere of Anne's pretty house calmed and restored Grizel. The best surprise on reaching Gideon Park was to find Lister, the faithful Glen Fada butler, and Beatie the maid installed in Anne's service. She had sent for them after her family left the Highlands, for when it was in her power to help their old servants she always set about doing so without fuss or self-advertisement. Now she occupied herself with looking after her sister, continually plumping up the cushions at her back as she sat in a cane chair on the terrace overlooking the flower-filled garden.

Grizel was beguiled by the scent of the climbing roses that clambered up the walls of the house and felt the tension of the past weeks flowing away. She was almost asleep in the sunshine one morning when she heard her sister's familiar footsteps. Then Anne was bending over her, the golden curls brushing her face and the soft voice coaxing her.

'Come out with me in my phaeton. I'll drive you round and let you see our countryside. It's very pretty.'

It was as if time had been turned back when Grizel sat at Anne's side in the high phaeton seat, watching her deft hands on the reins. But it was not a fat old Highland pony that she was driving this time. Between the shafts of the smart little carriage was a sleek-coated chestnut mare with flaring red nostrils and shiny flashing hooves.

It was not necessary to ask if Anne was happy. Contentment glowed from her. Her skin gleamed, her eyes flashed blue and laughter continually curved her mouth. Her dress was as untidy as ever but everything she wore was costly-looking.

She saw Grizel's eyes on her and smiled as she said, 'Yes, it's turned out well. I knew you were worried. I worried myself a little, but my husband's a good man. You can see that for yourself. Look how kind and considerate he is towards our mother although she was so bitter against him.'

Colonel Bingham's care of his fractious mother-in-law was so exemplary that she had completely changed her attitude towards him, speaking now as if it was she who promoted the marriage.

'I'm happy for you,' said Grizel truthfully. Nothing could be better for her sister than this peaceful rural life in a pretty house with a spreading park, a stable full of horses and servants in plenty to attend to her comfort. The only disappointment – though it did not appear to concern Anne – was the absence of babies. The Binghams' children were the foals which their brood mares produced every year.

'I admire you so much,' Grizel said. 'I wish I could be like you, but I'm not so brave. Too indecisive.'

'Nonsense! You feel much more than I do. Leaving Glen Fada must have broken your heart. I know how much you love it. I hope you'll find a husband who'll look after you, my dear, in the way you deserve. I'm sure you will in India.'

The latest addition to the East Indiaman fleet in 1827 was the *Mountstuart Elphinstone*, named in honour of the Governor of Bombay who retired that same year. It lay at anchor in Portsmouth Bay, paint pristine, decks scrubbed white as snow, its three tall masts shrouded with looped sails. Smaller ships clustered around it like an admiring throng of courtiers.

It was a glorious evening towards the end of September when Grizel stood at the window of their inn on Portsmouth harbour front, watching the activity on the decks of the magnificent vessel which would be her home for nearly six months. Now that the final leave taking was near, an unexpected excitement filled her. The pain of departure from Glen Fada was deep inside her now and she comforted herself with the hope that one day she would see her beloved home again. Soon they would sail away from present trouble and amazing sights and experiences lay ahead. The sight of the proud ship put courage into her.

Her mother, however, was pale and fractious, regretting now the step that would take her away from all those she held dear. There could be no eager anticipation of adventure in her heart while no news had yet been received of the whereabouts of her husband and youngest son. She did not know if they were safe; if they had successfully evaded the debt collectors who sought them on their way to France. She had no certainty that she would ever see either of them again.

With her family, she watched a neat pinnace scud over the water and head for the dock wall. It was to carry them to the sailing ship. The time had come for them to embark.

'I don't think we should go. We've heard nothing from Macalpine. What if we sail off to India without him?' Lady Macalpine fretted.

Colonel Bingham, who was standing behind the party in the window, came forward to reassure her. 'I'm sure all will be well, madam. Calm yourself.'

Patrick looked despairing. His duty was to put his mother and sisters on board and nothing must prevent the completion of his task. 'I'm sure he's not taken or some message would have come for us. You must go aboard, Mother. Father told me that you must sail. The bailiffs' men are out there, watching for him. One of them stopped me on the quay and asked where he was. They wouldn't bother if they'd already caught him, would they?'

From the window Grizel could see a trio of rough-looking men with the distinctive silver arrows of debtor catchers on their collars. They were staring up at the inn windows. All day they had haunted the dockside, intercepting every vessel that came from France in case their quarry was aboard.

A sudden rush of emotion almost choked her as she turned to her sister Anne and clasped her tight. They clung to each other, shoulders shaking, and neither of them could speak except to sob, 'Goodbye, goodbye. . . .' For the last time, she was clutched to the breasts of dear Annie and Aunt Lizzie. She was casting off her moorings as surely as the ship in which she was soon to sail.

One by one members of the family hurried away, wiping their eyes as they went. Lady Macalpine had asked them not to stay till the end. 'I don't want to look back and see you all standing on land. Please go before we do. Please go,' she pleaded.

Colonel Bingham led his weeping young wife away with an expression of deep concern on his face and Grizel felt a rush of gratitude towards him for everything he had done. She resolved not to burden him with any further outgoings so took from her purse a fold of banknotes which Aunt Maria had given her earlier that day. She passed these to Patrick with the whispered injunction that he was to settle the inn-keeper's bill and not allow Anne's husband to pay that as well.

He nodded and pocketed her money quickly. 'Make sure you pay the bill before the Colonel does,' Grizel repeated. He looked haughtily back at her, as if insulted that she should doubt him. 'Of course I'll pay it. I'll go and do it now,' he said.

Outside the door, however, he heard Colonel Bingham settling with the inn-keeper and slipped the folded notes back into his pocket.

Aunt Maria stayed till last. There had always been a strong bond between her and Jane, her youngest sister. They looked very alike, each tall and slim with thickly curling dark hair, flashing eyes and aquiline noses. Lady Macalpine would be rudderless in Bombay without her sister for even when they were apart, letters between Oxford and Glen Fada were exchanged every week. But India was a six months' journey away for passengers and post alike. Now they clung together weeping like bereaved children until Patrick, fearing that his mother would collapse, pulled at his aunt's arm and beseeched her to leave.

Maria's last words were to Grizel. 'Take care of your mother. Look after her, my dear child, and take care of Louisa too. She's much more grown up now, all this has changed her, but she'll still need help.'

Grizel's old reservations about her aunt were swept away in a rush of affection. Aunt Maria had her faults but she loved them in her way and her kindness and generosity in their time of trouble had been unstinting.

The noise on board was tremendous: clanking, bumping, creaking, shouting. Lady Macalpine was installed in the best cabin in the poop deck and her daughters had the one adjacent. They were to be attended on the voyage by two half-caste girls, engaged in London, who would work their passages home. All the furniture and the pianoforte which they had ordered was in place, and their boxes full of purchases from London suppliers neatly stacked. Normally the prospect of so many new and pretty things to examine would have entranced the girls but now they looked at them with indifference for under their feet they felt the creaking timbers of the ship as it swung round into the wind.

Finally, after Willie Crawford, Peter John's faithful clerk, had taken leave of them, they stood undecided in the middle of the swaying cabin floor.

'It's moving. We can't be leaving yet. Where's Macalpine?' cried his anguished wife.

'Do you want to go on deck, Mother?' Grizel enquired, but her mother shook her head.

'No. Go up and ask Patrick what's afoot. They can't sail yet.'

On deck they were casting off. Seamen were running here and there hauling on ropes and rattling chains. The other passengers were lining the decks, waving handkerchiefs towards people on the shore, weeping as they left their families behind. Patrick was standing slightly apart and Grizel rushed up to him, gasping, 'If we're sailing, surely it's time for you to go ashore, and Father's not here yet.'

'I'm to go out with you a little way and come back in the pilot boat,' he told her. The departure was obviously no surprise to him.

'But what about Father and John?'

'They're coming. Go and calm Mother. Put her to bed. Nothing will happen for a few hours yet. . . . Go away, Grizel. Don't make such a fuss.'

They were all abed in the softly rocking cabins but not asleep when there was another outbreak of shouting on deck. The darkness was total but Grizel groped about till she found a candle and a flint. Lighting the taper and drawing on a wrapper, she went to the cabin door to see what was going on.

By the light of the deck lamps she could discern a group of sailors gathered on the port side, hauling up the chair that was used for the embarkation of passengers while the ship was at sea. She ran to the rail and looked over. Against the darkness of the water winked the lights of a small boat. She could just discern outlines of men's figures moving about on its deck.

The swinging chair creaked slowly up the precipitous side of the ship. When it swung over the deck, it hovered for a few moments like a landing bird before being dropped with a thump. A man stepped out of it and almost immediately it was winched away again. The new arrival turned and walked towards the poop deck.

Grizel stared at him, rubbing her eyes with her hands. It couldn't be, but it was! Her father – tired and dishevelled but triumphant – had escaped his pursuers. He was safe!

Without speaking he walked up to her, put an arm around her and together they went to the door of his wife's cabin which he entered alone, leaving Grizel on deck. The chair was being raised again. This time the new arrival was John. Grizel looked lovingly at his thin, boyish figure and ran to him, arms outstretched.

'Oh, Johnny, I'm so glad you're safe. We're all together now.'

The little packet boat from Jersey that had brought Macalpine and his son aboard was to take Patrick away however. For their last few minutes, Grizel stood with her two brothers, clinging to their arms.

John, as usual, was calm but Patrick could not bear the parting. His voice thick with tears he said, 'I've got to go. There's not much time. Kiss Louisa for me.'

He ran into his mother's cabin where she broke away from her husband and held him to her, sobbing heart-breakingly over him. When he emerged, he could only hold out a hand in a last farewell to Grizel and John and, without speaking, run from them, his face ghastly in the flickering lamplight.

They stood by as he was lowered down in the chair. They watched leaning on the rail, until the little boat carrying him away was only a dark smudge on the surface of the moonlit sea.

Chapter Twelve

~⌒~

FOR A WOMAN who went into fits of hysterics if a carriage horse so much as stumbled, Lady Macalpine adjusted to the sea voyage with remarkable equanimity. Mercifully, it did not seem to occur to her that all there was between her feet and the bottomless ocean were a few planks of wood, and her peace of mind was helped by the remarkable calmness of the waters through which they sailed. They were blessed by the weather for every morning they were greeted by pale blue skies, aquamarine seas, piles of soft clouds on the horizon and, dotted here and there upon the shining ocean, other full-sailed ships India-bound like the *Mountstuart Elphinstone*.

Captain Hardwicke, the proud owner of the ship, kept a neat craft and his crew busied themselves throughout the day at their appointed tasks: holy stoning the deck, shining up the brass, preparing the meals which the passengers broached with appetites sharpened by sea air and walks round and round the deck, the only exercise they would be able to take for months.

Captain Hardwicke had been recommended to the Macalpine family as a reliable ship's master. Recommendations were necessary before booking a passage for the long voyage because some Indiamen captains were arrant rogues who charged high fares and provided poor and inadequate food. Travellers poured out tales of how, during the last weeks of their voyages, they were reduced to living on hard biscuits because the captain had economised on stores. Others were evil-tempered brutes who vented their spleen on crew and passengers alike as soon as they were on the high seas but Hardwicke, a mild-spoken and religious man, ruled his ship with a firm but reasonable hand. To John's approval, he read religious

services on deck every day and a blessing was always bestowed on
the ship in which they were sailing – a ritual which did much to calm
nervous temperaments like Lady Macalpine's.

Grizel, Louisa and John delighted in the life of a ship at sea. They
liked the different sounds that changed according to the time of day,
ranging from the cracking made when the direction of the sails was
changed to catch the most favourable wind to the lowing, baa-ing
and clucking of livestock quartered between decks, to be slaughtered
and eaten during the voyage. Some passengers complained about
the farmyard noises but the Macalpines enjoyed them because they
evoked memories of Glen Fada.

Grizel's endeavours in London had furnished their cabins with
sofa beds, dressing and washing tables, writing desks, a pianoforte,
comfortable chairs, soft rugs on the floors, pictures on the walls and
trunks full of their most prized possessions. Lady Macalpine's maid
Fatima, who had undertaken the voyage several times before, knew
how to organise things to make life as pleasant as possible. In the
hottest weather, the Venetian blinds were lowered at just the right
time over the large open window at the end of the cabin so that it
was possible to sleep in comfort, soothed by the sweep of a large
fan gently wafted by the maid servant.

'Mother's going to enjoy India. She's taking to the life of luxury,
that's plain to see,' remarked John one day. He and his sisters were
standing at the prow of the ship watching the spray break high on its
proud figurehead carved in the likeness of a bare-breasted mermaid.
The girls agreed with him. Their mother's contentment meant they
were free to wander the decks and make the acquaintanceship of
other passengers without having constantly to dance attendance on
her.

There were twenty-eight passengers on board, most of them
young men on their way to posts in the East India Company's
Bombay Presidency. Two pretty girls were a great lure for these
fellows who were only too aware of how starved of female company
they would be during the years that lay ahead. If they could catch a
wife at the last minute, they would be greatly in luck. The Macalpine
girls were courted assiduously by a succession of swains and though
Grizel took the flirting as a pleasant game, Louisa regarded the attentions much more seriously. She had never had a suitor before.

As Grizel watched her sister parading the deck with a trio of
gallants, she reflected on the improvement in her. She was still slim
from their last months at Glen Fada and by now looked extremely

pretty with her fair skin glowing from the sea air and flaxen curls tumbling round her cheeks. All the Macalpine girls had lovely hair but hers was the palest and most abundant.

'Isn't Louisa flourishing?' Grizel asked John one evening when their sister had distinguished herself by her spirited performance during an impromptu dancing party on deck.

He nodded. 'She's grown up at last. She'll never be a prodigy of intelligence but she can hold her own in conversation now. She's escaped from Mother's influence, thank goodness, and she's stretching her wings.'

'But she never wanted to get away before,' protested Grizel.

'She never had the chance,' said John. 'She's been kept at home like a toy dog. She's not an idiot, but because she's slower than the rest of us she was made to feel like one. No wonder she took solace in food! Now that she's happy she's stopped eating like a ploughman, haven't you noticed?'

The feeling of being happy was slowly returning to Grizel as well, and she tried to seize and hold it like someone catching a colourful butterfly in her hands. As each day passed she could feel her strength returning, filling her like a warm current.

On the day they sailed past the Island of Teneriffe, she stood on deck and watched the sun shining on the upper slopes of its snowcapped peak, tinting the summit the most luxuriant colours. Joy filled her. She wanted to dance and fling her arms in the air, rejoicing that Annie had been right. Life was not finished. There were wonderful things to look forward to after all.

Her smiling face and lightness of heart endeared her to the others on board and she quickly became a favourite with passengers and crew alike. One of her most fervent admirers was the chief mate, Black Sam, a rough-spoken man whose every utterance was accompanied by the oath, 'Damn my eyes.' When he spoke to Grizel, however, he tried to censor his conversation and bit back the words as they came, half uttered, from his mouth. Black Sam could always be found lingering on the poop deck when Grizel sat in the shade, practising on her guitar or singing, while Louisa played the piano in the cabin.

One of the other women passengers had brought a harp on board and they were able to form a small orchestra with Grizel on the guitar, John on the violin, Louisa on the piano and the harpist plucking away at her strings. The music of this ensemble wiled away many long, hot nights as they headed for the Tropics.

Fears of boredom during so long a voyage proved to be un-
founded. There were two small children on board and Grizel organised a school for them because she had always enjoyed teaching. In
the evenings there were card games, and one after the other, the
passengers threw supper parties. Lady Macalpine's were reckoned
to be the best of all. There were plenty of books to read for the Captain possessed a good library and the passengers exchanged books
among themselves; there were charts to keep as they traced their
progress down into the Southern seas; and every Saturday night
the Captain gave a supper party which was followed by a concert
in which both passengers and crew members took part. The sailors
danced with riotous energy or threw themselves about the deck in
athletic exercises. A solemn-looking civilian called Mr Grainger,
returning to his post in Bombay, sang ballads of unrequited love,
and Louisa and Grizel gave duets.

'Sing *Cuchulain* for me, my dear,' Peter John Macalpine begged
his eldest daughter one night as they sat in the warm moonlight.
Grizel was reluctant because she knew the music would fill her
with memories of the Highlands, but her father pressed her, 'till
she yielded. When the last notes of her song rang out the audience
sat silent for a moment and then began clapping delightedly. Black
Sam was so moved by the haunting music that he was seen to wipe a
surreptitious tear from his eye, and Grizel's father and mother wept
unashamedly at the emotions aroused by the familiar Gaelic song.

Arrival fever gripped both passengers and crew of the *Mountstuart
Elphinstone* twenty-four hours before they were due to make landfall
at Bombay. After the three-week voyage up the coast of Malabar
from Ceylon, everyone crowded on deck to enjoy the spectacle as
the stately ship swung like a dancer between little islands covered
all over with tangled trees. Passengers ran from side to side,
exclaiming and pointing out sights. 'Look, there are monkeys!'
cried the lady with the harp as they sailed close to one wooded
island. Mr Grainger, the ballad singer, made a face. 'You'll see
plenty of those devils soon enough. The place is full of them.'

Bombay was a large island ringed with hundreds of smaller ones
and set in an azure sea. Far away in the distance could be seen the
mainland of India with a range of purple mountains rearing towards
the cloudless sky. Grizel's first impression of the city itself was of
a church steeple rising high above a cluster of houses whose red
clay roofs seemed to burn like fire in the sun. Everywhere there

were trees, some with wide-spreading branches and others tall and plume-like. It was so brilliantly sunny and warm that it was difficult to appreciate the month was February. At home in Scotland the first snowdrops would be pushing their green tips through the frozen ground.

Grizel's eyes were wide with delight and surprise. Everything she saw intrigued her; it was all so totally strange and unexpected. Nothing had prepared her for the brilliance of the sun striking flashes like bolts of lightning off the surface of the water; for the close packed trees that covered the islands like giant moss; for the blackened little fishing boats with one large slanting white sail and huge eyes painted on their prows. They clustered round the *Mountstuart Elphinstone* in an eager escort as it made its way into the channel leading to Bombay harbour.

As they neared land, Grizel saw her sister Louisa and Mr Grainger standing close together in the bow of the ship. They looked easy with each other and Grizel knew there was something more than friendship between them, just as she had been the first to discern the stirrings of romance in Aunt Lizzie.

They sailed into the spreading bay very slowly, tacking gently in the breeze, and the crowd of attendant boats at their sides grew larger. Men in loincloths stood up in hollow-looking hulls, shouting through cupped hands at the people on board, offering their services as servants or porters. Soon they were close enough to see a long stone-built jetty sticking out into the water. At the far end stretched a line of buildings above a stout sea wall. The façades of the buildings were broken by arches and thick pillars like the buildings in Ancient Rome and the walls were painted a gleaming white that almost hurt the eyes. Everywhere there were crowds of people – jostling on the roadway, standing staring out to sea, waving their hands and watching the ship's safe haven.

When the family finally stepped ashore, heat reflected off the roadway and the building fronts hit them like slaps on the face. The breezes in which they had luxuriated out at sea had not prepared them for the ferocity of an Indian afternoon. Wiping the sweat from his face, Sir Peter John tried to pick out someone who would be able to help him. The *Mountstuart Elphinstone* had made good time and arrived several days in advance of schedule. Though he knew that his brother-in-law Edmund Godwin was awaiting their arrival, he might not be expecting the family so soon. At Macalpine's side stood his wife, staring around her in growing confusion. All at once she gripped his arm and said, 'Look at all those men. They seem to be coming towards us.'

He followed the direction of her gaze and saw a line of approaching natives in white and scarlet livery. They advanced, bowing, with their hands folded in front of their chests in attitudes of obeisance.

'They are coming for us. Who are they?' Jane asked in some alarm but before he could answer, the leader of the party made a deep bow and announced in broken but understandable English that he had been sent to receive them by his most respected master Godwin Sahib. From his high peaked turban, he pulled out a letter which he handed to Macalpine.

'It's from Edmund,' he exclaimed, passing the note over to his wife who read it with delight. The brother she had last seen fifteen years ago had sent a princely retinue of servants to escort the new arrivals to his house and a fleet of carriages were waiting to convey them there.

There was so much to see, so much to absorb, that Grizel was surfeited with the strangeness of it all. They were carried along a succession of broad tree-lined throughfares in which groups of ragged natives stood chattering or clustered before open stalls displaying brilliantly coloured fruit or flowers.

There were plenty of elegant carriages like their own plying to and fro filled with smartly dressed white people, and every now and again they passed groups of four running men carrying what looked like a large box supported on long poles over their shoulders. Through the box's open sides could be seen men or women reclining on a thin mattress with their heads propped up on their hands. The boxes were palankeens, a favourite form of transport in Bombay.

The sun was going down by the time their carriages started to climb the long winding hill that snaked upward from a horseshoe-shaped sandy beach about three miles from the harbour. Set back from the roadway were large houses with latticed shades over the windows and white-clad servants flitting about on the verandahs. Everywhere there were trees and flowering shrubs, springing up from the earth in glorious abundance, but the smells of the streets were often pungent and unpleasant.

At the top of the hill, Grizel gazed out from her seat in the open carriage and saw the lights of the vast city twinkling all the way down the hillside and in a long line along the horseshoe-shaped bay. They were now following a narrow road that twisted and turned beneath the dangling tendrils hanging from thick-trunked trees. Soon they were in a garden and she caught a whiff of the exotic flowers that lined the drive. Their heady perfume was so strong that it made her feel intoxicated.

The carriages turned a bend and they found themselves on a large circle of beaten earth in front of an imposing house. A flight of stairs led up to a wide verandah and on each step stood a servant in the same white and scarlet livery as the group that had met them on the quay. In every man's hand was a long gilded staff and the whole scene was illuminated by the blaze of torches held up by another party of men in the garden. As their carriages stopped, a dark-haired woman who looked as majestic as Mrs Siddons in one of her finest roles, appeared on the verandah and clapped her hands. At this signal, the servants on the steps stepped down in unison to open the carriage doors and form a guard of honour through which the awe-struck Macalpines mounted the stairs.

When Edmund Godwin left home he had been a leggy youth of nineteen, very like young John in appearance. The memory they retained of him was of a thin, tousle-headed lad so the portly, grey-haired man who came limping out to greet them was unrecognisable. It was only when, with a loud sob, he threw his arms around his sister that she was sure she had arrived at the home of her youngest brother. The woman who had given the signal to the servants was his wife Caroline.

They wept and talked, held hands and wiped away each other's tears. There was so much to say that sister and brother could have sat for days and nights pouring it all out but Caroline Godwin sensibly prevented them. After providing a fine dinner for her guests, she packed them off to bed, saying, 'You must rest now. Tomorrow will be time enough for talking. There's no need to rush.'

I'm happy, I'm happy. . . . The words ran through Grizel's head like a musical refrain as she sat in dappled shade beneath a huge banyan tree in the garden of the Macalpines' new home, The Retreat. A vast bungalow, it perched on top of Camballa Hill, overlooking the aquamarine Arabian Sea. Uncle Edmund had taken a lease of it for the family but he and his wife were no longer living in Bombay. Shortly after the Macalpines arrived, he had been been posted up the coast to Surat, a trading post several hundred miles away.

After the first rapture of their reunion, Jane Macalpine was dismayed to find that she and her favourite brother had little in

common any longer and she was intimidated by his forceful wife.
Caroline had been born in India, the daughter of an army officer,
and did not hesitate to parade her knowledge of the country which
irritated Lady Macalpine. On one thing however she could not fault
her sister-in-law; she had chosen The Retreat with care.

Within the long pendant branches that grew down into the
ground around the massive trunk of the banyan tree was a cool
and secret place where a seat had been placed to catch the fine
view of the sea below, stretching away like infinity. There was
a stone-built tank of water just below the house and on the worn
steps around it, busy crowds of women in brilliantly coloured saris
– purple, magenta, ochre yellow, searing green and scarlet – were
gathering water. They bore it off on their heads in earthenware pots,
swinging away with elegant assurance.

Grizel sat in the secret arbour, drinking in the scene. Too soon
she had to return to the house for this was the afternoon of Louisa's
wedding to Mr Grainger. The Macalpines had only been a fortnight
in Bombay but the couple saw no reason to wait. They were set on
marrying and the bridegroom, whose office was in the Fort, had
taken a house on Malabar Hill only a short palankeen ride away
from The Retreat.

The bride's parents accepted their daughter's wish to marry with
equanimity – and a certain amount of relief. Grainger was a solid
fellow, the son of a West Country parson, and though without
private fortune, he had been in the employment of the East India
Company for several years and would leave his new bride a three
hundred pounds a year pension should he be so unfortunate as to die.
Louisa had never been sought after at home, and it was a delightful
turn of events to find her snatched up so quickly in India.

The wedding was celebrated in fine style at St Thomas' Church in
the Fort, the building whose steeple was a landmark for approaching
ships. The Macalpines had already made many pleasant acquaintances in Bombay society and they turned up to swell the party.
Grizel was her sister's bridesmaid and was impressed at how calm
Louisa appeared as she stood at the altar, peering out from beneath
the thick veil that unbecomingly shrouded her head.

Grizel felt a strange sort of pity as she contemplated the match
her phlegmatic sister was making. Here was no passion, no pulsing
of the blood such as she felt every time she caught a glimpse of
Tom. Nor had there been for Anne. Grizel remained the unmarried
sister, the last left at home, yet she was the only one to have felt

the stirring of passion. She thrust the disturbing memories aside. It was easier to bear celibacy and spinsterhood if she did not brood about the past.

Throughout the ceremony, Louisa never once acted like a woman in love. She took everything calmly, as if she was entering into a satisfactory business contract. Perhaps she's doing things the right way. Perhaps it's safer to pick an unexciting man. Perhaps none of us will ever marry for love, thought Grizel sadly as she listened to the wedding service being read out to the couple.

The day after the wedding, Louisa and her Grainger set off on a short trip to the hills and young John took ship for Bengal, where a position had been found for him in the Company's administration. Grizel took leave of her brother with deep regret. To her he was still a little boy and she feared for him, turned loose in a cruel new world with only his religious faith to protect him.

He seemed to be able to read her thoughts, because he held her hand at parting and said, 'Don't worry about me. I'll be quite all right. I'm going to make a success of my life, Grizel. I'm determined on it.'

Life in The Retreat was busy and so eternally interesting that even Lady Macalpine rose at nine and dressed in her finery to wait for the troop of ladies who arrived to pay their calls every morning by the stroke of eleven. They came in carriages and palankeens, and their vehicles and palkie-wallahs waited at the foot of the verandah steps while they chattered and drank tea inside.

The Retreat was one of Bombay's finest houses but that was to be expected of a man with a salary of £10,000 a year. There was a thirty-foot long drawing room and a large dining room surrounded by wide verandahs where chairs and tables were arranged so that company could be entertained there in the cool breezes that blew up from the sea. On the first floor were enormous bedrooms with wardrobe rooms, dressing rooms and bathrooms attached. There was a separate wing for the servants and the kitchens. The buildings and compound were enclosed in a high wall and surrounded by terraced gardens where vegetables and flowers grew in profusion.

There never seemed to be a season when there was not something flourishing in the gardens, and the flowers glowed with the same searing colours as the saris of the woman water gatherers. Sweet pea shades so popular at home faded into insignificance in the brilliant Indian sun and to Grizel there was something energising about the profusion of colours all around her – garish zinnias, purple and scarlet sprays of bougainvillaea, scarlet hibiscus with bright yellow pistils. They woke a sensuous appreciation in her and this pleasure was heightened by the exotic scents that filled the house.

Beneath her bedroom window was a terrace of rose bushes with tiny bright pink flowers. They were unlike the luxuriant cabbage roses of home, but made up for their lack of size by their languorous scent for these were the famous attar roses of the East, the flowers from which the Mughal Emperors' perfumes were distilled.

When evening fell even the roses' scent was overtaken by the cloying smell of jasmine, the Queen of the Night. Its aroma crept into the house like a thief, lingering in clothes, wrapping itself around Grizel like the arms of a lover. She felt very strange on Indian evenings, changed and alien as if a part of herself that had long been denied was bursting into flower like the riotous garden.

'Mr Fanshawe called while you were out. He said he'd come back later.' Her mother's voice rang out from one of the cluster of lounging chairs on the verandah when Grizel entered the house after her morning ride.

'I don't care for Mr Fanshawe very much,' she said in reply.

Lady Macalpine pulled a face. 'You don't seem to care for anyone. People are beginning to gossip. We've been here for a month and you won't settle for any of the men who call on you, and some of them are very suitable.'

She started to reel off the names of presentable candidates for Grizel's hand. 'There's Colonel Outram, Major Knowles, Mr Thomas and his friend Mr Allison. They're all two and three thousand a year men with good prospects at home as well. What are you waiting for? Louisa found herself a husband before she even left the ship and it's not as if you're short of suitors. Your father and I can't keep you for ever.'

'Mother,' said Grizel, 'you know as well as I do that the moment I settle on someone, you'll change your attitude. You liked Louisa's husband well enough before they married. Now you haven't a good word to say for him.'

'What nonsense! My only complaint is that he keeps her away from me. She's so absorbed in Grainger that she doesn't spare a moment for her mother. Barely comes down here. There's a thousand and one things she could be doing for me.'

'Louisa comes down once a day, you have me at home to write your notes and an army of servants to fetch and carry for you,' said Grizel patiently.

But her mother was not to be convinced, and carried on with her complaints. 'What's once a day for about half an hour at a time when she only lives over the hill? Her poor mother abandoned in this alien place, among strangers! Anyway, you've avoided the question. When are you going to settle down with a suitable man, Grizel?'

At one time her mother's persistence would have made her seethe with inward fury but Grizel's old wounds were healing and she said in a joking voice, 'You know quite well that I'm waiting for Colonel Brown, Mother!'

This was a joke that had been started by Aunt Caroline before she left for Surat. When a name was suggested as a possible husband for Grizel, her aunt looked at her and said in a warning voice, 'Don't rush into anything, my dear. I'd like you to meet Colonel Brown. He's perfect for you.'

According to Caroline, this paragon was stationed in a remote place several hundred miles from Bombay and only came to the city occasionally. Grizel doubted if they would ever meet but had started using his name as a shield against her mother's matchmaking.

It was true that she was looking her best. Her flowering impressed everyone who met her because India, which sucked the life out of many European women, suited Grizel. Her blonde hair grew thick and glossy, her skin sparkled and her body became lithe with exercise. From their first days in Bombay, she and her father made a habit of riding out every morning as the sun rose in all its multicoloured glory over the mountain ranges that loomed behind Bombay island. Her old fear of horses was less inhibiting now but she was still slightly afraid of them and even the most polite animals tended to play the fool when she was in the saddle.

Her revived health and energy made her seem much younger than her age; people even thought she was younger than Louisa who was growing fat again and had quickly settled into a staid matronly existence.

A succession of suitors turned up at The Retreat, beseiging Grizel with invitations to balls and concerts, to soirées and picnics, to race meetings and to go out for drives – most of which she accepted.

Every evening she joined a party of young people who went out to 'eat the air' on the Promenade, where a military band played in an ornate open bandstand beneath the orange flower bedecked branches of the goldmohur trees. The gaiety she had last possessed at eighteen had returned, and Grizel rose every morning filled with happy expectations.

Her success, however, did not stifle her deep-rooted common sense. She knew she could have her pick of the eligible bachelors of Bombay but she drew back from commitment because she was looking for someone special. She did not have any preconceived ideas about what he would be like except that he must not resemble Tom Falconer – she did not want to suffer the same agonies of love again. She was looking for something different. Perhaps, like her sisters, she was seeking security, a man she could respect and whom she could trust to look after her well.

The summer crept on, growing hotter and hotter. The evening breeze was the only thing which made life supportable in the steaming weeks preceding the monsoon.

'This heat is quite suffocating. I'm in agony with prickly heat – my body's quite covered with it. My God, what persuaded us to come to this benighted place!' moaned Jane Macalpine as she lay on the verandah in her cane chair, ignoring the vast and colourful gardens spread out before her.

'But it's such a beautiful place,' protested Grizel, who, in spite of the blistering heat, still found herself bewitched afresh every morning when she woke up and looked out of her bedroom.

The front window overlooked the sea where little fishing boats with white sails dotted the flat water; the back window had a view up to a wooded rise topped by a stone watch tower. She loved the morning sounds – the hoarse voices of servants calling out to each other in their incomprehensible language; the swishing noise of the little brushes made of twigs with which they swept the floors and the dried earth around the kitchen compound; rustlings made on the roof by cheeky musk rats and the bird song that seemed to run continually through the air like background music. Even when the sun grew hotter and the humidity made her skin ooze with sweat during the stifling afternoons, she lay beneath the slowly waving curtain of her punkah, listening with delight to the world outside.

Louisa was not much company for either her mother or her sister. She and her protective husband retreated into their house as if into a fortress, not only because the heat made getting about uncomfortable but because Louisa was becoming more and more terrified of what she saw as the ever present violence of India.

'I don't like it when Grainger has to go to his office. I stay shut up in my room and wait for him to come home again,' she said in explanation of why she never showed her face outside unless accompanied by her husband.

'But your husband knows India. He worked here for ten years before you met him. Surely he can tell you that it's not dangerous? Everyone else goes out quite freely – more freely than they do in London,' protested Grizel.

'Grainger agrees with me. He says it's not safe for a woman. You shouldn't go out alone in your palkie, Grizel. They're savages and lust after white women,' was her sister's reply.

There was no arguing with Louisa who could be as intractable as a mule when she took an idea in her head. It was useless to point out that native women far outshone Europeans in their beauty, so why should any man in his right mind prefer a white-skinned woman? As she made further acquaintances among other European families, Grizel was intrigued to find that the women split into two distinct groups – those who, like Louisa, feared India and hid in their houses counting the days 'til they could return home, and the others who seized enthusiastically on the vibrancy of the strange country and blossomed in a society that was quite unlike anything they had known before. Grizel belonged to the latter group and, when she visited, tried very hard to coax Louisa out of her fears.

'Aren't you lonely here? Father has lent me his carriage. Come with me to pay calls. I'm going to visit Lady West.'

The reply was a shake of the head. 'I'm not well. It's rather delicate,' said her sister.

'You're having a baby!' Grizel was delighted for she loved children and the prospect of a baby to nurse and love filled her with delight.

Louisa, however, did not seem to share this enthusiasm. Her face was glum. 'It's so uncomfortable in this heat, and I feel sick every day. Oh dear, Grizel, I wish I'd never come to this terrible place.'

Grizel's next call was to The Hermitage, the house of Lady West, wife of her father's superior judge, Sir Charles West, who was Chief Justice of Bombay. When the two women met at the magnificent residence of Bombay's Governor, Sir John Malcolm, Lady West had taken a great liking to Grizel and implored her to pay a visit. Lady Macalpine was gratified that such flattering notice was taken of her daughter by Sir Charles's wife and ordered Grizel to make the call.

'Poor thing, she can't be much older than you and seems so
lonely. You must go and see her as soon as possible. It would be
a good thing if a social link could be made between our families
for there's so few people of the right sort in this city – most of the
women look as if their fathers were cheesemongers.'

Lady West's father most certainly was not a cheesemonger for
she was so fine-looking she resembled an overbred racehorse with
her gossamer fair hair and skin so transparent that the light seemed
to shine through it.

She was delighted to see Grizel and put down the book in which
she was writing to jump to her feet and lead her visitor to a
chair. The overfurnished sitting room looked as if it had been
lifted straight from an English country house and deposited in the
Tropics. Nothing it contained was suitable for the climate.

'I was writing up my journal,' Lady West explained. 'It's such a
help. I talk to it really – write down all the things I'd like to say.
There are so few people who understand.'

'I don't keep one. I wish I could but I never seem to have the
time,' Grizel said.

'Don't rush about so much. You must take care of your strength
in this hot weather,' warned her hostess. 'This is my third summer here and every year it grows hotter. There are always so
many deaths before the monsoon. Yesterday I heard about poor
Mrs Fairweather. She dined here on Thursday and on Friday evening she was dead! And last week it was Major Collins. The fever,
you know. It comes from nowhere. God preserve us from it.

'I worry about my husband having to go to the High Court
building. It's so crowded down there, right opposite the Dockyard
gates, with people going about in huge numbers all the time. The
infection is carried in the air, Dr Forbes tells me.'

She looked so piteous that Grizel reached out and took her hand,
saying soothingly, 'You mustn't worry so much. You'll make yourself ill. You're quite safe up here and your husband is a strong man.
The fever won't affect either of you.'

But Lady West was not to be consoled. 'It's not just us. There's
my dear little Fanny. She's only two years old and that's such
a dangerous age. Have you ever been to the European burying
ground? It's full of children's graves. So sad. Why did we come
out here? I wish we'd never left home.'

It was a very sobered Grizel who drove home for tiffin after her
visit. Although she had only been in the city a short while, she had

heard all the grim jokes about the graveyard, which locals called Padre Burrough's go-down. She had been told terrible stories of the cures against fever – red hot irons applied to the soles of the feet, leeches plastered to the throat, poultices that burned the skin off backs and bottles of claret that were poured down dying men's throats.

But the city that teemed like a sea around her carriage enthralled her. Despite herself, Grizel forgot her fear of contagion and leant out to watch the passers-by and the slowly wandering cows with their horns painted in coloured stripes and garlands of marigolds round their necks. She noticed that her imperious carriage driver, who was eager enough to crack his whip over the heads of people wandering aimlessly about in the roadway, drew on the reins and waited patiently to give cows their right of way. There was always something new to see in this amazing land providing your eyes were open and unclouded by fear or prejudice.

Her equanimity was challenged when she reached home, however. Her mother's maid came rushing out to meet her with the news that they had sent for a doctor to attend My Lady who was in a fainting fit.

Grizel rushed along the wide verandah to her mother's bedroom and saw her lying prone beneath the looped up mosquito nets. 'What's the matter, Mother? What happened?' she asked.

The only answer was a low moan. Before she could find out anything more, the sound of horses' hooves on the gravel below alerted her to the doctor's arrival. There was the sound of running footsteps and a grey-haired man came rushing into the room. The anxious expression on his face faded as he leaned over the body on the bed, grasped her wrist in competent fingers, listened to her heart beat for a while and then asked, 'Can you sit up, Lady Macalpine? You're quite well. Tell me what happened to make you faint.'

Grizel heard her mother's quavering voice saying, 'It was a human arm, doctor. It came floating down from the sky and landed on the grass almost at my feet. Right in front of me.' She gave a shudder and a sob.

A human arm from the sky? Grizel wondered if her mother was in the grip of some sort of mania and looked across at the doctor but, to her surprise, there was a faint smile on his face.

'Is that all?' he asked in a broad Scots voice.

Lady Macalpine propped herself up on her elbow and asked angrily, 'All? Do you think it normal for parts of the human body to rain down from the sky? It's enough to make a woman die, far less faint away.'

'Didn't anybody warn you when you took this house? You see that tower on the hill back there,' asked the doctor, pointing at the watchtower on the rising ground behind the house. 'That's the Parsee *dokhma*.'

'The Parsee what?' Grizel was curious and not in the least frightened by her mother's experience. Anything could happen in India, she had learned that already.

'Their *dokhma*. The Parsee people lay their dead bodies out on top of it and the vultures pick them clean. It's their custom.'

Lady Macalpine collapsed back against her pillows with a faint scream. 'Can't they be stopped? I'll ask my husband to stop it,' she gasped between white lips.

'Madam, they've been doing it for centuries, since long before there were any British people living in Bombay. They're not going to stop now.'

Grizel remembered that she had often seen crowds of bald-headed vultures roosting in the palm trees higher up the hill. The doctor was still explaining to her mother, 'It's a barbaric custom, I know, but it's part of their religion. There've been a lot of deaths recently from the fever; there usually are before the rains begin. It'll be better later. Anyway, the vultures don't often drop pieces. You were just unlucky, that's all.'

Grizel liked his attitude but her mother's response was predictable. 'Oh, my God, how I hate this place.'

This new acquaintance was none other than Dr Forbes, the man whose wife had given Grizel the piece of paper on board the packet ship coming down from Leith. He was a wizened little man who spoke with a broad Aberdeen accent and always had a merry twinkle in his eye. Grizel had liked him on sight and when he stepped out of her mother's room after prescribing a sleeping draught, they were able to talk to each other like old acquaintances. The first thing he sought to do was to reassure the girl about her mother's health.

'She's quite well but in a nervous state. That happens to lots of people in the hot weather and the heat's going to get much worse over the next few weeks. Why don't you all take a little trip to the hills? I always recommend Khandala to newcomers because it's not too far and the air's clear up there. It would set you all up.' Grizel said she'd suggest the idea to her father.

Before the doctor left, she gave him the paper on which his wife had written her name. As she handed it to him, she explained how it had come into her possession. Forbes read the scrawled words with an expression of such sadness that she almost wished she had not given him the paper.

'How did she look?' he asked after a pause.

'She seemed well,' Grizel replied, not wanting to mention the woman's thinness, her scarred face or pronounced limp. Perhaps he knew about these things anyway.

'Did she say anything about her family or where she was going?' was his next question.

'No, our conversation was very general, but she was sweet to me and very reassuring.'

'Tell me again her words when she gave you the paper,' he asked.

Grizel repeated the words as she remembered them. They seemed to please him. He folded the paper and put it carefully into his pocket. When he looked at her, his eyes were full of gratitude and he said, 'You can't know what you've done for me by bringing this, Miss Macalpine. My wife and I parted ten years ago. She couldn't stand it here – not after our child died of the fever and she was so ill with smallpox. Poor Mary. She'd been so beautiful.

'I wouldn't go back. My time here had only just begun and there was nothing to go back to. She went home alone and it seemed we were never to meet again. I've heard about her, of course, from time to time, but she never wrote. This piece of paper means more to me than you can imagine. It's a message to tell me to get in touch with her, I'm sure of it. This was a happy meeting indeed, Miss Macalpine, and I am for ever in your debt. If there's anything I can do to help you on the expedition to the hills, please don't hesitate to ask.'

Chapter Thirteen

LIKE HIS DAUGHTER, Sir Peter John Macalpine took to the idea of an expedition to Khandala. 'What a capital idea,' he said. 'We'll take Louisa and Grainger along as well. Do them good to get out of that house for a while.'

When the High Court adjourned for the hot weather in the middle of May, their party set sail across Thana Creek in a rough-looking dhow which was surprisingly spacious and comfortable inside. Once on the water, it was bliss to find themselves cooled and soothed by a soft breeze. They sat watching elegant flocks of white herons standing in the shallows of the creek that cut the island of Bombay off from the mainland, now shimmering in a heat haze.

On the shore stood a line of carriages, palankeens and horses, waiting with what looked like a vast army of servants who accompanied the convoy on foot. It was a slow journey across the baking plain to the dak bungalow where they spent the first night in spartan conditions that were forgotten like a dream when the brilliance of dawn woke them from fitful sleep.

By first light they could see the rampart of the Eastern Ghats rearing in front of them, a long line of mountains that rose out of the baking plain like a sheer wall. The mountain sides were thickly festooned with trees and creepers and the road they were to follow twisted and turned along the rock face like the track made by a mountain goat. The women were told to transfer into their palankeens because carriages could not negotiate the path up the mountainside. Grizel found it easiest to keep her eyes shut when traversing the most precipitous bends but her nervous mother insisted on getting out of her palankeen and walking along with

211

the bearers for she was convinced that a false step would tip her over into the abyss. Louisa stayed in her palankeen but moaned and sobbed throughout the long ascent. It was afternoon when they finally reached their tents, pitched on a platform of rock overlooking the plain. This was Khandala, their journey's end.

It was a place of magic. Everything had been carried up in advance and their tents were luxuriously appointed with carpets, beds and bedding, trunks of clothes, books, writing cases and medicine chests, even their table linen and cutlery, crested china and crystal glasses. The dinner table, when it was spread with candles glittering in glass holders, would not have disgraced royalty and was made all the more special because they ate in a tent with its sides open to the mysterious, rustling night.

In the morning, Grizel walked out of her tent door and found to her delight that she was standing practically on the edge of a precipice. There was an astounding clarity to the light. It sharpened her eyesight so that she could see far below her the twisting road like a line of string, and the tiny toiling figures of peasants tending their fields of pale green rice shoots. Above her head crested buzzards with huge wing spans were soaring serenely in thermal currents. Beneath, on the sloping mountainside, she could see the tops of trees, some of them brilliant with scarlet trumpet flowers and all threaded together with green lianas that twisted and turned from tree to tree and branch to branch in an impenetrable lacework.

As she gazed down into this forest, a troop of monkeys emerged into a clearing led by the oldest male, walking on its hind legs and leaning on a long branch as if it was a staff. There were other, smaller, solemn black-faced monkeys in the branches of the scrubby trees behind the tents, all of them watching her intently and, she was sure, gossiping about the strange looking people who had appeared during the night.

The best thing about Khandala however was the air – cool and clear and dry – free of the cloying dampness of Bombay's summer atmosphere. Intoxicated by the crystal freshness, Grizel wanted to run and jump and shout out loud with glee. The invigorating atmosphere even affected Louisa who agreed to accompany her sister on a walk during which they wandered along forest paths, picking purple grapes and gathering bouquets of orchids that hung in festoons from the branches above their heads.

When evening came, they sat in companionable delight around a fire that cast glimmering reflections over the white walls of their tents. Around them, servants' white-clad figures flitted to and fro and the shapes of their grazing horses could be seen tied up between the tents. The backdrop to the scene was the massed forest which seemed to creep nearer and nearer as darkness deepened.

Everyone went off to sleep early but Grizel was soon wakened by what sounded like the roaring of a waterfall in her ears. She rose and went to the open door of her tent where she found her way barred by the servant who had been appointed her guard. The whites of his eyes were rolling in terror and his sword hand shaking so much she wandered how much protection he could be.

'It's the great tiger,' he whispered. 'Go back inside, missie sahib.'

Just then there was another terrible noise, a deep-throated growl, immediately followed by the shrill screaming neigh of a terrified horse. Then came the sharp retort of a gun shot and Mr Grainger ran into the clearing between the tents, crying out to them not to be afraid.

'A tiger's been at the water tank for a drink but the shot frightened it away,' he called out.

The fact that a tiger had been near them at all was enough for Louisa and her mother. They went into hysterics, demanding to be taken home at once. No arguments could counter their fear so at first light camp was broken and everything packed up again for a return to the city.

They were a subdued group on their way down the Ghat. Grizel rode in her palankeen with the door half closed so that she did not have to converse with the others. She was bitterly disappointed at the abrupt curtailment of their trip for the glimpse she had of Khandala had whetted her appetite for a further glimpse of the hinterland. She was still silent when they mounted their carriages at the foot of the Ghat.

As they were crossing the plain to the first dak bungalow, a cry went up from the leading outriders. The lethargic Europeans roused themselves in their seats and saw a group of riders coming down the road towards them. As they drew nearer, Grizel recognised Forbes with the party and burned with shame that he should find them on their way home so quickly.

He made no adverse comment, however, but seemed pleased to confide in them that he was on his way to Poona where Sir Charles and Lady West had gone for the hot season.

'I've had a message to say that Sir Charles isn't well. He has a fever that won't go away and Lady West sent for me. When he's

better, I'll go on to Satara to meet my friend, Colonel Brown.
Now there's a man that would suit you, Miss Macalpine! You're
made for each other.'

In spite of her bitter disappointment at the curtailment of their
Khandala trip, she had to laugh out loud at this. 'Not you too, Doctor! My Aunt Caroline told me about Colonel Brown. It must be the
same man – there can't be two paragons with the same name.'

Doctor Forbes was quite serious. 'He'd suit you perfectly. He's
a man who's used to the country, and with him you'd be able to
take many trips like this for I can see how you enjoy them. Don't
engage yourself to anyone else 'til I introduce you and Brown to
each other. . . .'

Even Grizel felt exhausted and fractious as the heat rose to a
crescendo during early June. She fell sick with a liver upset and lay
in bed staring hopelessly at the rafters of the high ceiling, watching
little house lizards run to and fro above her head. It seemed as if all
her old worries were hovering above her in a black cloud, ready to
plunge her back into despair. Sweat soaked the thin wrapper which
was the only covering she could bear, and ran off her body into the
mattress. She felt the damp covering clinging to her limbs like a
winding sheet. In the next bedroom lay her mother, aflame with
the itching discomfort of prickly heat. Grizel pitied her father who
had still to work in these conditions and was further plagued by a
dispute he was currently engaged in with Malcolm, the Governor
of Bombay.

Even in the thick of his financial troubles, Sir Peter John Macalpine
had retained an equable temper and good humour towards his
family, but the Indian heat and this new trouble sharpened his
tongue and made him unusually fractious. He did not talk about
his latest problem to Grizel but she knew that he and her mother
discussed it. She heard their voices talking and talking for hours into
the night.

It was difficult to rest because just when Grizel was drifting off
into sleep she would be jolted back by the horrible screeching call
of the brain fever bird that rose and rose and rose to an unbearable
pitch before ending in an unearthly scream. Some of those birds
had taken up residence in the trees of their garden and refused to be
chased away. She could well understand how the bird had earned
its name because listening to it in the unrelenting heat of the night
made madness seem a very real possibility.

One night, when it seemed that the discomfort and lethargy engendered by the heat had been on them for a century, an ominous hush fell around the house and garden. After a few minutes' breathless expectancy, the sky was rent apart with thunder claps and lightning flashes so brilliant that they intermittently lit the bedroom, leaving a lingering smell of sulphur behind them. Although she had never been afraid of natural manifestations before, the Bombay storm made Grizel cower in bed with her head beneath the sheet, shaking in terror. Eventually it rolled away and was followed by a period of sinister stillness.

Then came a sound which she could not at first identify, a soft and swishing noise like the rustling of silk above her head. It took a few minutes before she realised that it was rain falling on the roof. The first shower soon became a downpour that drummed and thudded as it fell from the sky and filled her nostrils with the smell of damp earth, a sweet and refreshing scent that coaxed her from her bed and out into the garden. The ground beneath her feet was opening up to the rain, cracks in the baked red earth smoothed away by its benison. The very flowers and trees seemed to reach up to the sky in gratitude.

Grizel stood beneath the deluge, letting it pour over her till her clothes and hair were thoroughly soaked. Finally she walked back to the house, revelling in the feeling of water squishing between her bare toes as she stepped across the grass. What a blessing to feel cool again. When she reached her bedroom she could hear the sounds of merriment from the servants' quarters. They were all outside too, singing and dancing in the puddles.

Grizel enjoyed sitting on the verandah watching the falling rain. They had few visitors now but one day Dr Forbes called in with an urgent summons for her. 'Please go over to The Hermitage and see poor Lady West. She's just arrived from Poona and she's asking for you.'

Vigorously, he shook the rain off his coat as he spoke. Outside the monsoon was falling in torrents.

'I didn't know they were back in the city,' said Grizel, surprised.

Forbes looked at her, grave-faced. 'Brown and I brought her down yesterday. I've bad news, I'm afraid, Miss Macalpine – Sir Charles died in Poona. We tried everything to save him but he was too weakened. Lady West broke down completely when he died. She's near her time now and in no fit state to give birth.'

The palankeen men had to wade through knee high pools of water on their way to The Hermitage. Several times Grizel feared she would be swamped but they reached the house eventually.

Lucy West lay on her side in a vast bed, her white face half buried in the pillow. As the tears flowed unchecked down her ravaged face she reached out a hand and held Grizel's tight.

'I'm so sorry about your husband. It's tragic news,' said Grizel, kneeling by the bedside.

'I want to die, I want to die too,' Lucy West moaned, and shuddered convulsively. 'But there's Fanny. I want you to promise me that if anything happens to me, you and your father will look after her. My husband had a great liking for Sir Peter John. I want her sent home to my parents in Oxfordshire. Will you make sure that's done?'

Grizel did not wish even to talk of such an eventuality. 'You're going to be perfectly all right,' she soothed. 'Dr Forbes is confident of that and I'll stay with you. You mustn't give up, not now.'

'I'm going to die,' sobbed Lucy, 'but before I do I must make arrangements about Fanny. I must! Please help me. Say you'll take her.'

She had to soothe the frantic woman. 'Of course we'll take her – but isn't there someone else you'd want to be her guardian? Someone you've known longer.'

Lucy raised swollen eyes and stared at Grizel. 'Haven't you heard? Chambers, the other judge, is dead too. He died this morning. There's no one else. I know you'd be kind to Fanny. You must promise me you'll take her.'

Grizel ached with pity for the bereaved, frightened woman. 'I promise, but you're not going to die. This is a terrible time for you but it will be better one day.'

'I am. That's how it happens out here. I prayed that it wouldn't happen to us but now it has. Oh, this is a cruel place, so cruel. . . .'

Grizel stayed at The Hermitage for a week, helping to nurse Lucy who drifted in and out of consciousness after Dr Forbes had administered opium. Sitting by the bedside, holding the limp hand, Grizel's heart was heavy. It seemed that this beautiful country she had come to love had another face, one that was terrifying in its rapacity. With a shiver of foreboding she knelt and prayed for Lucy to be spared but when she saw Dr Forbes' grave face on his next visit, she dreaded that her prayers would not be answered.

In the middle of the eighth night, Lucy West was delivered of a baby which was born dead. The mother herself died the following day. In spite of everyone's pleas and efforts, she simply drifted out of life. Her burial, with her stillborn child at her side, took place that night. The funeral was a magnificent affair with the coffin covered with a gold-fringed black velvet cloth and drawn by horses wearing black plumes on their heads.

On the following Sunday, the Governor of Bombay, gruff-spoken Sir John Malcolm, delivered a eulogy in St Thomas' Church while a grim-faced Lady Macalpine sat with her daughters in the front row.

'How unsuitable for him to speak of the poor girl when everyone knows the trouble he caused her husband! And for my own, come to that. As I said to your father, the man's nothing but a rough peasant from Dumfries.' Solemn occasion or no, it didn't occur to Lady Macalpine to lower her voice. There was trouble brewing between the Governor and Sir Peter John. Jane Macalpine seemed positively to relish the prospect.

If Grizel had imagined her father's character would change when he came to Bombay, she was quickly proved mistaken. From the first weeks he had plunged into an intrigue that caused first faint stirrings of difficulty and then huge tidal waves of disagreement between the three man judiciary and the governing body of the East India Company.

The deaths of the other two judges of the High Court bench left Macalpine battling alone and with increasing fervour against Governor Malcolm over the implications of the Ramchandra affair, a custody case over an Indian minor.

Hearing rumours of the trouble from friends, Grizel attempted to remonstrate with her father, saying, 'This is India, not London or Edinburgh. The place works under different rules.'

He was adamant. 'I was sent out here by the King to administer justice, not to safeguard the privileges of the East India Company. Malcolm wants me to leave the Ramchandra case to be dealt with by the company agent in Poona.'

'But doesn't the boy in question live in Poona?'

Macalpine brushed that aside. 'It's a matter of right. Malcolm says we've no right to adjudicate in the matter because Poona's outside the island. But the writ of law should extend to all India, not just to the island of Bombay. He's treating me like a cipher and I won't have it!'

There, she thought, was the crux of the matter.

The orphaned Fanny had a small heart-shaped face and round blue eyes that anxiously interrogated every adult who spoke to her. She could not be persuaded to relinquish the hand of her ayah whose eyes were red with weeping. When Grizel knelt down to try and take the child in her arms she felt the little body stiffen and draw away from her.

'Don't be afraid, my dear,' she whispered. 'I won't hurt you. Come with me and I'll show you where you are going to sleep.'

Fanny looked up at her ayah, then at Grizel. 'Is Ayah coming too?'

'Yes, of course. Ayah won't leave you.'

'Where's Mama?'

Grizel and the ayah looked at each other. The ayah knelt down to explain: 'Mama's gone away. This lady will look after us now, baba.'

With that reassurance, the child allowed herself to be put to bed in the room which had been prepared for her in The Retreat, where she was to stay until instructions arrived from home and a suitable escort could be found to accompany her on the long voyage back to her grandparents. Because of the distance and the length of time it took to send letters, it would be many months before the people in England learned of the tragedy that had befallen their daughter in Bombay, and even longer before they were able to write back to the Macalpines with instructions on where to send the little girl. Her stay in The Retreat could be a long one.

Despite the sad circumstances, the arrival of Fanny and her attendant, who never let the child out of her sight and even slept on the floor beneath her bed at night, gave Grizel intense pleasure. The games she played with the child, the hours she spent drawing pictures for her and trying to teach her the alphabet, delighted her. Though Fanny was only three, she showed a precocious interest in books. As they sat together, Grizel was gripped with a deep yearning for a child of her own. She was painfully aware of how much her arms ached to hold a baby.

Her longing became even more intense at the end of the year when Louisa gave birth to a son. On the day he was born Grizel lovingly wrapped the tiny limbs in the softest cotton swaddling clothes and then held him up, laughing out loud with joy. When she carried the baby into Louisa's bedroom and laid him on the pillow, she wished with all her heart that she could have taken her sister's place. The faces, lying so close together, were so very alike. With a rush of love for her sister, Grizel bent down to kiss her. Louisa would be a good mother. She remembered the hours that had been spent at Glen Fada, patiently dressing and undressing the block of wood that was Louisa's first doll.

So devoted a mother was she, in fact, that her care of the baby, who was christened George, took over her entire life and energy. She even refused to engage an ayah to help care for the child.

'It's madness! You'll kill yourself doing everything for a child in this heat. White women aren't meant to exert themselves in this climate – and how will you be able to carry out your social engagements?' protested her mother.

Louisa put on her most mulish face. 'I won't go to any balls or tea parties,' she said flatly.

'And what about your husband? He'll be a cause of gossip if he's seen out alone.'

'He won't go out either,' said Louisa.

She and Grainger stuck to their isolation. No ayah was engaged and they retreated into deeper seclusion in their bungalow. When Grizel called, she tried to persuade her sister to venture out because she feared the effect such loneliness would have on her nerves but Louisa remained adamant.

'I don't want to. I hate society here anyway. It's so false. I want to go home.'

'But what about your husband's career? He can't throw away his prospects so easily.'

'His uncle died a few months ago and left him a small inheritance, not a lot but enough to keep us in reasonable comfort. He'll have to take me home.'

Grainger was a patient man but even he protested that he could not give up his career without good reason. His wife grew more hysterical and in her isolation allowed her mind to dwell on the sad deaths of Lady West and her husband. Self-imposed isolation and the looming prospect of another monsoon season in Bombay drove her distracted.

'If we stay here, we'll all die,' she announced flatly, and Grizel felt a chill of fear at the echo of the words spoken by the doomed Lady West. When hysterics did not work, Louisa tried another tack. One morning Grizel found her weeping pitifully.

'There's been a threat to my baby's life. Some wicked person wants to kill him,' she sobbed.

His aunt looked from the child kicking his legs around on the blanket she had spread for him on the floor and said in open astonishment, 'What nonsense! Who'd want to kill a sweet child like this?'

'We don't know, but someone does. A note was brought into the servants' quarters yesterday. It threatened our child's life.'

'I've never heard of such a thing. Let me see the note.'

'*You* may never have heard of it but things like that do happen. A child was stolen away from his parents last month somewhere up country and his body used in a heathen sacrifice. I read about it in the newspaper.'

Grizel truly feared now for Louisa's sanity but she tried to be reassuring. 'But who would want to take revenge on you? Neither of you ever go anywhere or antagonise anyone. Let me see the note.'

'It's been destroyed – I tore it up. Besides, it's not us they want to revenge themselves on but Father, because of that court case – the one that's caused all the trouble.'

Frightened, Grizel rose to her feet and handed the baby back to its mother, trying to sound comforting and sensible as she did so.

'You mustn't worry about such things. Your baby is perfectly safe. Father's court cases have nothing to do with you.'

But her sister was in floods of tears and moaning aloud: 'I want to go home. I want to go home. We'll all die here, I know it.'

Grizel had her doubts about the story of the note but felt that her sister was giving way to morbid fantasies rather than telling outright lies. Her intense desire to return home was painfully apparent. Grizel had seen too many cases of killing despair in her short time in India already, and sought out her brother-in-law at his office in the Fort in some concern. He was amazed to see a white woman being shown into his sanctum by the uniformed peon but politely busied himself, offering her a chair and sending out for cool drinks to refresh her after her journey from Camballa Hill.

'I've come about Louisa. She seems to be in a highly emotional state,' Grizel began.

Grainger spread his hands helplessly. 'I guessed that was the reason. It can't go on, I realise that. I'm going to have to resign. She'll never settle comfortably here now that the baby's come. She's obsessed with him, terrified of anything happening to him – and you know how dangerous it is for little children in this climate. If George became ill or died she'd never forgive me.'

There was obviously no need for her to plead her sister's case. 'I'm sorry,' said Grizel. 'I sincerely hope that this trouble of Father's hasn't caused any for you.'

Grainger shook his head. 'I don't believe there ever was a note, but for Louisa's sake we're going home.'

The Graingers left a month later, taking with them Fanny and her ayah whose terror of sailing over the black water was outweighed by her dread of losing the child she loved. When Grizel stood with her parents waving them off from Apollo Bunder her heart was full of sorrow, not so much at losing her sister who had been a poor companion during these Indian days but at being bereft of baby George and beloved little Fanny. She felt as if it were her own children she was sending away.

A few days later she met Dr Forbes at a reception held in the magnificent Government House, Parel, by the grim-faced Governor Malcolm. His previous affability towards the Macalpine family was now severely stretched, it seemed.

The doctor grasped her arm and said, 'I'm glad to see you here, my dear, but it's a pity your parents aren't present. By the way, my friend Brown's coming back to Bombay next week. Perhaps you'll be able to meet then.'

She was about to take the dance floor with an attentive young officer and smiled gaily at the doctor. 'I'm beginning to think your friend Brown's a figment of everyone's imagination. He's either just been or is expected imminently yet our paths never actually cross.'

On the following week, however, when she and her father were taking their early morning ride along the bay which led to Breach Candy Point, Dr Forbes approached from the other direction accompanying a tall, fair-haired, military-looking man who sat his horse with the casual ease of a cavalry officer. Grizel's father was leading because she, as usual, was having trouble with her horse, kicking it on without success for it was determined to proceed only at a slow amble and nothing she could do would speed it up. Ahead of her, the three men were talking and laughing together.

When they reached the fork in the sandy road that led up to Camballa Hill, the stranger turned his horse with a casual flexing of the wrist and trotted back to Grizel. 'Let me assist you, Miss Macalpine,' he said in a deep, pleasant voice, and reaching over took hold of the reins and led her slothful horse up to the others. She noticed how strong and well-shaped his hand was.

'You should be more firm with him,' he told her, meeting her eye directly when he looked at her.

To her surprise, she felt herself blushing. This stranger with his ease and self-confidence made her feel like a young girl again. Dr Forbes turned in his saddle and watched them approach together. 'See, Miss Macalpine,' he called, 'didn't I tell you that my friend Brown exists? You're not a figment of my imagination, are you, Brown?'

Grizel's blush deepened and she dropped her head in an effort to hide her confusion as formal introductions were made between them. She did not have to suffer her embarrassment long, however, because the doctor and Colonel Brown were taking a different fork in the road and soon cantered off. Grizel and her father stared after them.

'That's an interesting fellow with Forbes,' said Macalpine. 'He's Irish and seems a gentleman. We had a pleasant talk. He said he might well be exercising here again tomorrow.'

When they rode out over the following few days, Colonel Brown seemed to appear from nowhere and attach himself to their little party. As Grizel ambled along on her lethargic nag, he took it upon himself to improve her horsemanship.

'Drive him on with your heel, Miss Macalpine, take a good hold of his mouth, don't let him go along as he pleases. Hold your reins the same way as I do – look.'

He demonstrated how the leather rein was interlaced through his long fingers. She stared at his lean, capable hand and felt the colour rise in her cheeks.

'Like this,' he said, seeming not to notice, and leaned across to take Grizel's hand in his. As their fingers touched, both of them paused and there was silence for a second. She felt her stomach tighten as it had done on the day she saw Tom Falconer standing with his elbow on the parlour mantelpiece.

But to her chagrin the Colonel did not confine his interest to her alone on these morning rides. Sometimes he rode for a long time knee to knee with her father, talking earnestly, while she ambled along behind.

'What do you and Brown talk about? You seem to enjoy it, whatever it is,' she asked her father.

'He's very political but conservative like all those Northern Irishmen, an old-fashioned sort of fellow and a real Company man. I like him nonetheless. He's very well read,' came the reply.

'He doesn't talk to me about things like that. Perhaps he doesn't think women are capable of understanding such weighty matters!'

Her father laughed as he replied, 'Then you'll have to impress him with your intelligence, my dear.'

During her time in Bombay, Grizel had become accustomed to having men pay court to her. She enjoyed light flirtations, dancing and gossiping with her admirers and it piqued her that Colonel Henry Brown did not immediately fall under her spell as so many other bachelors had done.

She could not put him out of her mind, however hard she tried. She wondered what he did with the rest of his day when the morning ride was over. Where did he go? Who did he see? She knew that he. was on a short leave from his posting at Satara, a military station some two hundred miles away in the southern hills, and that he was staying with his old friend Dr Forbes in his bungalow at Byculla, but she never met him socially at any of the occasions she frequented. It annoyed her that he did not make any attempt to cross her path except on their morning ride.

As the days passed, she took more and more interest in her appearance, spending a long time at her mirror before riding out. She knew she looked particularly dashing in one particular hat with a trailing feather and she wore it proudly, hoping for a compliment from the Colonel.

The effect was as she had wished. When he saw her in it for the first time his admiration was plain to see. She gloried in the way his hazel eyes looked her up and down and her heart sang when he reined back his horse so that he could ride the whole circuit with her alone.

Now was her opportunity. She did not simper and flirt but talked soberly to him about books she had read in her father's library and the music she loved. They found they shared an enthusiasm for Shakespeare, and for his sonnets as much as for the plays. Laughing with pleasure they capped each other's quotations, and when they reached the Camballa Hill fork, Grizel had the satisfaction of knowing that the Colonel appreciated her as much for her mind as for her eye-catching appearance.

He bowed over her hand as he took his leave and said, 'Until tomorrow, I hope. We'll continue our discussion then.'

She stared after his erect figure, and her heart gave a leap of pleasure at the realisation she could once again thrill to the physical appearance of a man. She admired his broad shoulders and the set of his head. He was older than Tom and blond to her first lover's raven darkness, but there was a strength in his weathered face and whipcord body that set her pulses racing.

Morning after morning, the Colonel allowed her father to ride on alone and took his place by Grizel's side. In the second week of their acquaintance, he let Forbes and her father ride far ahead one morning, then put out a hand to grasp her horse's bridle, pulling it close to his leg.

'I hope you won't take this amiss,' he began, and she lowered her eyes in confusion. What was he about to say? Her heart was hammering in her breast as she smiled sweetly at him, encouraging him to continue.

'Could I ask you to do something for me?' were his next words.

Doubt crept into her mind. 'Of course, if it's in my power,' she said hesitantly.

'Could you intercede with your father over the Ramchandra affair? I know how much he respects your opinion. If you would ask him to consider Malcolm's side in the business, it would be a great help. The Governor's my friend and a good fellow – the way your father's behaving is driving him half mad. I told him what an unusual young woman you are, and he asked me to speak to you about it.'

She stared at the soldier by her side in genuine astonishment, hoping that her face would not reveal her grievous disappointment. So this was why he rode with her so assiduously every morning! He had been cultivating her on behalf of his friend, using her in the game of politics. She flushed painfully but collected herself sufficiently to nod and say shortly, 'I'll speak to my father, but I don't hold out any hope of being able to change his mind.'

Then, reluctant to prolong this humiliation a moment longer, she drove her booted heel into the horse's ribs. It was so surprised at her decisiveness that it took off in a canter, and seconds later she was riding alongside her father and the doctor.

Shame and rage held her in their grip all the way home. How foolish she had been to imagine that the Colonel's interest in her was romantic when all the time he had been softening her up on the Governor's behalf.

But he had asked her to do something and she had said she would. While the syces took the horses into the stables behind The Retreat, Grizel accompanied her father across the lawn towards the bungalow. She was too angry and distressed to try a diplomatic approach. 'Colonel Brown wanted me to ask you to consider Malcolm's opinion in the Ramchandra affair, Father,' she said baldly.

He gave an angry snort. 'Brown's a good enough fellow but soldiers should stick to fighting and leave the law to the judges. Don't bother yourself about it. I know what I'm doing.'

Next morning she sent an early morning message to her father, saying she felt too unwell to ride out. When he returned for breakfast he said, 'Brown was very disappointed not to see you. He's going back to Satara tomorrow. He'll be gone several months.'

Disappointment curdled her stomach and she pushed away her plate. 'Really?' was all she could say, for she knew her mother was watching her with lynx-like eyes.

'He sends you his best wishes and hopes that when he comes back to Bombay, he'll meet you again,' said Sir Peter John. He seemed totally unconscious that his daughter had been disappointed in her hopes of the Colonel.

'Dr Forbes has been here. There's some plan afoot for making an expedition to the hills.' Lady Macalpine was all smiles as her daughter came into the house a few weeks later, wiping her brow because the heat was once more building up to its summer crescendo.

A trip to the hills, where it would be cool and one could sleep at night without discomfort, sounded a wonderful idea to Grizel but she did not want to build up her hopes too soon.

'Surely you won't go,' she said, remembering the fuss about the tiger at Khandala, but Lady Macalpine gave a shrug of demurral. 'It's very hot here. Perhaps we should try the hills again. Anyway, I'm sure Forbes is far better at organising these things than poor Grainger. He suggests we travel to a place called Mahabaleshwar. The climate's wonderful, he says, very cool and fresh. Just the thing to cure my prickly heat.'

'But can Father spare the time to go travelling? He's alone on the bench now and so busy.'

Her mother smiled conspiratorially. 'I think he'll have time if he does what he's planning.'

When Grizel was helping her father with his papers that night, she broached the subject of the trip and he was full of enthusiasm.

'Yes, by George, we'll go! It's an excellent plan. I'll tell Forbes
tomorrow.'

'But what about all this?' His daughter indicated the piles of legal
papers on his desk.

Sir Peter John dismissed them with a wave of the hand. 'I'll close
the Court,' he announced.

'Close the Court! You can't do that.'

'I can and will. Malcolm's driven me to it by his lack of respect
for the law. I'm the only judge on the bench and if I were to fall
ill the Court would have to be closed. It'll soon be the hot weather
when it closes anyway.'

'Oh, Father, do take care. You mustn't fly in the face of established
practice. When we first arrived Sir John Malcolm was so kind. Now
people are drawing away from us. It's so distressing.'

Her father was incensed. 'The only people who draw away from
us are old-fashioned die-hards, Company men like Malcolm. Trade
and the Company are the most important things as far as they're
concerned. But justice is justice and as a judge I must stick to that.'

The same blinkered single-mindedness and sense of self-impor-
tance that propelled Macalpine into ruin at home was steering him
into trouble again. Grizel's heart sank as the old feeling of being
stalked by ill fortune returned.

Lady Macalpine's conviction that any expedition organised by Dr
Forbes would be well managed proved correct. Though he himself
was not able to accompany them, he engaged an escort and through
his various up-country friends planned every stage of their journey.

Feeling like potentates, they were escorted into a luxuriously
appointed boat to sail over the placid waters of the bay, seated in the
shade of fringed parasols. When they landed at a little village called
Lanowlie there was a contingent of gloriously uniformed Indian
troops waiting for them on a spread of unmarked golden sand.
Grizel felt a thrill of sheer romance at the sight of their escort, led
by a flashing-eyed young fellow in a scarlet turban. He approached
them on a prancing Arab stallion, made it rear into the air with its
hooves flashing above their heads, then leapt to the ground where
he greeted her father on bended knee.

A meal had been prepared which they were to eat sitting amidst
the ruins of an old Portuguese fort on the headland. Their guide
told them they should rest there until the evening when he and his
men would accompany them in their carriage to the next stopping

point. They viewed the magnificent spread of food with delight and afterwards sheltered within the thick walls of a crumbling tower which shielded them from the blast of the sun.

There were beds ready for them to rest upon during the afternoon but Macalpine was so excited and enthusiastic about the trip that he decided to ignore their guide's instructions. 'It's not too hot to travel. All this nonsense about sleeping half the afternoon annoys me. People here are much too lazy. We'll go on at once and reach the next point in good time.'

Not even the obvious reluctance of their escort dissuaded him and they set out beneath a blazing sun which grew hotter and hotter as they penetrated inland, across an enormous plain of rice fields baked into clay-like hardness by the intensity of the heat.

The passengers in the carriage lay back in their seats, sweat pouring from their bodies, in such discomfort that death seemed a preferable option. No carefully angled parasols, no waving fans manipulated by servants, could cool them. By the time they reached the bungalow where they were to spend the night, Grizel and her mother were on the point of collapse. Even Macalpine was ready to concede that ignoring the instructions had been a mistake.

At the bungalow, further careful preparations had been made for them. Another gloriously attired messenger arrived to explain that they were to undertake the last leg of the journey up the twisting mountain road to Mahabaleshwar in palankeens because the way was too narrow and twisting for carriages.

Their cavalcade set out in the early morning with the curvetting horses of the escort looking like illustrations from a Persian manuscript. Their harness and trappings were multi-coloured and rich with gold braid, rosettes, tassels and scarlet cords; the clothes of the riders were pristine white with scarlet and gold sashes and huge magenta turbans set with plumes in front. In the middle of this glorious crowd three wan-faced Europeans travelled in deep cushioned palankeens with rattan cane sides to allow the free passage of air. Surrounded by all the glory of the escort, they felt like dowdy mice.

Grizel wanted to see everything. The sliding panels of her palankeen were left open so that she could gaze out in wonderment. They passed deep gullies, so thickly forested that from above they looked like cushions of green velvet. She saw the course of waterfalls where only a trickle of water was flowing now but which in the rainy season would gush with cataracts, and admired the variety of trees that clustered close to the path. From their branches exotic blossoms drifted down on to the roof of her palankeen. Native women and children came out of clearings to watch the procession pass by. Though Grizel smiled at them, only the children smiled back, eyes dancing with delight and white teeth flashing. The women remained mute and expressionless.

Sometimes the cavalcade passed holy men stalking along completely naked. Their tangled hair grew down below their shoulders and they wore necklaces of huge beads that looked like small skulls. In their hands they carried long staffs like Highlanders' crooks but instead of a carved horn on top, their sticks were surmounted by a trident, the symbol of Neptune and of Shiva.

This journey made Grizel feel that at last she was seeing the real India. It was as if a magnificently illustrated book had been opened and she was being granted a fleeting glimpse of the treasures it contained. While she was carried along in the swaying palankeen, she fell deeply in love with the strange country to which Fate had brought her.

For Grizel, Mahabaleshwar – the name meant All Powerful God – was almost as magical a place as Glen Fada.

Lansdowne Lodge, the grandly named bungalow that they rented for their sojourn in the village, was a miniature and rougher version of The Retreat in Bombay but its view was even more magnificent because it stood on a rocky point of hill, teetering on the edge of an abyss. When Grizel leaned over the verandah rail she felt like an eagle staring down, down, for a giddying distance to the baking plain four thousand feet below.

Even Lady Macalpine appreciated Mahabaleshwar. In the cool of the evening, wrapped in a long fringed Kashmiri shawl, she accompanied her daughter and husband on a stroll through the village bazaar where goods were laid out in colourful heaps on the ground – strawberries in tightly woven cane baskets; tomatoes; pyramids of oranges; piles of dried lentils and rice; bales of brilliant sari cloth; native medicines that looked like bundles of dried twigs; household goods, tin buckets and elegant earthenware pots for carrying water.

This tranquil place entranced and delighted Grizel. The good looks that had faded during the stifling Bombay months were restored to her. All her worries over her father's intrigues, even the disappointment about Colonel Brown, seemed less painful as she rode bridle paths beneath close-crowding trees or paused at

viewing points where lush banks of ferns mingled with the carpet
of wild flowers at her feet. She went out every morning while the
dew still glistened on the grass. She felt quite safe accompanied by
a syce who rode at her back, his head wrapped against the chill in a
thick woollen scarf.

On the fourth morning, they did not follow their usual path. The
syce, who spoke no English, pointed in the opposite direction and
said something that sounded urgent. She peered in the direction he
was indicating and could see a narrow path, almost overgrown with
flowering bushes, snaking off into deep woodland.

'Do you want me to go that way today?' she asked in English.
The syce pointed again and smiled reassuringly. Grizel urged her
horse on to the path which seemed little used. As she rode along,
branches of the scrubby trees whipped painfully into her face.
Behind her came the syce on his pony, pressing on, driving her
forward. Where to? She gazed around at the encroaching trees and
a tremor of panic seized her.

I've been foolish. I shouldn't have come here, she told herself,
reminded of Louisa's terrors. She turned nervously in the saddle
but the syce was still smiling and pointing ahead. They had not yet
reached their destination, it seemed.

For another ten minutes, the path went on twisting and twining
its narrow way, half in darkness from the creepers that looped over
the branches above her head. When Grizel was on the point of
galloping past her guardian and retracing her route, a huge black
stone building loomed up before her. It had a domed stone roof
and walls streaked with green lichen. Two statues of massive
crouching bulls were set on plinths at the small entrance door
which was approached by a flight of shallow steps. Grizel saw it
was a native temple.

The syce drew rein in a clearing before the building, put a hand
to his mouth and gave a high-pitched cry. The hairs on the back
of Grizel's neck bristled with terror. She was really afraid now for
she had no idea where she was, and knew that if she screamed no
one would come to her assistance. She gripped her riding crop
determinedly, ready to slash it across the face of anyone who
approached her.

She heard the sound of a horse crashing through undergrowth
ahead and, as she stared fearfully, caught a flash of scarlet and gold.
A soldier in the East India Company's brilliant uniform rode out of
the shadows on a tall grey horse and reined in beside her.

'Good morning, Miss Macalpine,' said Colonel Henry Brown, 'I was afraid that the syce wouldn't manage to persuade you to come. This is a very holy place. Hardly any Europeans know about it.'

He dismounted from his horse and held her stirrup.

'Did you tell him to bring me here?' she quavered as she slid down from her mount.

'Yes. I wanted to speak to you without fear of any interruptions. Grizel, I'm sorry about what happened in Bombay. It was only afterwards that I realised you might have misinterpreted my actions.'

'Not at all!' she bristled. 'What was there to misinterpret? You were acting for your friend Malcolm, and made that very clear.' For a long time he gazed at her without speaking. Grizel glanced aside, foolishly convinced he could read her mind. 'You did misinterpret things,' he said. 'I didn't meet you every day to press Malcolm's case. I met you for my own sake.'

She stalked ahead of him to the temple steps where the two bulls watched from slanted carved eyes. The syce was nowhere to be seen.

'And is it for your own sake that you've had me brought here today?'

Henry Brown nodded. He followed her and put a hand on her chin, turning her face up towards his. 'Your eyes are so very blue,' he murmured. 'A lovely colour, like the sea.'

She was still angry at the surprise he had sprung, having her brought to him like this, but her legs felt very feeble and she had to sit down on one of the plinths. Brown drew back from her again, seeming to regret his familiarity, and became more formal. 'Let me show you the temple. It's a very special place.'

With a courtly gesture he held out his arm and she rose to take it. Together they walked into the temple courtyard where there was a huge stone tank of water, all green on the top with water weed. In a corner stood the statue of another bull. This one had its mouth wide open and from it poured a glittering cascade of liquid that ran off into the jungle through a carefully laid water channel.

Leading her to the edge of the temple terrace, the Colonel pointed out the same stream tumbling to join a river that snaked over the brown plain below.

'Krishna, the sacred river, and this is its source,' he said.

Chattering monkeys ceased their games on the temple walls and sat solemnly watching as Grizel raised her face to his and they kissed for the first time.

When she found out that the bazaar's official name was Malcolm Peth, Lady Macalpine lost her pleasure in Mahabaleshwar. 'This place is given over to the man – his name's everywhere! My maid told me yesterday that the local people's cure for fever is to call out "Malcolm, Malcolm, Malcolm" three times over the sufferer. Did you ever hear such nonsense?' she asked her daughter.

Governor Malcolm, whose patronage had given the hill station its popularity with the residents of Bombay, was the local hero, as great a favourite with the native people as they were with him. He had laid the road to their village from Satara and for several years made his summer headquarters at Mahabaleshwar. One of the favourite viewing points was named after his daughter Kate.

When the Macalpines settled into Lansdowne Lodge, the community was eagerly awaiting Malcolm's arrival for he always came when the torrid heat of April held the plains in its grip. Grizel feared that it would take some organizing for her father and Malcolm not to bump into each other in such a tiny place.

Brown's courtship was continuing at a headlong pace now that he had managed to convince her he was not only interested in her on Malcolm's behalf. Each morning they rode out together in the dawn, and in the afternoon he called on her at Lansdowne Lodge. Now that they had discovered their true feelings for each other, they were anxious for a resolution to the Ramchandra affair for their own sake.

'If your father and Malcolm could only talk quietly together, without outside influences coming to bear, it would all be over in half an hour,' Henry said.

By 'outside influences' Grizel knew he meant her mother who actively stoked the fires of her father's resentment.

Unfortunately Lady Macalpine's campaign was greatly aided during their stay at Mahabaleshwar by an article in a Bengal newspaper, sent on by John, which quoted letters between Malcolm and the Court of Directors in London. The senior Macalpines were vociferous in their indignation when they saw a reference in one of Malcolm's letters complaining about 'quibbling, quill pushing lawyers'. He had written that he wanted amenable replacements to be sent out for Chambers and West so that Macalpine could be restrained, 'like a wild elephant between two tame ones'.

'A wild elephant! Imagine calling you a wild elephant,' cried Lady Macalpine. 'And him only the son of a Dumfriesshire tenant farmer! He's jealous of your position in life, that's why he's doing this, that's why he's allowed those insulting letters to be published.'

Her husband believed what she said. He had earlier lobbied his contacts in London for promotion to the position of Chief Justice of Bombay but those hopes were dashed when a missive in his mail bag told him the appointee was a Malcolm man and one much younger than himself. He had been deliberately slighted.

The Governor's nickname was 'Boy' and Grizel asked Colonel Brown the reason for it. 'Was it because he was only thirteen when he came out to India?' she wanted to know.

'Only partly. When the Directors interviewed him, they thought he was too young to come out because he was such a skinny little thing but they changed their minds when he was asked, "What would you do if you met Hyder Ali, young man?" and Malcolm answered in that Scots voice of his, "I'd cut aff his heid!" Just like the Boy David.'

'I hope he doesn't try these tactics on my father,' she said with a laugh.

'No, he won't. He's anxious for a reconciliation. In fact, he's written a note to your father about that newspaper article. Will you give it to him when he's able to sit down quietly and read it alone? I'll come tomorrow afternoon to talk things over with him.'

'What things?' she teased.

'The note, of course! All right then, us as well. I'm going to ask your father for your hand in marriage. I think we'd make a good pair, don't you?'

Grizel had resolved to accept him from the moment he kissed her. Henry was no longer young at forty-one but Grizel, though she'd kept her looks, would not see thirty again – a great age to have reached before marrying. But Henry made her feel young again. Her heart beat faster when he stood by her side and her sleep was broken by tantalising thoughts of love. . . .

Later that evening, Sir Peter John took Malcolm's note from her and scanned the words quickly before slipping it into his pocket.

'Consider it well, Father,' she whispered, glad to see that he was in a mood to be receptive to the olive branch the Governor was extending. In the next room, Lady Macalpine sat sewing. When her husband and daughter joined her, she spotted the piece of paper carelessly thrust into Sir Peter John's pocket. 'What's that? Is it a letter from John?'

'No, a note from Malcolm. He thinks we can settle this Ram-chandra affair – says it's been a misapprehension.'

Malcolm had tried to find a way out for both of them but he had not counted on Macalpine's wife. 'Misapprehension? Don't be silly! There was no misapprehension when he was calling you a mad elephant. He's manipulating you. He doesn't appreciate how much work you've done since you came here. Let me see that note.'

Assiduously she read double meanings into every word until she had roused her husband to fury again. The chance of reconciliation was lost and by the time evening fell they had decided between them that if Malcolm did not yield every point and make a public apology, Macalpine would keep the court closed. He might even resign his position as a judge.

Grizel was appalled at this. She could not believe that her mother would be so stupid as to encourage her father in his foolhardiness. 'You can't go home,' she reminded them, 'there are still too many debts outstanding.'

'We'll go to Calcutta,' announced her father, 'I can practise at the Bar there. There's plenty of work. Men without any legal qualifications at all are making fortunes as barristers.'

Grizel decided that the moment had come to break her own news. She could not wait for the Colonel to break it for them.

'I won't be with you in Bengal,' she announced, and her father's face clouded. He had guessed there was something afoot with Brown but had always dismissed the possibility of Grizel's leaving home to marry after so many years of spinsterhood. Now it seemed there was a real danger of losing her and Sir Peter John grew still and silent.

'And where will you be?' her mother taunted.

'I'm thinking of marrying.'

Lady Macalpine laughed. 'Don't tell me you're going to throw yourself away on that scheming soldier, that low-born fellow who came out here as a cadet?'

'He's not low-born! His brother owns an estate in Ireland, and he comes from as good a family as you, Mother.'

'He's just making use of you,' her mother sneered, 'plotting with Malcolm against your own father – and you can't see it! Anyway, I don't understand this craze for marrying. Other people have daughters who stay with them – why can't I?'

Grizel remembered how Anne had withstood the storm when she had announced her marriage plans and now she copied her sister's method, hardening her heart and saying: 'You prevented my marriage to Tom Falconer. You will not do the same again.'

In this testing time Grizel found unexpected reserves of courage to carry her through. There were no divided feelings, no doubts, no pull of old loyalties. Although she had not expected such a turn in her fortunes, she had found the man she wanted and bitter memories of her unhappiness over Tom strengthened her resolve.

'I will never find a husband like Colonel Brown again. I'm marrying him whether you like it or not. The announcement will be made tomorrow.'

She composed her face and left her parents to accustom themselves to the prospect – Lady Macalpine with tears and protestations; Sir Peter John in suffering silence.

Grizel was sorry to cause her father pain, but realist enough to see that to remain at home, the spinster daughter ever at the beck and call of her parents, would cause her infinitely more.

Besides, Henry and she had so much in common. They could talk easily to each other, sharing the same outlook on many things. She prized his polished manners, well-bred appearance and calm temperament. He was not Tom Falconer but the fierce flare of that earlier attraction was in the past now. Colonel Henry Brown was to be her bright new future.

Chapter Fourteen

To GRIZEL'S SURPRISE, her newfound resolution had her parents on the run. Her mother, with her desperate need always to present a gracious social front, could not allow the rift inside their home to become common knowledge. No matter how she raged and lashed Grizel with her bitter tongue behind closed doors, she was as reserved and ladylike as ever when they went abroad.

Next morning, reunited for their early morning ride, Grizel and the Colonel met Governor Malcolm. He beamed at the sight of them, riding alongside Grizel and engaging her in conversation with real warmth and friendliness. It was obvious that he was not going to hold his trouble with her father against her and she was particularly pleased when he congratulated her on her choice of a husband.

'Brown's a good fellow, and an excellent soldier,' he said. 'There's word that his Regiment is to be moved from Satara next year. Just let me know where you'd like to go. Ask around and find out which posting would suit you – tell me and it'll be arranged.' Before they parted he took her hand and said, 'I'm sorry about the trouble with your father. I only wish he'd had you for a wife instead of a daughter then things would not have reached this sad pass.'

Grizel and her Colonel wanted to be married in the little stone church that stood on a hill in the middle of Mahabaleshwar. Its cool interior reminded Grizel of the little church at Glen Fada.

'It would be perfect to marry here,' she sighed, taking Henry's hand.

He bent to kiss her cheek. 'Then we shall,' he promised. 'We'll arrange the ceremony for next week. I've waited a long time to find you. Why wait any longer?'

When the news of their plans was broken to Lady Macalpine, she had hysterics, throwing herself back in her chair and going blue in the face with fury.

'You can't do that. What will people say? No, you'll go down to Bombay and marry in the cathedral as your sister did. It's the very least you owe us in this whole unsuitable affair.'

Peter John Macalpine rushed to soothe his wife and plead with Grizel, 'If you must marry this man who's our enemy, at least do it in the proper way. Your mother's right. Though it would be far cheaper for me and a lot less trouble for your poor mother, the ceremony must be held in Bombay.'

'You're only concerned for the look of things! If we marry here, Henry won't need to travel back to Bombay. His duties at Satara have been neglected these past few weeks and he's anxious to return there. Can't you consider him in all this?'

Her mother returned to the offensive. 'He's only thinking of himself, not about you and your standing in society. He should consider the scandal – but perhaps he's not concerned how *you* will feel, being branded a hasty bride!'

This barb struck home but the reason Grizel gave in and agreed to marry in Bombay was because she saw that her parents no longer objected to the marriage itself. Having won that victory, she was prepared to give in over where it took place.

'Such trouble for me! Marriage doesn't seem to have done any of my daughters much good,' Lady Macalpine's litany of complaint continued, day after day. It was partly quietened by news of the death of the Colonel's brother in Ireland. Grizel would not now be marrying just a Company soldier but a man who owned over four hundred acres of rich farmland on the borders of Armagh, yielding a good return in rents.

As the day of her marriage drew near, Grizel's mind returned over and over again to thoughts of Glen Fada. This step she was taking would cut her off from her beloved home. If she and Henry ever left India it would be for Ireland and not to return to her old home in the valley of the rushing, turbulent, eternally fascinating Spey. Her future visits to Glen Fada would be as a stranger, an outsider. The thought stung but all doubts were swept aside each time she saw her husband-to-be. The better she came to know Henry, the more astounded she was by this change in her luck. Every time they met she found out something new and fascinating about him. His knowledge of India and his manly self-possession delighted her. To spend the rest of her life learning from him seemed the most delightful prospect in the world.

Over the years Grizel had developed the ability to turn a deaf ear to her mother's malice. It stood her in good stead now. She went calmly through the preparations for her marriage – the drawing up of a wedding contract; the preparation of a trousseau. The latter was not an arduous task. Her father had stiffly informed her that she would oblige him by not asking for new clothes as his funds would shortly be depleted by resignation from the judgeship. His gift to her on the wedding morning was a purse containing twenty gold moidores, the equivalent of forty guineas English money. Her Uncle Edmund had already sent her ten and Colonel Brown presented her with another thirty as his wedding present. Even stripped of the dowry and trousseau she might once have expected, Grizel felt truly rich for the first time in her life.

The wedding gift from her mother was a riding habit Lady Macalpine had ordered for herself before they left London but had never worn, and a magnificent hat of wired gauze and ostrich feathers that had been shipped out from home just before the ceremony. It did not suit the mother so was passed on to her daughter. Fortunately it became her magnificently.

The most unexpected present was announced in a letter from Sir John Malcolm.

My Dear Miss Macalpine,

During our rides in Mahabaleshwar, I noticed that you were nervous of horses and since your new life is taking you to a place where you will have to do a great deal of horse back riding, I'm sending a mount called Donegal to await your arrival at Satara. He is my wedding present to you because he is the best mannered, most sagacious horse I've ever owned. I've told him to carry you with care. . . .

The wedding day was the first of June, a day of heat and stifling humidity. Beneath waving punkah curtains that only stirred the clammy air about like soup above their heads, Grizel Macalpine and Henry Percival Brown stood up together before the altar of St Thomas' Church and became man and wife.

When she had time to reflect upon it afterwards, Grizel realised with regret that she retained little or no memory of her wedding day. Throughout it all she was in a daze, moving to order, speaking the right words, but doing everything automatically. She retained only brief pictures in her mind of her own figure in white muslin and lace, with pearls around her neck and flowers in her hair, standing beside the groom. Henry, with his leonine head and brilliant uniform, overtopped everyone else present. Grizel recollected that her father and mother wept in their pew as if she were being taken away to be buried instead of beginning a new life, but all she remembered of the wedding party, which was of short duration, was the searing heat that stifled appetites and stained everyone's clothes with disfiguring patches of sweat.

Yet it was a cordial and happy occasion. After the ceremony, even Grizel's parents seemed to enjoy themselves and when the time came for the newly married pair to leave, their embraces were heartfelt and genuine. Doctor Forbes, the groom's man, was at his most brilliant and kept shaking his friend's hand, congratulating him on having won the finest girl in Bombay Island as his wife.

Finally, without really understanding how the hours had slipped away, Grizel found herself being escorted to the dockside and boarding a felucca with her groom.

The ship slipped like a wraith between the green islands while the couple stood waving at the little party on the quayside. Then they clasped hands, each staring with astonished delight into the other's face. After all the trouble, all the uncertainties, they were truly man and wife.

The sailors had tactfully removed themselves to stand on the high prow, well out of earshot. Henry Brown raised one of Grizel's hands to his mouth and kissed it. Her heart began thumping fast as he stepped closer to her and gently unpinned her elaborately upswept hair. 'My darling,' he said urgently, and pulled her to him, burying his face in the tumbling golden mass of her curls.

Wordlessly, they turned from the rail and walked across the deck. Under the striped awning, a laden table stood ready for them but they did not pause beside it. Henry grabbed a bottle of champagne by the neck and Grizel, with a smile, lifted two long-stemmed wine glasses. Then they climbed down into the dark shuttered cabin where a silk-covered bed awaited them.

Henry closed the cabin door with a careful hand then turned to gather his bride in his arms. She yielded to him with a sinuous movement, like a slender tree bending in a breeze. He kissed her, she closed her eyes, and when he paused to look closely at her she gently pulled his head down again.

'Don't stop,' she told him. 'Don't ever stop.'

Marriage suited Grizel. There was the nightly joy of sharing her husband's bed, and day to day pleasures such as the journey they were forced to make back to Satara. They cantered along with a glamorous escort of native Lancers who sat easily in their saddles, loose white trouser legs flapping in the breeze and long staffs holding proudly waving banners above their turbanned heads. The romance of it all made Grizel feel like a princess from an *Arabian Nights* story. Liberated by loving and being loved, she rode in the middle of the cavalcade with her golden hair freed from its pins and flowing down her back. She looked so much the part of the fairy-tale heroine that parties of natives they passed on the road stared after her with open astonishment.

In Satara at last, Grizel arrived with infinite gratitude at the door of their first home. It was the usual Indian up-country bungalow – two reception rooms, bedrooms with bathrooms at the back, and a verandah running all the way round – but to her it was magical, the first of the many homes she hoped to share with Henry, wherever his postings took them.

The greatest glory was the garden, a miniature paradise of flowers and shrubs that seemed intent on climbing over the verandah rails into their drawing room. There were sweet-scented roses and gardenia bushes with glossy leaves and startling white rosette-like flowers that gave off a heavenly perfume. A huge gulmohur tree stood guardian over their gate and branches of pink and purple bougainvillaea arched across the front of the house like protective arms.

The English community at Satara numbered less than twenty, including wives and children, and accepted any newcomer with alacrity. Dinner parties and card games were held every week, the wives visited each other during the day and delighted in the arrival of visitors from the world outside. To a person fond of smart society it would have been a cruel exile but station life suited Grizel well. She was by now deeply in love with her husband and their secluded domesticity suited both of them very well. They liked nothing better than to sit together on their verandah in the evenings with him smoking his sweet-smelling cheroots and Grizel mending his large and tattered wardrobe which showed sad need of a woman's care.

'I cannot imagine how you managed before you married me,' she joked as she stitched away, and Henry laughed and leant over to kiss her.

'I can't imagine either, my dear.'

She made friends, avoided the few people she disliked, never gossiped and amused herself in the garden or with household chores. At night, while the moon silvered their bedroom and owls hooted in the garden, they made love and Grizel was awakened to the pleasures of a sensuality which she had never imagined existed within her.

Sir John Malcolm was as good as his word and Donegal, complete with a fine bridle and a side saddle made of the softest suede, was waiting for Mrs Brown when she arrived at Satara.

'He's enormous, I'll never manage him,' she gasped in horror as she looked at the horse which stood almost seventeen hands high.

'No, no, mem sahib, this is very peaceful horse, very kind,' assured the syce. As if to confirm the groom's words, Donegal bent his head down towards her and whinnied softly through his nostrils. Grizel put up a hand and stroked the velvet muzzle, feeling the lips nuzzling softly at her palm, looking for a tit bit. Donegal, despite his size, was a pet, a gentle giant with a sagacity honed by twelve years as a parade horse. He could have been trusted to carry a little child.

The rains were late that year and did not break until the end of June. When the heavens darkened and thunder announced the arrival of the deluge, everyone greeted the change in the weather with delight though it meant that the paths of the station turned to red mud and sheets of rain confined the women to their homes. In July a three-year-old child belonging to a young lieutenant and his wife died of the ague, and Grizel faced her first serious duty as the Colonel's wife, commiserating with the stricken parents and daily going in a mud-splashed palankeen to sit with the sorrowing mother.

The death made her acutely aware again of the hidden face of India, conscious that behind the beauty and the colour there was a secret world that Europeans had every reason to fear, a world of illness, disease, death and sinister gods; a world that was commonplace to the servants and native soldiers but was closed to the British people who ruled over them.

She lay awake in bed at night listening to the frantic drumming that would suddenly start up in the native lines. What were they doing? Were they propitiating a scowling goddess with severed heads in her many hands, or celebrating something that none of the British inhabitants could understand?

But with the return of good weather, the lightening of the skies until they were once again unmarked cerulean blue, all Grizel's morbid thoughts disappeared. Once again she was able to ride out on Donegal, or sit in the arbour the Colonel had built for her beneath the flowering trees, reading her books and making sketches of the people passing by beyond her garden gate.

There was a great deal of activity in the station during October because the regiment was planning a sixty-mile journey to Poona to take part in a Grand Military Parade there. Sadly, Malcolm had announced his intention of retiring from his post. Though he would not actually depart for another year, he was spending the intervening time touring the districts and taking his farewell of the widespread lands of the Bombay Presidency. The display would mark the region's farewell to him. As well as the Company regiments, it was said that various friendly rajahs intended sending their irregular regiments to the Review, as tribute to Boy Malcolm.

'Some of them make a wonderful sight, especially the ones that have British or French officers. You must remember to look out for them, my dear,' the Colonel told his wife.

'Then you're not going to leave me behind? You'll take me with you,' she said in delight, for the prospect of a visit to Poona thrilled her. Henry was just as keen for her to go. He wanted to show off his golden-haired bride to all his old bachelor friends.

Preparations for the trip took all Grizel's time and attention for several weeks. Among the clothes she packed for herself was her mother's fine hat. There had been one or two occasions in the past months when she had suggested giving it an airing but her husband, who hated ostentatious display or making oneself conspicuous, was reluctant to see her wearing it on the station.

'It might seem too flamboyant to the other wives. They never wear anything but the simplest bonnets. Perhaps it would be more tactful not to wear it here,' he'd told her.

If it's not suitable wear for Satara, at least I'll be able to sport it in Poona, thought Grizel, lovingly stroking the curled feathers as she put on the hat and posed before her mirror. To her delight it seemed to become her even more now that she was a married woman.

Nevertheless, afraid that the Colonel might not want the hat to appear in Poona either, she hid the hatbox beneath a pile of bundles and smuggled it aboard the baggage waggon when they set out.

They arrived to find Poona *en fête*. Regiments from all around the West coast of India – from Surat, Baroda, Ahmednager, Ratnagiri and Sholapur, as well as Satara – were there to show themselves off. Each was intent on outshining the others and the amount of cleaning, polishing, grooming and drilling that went on before Parade Day was ferocious.

The officers and their wives were accommodated in a village of white tents on the field adjacent to the parade ground. Each was luxuriously equipped and hung nabob-style with carpets on the walls as well as on the floors. Grizel took a great delight in living in a tent, for it was much cooler than a house. The breeze fluttered its canvas walls, and the sound of the regimental pennant, flapping to and fro on the top of the tent pole, made a regular lullaby for sleepers below.

They spent the few days before the Parade paying calls, meeting old friends and hearing all the gossip. Grizel's father had recently announced his intention of resigning his judgeship but, though she knew it was the talk of the Presidency, everyone tactfully avoided the subject in her presence. Her parents were still in Bombay, packing up their possessions and preparing for the journey to Bengal. She hoped to persuade her husband to take her down to the city to see them before they left in December.

On Parade day, Henry rose from his cot and donned his finest uniform by the light of dawn. Grizel rose later and dressed with care, stifling a feeling of guilt because she had not warned her husband in advance that she intended to wear the wonderful hat. As she skewered it to her hair with long pins, she knew she looked ravishing in it – like the Duchess of Gordon, she decided as she peered into her glass.

Donegal was to carry her to the Parade ground where she would sit on the side-lines among the other officers' wives. When he was led up to the tent door, she thought he looked fit to carry a king. The old horse's coat shone like satin, his kind eye was lambent and brown as he gazed at her, and she could see he at least approved of her hat because as her head passed his muzzle he lifted his lip in an attempt to taste one of the trailing feathers. His flanks were heaving slightly with excitement but he stood rock still while the syce took Grizel's boot in his hand and helped her into the saddle.

Grizel gathered up the reins and urged him gently forward with her heel but Donegal needed no telling where to go. He turned smoothly and set off at a steady pace towards the teeming Parade ground. Ahead of her she saw the mounted figures of her women friends and trotted on to catch up with them. Her horse performed perfectly, falling in line courteously, and when they reached their appointed places at the side of the grassy arena he stood like a gentleman, head erect, neck flexed and mouthing gently on his bit.

Grizel's fears disappeared and she relaxed in the saddle, receiving with delight the compliments of her friends on her magnificent hat. Her hands lay loosely on the saddle pommel as she strained her eyes for the first sight of her husband and his men. In the distance, she heard martial music and a line of bandsmen appeared, marching across the field towards Malcolm's viewing platform.

The sun was glinting on their brass instruments and at the sound of the band, Donegal lifted his head and stared ahead. She felt him quiver slightly beneath her. He's enjoying the music, she thought and patted him gently on the neck, speaking soothingly to him.

The lines of bandsmen seemed to stretch for miles and were followed by an escort of officers from the Bombay Infantry in scarlet and gold, riding on prancing chargers. Behind them came a mounted bugler who, as he passed the watching women, put his silver bugle to his lips and sounded a rousing note.

It was too much for Donegal. His days as a parade horse were not forgotten. With one bound he leaped forward and galloped into the middle of the ground while Grizel clung with one hand to her saddle pommel and used the other to hold her hat on her head. Donegal knew where he was going. He recognised old friends in the leading contingent of riders, the Governor's escort. He kept on galloping until he caught up with them and then fell into a curvetting canter. Donegal and Grizel had joined the Grand Parade!

Frantically she pulled on the reins but her mount had the bit between his teeth and ignored her as completely as if she were an ant sitting on his back. Grizel's face was scarlet with mortification while they cantered round and round with the soldiers, who were having a hard time concealing their laughter. She was shedding impotent tears when a figure on a small pony dashed up alongside Donegal and a hand reached out to pull on his bridle. Without any fuss her saviour led Grizel and her disappointed horse to the side of the Parade ground. 'Are you all right?' a concerned voice asked. 'I'm afraid he gave you a bit of a scare.'

She had been trembling but the voice magically soothed and reassured her. She adjusted her hat which had slipped over her eyes
and collected herself enough to reply: 'I'm perfectly all right now.
Thank you very much for stopping him. He's an old parade horse,
you see, and he must have thought. . . .'

There was laughter in her rescuer's voice as he wheeled about to
rejoin the parade, calling over his shoulder as he replied, 'Oh, he's
a canny old horse right enough. Keep a firm hold on him now in
case he tries the same trick again.' And then the man on the pony
cantered off and was swallowed up in a group waiting to take their
place at the back of the parade.

When Grizel alighted from the saddle her legs were trembling so
much that she couldn't stand. A woman friend rushed forward to
help her into a chair where she sat in abject shame till the Parade
was finished. She was so shaken that she did not see her husband
and his men ride past and certainly could not have recognised the
man who rescued her.

Fortunately her interruption of the Parade was taken in good part.
Even Henry was laughing when he came up after the ceremonial
salute was over and put an arm around her shoulders. 'At least
you made a great appearance out there,' he told her, eyeing the
hat.

As they walked across to the largest marquee, she asked, 'Who
rescued me? I must thank him.'

He frowned. 'I didn't see it myself but one of the other fellows said
he was from a native state – Aundh or Jhat, I think. Both Rajahs are
here with their contingents. I'll make enquiries.'

A huge crowd had collected around Governor Malcolm inside the
tent but when he saw Grizel come in, he made his way towards her,
full of apologies for Donegal.

'I never dreamt he'd be so carried away as to carry *you* away!' he
laughed.

'Poor Donegal. When he heard the bugle, his blood was up.'
Grizel could laugh now that her fright had subsided.

'It was a good thing Aundh's fellow stopped him, though.
Donegal hadn't a chance against that pony. They're like needles –
flash in and out so quickly. They're hard to fight against, too, I can
tell you!'

'Where is Aundh's man? I didn't thank him at the time,' Grizel
asked, looking around.

'He's over there with his Rajah. I'll take you across to them.'

The Rajah of Aundh was impressive, a pale, moon-faced man with pursed lips and flashing, kohl-rimmed eyes beneath a turban of blue silk. He sparkled with jewellery. In his turban was a huge golden lion's head studded with precious stones that flashed and sparkled in the sunlight. The hand he extended to Malcolm was heavy with rings – he even wore them on his thumbs – and in each sparkled a spectacular gem stone. The lobes of his ears were pulled down with pendant pearls like pigeon eggs and on his brocade tunic he wore a breastplate of gold in the shape of a peacock inlaid with fine enamels and more rubies, diamonds and emeralds. He wore enough finery to keep a London jeweller in stock for years.

Behind him stood a stocky figure dressed in native costume. He was European though that was not at first obvious because he was deeply tanned and his head was wrapped in a purple and yellow striped turban with a white egret's feather in front fastened by a diamond pin. He wore the same style of long fitted coat and loose baggy trousers as his ruler but his jewellery was plainer. A heavy linked gold chain hung around his neck and a scimitar with a jewelled hilt swung from an inlaid scabbard at his side.

There was amusement in his eyes when he looked at Grizel. She flushed when she caught his gaze but collected herself sufficiently to deliver her thanks in a gracious way.

'It was a pleasure. You never were much at ease with horses, were you, Miss Grizel?'

He spoke in a Highland voice, the sibilants soft and almost caressing, the voice of the people of the Spey valley.

'You're from Glen Fada?' she asked in wonder.

'Not exactly, but I know it well. Don't you remember the week-ends when my father and I used to come down from Duthil? I led you out on the old white pony.'

At the memory, tears rose in her eyes and she was overwhelmed with memories of her old home.

'Murdo Grant, the minister's son!' she gasped. 'Oh, Murdo, imagine meeting you here. My sisters and I always wondered what happened to you.'

'And isn't it fitting that I should be the one to lead you around on a horse again!'

Grizel wanted to talk to him, to find out what had happened since they last met, but his Rajah was anxious to set out on the return journey to Aundh immediately. Murdo smiled regretfully at her as he said goodbye and told her, 'I could hardly believe my eyes when

I saw you in the middle of the parade ground. I knew you at once Miss Grizel – it's the hair. You always had such bonny hair.'

At this point, while she and Murdo were still saying goodbye, Henry arrived and took his wife by the arm. With only a cursory nod to the Rajah and Murdo, he said, 'Come along, my dear, there's someone I want you to meet.'

She was angered by his rudeness and when they were alone, charged him with it. 'You shouldn't have dragged me away like that. The man I was speaking to was the son of our old minister at Glen Fada. He's a childhood friend.'

'You almost fell into his arms!' Henry said stiffly. 'It was most unseemly. Besides, those mercenary fellows are hardly gentlemen. Most of them have Indian wives and half caste children. That fellow's as bad as the rest, I'll be bound.'

The Colonel was obviously jealous!

Grizel placated him with kisses and by saying, 'You needn't worry, I'll never see him again.' But often, when she was alone, she wondered about Murdo Grant and wished she could have talked with him longer. The sight of him had wakened memories long dormant and in her dreams during the nights after the Parade, she was carried back to happy familiar scenes from her childhood.

When they returned to Satara, there was a worrying change in Henry. He appeared sunk in depression and his usual energy left him. This continued for several days before the explanation became apparent. In the middle of the night he was stricken with a severe attack of asthma, a malady which he told Grizel had assailed him intermittently during his time in the East.

She had never seen anyone suffering from an attack before and was driven to distraction by his strangled gasping and painful struggle for breath. She sat beside him till daylight, holding his hand and suffering every spasm with him. When the doctor arrived, he prescribed that the patient inhale the fumes of burning datura leaves. Fortunately Grizel's servant knew where the plant was growing in the forest so a party was sent out to collect some.

The smell of the burning leaves was pungent. Even though she did not inhale it directly, Grizel felt her head swim as she went in and out of the bedroom to tend the invalid.

When she complained to the doctor of giddiness and light-headedness, he explained, 'Don't worry, it's natural. Datura's a strong narcotic. It has a very relaxing effect even on people who only catch a little of the fumes.'

The cure was effective and the Colonel's illness subsided sufficiently to allow him to sleep but, to their great disappointment, on the next day his asthma returned even more severely. Grizel feared that he might die, so agonising was the attack. He lay gasping, his lips blue, and his hands gripping hers tightly as each spasm seized him.

'It's the worst he's ever been. There must be something upsetting him. I can't understand it. Did anything happen to derange his constitution in Poona?' the doctor asked, but she shook her head. Surely jealousy over Murdo wouldn't bring on asthma?

The coughing and choking went on day after day without cease until it was decided that the patient had to be moved from Satara. 'Take him down to Bombay for a change of air and see how he settles there,' suggested the station doctor.

Once again their bags and trunks were packed; once again the horses and carts loaded up. A two hundred mile journey lay before them and again they climbed into their palankeens – the Colonel lying flat in his. Grizel was sorry to leave Satara where she had been happy but her mind was too full of anxiety for her husband to dwell on regrets.

Fortunately the weather was cool and travelling was not arduous. When they reached the coast three days later Henry was so much better that he was able to walk on to the boat like a new man. The respite was only fleeting however. On the second night of their stay in The Retreat, which was also being packed up for removal to Calcutta, the asthma returned with such force that a messenger had to be sent off in the early hours of the morning for Dr Forbes.

'I'm afraid it isn't good news, my dear,' he said privately to Grizel after his examination of the patient.

She stared back at him, eyes wide with fear. 'He's not going to die, is he?'

The doctor shook his head. 'Oh no, not that – provided he leaves India. But he'll have to go home, I'm afraid. His health has been undermined by this climate. He's been here without a break for over twenty years, remember. The stomach is totally disarranged and so is the liver. Asthma is only part of the problem.'

'But he's always been so strong!' she exclaimed. 'Perhaps I could take him to the Nilgiris Hills, plenty of people have their health restored there,' she suggested, unable to grasp the seriousness of the doctor's warning.

Forbes shook his head. 'I don't think that would be sufficient, but of course you must seek a second opinion. I'm sure the verdict will be the same as mine though – your husband must leave India if he's to live another year.'

The second opinion was the same as Dr Forbes' and so was a third. There was no alternative. Though neither of them wished to return home, they knew they would have to. Henry continued to gasp and fight for breath, the least exertion exhausting him. At the same time, Grizel's mother and father were in turmoil because of the move to Calcutta. She was at her wits' end trying to cope with her own problems and the demands of her parents when, like a saviour, John arrived from Calcutta.

The change in him was astonishing. He was even taller than before and as thin as ever but his assurance and self-confidence were those of a man far older than his years. He had done very well in the Bengal service and had been appointed to a position in the Governor's entourage. Everyone who knew him said that a brilliant future lay ahead for young Macalpine. Men many years his senior treated him with respect.

Because Henry was so ill, it was John who took over the arrangements for the Browns' trip home. He also managed to bring some order into his father's chaotic affairs. Though Peter John went bustling around, issuing orders and then countermanding them, it was John who ensured that everything proceeded smoothly. When it seemed that the senior Macalpines were going to leave Bombay under a cloud of official disapproval, John went privately to call on Sir John Malcolm and managed to smooth over the long standing dispute. It was impossible to make his father apologise but his son did it for him and ensured that the departure from Bombay could be made with some vestige of dignity.

As she watched her brother in operation, Grizel was filled with admiration. Mr and Mrs MacIvor's faith in him had proved well placed. Her old regrets that she had not been the heir to Glen Fada gave way to a wish that John had been born in Patrick's place. He shared her devotion to their Highland domain and when they talked of it, asked her, 'If it's possible, try to take a trip home. I feel so far away from Glen Fada, and often wonder how things are there. I've been sending money back to make sure it doesn't go to rack and ruin.' From John that short statement was of more value than an hour-long oration from her father or Patrick.

'I don't think I'll manage a visit,' she told him regretfully. 'Henry's so ill and his estate is in Ireland. We'll probably go straight there.'

John nodded. Unlike the other men in the family, he knew when protest would be unavailing. 'Then tell Anne that as soon as I'm able, I'll send more money. She's keeping an eye on Glen Fada, you know.'

'What about Patrick? What's he been doing?' Grizel asked. For some time the arrival of the eldest son in Bombay had been expected but his departure from home kept on being postponed.

John grimaced slightly. 'Haven't you heard the latest news? He's involved in a romance at the moment. Father told me Patrick wrote to say he wants to marry Sally Siddons.'

This item of news had been kept from Grizel by her parents. Her eyes widened in astonishment. She remembered pretty little Sally well. During their stay at Picardy Place she had been in their house every day and Patrick had been taken with her then. Her mother, the actress, was the star of Edinburgh's Theatre Royal.

'She's a very pretty girl,' said Grizel tentatively, but it was obvious that an alliance with the Siddons family was not to John's taste.

'I don't approve of stage people. They're not respectable,' he said firmly.

'Mrs Siddons was always very respectable. There was never a word of scandal about her,' Grizel protested, but her brother's Presbyterian intransigence had not weakened with the years. 'They're not godly,' he announced.

Later, when she asked her father about Sally, he made a face. 'Poor Patrick! Mrs Siddons is making a great fuss about her daughter wanting to marry him. She doesn't think he's good enough.'

Grizel laughed. Now she knew why Patrick's marriage problems had been kept secret. Her snobbish mother must have been shocked by the actress's effrontery – disdaining a Macalpine indeed!

'Will they be very poor if they marry?' she asked.

Her father shook his head. 'No, that's not the problem. Sally has a fortune of ten thousand pounds. That's what worries her mother, apparently. She thinks Patrick rather careless about money.'

'Rather careless' was a kind way of describing Patrick's financial incompetence, thought his sister, but it was obvious that the ten thousand pound dowry had sweetened their parents towards this alliance with the family of an actress.

As poor Henry continued to wheeze and choke through the days and nights, Grizel herself began feeling strangely unwell but she thrust the trouble out of her mind. For a long time she had yearned to have a child, longed to hold a baby in her arms, but now that it seemed a possibility she hoped against hope that her symptoms were not those of pregnancy. The time was not right. Her husband needed her full attention and would need it for a long time to come.

But her face grew paler, her luxuriant hair hung lank and lifeless, her energy disappeared. Every morning she rose at dawn to retch into a basin that the maid left beside her bed. Food nauseated her, the heat oppressed her more than it had ever done, and as the days passed, she knew with certainty that she was having a child.

When she confided her fears to Dr Forbes, he nodded sympathetically and said, 'I thought there was something and feared it might be that. But you're not to worry, my dear. God be praised I'm sailing on the same ship as you and your husband. I've been long enough out here and my wife and I have been communicating recently. Thanks to you, we've mended our old differences.'

Grizel was delighted. 'Oh, that is good news. I'm so glad you're going to be together again.'

Forbes smiled. 'When you brought me that piece of paper, I wrote to her and we've been making our arrangements ever since. It's an added happiness that I shall be able to care for you and my friend Brown on the journey.'

On her last day in Bombay, Grizel sought out her father to say her farewells to him privately. They held each other's hands and wept openly.

'I'm sorry ever to have done anything that caused you pain, my darling. You've always held a special place in my heart. Perhaps I've not been able to show that properly but I want you to know how much I prize you,' Peter John told her brokenly. 'It's my mistakes have brought us to this pass. Things should have been so different for you. Sometimes I think about what might have been and regret burns me like a fire.'

It was the first sign he had ever given of wishing his life had been different, and Grizel longed to reassure him. 'Don't say that, Father. I've been happy in India. If I'd never come here I wouldn't have met Henry. He's a good man, and our life from now on will be contented, I'm sure of it.'

Her father looked relieved. 'I often worried about who you'd marry after – after the Edinburgh business. I'm glad to know you've found happiness, my dear.'

They had never talked about Tom, never mentioned him by name, but in the last hours with her father, Grizel was determined to solve the mystery of his animosity towards the Falconer family.

'Why were you so against my marrying Tom, Father?'

His gaze slid away from hers and he looked away, muttering, 'It was an old feud between his father and myself. We were boys together, just silly lads. Falconer took something in bad part.'

'What happened?' Grizel pressed him.

'It was over a girl. I was eighteen and so was he, the age when you fall in love for the first time and think you'll never fall in love again.'

She nodded. She had been eighteen when she fell in love with Tom and remembered the pain.

'We were both taken with the same girl. She was a coquette, I'm afraid, and played us off against each other. We fought about her, and it finished our friendship.'

With a feeling of numb disbelief she asked, 'What happened then?'

'Nothing. I told you – we fought. I gave him a black eye and he bloodied my nose. I thought it was broken, in fact.' He fingered the bridge of his nose as he spoke.

The words stuck in her throat but she had to say them. 'Do you mean to tell me that you and Tom's father broke our attachment because of a schoolboy quarrel?'

Her father puffed up with annoyance. 'I was very hurt at the time. The girl meant a lot to me.'

Grizel's face was grim as she struck home. 'What was her name?'

Peter John thought for a bit. 'Do you know,' he said finally, 'I can't remember.'

She rose from her chair, unable to utter the words of bitter recrimination which threatened to choke her. To think that she had undergone such agony, given up her lover at her father's request, for something so trivial!

In the doorway, she paused and looked back. Her father stared helplessly after her. Under the grey hair and wrinkles, his face was that of a puzzled boy. It was as if their roles had been reversed. With adult eyes, Grizel saw through Peter John's public face to the lonely, bereft child still visible beneath the pride and bombast. He'd be lonelier still when she sailed away. In all likelihood they would never meet again.

Running back, she knelt beside his chair and kissed his hand.

'Don't worry any more about it, Father. I found Henry and I'm happy with him now – that's all that matters.'

Embarkation on board the *Centaur* was one of the most painful experiences of her life, rivalling in sorrow even the last day at Glen Fada. She embraced her parents and John over and over again, even feeling genuine regret at leaving Jane.

She's my mother after all, I'll miss her, Grizel thought as she stood on the deck waving goodbye to the three figures on the dock as the huge ship tacked about and sailed out of the bay. Her sorrow was compounded by the fact that she was leaving India. The country held so many mysteries and such exotic appeal that if she'd lived there until she was a hundred years old she'd still only begin to understand it. Now she would never get the chance. She stood, her ashen-faced husband leaning on her arm, and gazed at the purple outline of the hills far away upon the eastern horizon. Beyond lay Satara and lovely little Mahabaleshwar with its dark temple; palaces and pleasure gardens, delights she would never see again.

The *Centaur's* voyage was interrupted by calls at Ceylon and at the Cape of Good Hope. After that, they made good time until they were well up the coast of Africa where they ran into a fearsome storm. Huge waves tossed the ship around like a nutshell, throwing the furniture about in the cabins and breaking almost every piece of china on board. Grizel was severely sea sick for a whole week, but in spite of her own nausea, continued to rise and tend her ailing husband for his asthma had not responded as well to the benefits of a sea voyage as the doctors had hoped.

Her hopes rose at Ceylon where Henry was well enough to go ashore and enjoy a few days in the island of Serendipity but were disappointed as soon as they were under sail again. When the storm struck, Henry was so ill that he found it impossible any longer to share a bed with his wife and insisted on a hammock being strung up for him from their cabin roof.

It was uncomfortable inside the cabin not only because of his hammock but because Henry continued constantly to inhale datura fumes in an effort to ease his breathing. The fumes stifled her, and when Henry was under their influence it was impossible to talk to him because he lay semi-conscious, barely able to mutter replies to anything she said. Grizel crumpled the dry datura leaves in her hand and remembered how she had seen them growing in the forest near Satara. Their tall trumpet-like flowers had smelt so sweet and looked so majestic but now she thought them flowers of evil omen.

In his periods of lucidity, Henry worried about her. 'Are you taking enough rest? Are you feeling better? I've told Forbes to take care of you – if anything happens to me.'

She was anguished but hid her fear. 'Nothing's going to happen to you, my darling. When we reach England, you'll be strong and well again. You'll have to run around with our baby. I'm sure it's going to be a boy. You must teach him to ride and shoot.'

The thought pleased him. 'A son! He'll like Armagh. There's good hunting and fishing there.' Then he put out his hand and touched Grizel's cheek lightly. 'And if the baby's a daughter, I hope she looks like you, my lovely one.'

As they sailed nearer and nearer to colder climes, Henry's illness intensified until he was unable even to lie down in his hammock. He spent his days and nights sitting upright in a chair, wrapped in a blanket and fighting for breath. She had managed to buy a goat at the Cape and it was quartered below decks where she went to milk it every day, feeding her husband on gruel and custards made from its milk. In spite of her care, however, his tall frame was becoming emaciated and the haunted look in his eyes as he strained to breathe normally was deeply distressing to her.

'Tell me the truth,' she pleaded with Dr Forbes one day when he came out of their cabin looking very grave, 'is he going to die?'

'There's cause for concern,' he admitted. 'If this voyage doesn't end soon, I fear his constitution won't sustain him through it. I told you his system's badly broken down after all those years in India. The suffering he's enduring now is putting a great strain on his heart.'

Grizel wrung her hands. 'Is there anything I can do? How can I help him? Just tell me. I'll do anything.'

The doctor looked at her swollen figure. 'You should be resting and building up your own strength. It's only to be hoped we reach England before your baby is born.'

The child was due in May and the ship's arrival scheduled for late March but the storm delayed them badly and they were still wallowing about in heavy seas, making little headway, when February ended.

Grizel's anguish increased as each day passed with little progress made. Her greatest support, apart from the continued attention of

Dr Forbes, was a giddy young woman called Mrs Gainsborough
who had greatly entertained the passengers by her amatory adventures during the earlier part of the voyage. She was a pretty flirt
who conducted one affair after another with the male passengers
and ship's officers until she was the cause of much dissension
and even a projected duel, only prevented by the Captain's firm
intervention. He threatened to put the protagonists in chains if they
tried anything so stupid. At first Grizel had been scandalised by the
young woman's wanton behaviour but when she needed a friend, it
was Mrs Gainsborough who proved to be the most attentive of the
women passengers. Every day she came to sit by Grizel, soothing
her worries about the Colonel and helping her stitch away at baby
clothes.

One stormy morning Mrs Gainsborough was on deck when Grizel
came out of the cabin and leaned her head wearily against the door
post. From inside could be heard Henry's terrible wheezing for
breath. Grizel looked up with drawn face and saw her friend beside
her.

'My dear, you look so tired. Have you been awake all night?
Come into my cabin and I'll give you a glass of Madeira.'

Shakily Grizel went into Mrs Gainsborough's prettily furnished
cabin and sipped gratefully at the wine. Although she had not
yet eaten any breakfast, it settled her stomach and made her feel
stronger.

'Don't lose heart,' her friend said comfortingly. 'The voyage
won't last forever.'

'But he's so ill. He can't draw a breath without agony now.
Everything seems to make him worse – even the datura has lost its
effect and we haven't got much of it left anyway. I know Dr Forbes
is at his wits' end but he tries to hide it.'

Mrs Gainsborough put an arm around her. 'Your husband's a
strong man. He'll recover. The captain said this morning that there's
better weather ahead. He's always better in fine weather, isn't he?'

'Fine weather, foul weather, it doesn't seem to matter any more.
He's bad in both.' Grizel held her head in her hands and wept. Henry
was so short tempered in his illness for pain and distress had robbed
him of his easy-going manner. When she tried to spoon some milk
into him that morning he'd swept her hand away but, poor man,
how could she blame him? With every painful gasp of breath he
drew, she felt a spasm of sympathetic suffering.

'His lips were blue this morning, bright blue. He doesn't seem to know me any more.' Her friend held her hand and let her weep. Even Dr Forbes had stopped trying to reassure her. He seemed to be preparing her for something but she would not allow herself to consider what it might be. As she sat in her friend's cabin, the door opened and the doctor's head peered round. 'Grizel,' he whispered, 'I think he needs you now, my dear. Come with me.'

Heart thudding, she went out followed by an anxious Mrs Gainsborough, who waited outside while they went inside the cabin and shut the door.

Henry was propped up in the chair, a blanket round his shoulders and his face a frightening livid colour. When he saw Grizel come in, he reached out a hand towards her but no words could come. She knelt at his knee and held his hand in hers. With a superhuman effort, she did not weep but composed herself and said, 'Is there anything I can do for you, my dearest?'

Very slowly he shook his head. He gazed at her for a long time and there was love in his eyes, but he only managed to croak out three words, 'Stay with me.'

Behind her, Dr Forbes was desperately hurrying to prepare a draught for the invalid. He passed it to Grizel who attempted to pour some between her husband's parted lips. He could not swallow. Each rasping breath pierced her like a stab to the heart.

Without warning, Henry pitched forward. The doctor hurried forward to support his long, pitifully thin body. When her husband's head was raised Grizel saw that his eyes were open and staring, his face the same heliotrope colour that had terrified her when she viewed old Geordie Dunn's corpse. The cabin was quite silent, she realised, before a woman's voice rang out. 'Oh no, no! It can't be true. Speak to me, my darling. I love you. I love you. You can't leave me.' It was her own voice.

Dr Forbes tried to lead her out but she wouldn't go, weeping hysterically, all restraint gone.

'Help her. He's dead,' the doctor told Mrs Gainsborough in a sharp voice.

Her friend tried to lead Grizel away but she fought free and dashed back into her own cabin, calling, 'I must speak to him. I'll help him. I can't leave him now.' Kneeling by the chair in which her husband's body was slumped, she took his cold hands in hers and chafed them frantically. 'Don't die, my dear, don't die. There's so much for us to do.'

But he was beyond listening, beyond helping. Grim-faced, the doctor came up beside her and laid a white cloth over Henry's face.

Even in a winding sheet of stiff tarpaulin, Henry Brown's body looked dignified and military – long, straight and spare with the outline of the stiff chin sticking up bravely under the dark green covering. His widow stood on deck beside the bier, her shawl wrapped tight against the wind and her face white and set. When people offered their sympathy, she thanked them gravely and with composure. The hard won veneer of self-possession was once again intact.

During the twenty-four hours since her husband's death, she had ranged through a gamut of emotions from disbelief to dry-eyed despair until she reached her present condition of numb misery. Dr Forbes and the Captain had been kind. Very tactfully they asked her about the body.

'Do you want to take him home? He could be sealed up in a cask of spirits for burial in England,' they suggested. She shook her head. It seemed too undignified to store Henry inside a cask. 'No, I'd rather bury him at sea.'

The Captain was to read the burial service. It worried Grizel that there were no flowers for the committal. Then she remembered that she had packed some artificial flowers beside her fine hat and dug out the box to find them. When she opened it, there was nothing inside but a heap of dust. Her glorious hat, the one she'd worn to the Ceremonial Parade, had been eaten up by India's voracious insects. Her maid could not have sealed the box properly.

Mrs Gainsborough brought out some pretty artificial flowers and a tribute was made out of them. Grizel stood with the little bouquet in her hand as the solemn words of the committal service rang out over the steel grey ocean.

When the Captain intoned: 'I now commit you to the deep,' she lifted her head and watched in silent anguish while a trio of stout seamen lifted the body of her husband in their arms and launched him over the side. There was a splash. For a few moments the tarpaulin-shrouded corpse floated on the surface, and then, very slowly, it sank from view. Grizel stared at the rippling water, imagining her dear Henry sinking down into the world below, among fish and forests of waving seaweed, caverns of coral and caves of pearl. She stepped forward and threw the flowers after him. They did not sink but bobbed around marking the spot where he had disappeared. Grizel and Doctor Forbes stood in the stern of the ship, staring after them, until Henry's last resting place was lost for ever.

For days afterwards Grizel lay in her cabin, staring dry-eyed at the wooden ceiling, while her heart cried out in agony. The pain of losing her husband was compounded by anxiety for her unborn child. As she mourned, it heaved and turned within her like a dolphin. She put her hands on her distended belly and felt the movement. Then her tears broke in a torrent. She was crying for the child as well as for herself. She had lost a husband, her baby a father. 'What is going to happen to us?' she cried aloud.

It was another two weeks before they sighted England. For all that time Grizel stayed in her cabin. Mrs Gainsborough tried to divert her but Grizel could think only about her loss.

'Why, why, why . . .?' she asked over and over again. There was only one possible answer. 'I'm unlucky. I've been unlucky since the day I was born. My mother was right to blame me for the carriage accident. I cause terrible things to happen. I must be cursed.'

'Oh, my dear!' cried her friend. 'Of course you're not. You're still young. In time you will recover from this terrible blow, and there's your baby to think of.'

'My poor baby . . . how will I manage to care for it? Oh God, what will happen to us both?'

By the time the voyage ended, however, Grizel seemed to have regained her composure. She stopped speaking about her fears and instead hugged them inside like a secret. To her friends on board, she appeared to accept her husband's death in an exemplary manner – bravely, without making a fuss – and was greatly admired by men and women alike.

They docked at Portsmouth. From the deck she could see the inn where she had given her brother Patrick money to pay the bill. Everything looked the same; only Grizel had changed.

In the boat which ferried them to the shore, she sat with her hands knotted in her lap and prayed, 'Let there be someone to meet me. Let there be someone to help me.' The news of her husband's death could not yet be known to anyone on land and she feared that the delay in their arrival meant that no one would be waiting for her.

Dr Forbes guessed how anxious she must be and leaned forward to pat her hand. 'I'll make sure you reach your friends before I leave you, my dear.' She smiled at him gratefully. He had been a great source of comfort and reassurance during the terrible voyage. Without him she could not have born her terrible burden.

He assisted her up the steep stone steps to the jetty for she was heavy now and it was difficult to move. He guided her towards the Customs House and then the door was opened. Grizel was immediately seized in a pair of loving arms and a familiar voice cried over her, 'My dear, my darling! We've just heard the news from one of the seamen. Oh, Grizel, you're not to worry, we'll look after you.'

Through blurred vision she saw the face of her sister Anne, red-eyed with weeping but still beautiful, still young. Behind her stood the ramrod little figure of her grey-haired husband, dear Bingham. Grizel held out a hand to each of them, took a step forwards and fainted dead away.

Chapter Fifteen

FROM TIME TO TIME she drifted into consciousness and heard her sister's anxious voice. 'Grizel, Grizel, speak to me.'

She wanted to say something. Words formed in her mind but before she could speak them, she drifted off again. As if in a dream, she was dimly aware that someone was feeding her, propping her up and gently spooning gruel between her lips. Sometimes competent hands smoothed her pillows or changed her nightclothes; she allowed herself to be handled like a baby.

One morning, she opened her eyes and blinked as sunshine fell full on her face. She slowly gazed around, taking in the luxurious fittings of the bedroom: the heavy framed pictures on the walls, tapestry bed curtains and gleaming furniture. She had never seen any of it before.

'Where am I?' she whispered, and the woman sitting by her bed jumped up and pulled a bell pull by the fireplace. 'Where am I?' whispered Grizel again but before she could be told, the bedroom door opened and Anne rushed in.

She bent over her sister and cried out in relief, 'You're awake! You've come back to us. You gave us such a fright.'

Grizel was at Anne's home, Gideon Park, and her friends were around her. One by one they came tip-toeing into the bedroom, their concern plain to see for though she had regained consciousness, she was still very ill.

Apart from her sister, the person that she was most grateful to see was dear Annie Arkwright who had shared the nursing with Anne. In her delirium Grizel had dreamt she was with Annie, and, when she came back to awareness, was glad to realise it was true.

'We're going to take care of you,' said Annie in her reassuring voice and, comforted, Grizel drifted off into calm, restorative sleep.

Aunt Lizzie came, bearing gifts, as did Louisa and Grainger. They were living in a cottage in the grounds of Gideon Park. Domesticity and the arrival of another child had made Louisa fatter than before and she seemed a good deal older than Anne. Her sweet-tempered husband, however, remained attentive, devoting his entire time to diverting and amusing her.

Though Grizel was not able to talk much, Anne sat by the bed and told her snippets of news. She was full of information about Patrick. He had not been able to tear himself away from England apparently, but had married Sally – whereupon they had both embarked on a spending spree and between them were fast dissipating her dowry!

He came to see Grizel and brought his sweetly pretty wife with him. Neither of them knew what to say to the sick woman propped up in bed, and stood by her in embarrassed silence hunting for topics of conversation that would not remind her of Henry's death or the approaching birth of her child.

'They make a handsome enough couple but they're like a pair of children. Sally's money's only given to them in small amounts but Patrick swells it by living on credit. It's all going to catch up with him one day,' Anne told Grizel.

Her brother's inept stewardship of Glen Fada had caused her final disillusionment with him. Patrick had shown himself only interested in collecting the rent from the Duke of Bedford, who now leased the house. He never went to the Highlands and did nothing to plough funds back into the estate. The huge burden of debt was undiminished.

In spite of her apparent indifference on the day of her wedding, Anne was in fact devoted to her home. She wrote voluminous letters to John on estate affairs and sent money to Glen Fada for the support of poor pensioners. Lister and Beatie were still in her service, and, though their shortcomings had grown more noticeable with age, she would never dispense with them.

During her illness, Grizel was treated like a piece of delicate porcelain. Though they did not openly show their concern, Anne and Annie were deeply anxious about her.

'She mustn't be worried about the least thing,' said a determined Annie. 'There's no problem about money,' she reassured Grizel.

'My husband's making arrangements about Brown's pension, and he's written to the agent in Ireland about the estate.'

'Have you any idea if that estate of Colonel Brown's was entailed?' she asked Colonel Bingham privately.

He shook his head. 'As far as I know, Henry Brown inherited from his brother. I don't know whether *he* was married or not.'

'If it is entailed, let's hope that Grizel has a son, and that her father drew her up a watertight marriage contract,' said the ever practical Annie, but allowed no hint of her concern to show before her friend.

Neither Anne nor Annie had ever carried a child and they hovered over Grizel like anxious angels. Sometimes Anne would lay a hand on her sister's heaving belly and ask in wonder, 'What does it feel like? Is it sore?'

Grizel shook her head. 'No, it's not sore. I feel as if I know this child already. We've come through so much together.'

Anne's face was sad. 'I've never been able to have children. Perhaps it's just as well. Bingham says it wouldn't be right for a child to have a father old enough to be its grandfather and I agree really but sometimes. . . .'

She and Annie looked at each other in silence till Annie said briskly, 'Let me give you some beef tea, Grizel. You've got to be strong when the baby comes.'

Elizabeth Anne Brown was born in the early hours of a May morning while sunlight glinted on the diamond drops of dew silvering the lawns and harebells clustered in drifts beneath the trees. In spite of the trauma that Grizel had undergone while carrying the child, the birth was easy. After sleeping soundly for most of the day she woke in the evening to find her beautiful new daughter in a lace-trimmed cradle by her bedside.

When the baby was placed in her arms, a feeling of exultant wonder filled her heart at the perfection of this new person she had brought into the world. She slowly uncurled the tightly folded little fists and admired each shell pink finger. She played with the baby's tiny toes and gasped in wonder at its cherubic face and thatch of blonde hair. As she gazed in adoration, her daughter opened her mouth to give an enormous yawn. A rush of emotion filled Grizel's heart, a first intimation that one day she might regain a measure of happiness.

The summer was fine but Grizel's strength was slow in returning. Confined to bed still, she delighted in her child who was in the care

of a devoted wet nurse and the whole of Gideon Park revolved
round the baby and its mother.

Annie Arkwright came down frequently from her northern home
and for a while managed to conceal from Grizel that there was a great
deal of trouble about her husband's estate. It was General Arkwright
who finally broke the bad news. He came and sat beside Grizel's bed
and put a sheaf of papers on her knees, saying, 'I have to explain
how you're placed financially, my dear. Do you feel strong enough
to listen?'

She nodded. 'I'm getting better every day, but I have been
wondering what's going to happen in the future. I can't live here
with Anne for ever.'

The General's face was grave as he began, 'Unfortunately your
husband's estate was entailed. His elder brother was married with
a daughter so she couldn't claim the property on her father's death.
That's why your husband inherited it. If you'd had a son, he would
follow automatically as the owner but, because your child is a girl,
the nearest heir is a twenty-one-year-old nephew, son of Brown's
next brother. He's being rather difficult, I'm afraid.'

A rush of anxiety filled her. 'In what way?' she asked.

'His lawyer says the elder brother's daughter is already receiving
an income from the estate and therefore it can't meet any claim from
you. All it yields is rents and Irish farmers are apparently very slow
at paying up. The place is in debt and the new owner gets the benefit
of little more than a crumbling old castle. My lawyer thinks we can
force him to give you a stipend but it will be very small. There's no
likelihood of your receiving any worthwhile income from Ireland.
You could go to law over the matter but the case would drag on
for years and you might be worse off in the end than you are at the
moment.'

'But my father drew up a marriage contract for me!'

'Oh, the contract's good enough, but if there's no money to
pay you, even the best drafted clauses mean nothing. You'll have
Brown's Company pension though.'

'How much is that?' she whispered through dry lips.

'Less than four hundred a year, I'm afraid. It's enough to keep you
and the child but not in any style.'

Grizel's health had been improving until this news was broken to
her. Afterwards, though she did not show it outwardly, she took
to worrying in secret, going over and over her situation during the

night as she lay sleepless in bed.

'Where can I go? Perhaps I could find work. . .I might be a lady's companion. But what about Elizabeth? I can't leave her, she's all I have.'

When she tried to broach the subject with Anne, her sister was brisk. 'You can stay here for as long as you like – for ever, if necessary. You don't have to worry about finding anywhere else to live. The pension is money enough if you stay with us. I enjoy your company, and little Eliza is like our own child. Bingham and I adore her.'

It was true. They hung over Eliza's cot like worshippers. When the weather grew warm, Anne took her out each day in a basket-work cart drawn by a grizzled old donkey. But Grizel longed for independence. She wanted her own home. She dared not think about her dead husband or the brilliant sun of India for the pain the memories brought in their wake was almost insupportable. Gideon Park was beautiful but she found it too douce, too pallid for her taste, preferring the savagery of the Highlands or the exotic impact of the East.

Anne was concerned when Grizel became weak again. She tried everything to cheer her and restore her energy. 'What about taking a trip North? We could stay with the MacIvors at Carn Dearg,' she suggested, but Grizel shook her head.

'I'm not strong enough yet. Besides, I don't want to go back and see Glen Fada being lived in by other people. I don't want to be a stranger in the valley.'

It was better to cherish memories than to return and find that enchantment had faded. Her treasure, her jewel, her most engrossing interest was the baby. She loved the child with a passion that was moving to see.

When the summer failed to revive her, a succession of doctors were called in. They advised all kinds of treatments but nothing helped. One morning when Grizel awoke, she found that she was unable to stand. Her legs failed her as if they were stuffed with wool. Furious at her own weakness, she tried to stand up over and over again but each time collapsed in a heap on the floor. Anne, distraught, summoned more doctors who pronounced themselves baffled.

The most eminent physician of the time came down from London to look at Grizel but could say only, 'The poor woman's physically and emotionally exhausted. She wants to walk right enough but her nerves won't let her. She'll have to rest until the paralysis disappears.'

'Will it?' asked Anne.

He pursed his lips. 'Sometimes it does. Sometimes it doesn't. It's impossible to tell.'

When spring came it was difficult for Grizel to move at all. She spent her days on the sofa in Anne's drawing room, carried up and down stairs by the devoted Lister who treated her as gently as if she was a china doll.

'I want to walk so much. I must walk,' she said through gritted teeth. At night she lay beneath her embroidered bedcover and willed her legs to come back to life, willed her body to respond to her mind's prompting, but still the strange paralysis held her in its grip.

Her chief delight was to watch her daughter growing into a chubby, happy child with the reddish-gold hair of both her parents. She walked very early and loved to linger beside her mother, stroking her hand and making cooing sounds of endearment.

Louisa had less patience with the invalid than Anne. 'You're indulging yourself! You could walk perfectly well if you wanted to. You can't go on lying here. Get up and get back into life,' she said crossly one day.

That night Grizel tried to get out of bed. She levered her feet to the floor and, using the bedstead, pulled herself slowly upright. When she did not fall, she reached out for a small chest of drawers that stood on the other side of the room and miraculously managed to reach it, only to collapse while trying to return to the bed. She lay unable to drag herself further and was found half frozen in the morning by the maid.

When scolded for foolhardiness, she said, 'But I want to walk. I'm not pretending. I've never been a weak-willed woman. I must make myself walk again.'

News of her paralysis was sent to Dr Forbes, now happily reunited with his wife and living in Scotland. He came to Gideon and set about encouraging Grizel to exercise her useless legs. While she flexed and unflexed the limp muscles, she talked to him about the things that filled her mind, all the pent up worries and secret thoughts flowing out in a torrent. She found herself talking freely about things she thought long forgotten: about growing up in Glen Fada, the coach crash that had killed her grandmother, the constant jibes and accusations that she was sly and jealous of Anne.

'But it wasn't true. I was so shy and frightened that I was afraid to show how I felt. I was never jealous of Anne. I've always loved her dearly.'

Dr Forbes' face was grave as he listened. He knew Lady Macalpine well and had formed his own opinions about her character but said nothing to interrupt Grizel, only nodded and made encouraging noises. He realised that if she was ever to recover her health, she must first free her spirit.

She told him of her slow disillusionment with her father; of her shame at having to negotiate with people to whom he owed money and the years she had felt herself responsible for him rather than the other way around. Still, for all his faults, she loved and missed him.

She talked about Tom Falconer and as she relived that episode, a weight was lifted from her heart. It truly did not hurt any longer. She talked about her puritanical brother John and about Patrick. Words flowed from her like the water that came gushing from Loch an Eilean to carry away the felled logs from the forest.

Eventually the doctor encouraged her to talk about India and Henry. When she relived the death of her husband, she wept sorely. 'I wish I could turn the clock back. I wish I'd never agreed to our leaving India. I feel so guilty. If Henry had stayed, perhaps he wouldn't have died.' Then she turned harried eyes on Forbes and whispered, 'Most of all I worry in case I killed him.'

Shocked by this, the doctor protested, 'That's nonsense! Of course you didn't kill him.'

But Grizel's eyes held his as she said, 'He'd never had asthma so badly as he did after we married. It was as if I made it worse.'

Forbes grasped her hand in reassurance. 'Brown had asthma for years. It had already injured his heart. Perhaps I should've advised him against marrying at all but I thought you'd make such a splendid couple. I admired you both.'

'Are you sure I didn't make him worse?'

'Of course not. You must put that notion out of your head,' he told her. 'You're still a young woman and you've a daughter to care for now. There's a future ahead for you both. Try to remember that.'

His words encouraged her and she resumed her attempts to walk a few yards every day. As Anne watched her painful efforts, she longed to rush over and help but the doctor had said that Grizel must be left to find her own feet.

It was decided that she might benefit from a change of air so
Annie Arkwright arrived in a huge brougham with deep cushioned
seats and conveyed Grizel and Eliza away to Nottinghamshire. For
the first time since her return from India, Grizel's face looked less
drawn and her natural colour was returning. Annie reached out a
hand to tuck in a tendril of hair that escaped beneath the frill of
the lace widow's cap Grizel wore and said, 'You're looking better,
almost your old self, my dear.'

'I feel as if I've come through fire and been reborn.'

In spite of the improvement, she was still an invalid and her
strength was easily exhausted. After lunch every fine day she was
wheeled into a sheltered corner of the garden, tucked up beneath a
thick rug and left to sleep in peace. One afternoon she was wakened
by a voice softly speaking her name. 'Grizel – Grizel Macalpine.'

She thought she had dreamt it but when she looked up, found
herself gazing into two hazel eyes. A face was bending over hers.
Her gaze travelled slowly over the features; curving mouth, proud
nose and eyes with flecked golden lights in the irises. . . .

'Where's that turban?' she asked. 'It suited you very well.'

Murdo Grant leaned back on his heels and laughed. 'Did you like
it? I liked your fancy hat too. What are you doing lying in a wicker
chair like an invalid?'

She sat up straight. 'I'm resting. I've not been very well but I'm
better now. What on earth are you doing here?'

'I knew General Arkwright in Cawnpore. He keeps a sort of
clearing house for old India men who come back and don't know
where to go – he gives us advice.'

She was delighted to see him again. He evoked so many
memories.

'Let's go for a turn round the garden,' Murdo said, holding out
his hand. She was filled with indecision. Could she walk with him?
She had not gone more than a few steps at a time since arriving at
Annie's house but did not want Murdo to think her a feeble invalid.
She stood up, laying her hand on his arm. His muscles were strong
and firm as she leaned trustingly on him. She knew she wouldn't
fall when he was there.

They walked very slowly for a short distance before he seated
her beside a clipped yew hedge on the other side of the lawn. She
could not tell whether Murdo knew of her illness or not. He seemed
determined to divert her, accounting for himself in lively fashion.
'I came home because my Rajah died – poisoned, I suspect. There

wasn't much point in my staying with his successor, a wily fellow if ever there was one! I didn't want to end up with ground glass in my curry so I retired and went to Calcutta. But it wasn't like Aundh. I didn't like it, so I booked myself on a ship for home.

'Before I left I met your brother John. He told me your husband had died. I'm very sorry, Grizel. People tell me he was a good fellow and a fine soldier.'

She nodded without speaking then, out of the blue, flabbergasted him by asking: 'Did you have an Indian wife, Murdo?' She remembered Henry saying all the mercenaries married local women.

'Yes,' he said, looking sharply at her, 'but she died. Her name was Begum Sumroo.'

'Have you any children?'

He shook his head. 'My only son died with his mother when he was three. One of those relentless fevers. I was grief-stricken.'

'I'm sorry,' she said, and they sat silent for a while until he stood up again and extended a hand to her. She walked fearlessly, watching her feet in their soft slippers treading the moss-covered path. It felt like a miracle to be walking again and the triumph filled her mind to the exclusion of everything else. How wonderful to feel the possibility of life and energy returning!

'What is it about you? Every time we meet you lead me around,' she said to Murdo when they passed her invalid chair.

He laughed lightly as he replied, 'Perhaps that's my function in your life.'

Annie Arkwright woke her next morning with bad news. 'Wake up, my dear. Something terrible has happened.'

Grizel opened her eyes and gasped in fright. 'Not Eliza?' She sat up in bed, casting terrified glances around her room, but her fear subsided a little when she heard her daughter laughing in the nursery next door.

Annie was quick to reassure her. 'No, it's not that. I'm sorry I woke you so suddenly but it's Colonel Bingham. A messenger's come from Gideon. He's dead, poor thing. It was an apoplexy, quite unexpected.'

A letter arrived from the ever practical Anne telling Grizel to remain with Annie until the funeral was over. The same iron resolve that had carried her through her wedding sustained Anne through her bereavement. When she arrived at the Arkwrights' ten days later

she was bleak-faced but controlled, resolute and determined. Everything was decided by her alone without reference to anyone else.

'I'm giving up Gideon Park and returning to Edinburgh,' she
told Grizel. The city had always been a favourite with her and
throughout her marriage she'd kept up links with old friends there.
It held no ghosts for Anne as once it had for her sister. 'I'm buying
a house in Queen Street,' she continued. 'James Guild is handling
the business side for me. I've been left comfortably off because
my poor Bingham was careful with money and made some very
good investments. Then there's the estate and our stud – they'll sell
well. I've already told Louisa and Grainger and they're looking for
a small place in Hampshire but I want you to come with me, Grizel.
Will you, please?'

Her mind's eye was filled with pictures of Edinburgh, city of grey
stone. She saw again the craggy outline of the Old Town creeping
up the spine of rock towards the brooding castle. Clinging to its
skirts was the regular, orderly New Town with its leafy squares
surrounded by crescents of imposing houses. To her surprise she
found that the prospect of living there and meeting old friends again
appealed to her, now that the thought of meeting Tom no longer
filled her with dread. He was someone she had loved when she was
young, before she really started to live. The woman she was today
and the girl she had been then were very different.

As a rich widow, Anne Bingham quickly took up a premier position
in Edinburgh society. She always found it easy to make friends and
as soon as her period of deep mourning was over, the house she had
bought in Queen Street was filled with people taking tea, playing
cards or listening to music. Every day she went out driving and
paying calls on her numerous acquaintance.

Grizel usually stayed at home for her strength was still easily
sapped. An hour of company tired her out so much that she was
forced to spend the following day in bed. The doctors assured her
that she was mending but she was often depressed by the inability
of her body to cope with things that others took so easily in their
stride. It was still difficult to walk far and she dreaded a return of
the strange paralysis.

A frequent visitor to Anne's house was James Guild, son of their
father's lawyer, now successful in that field himself and still a bachelor. He often talked to Grizel about the library of books he bought
at the auction of the Glen Fada effects and once or twice, when she

recalled a particular volume, he lent it to her. She appreciated these kindnesses but they did not greatly increase her liking for him. He had an air about him, cool and self-satisfied, that prevented her from warming to him but her sister obviously enjoyed his company and, as the months passed, Grizel saw their interest in each other increase. It was not too cynical, she thought, to reason that Anne's fortune would increase her appeal to the canny minded Guild. Yet if the Bingham fortune was to be entrusted to anyone, it could not be in better hands. At least James Guild would see that it did not depreciate.

Once or twice they were paid a visit by Murdo Grant but James Guild and his friends made no secret of their distaste for him. An Indian mercenary soldier, whose father had been an out-at-elbows minister. Their interests – who was suing whom, which estate was gaining most by various bequests or careful investment – were equally devoid of appeal to Murdo and his visits usually ended with a private audience in Grizel's parlour where his stories about elephants and the Rajah of Aundh met a spellbound audience in Eliza.

'Why don't you go back to India?' Grizel asked him one day. 'You obviously love it very much.'

'I'm too old to start all over again.'

She was shocked by his reply. He'd seemed the pattern of strength and vigour to her and she'd thought his energy well-nigh inexhaustible for he was always dashing hither and yon on mysterious business.

'You can't be forty yet,' she said accusingly. 'My father was well into his fifties when he went to India for the first time.'

'Forty is old for a mercenary soldier,' Murdo said solemnly. 'Anyway, I've lost my taste for adventure. I'm looking for something different now.'

I'm thirty-six myself, a vast age, thought Grizel. She studied him closely. He'd been such a carrot-headed, freckle-faced boy but now the hair had toned down, the freckles disappeared, and he had the seasoned look of a man who had won through.

It struck her suddenly that Murdo was the sort of man that women were drawn to. Why had he not married again? she wondered.

When he did not return to the Queen Street house for many weeks, she was decidedly piqued. On Eliza's behalf, she told herself. The child so missed his stories of Aundh.

A cold wind was whistling along Queen Street, blowing the last
sere leaves off the trees that faced Anne's house, when Murdo finally
reappeared. He turned up wearing a huge travelling greatcoat with a
caped collar. As he held out his hands to the fire that burned brightly
in Grizel's sitting room, he said, 'You'll never guess where I've been
for this past six weeks.'

'Tartary,' she suggested in a joking tone.

'Not so far. I've been to the Spey, to Inverdruie and Kingussie
and Aviemore. I went to look at Glen Fada and walked around all
the places we used to visit.'

Her face clouded. The memory of the Highlands haunted her but
she still could not face a visit. Murdo did not appear to notice her
change of mood for he continued talking about his trip. 'I went to
Loch an Eilean where we used to go with that pony of yours. It was
lovely in the autumn sunlight. Nothing's changed, Grizel.'

'I have.'

'You'd be cured if you went back, you know,' he said solemnly.
'The mountains would see to that. The Highlands would heal you.
When I stood on the banks of the Spey, I felt the strength of the earth
beneath my boot soles. It was very strange.'

'The old earth magic,' she cried. 'My first nursemaid once told
me that all true Highlanders feel it. She said newborn babies are
given a spoonful of earth with their first feed. I think she must
have given some to me because I've felt it too, just the way you
described.'

He came over to her chair. 'Why not go back?' he urged her.
'There are so many places where you could live. Your brother
would give you a house on the estate.'

'I'm afraid to go back. I still remember the pain I felt when I
left. Perhaps it's best to remember it the way it was. They say the
Duke of Bedford's made a lot of changes to the house. Everything's
different, all the old people are dead or gone away – Betty's dead and
so's her husband and the piper and our old boatman. I don't want to
see the valley without them in it. I don't want to see the changes.'

'You want to go home, don't you?' she asked him. 'It's why
you've not returned to India, isn't it?'

His eyes were brooding as he replied, 'I love India. You know and
understand that because you loved it too, but it's not our country.
The way I feel about the Highland earth is the way Indian peasants
feel about their land. I sometimes used to see them lifting it up by

the handful and letting it drift through their fingers as if they were handling silk. I did the same thing at the side of Loch an Eilean and I knew what it meant.

'I don't go back to India because there are things for me to do here. Besides I'm a very rich man, Grizel. I made a fortune in the East. My Rajah was generous. It makes me laugh inside when I listen to Guild and his friends talking in thousands. I don't want to boast but I could buy them all up and still have change!'

She stared at him, amazed. It had never struck her that this son of the Duthil minister had become a nabob. She'd thought of him as a lad o'pairts because he retained his down to earth attitude along with his Highland accent, but now he was showing her his other side, the side that had made him a successful mercenary general.

She thought over what he had said during the weeks that followed and was disappointed to receive no further visit from him. Once again he seemed to have disappeared.

At Christmas time Anne announced, in characteristic take-it-or-leave-it fashion that she was to marry James Guild. 'And before our wedding, we're going to pay a visit to the Highlands. I want to show James our old domain,' she said. Grizel noted that her sister did not call this husband by his surname as she always had when referring to Bingham. Anne smiled at her warmly. 'We want you and Eliza to come with us. It's time she saw her mother's birthplace.'

The trip did not seem impossible this time, and Grizel asked, 'When do you plan to go?'

'In the spring, when the danger of snow is past. Then James and I will come back here and marry quietly. We don't want any fuss.'

Spring came early in 1835. By the first week of March, carpets of crocuses showed white, yellow and purple beneath the trees in Queen Street gardens. Banks of daffodils gleamed bright as James Guild's gleaming barouche took the high road heading for the Queen's Ferry. Grizel found she was enjoying the journey for the country looked beautiful in the pale sunlight. Lambs skipped about in the fields and the trees showed the first glimmerings of green.

In delight she pointed out the sights to her daughter and told stories about the places they passed on the way. At Inver, she remembered hearing Neil Gow play his fiddle; at Killiecrankie, she recounted the tale of the last stand of Bonnie Dundee; when they passed Blair Castle she told about Prince Charlie and the '45 rebellion, but when they crossed the fateful bridge she said nothing of the carriage accident that had killed her grandmother.

My poor mother, it was such a terrible thing to happen but why did she think I was to blame? I'd never be able to sustain such a feeling towards Eliza. Silently she hugged her daughter close as the horses' hooves clattered over the stone surface of the hump-backed bridge.

Their leisurely trip lasted four days. Eventually they drew up before the imposing portico of Carn Dearg. As she stared up at it Grizel felt that time had stood still for the house and its gardens seemed exactly the same as the last time she saw them. Only the two people who came rushing out to clasp the visitors in fond embraces had grown older. Mrs MacIvor's crow black hair was white and her husband looked shrivelled and bent but their delight at the girls' return made them leap around like children.

Next morning, Anne asked if a horse could be yoked to the MacIvors' light gig, then drew on her cloak, announcing, 'I'm going to drive down to Inverdruie. Put on your cloak and come with me, Grizel.'

But her sister hung back, heart fluttering wildly as she protested, 'You'd better go without me. I'd rather stay here.'

'Nonsense! You must come. You've got to see Glen Fada again. I haven't brought you all this way to duck it. You'll never be really well again until you do,' said Anne, obviously not prepared to brook any objections.

She half pushed Grizel up the carriage step and Eliza was lifted up to sit between the sisters. James Guild stayed behind to talk to his host about shooting. Grizel felt sure that her sister had deliberately left him out of the party so that they could go home alone.

The familiar road twisted along the river bank. Everything seemed unchanged – the same bits of broken fence posts, the same gnarled tree trunks, the same heaps of tumbled stones lying at the roadside. The last sad trip along that road with their mother, Louisa and Patrick came vividly to mind. Grizel held her daughter's hand tightly as the hill that backed Kinrara loomed up in front of them. On its top stood a monument to the memory of the Duke of Gordon who had died after the Macalpines left Glen Fada.

As they drove she saw Anne's eyes sliding towards her and knew that her reactions were being checked because the next sighting would be of Glen Fada itself. Grizel wanted to close her eyes but something drew them inexorably towards the far bank of the river.

There were the gleaming little lochans that flooded every winter; there were the banks of broom soon to be yellow with flowers and the lines of silver-trunked birch trees. The forest was thickening again with the passage of years. Through the scrub she caught a fleeting glimpse of Glen Fada church. Her heart started thudding wildly. It was coming closer. . . . Suddenly she saw the house itself – huge, bigger than she remembered, and pristine white, its paint and windows glistening in the sunshine. A new white-painted picket fence surrounded the spreading gardens. Filled with relief that the sight did not kill her with pain Grizel leaned forward in her seat to take a closer look.

Anne's hand fell on hers and her sister whispered, 'It looks well. I told you, it's in good hands.'

Their gig was manhandled on to the ferry at Inverdruie by men who remembered them and whose rugged, tanned faces split into smiles of genuine welcome. They crowded around the laird's lassies and poured out stories of what had happened in the valley since they went away.

'Your ferryman went to his grave wrapped in the plaid your mother put on his shoulders the day she left the house. He treasured it,' said one sturdy fellow whom Grizel remembered as a wild little lad employed at their farm to scare crows.

Both she and Anne were weeping unashamedly when they reached their own side of the river. Word of their arrival spread like lightning for before they were back in the gig, people came rushing to the roadside, waving their hands and smiling as if time had turned back to the days when the laird and all the family were deeply loved. It was obvious that they were well aware of Anne's continuing care for the estate and appreciated her kindness.

'Mama, is a king coming?' asked Eliza, waving back at the cheering people.

Grizel hugged her and asked her sister, 'We can't go into the house, can we?'

'No, I'm afraid not. Patrick made some trouble with the Duke about his tenancy and I don't think he'd be too happy to see any of the family, but there's somewhere else I want to go – somewhere that you'll enjoy seeing again. Don't ask questions, just sit back and enjoy the view.'

Grizel did as she was told, breathing in the sparkling air and gazing at the distant mountains standing out blue against the horizon. She felt the old awe of them fill her and every breath of air she drew into her lungs seemed to make her stronger. She felt she could have leaped out of the carriage and started one of the long walks she used to love so much. Anything seemed within her capabilities now and lifting her face to the sun, she said aloud, 'Thank God I feel well again. I feel as if I've been made whole.'

Anne said nothing but tears filled her eyes.

The lane leading to Loch an Eilean was flatter and more easily negotiable than it had been in the past. 'It looks as if someone's been making a proper road here,' said Grizel to her sister who was, as usual, handling the trotting horse and the gig with masterly aplomb. Anne nodded but made no comment, driving on by the side of the chattering, frolicking little river.

The forest closed in around them and the road became a lane banked on each side by dry bracken. Grizel's heart gave a leap when she saw a silver glimmer of water through a clearing in the trees. In a sudden panic she closed her eyes and whispered, 'Go back, Anne, don't go on. If I see it again, it'll be agonising to leave. I've dreamed about it so many times since last I was here.'

But Anne was urging the horse along with practised hands, her eyes fixed on the clearing in front of them. Though Grizel put a hand on her arm, her sister appeared unconscious of any attempt to restrain her.

They rocked perilously around the last corner and the loch spread before them like a silver bowl. Tall firs with blackened clawing roots huddled at the water's edge; purple mountains rose above the treetops like watching guardians, a faint blur of cloud drifting over their summits like blowing hair. It was as beautiful as Grizel remembered. Through dazzled eyes she saw the ruined castle, rising majestically from its island in the middle of the still water.

Everything was exactly the same. A day or a century might have passed since she was last there for time meant nothing in Loch an Eilean. Still the ospreys slowly circled the crumbling battlements and the tips of intruder trees reached up within the curtain wall.

The blood in Grizel's veins pulsed with a strange intensity. After all her wanderings, she had finally come home. The loch and its castle took her in and held her safe. This was her land, the land of the people from whom she had sprung, the land that had given her birth and would receive her body when she died. She wanted to get down from the gig and kneel on the ground to scoop up water from the loch and pour it over her head like a libation.

When she looked at her sister she saw that Anne too was deeply affected. Tears were running unchecked down her cheeks and she let her hands fall from the reins so that the horse stopped. The sisters clung to each other, weeping, but their tears were not sorrow but an outpouring of emotions that went so deep they could not be named.

They collected themselves when they saw a man walking towards them from the lochside. He was plump and short statured, wearing white breeches and half boots under a dark jacket with shining buttons. From a distance he looked like any gentleman's servant but when he came closer, Grizel blinked and gasped: 'He's an Indian. That man's an Indian!'

The stranger came up to the horse and put a hand on its bridle. 'Come this way, ladies, my master's boat is waiting,' he said in a sing-song voice.

Feeling like someone in a fairy tale, Grizel descended from the high gig seat and, taking her daughter's hand, walked up the path behind him. Her feet seemed not to make contact with the ground; she felt she was floating a few inches above the earth.

When they neared the water's edge she saw a little rowing boat with scarlet cushions on the seats tied to the roots of one of the trees. The solemn Indian helped them aboard and, when they were comfortably settled, climbed in himself and took up the oars. No one asked where they were going but sat gazing in silent wonder towards the castle.

It was a dream, Grizel decided, and dipped her hand into the glassy water. Its chill froze her fingers. If this was a dream, it was a waking one.

Their guide pulled them rapidly over the water. They skimmed along almost soundlessly. As they passed a little headland, they looked towards the shore. Their play cottage was still there.

'Look, look,' gasped Grizel excitedly, pointing towards it. 'It's been painted and tidied up. Isn't it lovely?' The paint was shining fresh and bright in the sunshine and the long slope of lawn facing the water was soft and green as a carpet and studded with white daisies. She leaned forward in her seat and exclaimed, 'But it's much bigger! New wings have been added and someone's made a lovely garden. I wonder who lives there now.'

Anne smiled but said nothing. Grizel could not stay silent. The words came bubbling out of her, 'Oh, look, Anne! There's a new landing stage. And they've built lovely verandahs all the way round, just like an Indian bungalow. Look at the creepers growing up the verandah rails. It's beautiful.'

When their boat ground its keel into the pebbles at the landing stage, their guide helped them on to a little jetty and Grizel stood gazing at the transformed play house. The central portion was their old cottage with the same door and two windows glazed with criss-crossed lattice bars, repainted and mended of course but recognisable.

On each side of the cottage, however, stretched new long wings with verandahed fronts facing south so that they could catch the full sunshine. 'How cleverly it's been done!' she sighed. 'I wonder if the Duke of Bedford is responsible.'

Anne shook her head and spoke for the first time since they got into the boat. 'No, it wasn't him. Let's go up.'

Only a few days before Grizel would have found it impossible to climb the slope to the house without a terrible weakness sapping her strength. Today she felt miraculously restored and reached the verandah without pausing for breath.

The sound of a door opening and a man's voice startled her. 'Welcome, come in and sit down. Krishna will bring us something to drink. There's champagne on ice. I hope you're not tired.'

Grizel swung round, her face alight. 'Murdo Grant, it's you who've done this! You're a magician.' She laughed in delight and swept open her arms, encompassing the treasure box of a house, its gardens and lawns, the whole lake in her gesture.

Like someone who has given a child the toy of its dreams, he beamed with pleasure at her reaction. He took the three steps from the door with arms extended, as if he meant to hold her to him, but recollected himself at the last minute and let them drop by his sides.

'I'm glad you like it,' he said formally.

'It's beautiful. If you're going to live here, you couldn't have picked a better place in the whole Highlands.'

'It's not mine. It's yours. I planned it all for you – you and Eliza,' he replied, leading her on to the verandah.

She stared at him with an expression of outright astonishment and sobered immediately. 'But you can't do that. You can't give me this house. It must've cost you a fortune and, besides, it's part of Glen Fada estate. How can you give me what belongs to my father?'

'I arranged it with him. I bought a stretch of forest on the other side of Inverdruie and exchanged it for this house and a parcel of land. It'll stay in the family anyway because I've gifted it to you.

I know how you feel about your own domain. Please accept it, Grizel.'

In bewilderment and confusion, not knowing what to say, she looked across at her sister and saw a strange expression on Anne's face. It was a look of love and sympathy mixed with admiration and a tinge of envy. 'You knew about this, didn't you? You knew all the time. That's why you insisted on my coming back,' she whispered.

Anne nodded. 'Yes, I'm afraid I did. We've been organising it for a long time. You'll be happy and grow healthy again here. This house will heal you, Grizel. Mr Grant's gone to a great deal of trouble to make everything right.'

'So you think I should accept it?'

Anne looked straight at her sister and nodded firmly. 'Yes, you must. It's been done with you in mind all along.'

Grizel turned and looked out across the loch. With a sudden decisive gesture she untied the strings of her bonnet and took it off. Tendrils of golden hair escaped from their close imprisonment. She shook her head so that the whole mass of her disordered hair tumbled down to lie free upon the grey silk of her dress.

Grizel put her hands on the verandah rail and gazed like a pagan priestess out across the water to the island, giving herself up to the land that she loved. She knew that if she wakened in this place every morning, all pain and trouble, every last haunting memory would be soothed away 'til only happiness remained.

Murdo Grant was standing directly behind her. She glanced around and saw a deep furrow between his brows. His eyes were guarded, as if he was afraid of revealing his true feelings. She felt at ease in his company, filled with the same trust he had inspired in her in childhood. Then she smiled as she realised that her regard for him was fuelled by more than trust. She liked his strong, sturdy Highlander's build, his open, honest face and the burnished cap of auburn hair; she liked his natural, unaffected response to things. She felt that they were united by a strange bond that time and distance had never broken. Pride of birth, inculcated into her by her mother, became a hollow pretension in the face of someone like Murdo Grant.

Walking towards him, she held out her hands, saying, 'It's a beautiful house, but how can I accept it from you? I can't allow you to spend so much on me. I could never repay you.'

'I don't want repaying,' he said. As his hand reached out for hers, she knew with certainty that there was another request she must make of him. With an air of gaiety, she held him prisoner and said, 'But I wouldn't want to live in this house, lovely as it is, alone. Would you consider marrying a widow lady of uncertain age, with little money and no prospects?'

Murdo reeled slightly then put his other hand over hers, laughed his great laugh, and told her, 'Why, thank you very much for the proposal. I accept. Nothing would please me better.'

Anne ran up to Grizel and threw her arms around her, sobbing for joy. 'Oh, I'm so happy! I knew you were perfect for each other but he was afraid to ask you. Didn't I tell you everything would be all right?'

The last question was directed at Murdo who nodded and said, 'Yes, you did. But it didn't seem possible that Miss Macalpine of Glen Fada would marry the minister's laddie!' He turned to Grizel and said earnestly, 'It wasn't part of my intention in giving you this house to bribe you to marry me, Grizel, I promise you that.'

'I'm not for bribing,' she said. 'I'd marry you, Murdo Grant, if you offered me a dog kennel.'

They stood looking into each other's eyes, completely oblivious to the presence of Anne, an open-mouthed Eliza and the smiling Indian servant. Enchantment held them in its grip and Grizel felt she was eighteen again and in love for the first time. Murdo filled her vision, blotting out even her beloved loch, its island and the sunlight. They would be happy, she was confident of that. They would live together in their jewel box house 'til they were very old, and nothing would ever harm or hurt her again now that she was safe with him.